BUTCHER

Detective Sergeant Lou Perlman is an outcast from police HQ, doomed by the chief superintendent to a seemingly infinite 'sick-list'. He's barred from investigating the bloodbath that has rocked the foundations of the city's lower depths. A new man has powered his way to the top of Glasgow's gangster fraternity: Reuben Chuck is a villain who promotes cruelty and murder whilst he pursues an inscrutable religious awakening of his own. A gruesome discovery made in Perlman's own house launches him into an enquiry that becomes fraught with perplexities — the whereabouts of his missing love, Miriam; body parts; a seemingly haunted house; dubious part-time surgeons; a mob of dangerous hooded teenagers; and his own family's history — all leading, inexorably, to the deathly terrain of Reuben Chuck.

Books by Campbell Armstrong
Published by The House of Ulverscroft:

CONCERT OF GHOSTS
DEADLINE
THE LAST DARKNESS
WHITE RAGE

CAMPBELL ARMSTRONG

BUTCHER

Complete and Unabridged

CHARNWOOD
Leicester

First published in Great Britain in 2006 by
Allison & Busby Limited
London

First Charnwood Edition
published 2007
by arrangement with
Allison & Busby Limited
London

British Library CIP Data

Armstrong, Campbell
    Butcher.—Large print ed.—
    Charnwood library series
    1. Perlman, Lou (Fictitious character)—Fiction
    2. Police—Scotland—Glasgow—Fiction
    3. Missing persons—Investigation—Scotland—Glasgow
    —Fiction 4. Organized crime—Scotland—Glasgow
    —Fiction 5. Detective and mystery stories
    6. Large type books
    I. Title
    823.9'14 [F]

    ISBN 978-1-84617-723-1

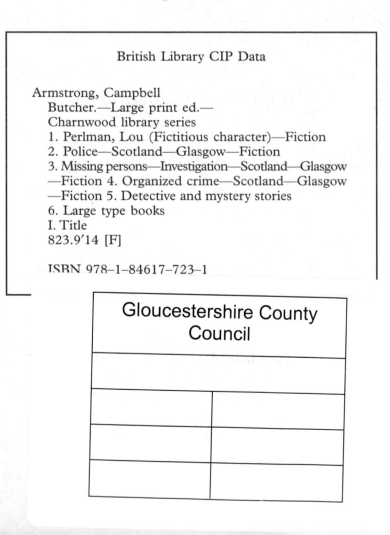

Gloucestershire County
Council

The author thanks the following people:

Superintendent Iain Gordon, Strathclyde Police,
for his endless patience with my questions
Alex Reilly, for the illuminating tour
Ed Breslin, for his encouragement
Netta White, and Hazel Frew, for their
help with Glasgowspeak
Fraser Campbell, for his memories
and *bon mots*
Patrick Killian, master locksmith
and Detective, for his skills
The Editor of *The Jaggy Thistle*, for fun
Marie-Caroline Aubert, for her kindness
Susie Dunlop, for taking a chance
Dave Read, for Manning the Web
Jarno Mattila, for the Korskenkorva
Wilma McFarlane, for research
Sam Sinclair, for the Dolmio
Erl and Ann, for accommodating me
Elsie B, specially, for the stones

1

It was time. He'd watched bosses rise and fall and others emerge to take their places. He'd seen fragile allegiances forged only to disintegrate in squalls of treachery and violence. He was forty-five and primed for advancement and he'd waited years for his moment.

He stepped out of his Jaguar at the top of Hill Street. He wore a full length camel-coloured cashmere overcoat against the cold October night. Beating his gloved hands together, he surveyed the city spread beneath him — the intricate splendour of St George's Mansions lit by red floodlights, the towers of Trinity, the electric clusters of Maryhill, the dark pool that was Kelvingrove Park. Beyond lay Partick, Broomhill, Hyndland. He heard the roaring motorway ferry cars and trucks to Anderston and the Broomielaw, and then across the narrow water of the Clyde to Kingston and Kinning Park, Govan and Pollok, and beyond.

So much buzz, so many lights, so many pockets of darkness.

This city is mine.

Reuben Chuck took his mobile phone from his pocket and punched in a number and said, 'Start movin.'

★ ★ ★

Jimmy 'Bram' Stoker sat in his usual private dining room at the Corinthian, a restaurant and club in an ornate Victorian building that was once the Glasgow Sheriff's Court. His ulcer, that wicked wee cunt in his gut, was acting up. He'd eaten curried bream, and the taste kept coming back at him. Never trust bream. Specially *curried*.

He finished his brandy and rose from the table and looked at his guests, a Texan called Rick Tosh and a local girl, Patsie, who'd been brought along for the American's amusement.

Stoker said, 'I'll leave you two. Enjoy.' He made an expansive gesture, indicating that he was bestowing on them not only the finest of meals and the best wines, but also any pleasures the rest of the evening held.

'Jeez, it's only what, ten o'clock?' Rick Tosh, a leathery man with a neck so gnarled the cords were like stretched brown rubber bands, protested mildly. He had one liver-spotted paw on Polly's compliant knee under the table. He planned to reach the inner thigh soon as Stoker had split.

'We'll talk business in the morning,' Stoker said. 'Tonight's for enjoyment.'

'Place like this, gal like this, a guy'd have to be a goddam Baptist not to enjoy.' Rick Tosh had a silent laugh. His head went up and down like a man dooking for apples, and his mouth opened and his shoulders shook, but no sound emerged.

Jimmy Stoker inclined his body toward the girl, and whispered in her ear. 'Treat him well, lassie.' Her perfume was so overwhelming he suspected prolonged exposure to it would collapse his lungs. He shook Tosh's left hand, knowing the right was otherwise engaged. 'I'll send somebody at 10 a.m. pick you up at your hotel.'

'Looking forward,' the Texan said. 'Adios.'

'Aye, adios.' Jimmy Stoker moved away from the table. Simultaneously, two young men who'd been standing at the bar all evening left their drinks unfinished and followed Stoker to the cloakroom. One claimed Stoker's coat and hat and helped him into it. He'd give him the hat outside if there was inclement weather, the only time Stoker reluctantly acquiesced to covering his thick white blow-dried hair, his pride.

'Nice night, Mr Stoker?'

Stoker belched. 'Texans are all fucking windbags. Oil this, oil that, and if it isny oil it's cattle, and who knows how many million head and how many million acres. You could build a city size of five Glasgows on his land, he says. He's a blowhard. Soon's you let Americans get their mitts into your business, they're leeches. Give em an inch.'

The young man checked the street from the front door and said, 'All clear, Mr Stoker.'

'Righto,' Stoker said.

The door was held open for him. The two young men flanked him as they moved along Ingram Street toward Stoker's parked Daimler. One opened the back door.

Stoker climbed in and said, 'Take me home, country roads.'

The young man who'd opened the door

settled into the passenger seat, the other got behind the wheel. The car rolled past the Italian Centre and down Glassford Street in the direction of Argyle Street. Glassford wasn't very well lit; dark buildings on either side, old warehouses transformed into shops with flats above them.

Jimmy Stoker tasted bream again. It was like the fish had come back to life and was swimming up his gullet on a cloud of aqueous gas. He belched profoundly a couple of times and said, 'Never eat curried bream, boys. I swear to God.' He undid the buttons of his grey single-breasted suit, and loosened his belt. He also popped the top two buttons of his trousers.

The young man in the passenger seat looked round. He still had Stoker's hat, and he held it out to him. 'Here's your hat, what's your curry.'

Stoker leaned forward. 'See you, Jack. The last thing I need is any of your rotten jokes. See if there's Rolaids.'

Jack opened the glovebox and a little lightbulb glowed. He rummaged around. 'None, Mr Stoker.'

A car coming the other way angled abruptly into the Daimler's path. Stoker's driver braked to avoid collision and said, 'Fucking *bampot*.'

The other car stopped and doors swung open and three men jumped out into the glare of the Daimler's headlights.

Stoker shouted, 'What the fuck is this?'

Jack was reaching for a gun he kept under the passenger seat as the windscreen cracked and collapsed. Jack fell sideways. A piece of his scalp was blown into the back seat and blood splashed into Stoker's eyes. The driver tried to squirm down in the seat and take the gun out of Jack's dead hand but a second shot blew through his jawbone and he slid silently away from the wheel. Stoker opened the back door, stumbled out of the car, felt his slackened trousers begin to slide from his hips. He tripped on the pavement. He blinked, Jack's blood blinded him. He tried to get up — if I run, if I run *hard* enough.

'Don't even think about it,' somebody said.

Stoker did think about it — and decided he wasn't going out like a snivelling wee boy. He grabbed the top of his falling trousers and rose, thinking he'd make a mad rush into a dark side-street, but he stumbled again. Ah shite.

Cardamom ginger chillies and fish flakes clotted at the back of his throat.

Jesusmaryjoseph.

⋆   ⋆   ⋆

'*Move Over Darling*,' Eve Curdy said. 'That's my favourite.'

'Nope, has to be *Pillow Talk*.'

'When you get down to it, Gordy, is there a difference between the two?'

'Get down to it?' Gordy had a big smile. 'How far down?'

'Oh you — you know what I mean.'

Gordy Curdy said, '*Pillow Talk* has that extra magic.'

They were lying on loungers in the room Gordy Curdy called The Kon-Tiki Room, created out of what had once been the cellar of his house in Newton Mearns. Both Curdys wore identical khaki shorts, red and yellow Hawaiian shirts, and they had tanning-salon tans. Somebody had once referred to them as The Trader Vics Twins.

The décor was ersatz Hawaiian: plastic palm trees, a cocktail bar with a pineapple-shaped ice bucket, and brown hula girl swizzlesticks that fitted nicely between thumb and forefinger when you stirred. It was a cosy warm place where Gordy loved to invite clients and friends, showing them with enormous pride how an ordinary basement could be transformed, with a little imagination, into an exotic South Sea island retreat.

On the 52 inch plasma screen Tony Randall was having a nervous breakdown. Big Rock was trying to console him. Curdy preferred the scenes between Big Rock and Doris. Doris had that special *sparkle*.

He said, 'Rock was a good actor. A poofter playing a straight guy. That's got to be hard.'

Mrs Curdy looked at her husband. 'Hard?'

'Oh very hard.'

'And how hard is very?'

'Rock.'

Eve Curdy slid her feet out of her fuzzy slippers. Her toenails were bright red. She wiggled them. 'Know that rock near Dumbarton?'

Gordy nodded. 'They say it's an old volcano. Inactive. Except you never know where you stand with volcanoes.'

'And exactly *where* do you stand with volcanoes?'

'That's just it. They're unpredictable. They can erupt any time.'

'Erupt any time, mmm.' Eve Curdy narrowed her eyes. 'Isn't there a lighthouse on that rock?'

'You're thinking Edinburgh. Bass Rock. That lighthouse is a firm big thing, rises tall out the sea.'

'Oh it's tall, I remember that,' Eve said.

Gordy watched Doris on screen. She was talking by phone to Big Rock, who was conning her as he always did. 'Doris never gets it, does she?'

Eve said, 'She gets it eventually.'

'I fucking hope she does.'

'Oh so do I, so do I. Sooner rather than later, Gordy.'

'My money's on sooner every time.'

She finished her drink, looked at her husband with head tilted. He knew that expression. I'm on to a winner here.

'Get me the same again, would you, Gordy?'

Gordy Curdy rose and took his wife's empty glass to the cocktail bar. He fixed the concoction just the way she liked it except he added a little more rum than usual. And bagza ice cubes. The rest was just for colour.

He opened a Miller's Light for himself. The can popped, fizzed, spluttered out foam.

Eve said, 'I like that sound, Gordy.'

'Pop fizz, aye. Reminds me of something.'

'Does it?'

'Trying to remember what . . . '

'Try harder, lover.'

7

★ ★ ★

The intercom buzzed.

Eve Curdy was annoyed. 'Oh Christ, who's that at this time of night? I don't suppose you can ignore it, Gordy.'

The intercom buzzed again. 'No, but I'll deal with it fucking *fast*.' Gordy flipped a switch.

'Somebody here to see you.' Mathieson's voice came through the system as if he had a clothes-peg clamped to his nostrils.

'Who?'

'Only Soutar.'

'Send him down.' Gordy flicked the switch back.

'Soutar, he's an annoyance,' Mrs Curdy said.

'He'll only be here a minute.' Gordy Curdy saw that Doris was crying now. Big Rock had cut her to the quick. 'Soutar brings me a lot of business.'

'Frankly Gordy, I don't like the way he squints. And why do we need Mathieson all the time?'

'Home sec,' he said.

'But he's always here, or somebody like him.'

'He's a status symbol, sweetheart. Round-the-clock on-site protection. You want nasty big Alsatian dogs? Or that bloody awful fencing?'

'Frankly, Gordydear, I think we should do something *off the fucking wall*. Build lighthouses in the front and keep them on a really low romantic glow. I could look out the window and enjoy them.'

Gordy said, 'Great. Hold the thought, lover.'

8

'I'm holding more than that,' she said.

The door opened and Soutar came in. He was dressed in a black blazer and grey slacks and carried a black leather briefcase. He was a short bald man with one eye that didn't open all the way. Gordy Curdy never thought of it as a *squint*. It was a lazy lid. Lots of people had them.

'Soutar, how are you?'

'Sorry to disturb. I just have some papers for you to sign.'

'Aye, fine. I'll have a gander.'

'Hello Mrs Curdy,' Soutar said.

Eve Curdy nodded coldly. 'Hello Soutar.'

Soutar opened the briefcase. Mrs Curdy watched Doris Day and thought about lighthouses and rocks and planting plum trees in the backyard and having a whole harvest of plums every year. Gordy Curdy thought about cash, making cash, fucking *volcanoes* of cash.

Soutar took a gun from his briefcase.

Gordy Curdy smiled in surprise, then lost the smile when he looked into Soutar's eyes. He didn't like what he saw there. The lazy lid pulsed strangely and Soutar's eyes were darkly earnest.

This is no joke, Soutar's no joker.

Panicked, Curdy stuck a hand out defensively.

Mrs Curdy only turned away from the plasma screen when she heard the gunshot. She saw her husband fall and blood pump through his Hawaiian shirt.

Soutar shot her in the head.

The bullet knocked her up and out of her lounger with such force her head broke the

9

plasma screen and compressed gas blew across the room amidst a hail of shards. Her head was trapped in the shattered frame.

Rock Hudson's voice said, '*I'm a sensitive man.*'

Then the audio died.

Mathieson, who had the razor-cut look of a young marine, entered the room.

'Done,' Soutar said.

'OK. Let's fuck off.'

'She looks good in the telly.'

'A star,' Mathieson said.

Both men left, closing the door behind them.

On the way out of the house Mathieson said, 'I better phone the man.'

★　★　★

Reuben Chuck stood in the living room of his riverside penthouse apartment and spooned an organic mix of chopped bananas, muesli and goat's yoghurt into his mouth. He gazed down at the Clyde where lamplight curdled on water. He felt calm, confident. When his phone rang he was in no hurry to pick up.

When he did he heard Mathieson say, 'Done, dusted.'

Reuben Chuck put the phone down without saying anything. Dusted. Stardusted. The old order changes. There would be other phone calls in the course of the night. By morning he'd be calling all the shots and gathering all the booty.

2

'I left my heart at Woodstock,' Betty McLatchie said.

Lou Perlman wondered how she'd drifted to the subject of Woodstock. Maybe he'd absent-mindedly missed a beat. She'd arrived, prompt at 10 a.m., with mop and bucket and assorted detergents, and *he* certainly hadn't mentioned music or festivals. She was small, somewhere in her late forties, bright turquoise eyes, a smile that would crick a celibate's neck. Perlman detected a lively shade of her younger self.

She wore her yellow-grey hair piled up and held in place by clasps, an intricate arrangement. Her faded blue jeans, adorned with trippy little zodiac patches, were strapped to her hips by a thick belt with a fancy bronze buckle. Her clothes told the story: unrepentant hippy.

'It was the time of my life, Lou. We were all so bloody young and free back then. We kicked ass.'

'I remember being young,' Perlman said. And he did, through an old Glasgow fog.

'I get so *embarrassed* when I think of the things I did,' Betty said, and laughed at past follies. 'I had a fling with Country Joe. *And* two of the Fish.'

Perlman was intrigued by her candour. 'I thought there were *three* Fish. One got away?'

'I tried, mind. Oh I tried.'

'Did you see Bob Dylan?'

11

'He didn't appear at Woodstock. People always make that mistake.'

Dylan, formerly Zimmerman. Perlman wondered if a name change would work wonders for him as well. Lou Perlman becomes Hamish McKay, say. A name denoting tweeds and sensible brogues and maybe a wee terrier dog. 'About this house . . . '

'It's a pigsty, Lou. Don't mind me saying. I'm just being truthful. Your Aunt Hilda told me to expect the worst.'

Lou's Aunt Hilda was known for exaggeration, but perhaps not in this case. 'I live alone . . . ' As if that explained everything.

'Where do I start? This'll take weeks.'

Perlman shrugged. 'Anywhere you like, Betty.'

He scanned the living room. Pigsty, well . . . He'd let the place go year after year, and apart from the occasional desultory attempt at dusting or knocking spider's webs down, he'd done pretty much fuck all.

Now Betty McLatchie was here to transform the place, at the behest of Perlman's aunts on the Southside, who worried about his well-being. They were kindly women, his aunts, although their concern sometimes became meddlesome.

He gazed at the collection of WWI medals he'd bought at a jumble sale because he felt sorry for the poor long-dead sod who'd gone through shite and shellfire to earn them; the big glass jars of pre-decimal coins, those huge brown pennies and tarnished florins he'd had since childhood; the vinyl albums long parted from their sleeves and the CDs that lay in silvery layers on the floor around the miniaturized sound system.

He dreaded the idea of all this being disturbed — but it was time for change. Time — he had time in spades right now.

Betty McLatchie said, 'I'll get started then.' She produced a canister of air freshener and sprayed the room briskly. Off guard, Perlman tried to dodge the scented mist but felt a few drops of moisture fall against his face.

'I know spraying's superficial, but I always say freshen the air before you start in earnest.'

'Is that what you always say.' Perlman could taste the stuff on his lips. 'What is that?'

'Ocean Breeze.'

'Ocean? It's no ocean known to man,' Perlman said, giving in to a brief coughing attack. 'I'll let you get on.'

He went inside the kitchen and opened the door that led to a backyard. A tangled sanctuary of great ferns, old rhubarb stalks, a couple of maniac hawthorns beyond pruning. He lit a cigarette and made his way through the jungle where he knew there was a relic of a wooden bench somewhere. He pushed long hanks of obstinate grass aside and sat gazing at the back of his house. Black stone stained by a hundred years of the city's effluents. The window frames needed paint. A drainpipe was loose and rusted. Starlings bred there.

This catalogue of neglect and carelessness weighed on him. *I'm never here much. It's a place where I sleep and change clothes.* Excuses. He smoked the cigarette down to the filter. He

13

listened to the wind in the trees and the way it slapped ferns and grass: one of those unpredictable Glasgow afternoons when the weather could go any direction. The sky was glowering, and grey as ash.

He thought, as he often did, about Miriam: his regular haunting. The last postcard he'd received had come four weeks ago from Copenhagen, a terse message with no suggestion that she was coming home to resume where they'd left off — wherever that was. A kiss, a light caress of her breast, vague suggestions of a possible future. Or else he'd misconstrued the situation, reading far too much into it. He wasn't sure about anything save his feelings for her, and sometimes even then he had moments of uncertainty.

She'd written: *lovely city, fond wishes.*

Four words, followed by M.

Fond, oy, what the fuck was *fond?* It was a word you'd use about a favourite uncle or a soup you liked. Four weeks. Had she forgotten the romantic dinner at La Fiorentina, and how they'd lain close together on the sofa in her loft-studio and he'd wondered if love was finally breaking through like a half-remembered song?

She needed time, she'd told him. He'd been sympathetic, of course: love was a serious commitment, a matter of the heart, an organ about as predictable as this city's weather. He was always so damned acquiescent where Miriam was concerned, so patient.

I never carped the fucking diem.

He thought: let it go. Miriam, *neshumela.*

He'd loved her so many years in silence he could go back to silence again. He'd be all right. He'd be OK, he was a survivor. But.

He heard the whine of a vacuum cleaner inside the house. He got up from the bench and wandered the thickets for a while like a melancholic poet in search of inspiration. Lou Keats. At the first drop of rain he went back indoors where music played over the drone of the antique Hoover. Betty McLatchie smiled at him and gave him a thumbs up.

'I work better to music,' she shouted.

The song was 'Hotel California'. The Eagles.

Perlman picked up his raincoat from the back of a chair. 'I'll leave you to it, Betty.' He fumbled in his pocket for his keys, slipped one from the ring, and handed it to her. 'Here. You should have this. If I'm not around, be sure you lock the front door before you leave.'

She took the key. 'Fine.'

He went down the corridor, stopped in front of the mirror and thought about brushing his hair but some days all the brushing in the world failed to improve his appearance. What was it Miriam had said about him? *You have that just out of bed look*. He scowled at his reflection, stroked the stubble on his chin, then left the house.

Outside, he saw no sign of his old Ford Mondeo and for one panicky moment he thought, some *gonif*'s nicked it — but then he remembered he'd traded it for a used Ka only days ago, a balloon of a thing the salesman had talked him into buying. *Very popular wee car,*

Lou. Easy on the juice, but zippy. Perlman understood zero about cars. A good car was one with a music system and a capacious ashtray. He drove down Dalness Street to Tollcross Road.

The Jew zips out of Egypt, smoking furiously.

3

Perlman walked through the Buchanan Street Galleries. Bright new Glasgow, scores of shops operating in fluorescent haze. Mango, Next, Habitat. He looked in the window of Ottakar's. He was tempted to go in and sniff among the stacks. He loved the smell of books. Sometimes he'd open one just to inhale the scent of the binding, the whiff of paper. But today he had a lunch with Sandy Scullion — the highlight of the week, the month.

A kilted piper played 'Amazing Grace' outside the Buchanan Street subway. Perlman paused on the corner of Bath Street. His instinct was to turn right and walk where he'd walked more than a thousand times, up the hill to Pitt Street HQ. The magnetism of old reflexes. Not today, not tomorrow. He didn't know when he'd go back. It was like being barred from a club you'd joined more than twenty-five years ago.

He headed past the old Atheneum, formerly a drama college, a wonderful red sandstone building now occupied by a company called Townhouse Interiors. He glanced at the Church of Scotland on the corner of Nelson Mandela Place and went down Buchanan Street in the worst kind of drizzle, omnidirectional, swirled by a slight wind. Buses roared in his ears. Taxis went past in sleek sharklike streaks. Pedestrians bustled around him. The natives, faces determined and toughened and fatalistic, looked like descendants of foundrymen, shipyard workers, grafters.

He loved the faces of Glasgow.

He crossed the street. Sandy had said one sharp. Perlman would be punctual. He had no excuse not to be. His life, formerly so crowded, so intricate, was flat as day-old Irn-Bru.

Princes Square was a flash place of boutiques and cafés under a glass Art Nouveau roof. He saw Scullion at a table outside the Café Gerardo.

Perlman sat, shook Sandy's hand.

'Good to see you, Lou.'

'Is that a wee tash you're trying to grow, Sandy?'

Scullion fingered his lip. 'I'm giving it a shot. Madeleine likes it.'

'Wives are biased.' Perlman picked up a menu. 'I counted how many times in my life I've shaved. I got a figure of close to fourteen thousand. That's a lot of razor plus a lot of cuts. So now I think, what's a bit of scrub?'

'Counting shaves is a sign of . . . ' Scullion didn't complete the sentence.

'I know already.' Perlman looked at the menu. 'Why do chefs put soy and bok choi into everything these days? Take a perfectly good omelette and turn it into an oriental egg fuck.'

'You prefer we go where you can get a deep-fried Mars bar?'

'Death by grease.' Perlman put the menu down and looked at the Inspector. His thinning sandy hair, which he used to comb with a side parting, he now wore cut short into his scalp. He looked harder, tougher, more polis-like. His pink

18

skin had a glow of good health and good deeds. He was happily married, and there were two kids. Scullion had a full life. He could switch off when he went home at nights. Crime wave, what crime wave? Perlman had never been able to put work behind him. Even now, when he was on 'sick leave'.

'How's the shoulder, Lou?'

'Some days nothing. Other days I take a painkiller.' He didn't want to talk about the bullet that had passed through his shoulder. He dreamed sometimes about the way he'd been shot, and in the dreams the bullet always found its intended target, his heart. He died and saw his own funeral. Miriam wasn't among the mourners, but his aunts wailed in the background like a bad Greek chorus.

He scanned the menu again: *smoked haddock and ratatouille en croute*. 'Does anybody ever ask about me, Sandy?'

'Superintendent Gibson always does.'

'A sweetheart. She phoned me once a while ago.'

A waitress with dyed black hair and a tiny silver nostril ring stopped at their table.

Scullion said, 'I'll have the pasta with tomato and basil. Lou?'

'Burger and chips,' Perlman said. He looked at the waitress. 'I don't want any fancy sprinkle of soy and mustard on my plate.'

The waitress smiled. 'Burger and chips is burger and chips.'

'I'll also have a lager, please,' Scullion said.

Perlman asked for sparkling water.

'Right away.' The waitress went off.

Scullion propped his elbows on the table. 'Mary Gibson's always had a completely inexplicable soft spot for you. But Tay — he's like a cat with a lifetime supply of free cream. He's delirious he doesn't have your, er, troublesome presence around Pitt Street.'

William Tay, Chief Superintendent, a dour concrete man who was rumoured to smile every ten years or so, had been marinating all his life in joyless Presbyterianism. He was a Christian soldier in the Onward sense, battling the forces of darkness in Glasgow in God's name.

'He's an anti-Semite,' Perlman said, and made a *phooo* sound.

'Rubbish.'

'He reminds me of Goebbels. I always feel he's about to lecture me on the master race . . . I could go back to work tomorrow, Sandy. For Christ's sake, I'm OK. Really.'

'It's not going to happen, Lou. Tay has the medical people dancing to his flute. They wouldn't wipe their arses without his say-so. You won't pass a physical in the near future. Count on it. Tay's never liked you. And he likes you even less ever since Miriam's trial.'

'I'm ostracized,' Perlman said. He didn't want to rehash Miriam's trial. Anything to do with Miriam was like cutting a vein. 'So what the *fuck* am I supposed to do with myself?'

The waitress appeared, set the drinks down.

Perlman looked at her apologetically. 'Pardon my language.'

'I'm the brass monkey that hears no bad

20

words. Your food's coming right up, guys.'

Perlman watched her go. 'I like her. Leave her a sizeable tip, Sandy.'

'You said on the phone this was your treat.'

'A Jew and a Scotsman haggling over who pays the bill? There's a bad joke buried in there.'

Scullion lifted his glass. 'Cheers, Lou. For what it's worth, I wish you were back.'

'I appreciate that, Sandy. Now what about my question?'

'Find a hobby. Go to football matches. You used to do that a lot.'

'When men played. Now it's fashion models with poncey tinted hair and Boss jackets and unsavoury incidents in night-clubs.'

'Then get out of town. When did you last leave Glasgow?'

Perlman was always uneasy out of the city. 'Can you see me at the top of the Eiffel Tower grinning like a doolie? I ask for an idea and what do I get? Mince.'

Scullion looked inside his beer. 'Then I don't know, Lou.'

The clouds in Perlman's head massed darkly. He'd never been a man to despair, not even when he found himself confronted with the most base acts of his fellow human beings — but now he yielded all too easily, and uncharacteristically, to the glooms. 'I'm just a wee bit lost, sonny boy,' he said.

Scullion frowned. 'Come round for dinner some night, Lou. Madeleine's always on at me to invite you.'

'Fish pie?'

'I swear, no fish pie.'

Madeleine's fish pie had become a routine between them. Perlman couldn't remember how the pie banter had even started. He was losing touch, an idle mind forgets.

The waitress brought their food. Perlman surveyed his burger and chips. Scullion curled pasta strands round his fork.

'I just realized you're not wearing glasses, Lou.'

'Well done, Sandy. One day you'll make a fine cop. I replaced the Buddy Holly specs. The contacts sting sometimes, but at least I'm not carrying the stigmata of those heavy old frames on my hooter.' Perlman stuck a chip in his mouth. 'Tell me stuff. I'm deprived.'

'Junkie teenage mother puts baby in spin-drier. Headless man in clown costume found on the banks of Hogganfield Loch. Two victims of apparent spare-part surgery operations discovered, one in Barlanark, the other in Possil.' Scullion spoke in tabloid headlines between bites of pasta. 'And the gangland slayings.'

'Some villains got it, big deal. No matter who took over, eventually some other gunslinger will come in. Anyway, who's going to miss bad bastards like Jimmy Stoker and Gordy Curdy? Racketeers and hoormeisters and killers.' He stuck another chip in his mouth, felt he was heading for a rant, changed the subject. 'I read about the headless clown.'

'An odd one.'

'What was he doing dressed like that? And who chopped off his head?' Perlman poured

22

brown sauce on his burger. He was boiling with the need for action, and falling out of harmony with the things that mattered to him. This headless clown took his fancy. He picked up his burger, tasted it. The blandness of factory beef. 'Mibbe he was on his way to a fancy-dress party. Or else it was a case of goodbye cruel circus, I'm off to join the world.'

'He hasn't been ID-d, and the head hasn't turned up either.'

'Was it a clean cut or a hacked job?'

Scullion dabbed his mouth with a napkin. 'This isn't doing you any good. It's unhealthy.'

'So? I've spent my life exploring the unhealthy.'

Scullion's mobile rang. 'Excuse me.' He took the phone from his pocket. Perlman looked round Princes Square. He fixed his attention on an aged man sitting at a table outside one of the other eateries. Talking to himself. Or an imaginary companion, a dead wife, or just praying somebody would come along and help him out of his solitary conversation.

Scullion tucked his mobile phone away. 'Shite. I have to go.'

'I hope it's something tasty.'

Scullion stood up. 'Routine. You remember routine, Lou? I think you've forgotten the humdrum of every bloody day. It's not all headless clowns and gangland slayings and mystery.'

'It is for me.'

'I'll call about dinner.'

'I'll be by the phone, paralysed.'

Perlman hung around for a couple of minutes after Scullion had gone. When he asked the waitress to get the bill, she told him that lunch had already been paid for.

'Did he leave you a good tip?'

'Very generous.'

Perlman got up. He dropped three pound coins on the table.

The waitress said, 'You don't have to. You didn't even eat your burger.'

'No appetite, love.'

He walked up Buchanan Street where the afternoon light was already shading toward dark. He raised the collar of his coat and went in the direction of the Galleries: a dead clown, a rainy city.

*   *   *

Instead of driving back to Egypt, he crossed the Clyde and travelled south to Ibrox, passing the monolithic red-brick stadium where Glasgow Rangers played football. About a quarter of a mile from the stadium he parked outside a bar in a street of grey sandstone tenements and sat smoking a moment in his car. Then he flicked his cigarette out the window and punched in a number on his mobile.

He said, 'Meet me. I'm outside The Jaycee.'

'Gimme five.'

Perlman closed the connection. He saw two stout girls, faces flushed from a heavy midday session, come out of the Jaycee Bar, arguing. Identical twins, he realized, each wearing the red

24

white and blue scarves of Rangers' fans.

One said, 'Brian Laudrup's the best we ever had at The Brox.'

'Away to fuck, it was Davie Cooper, Coop, go wee man.'

'Za matter of opinion.'

They squared off, fists raised, then apparently thought better of it and went back inside the bar for another drink.

Perlman saw The Pickler approach from the other side of the street. Perlman beeped his horn lightly and The Pickler stepped toward the car and peered in through the window. Perlman reached across, unlocked the door, and The Pickler slid into the passenger seat.

He smelled overpoweringly of mothballs.

'New car, eh, Mr Perlman? Very nice. What does she get to the gallon?'

'How should I know?'

The Pickler examined the instrument panel, touched the dashboard, opened the glovebox and took out the Owner's Handbook. 'What's the cubic capacity of the engine? Is it a 1297 cc?'

'I never read the book,' Perlman said, bored with car talk already.

'You should, Mr Perlman. I'd be asking questions. MPG. Horse power. I think she's 68 or 69 bhp. Standard tranny, I see. Four cylinders, right?'

'Gimme a break,' Perlman said.

'You want me to look under the bonnet?' The Pickler was already halfway out the car.

Perlman tugged him back. 'The car runs. I'm satisfied.'

The Pickler settled back in his seat. 'I'm no delighted with the colour, have to say. Purple's too . . . soft.'

'Vermilion,' Perlman said.

'Vermilion, eh?' The Pickler jiggled the gearstick. 'So how's life anyway?'

'You tell me.'

Perlman regarded The Pickler a moment, who was fingering buttons on the dashboard with great interest. A squat man with a collection of sagging chins, he wore an ill-fitting old brown suit and an old-fashioned collarless shirt — clothes that had never been his to begin with, inherited, borrowed, or shoplifted from Goodwill.

'I hear you're no back on the job yet,' The Pickler said.

A man with sources, Perlman thought. 'Not yet.'

'You're outside looking in, eh? Here, that could be my job description as well.' The Pickler chuckled.

Perlman didn't want to dwell on the subject of his exile, nor any similarities between himself and his snitch. 'This headless clown,' he said.

'Oh aye, I read about him.'

Perlman took out his wallet and gave The Pickler a twenty. 'I'm mildly intrigued.'

'OKdoke. I'll sniff aboot, see whit I can find.'

Perlman saw the note vanish in the depths of The Pickler's pocket. You're sucking thin air, Lou, dying from lack of a fucking purpose and trying to buy your way into a world where something, *anything*, intrigues you.

26

'Upfront with you. It's gonny be tough, Mr Perlman. That place where they found him is way oot my territory.'

Perlman said, 'It's less than twenty minutes on a bus.'

The Pickler laughed. 'When were you last on a bus, Mr Perlman?'

Perlman gave The Pickler another ten. 'I'll phone you in a few days.'

'Right you are.'

The Pickler started to get out of the car. 'None o my business, but if you're on leave, how come you're asking about this clown?'

'Keeping my finger in,' Perlman said. 'You still going to meetings, I hope?'

'Oh aye, when I'm sober enough to remember.' The Pickler laughed again, a coarse good-natured chortle. He was a man who knew his weaknesses and tried to accommodate them. He took one last gander at the car and said, 'Vermilion, did you say?'

'Right.'

'Mair like purple.'

Perlman drove off. In his rear-view mirror he saw The Pickler waddling down the pavement. Choked by camphorated air, Perlman thought: Desperate times. Digging up dead clowns.

4

Betty McLatchie vacuumed and dusted, then polished the big glass jar with all the coins in it. She remembered the old money. What a penny bought when she was a kid, a bag of sherbert, a jawbreaker. Two pennies would get you a loosey. A florin would buy you a whole pack of cigs.

She rearranged all the CDs and found sleeves for about a third of the vinyl albums. Perlman had a mixed collection. Jazz, fifties and sixties rock, classical. She slipped Sinatra into the CD slot. 'Fly Me to the Moon.'

Fly me, Frank. She danced into the kitchen. Soiled tea towels and an ashtray full to overflowing and a piece of hard toast with a single half-moon bite out of it and some spilled egg turned to glue. The tiled floor needed a serious mop attack. This shambolic room required the full elbow grease.

Obviously Perlman didn't think it important to keep up domestic appearances, which meant he had few visitors — certainly no women he wanted to impress. Once or twice she'd overheard his aunts talk in a disapproving way about a woman Perlman was said to love, Miriam. She isn't the one for Lou, Hilda would say. And Marlene would agree. You love a man, you don't fly away leaving him stranded like a starfish on a beach. Now Lou mopes, and he's too easily depressed. Also that part of the city

28

where he chooses to live isn't for him either. Egypt, what's wrong with Shawlands or Giffnock? They analysed the condition of Lou's existence regularly, sighing, headshaking, such a man deserves better than to live alone.

Betty remembered a call she'd been putting off. She bit on a fingernail and stared at the phone on the sideboard. She picked up the handset, then felt like putting it down again. But she dialled.

Debbie the Dreich answered, second ring.

'This is two three one — '

Betty said, 'Hello Debbie. Is my son there?'

'No your bloody son's bloody no here. Three days. Not a rat's squeak outta him.'

Betty pulled on her lower lip. 'I get worried.'

'Why waste yer time? He's done it before.' Debbie spoke with all the icy resentment of a wife accustomed to abandonment and neglect. She was a talking popsicle.

Betty said, 'Have you no idea?'

'Oh I've got an idea all right. I'm thinking I'll bugger off and leave him.'

'Ah, no, you need to give him a chance.'

'He's had chance after bloody chance. You spoiled him all his life.'

'I'm a mother who just happens to love her son.'

'He's a brat. And you made him that way. Sun shines out his arse.'

Don't get me started, Betty thought. Or I'll tell you what I really think about you, Missus Debbie McLatchie *nee* Grierson. Kirk saddled the wrong pony when he married you. The way you slurp soup, and that neighing laugh of yours would get on anyone's nerves, and as for your temperament, well, you could curdle milk just by looking at it —

'Listen, Deb, I'm working for this cop right now. Mibbe I can talk to him.'

'Polis never listen.'

'No, he's OK. He's nice.'

'See you, you think everybody's nice, so you do. You're living in a dream, Betty McLatchie. I don't believe your Woodstock stories and you shagging these bands. I don't even believe you *went* to Woodstock — '

'Believe what you like. I'm no in the mood for fighting.'

Whack. Debbie hung up.

Betty said, 'Bad-mannered cow.' She had a menopausal flush, her private sauna. The surface of her face felt hot.

Debbie was Mrs Brillo Pad, abrasive. Talking to Debbie always made her tense. She pulled a cigarette packet out of her hip pocket and opened it. Inside was half a joint. She lit the doobie with her mini red Bic and took a few hits. Kirk should never have let Annie drift out of his life. Big bloody mistake that. Lovely lively Annie — what had become of her anyway?

She let the joint go out, then stuck it back in the pack. The smoke was just enough to loosen the muscles. And she needed that feeling, the nice blur that buffed the hard edges of things.

When she heard Perlman unlock the front door, she quickly sprayed the kitchen with Ocean Breeze, then she slipped back into the living

30

room in time to greet him. His coat was wet with rain and his thick black-grey hair, which was all over the place, sparkled.

He looked around, pleased and surprised. 'Excuse me, I'm in the wrong house. I thought a certain Perlman lived here.'

She laughed. 'I've been busy.'

He ran a fingertip along a polished shelf. 'A miracle. I can see my reflection in wood.'

He smiled, which changed his face entirely. That shroud of sadness he carried fell away and he looked like a boy waking on his birthday filled with expectation.

Betty felt the grass ease through her head. 'Mind if I ask for some advice?'

'Ask away,' he said.

5

Dorcus glanced from the window at the towers glowing in the early dark. Scarred here and there by fire, studded with satellite dishes, they stood only five hundred yards from the walls of his house. He drew a curtain swiftly across the window and motes of old dust scattered all around him.

You don't have to look now.

But you can still hear the non-stop noise of the tower inhabitants, the Slab People. Stomping rock music glass shattering motorcycles roaring babies crying dogs barking drunks vomiting men and women fighting.

Nurse Payne called out from the top of the stairs with some urgency in her voice. *Prepped and ready.*

He hurried upstairs, passing the cold spot where he always shivered, then entered his surgery. The slatted white blinds were shut and the lamps lit. Mahler's *Kindertotenlieder* was playing on the stereo. Sweetly tragic.

He remembered something his late father, Judge Dysart, had said once. *I live in the afterlife, Dorcus, which is my tragedy. And, unfortunately, yours.*

Forget that, concentrate on the job now.

He scrubbed his hands scrupulously with Dettol. He pulled on his surgical gloves and admired his flesh through them, white and germ-free. When he thought of germs his head filled with blown-up images of clustered *staphylococci* or the flamingo-pink rods of *E-coli*. These insurgents in the blood were his enemies, and he had to maintain a constant vigilance.

He washed his hands a second time before slipping the mask over his face. He liked to feel his breath against the cotton fibres. He brushed his teeth three times a day and mouthwashed night and morning with Corsadyl.

He stood at the table. The flaccid face below him was ageless. It was an ordinary face. If you saw it in an old school photo you wouldn't pause over it, all you could imagine for this person was a future of drab anonymity. Dorcus reached down, touched the face gently, and marvelled at the resilience and purpose of skin: it kept blood and organs from spilling out and rain from getting in. But it was delicate and so easy to puncture, a shard of glass, a skelf of wood, even an edge of paper would draw blood. Dorcus thought: poor thing, life hasn't been generous to you, has it?

Scalpel, Nurse Payne.

Scalpel, Dr Dysart.

He adored Nurse Payne. He looked into her eyes as he took the scalpel from her. The connection was difficult to break. The darkness in her eyes trapped him. She knew how he felt. She was the only emotional certainty in his perilous world.

Now he had work. This body.

The steel blade cut a neat incision from belly button to sternum, and after a second blood flowed cleanly through the slit.

6

Perlman asked, 'When did you last see Kirk?'

Betty McLatchie frowned. 'Three days ago he came round my flat and we had a cup of tea.'

'Did he say he was going away?'

'Nope.'

Perlman took off his coat finally and threw it over the back of a chair. Betty McLatchie picked it up and carried it out to the hallway where she hung it on a peg. He tried to imagine Miriam doing this kind of thing, hanging up his coat or making sure he wore socks that didn't have holes in them. He couldn't see it. At times he thought: I'm *meshugane* to love her. Other times, he condemned her for being a cold-hearted bitch who just upped and left, without a word of cheerio. He was dogged by the idea she'd found a lover elsewhere, which caused him to feel that his heart had capsized.

'Does Kirk drink?'

'Now and then.'

'Does he have a girl on the side?'

'I don't think he screws around, Lou. He's never been a ladies' man.'

Perlman felt a small ripple of interest at the back of his head; he heard the old metronomic rhythms of Q & A. Worried mother looks for son. OK, so it's not hotshit-news gangland violence, and it doesn't have the strange allure of a decapitated clown, but sometimes a mystery

34

opens up like a night flower. Or maybe not, and the guy will just reappear with vague explanations and one shoe missing and a black eye.

'What about his friends?'

'He's the only one of his crowd married. I keep thinking he must be on the razzle with some of them. One thing leads to another, and you wake up in a strange room in another town with a hangover, and you think, well, I'm already in the doghouse, I might as well stay away for a while.'

'SMP. Standard Male Response. Problem: I'm in shite. Solution: ah screw it, why not make it worse? It's the way men are wired, Betty.'

'Is that how *you're* wired?'

He gazed at her. She had a frank look he found challenging. She asked a straight question with every expectation of receiving a straight answer. The unblinking blue eyes never left his face. 'Some days I don't think there are any conduits up here at all,' and he tapped his skull. 'Other days I believe they just fritzed.'

He lit a cigarette, offered Betty the packet, she shook her head. He walked round the room, this glossy, waxy, reinvented room.

'You'll need an ashtray,' Betty said. 'Over there.' She pointed to the wooden sideboard where a shiny glass ashtray was placed.

Perlman obeyed, making a big play of getting the ash dead centre.

She approved. 'I had a sneaky wee feeling you were trainable.'

She has mischief in her all right. Perlman folded his arms, gazed at the immaculate stack of

35

his CDs. I leave a wreck, I come back — a showroom. 'What about Kirk's father?'

Betty made a face like a woman crunching a sherbet lemon between her teeth. 'Kirk's never even met his father. One-night stand. Two drunk people in undying lust.'

'Give me Kirk's address.'

'Duntarvie Avenue . . . number 33. Easterhouse.'

'I'll phone the office about your boy. They can check accident reports, hospitals, arrests . . . '

Perlman noticed she looked disappointed. Is this all, Sergeant? Is this as far as you go? 'I'd pop down to Pitt Street myself, Betty, but I'm on sick leave.' Like a man with the plague. Here's fucking Bubonic Lou coming, quick, bar doors, lock the windies, get antibiotics, and somebody call a priest to bring a bucket of holy water.

Betty said, 'You don't look sick.'

'Don't be deceived by my healthy East End glow,' Perlman said. It's deeper, Betty McLatchie, it's not something you'd notice on the surface. But he wasn't about to unload the current state of his psyche on her, nor involve her in a narrative that included a gun being fired in this very room by a sick criminal, and his rough treatment at the hands of the Nazi Tay. 'If I don't hear anything from HQ . . . ' He hesitated. He was on the point of making a promise he wasn't sure he could keep. 'I'll poke around, see what I can do.'

'Would you?'

'It's nothing. I'm sure the boy's all right.'

'I hope so. Thanks for taking time.' She

wheeled the vacuum cleaner across the floor. 'I was thinking I'd leave the kitchen for tomorrow because it's an all-day sort of job. So I'll go upstairs and knock your bedroom into some kind of shape. Is that OK with you?'

'Anything you like. Here, let me take the Hoover for you. Then I'll make that phone call.' A moment of gallantry. Perlman puffed as he hauled the heavy old machine up the narrow staircase.

'You know they make them lightweight nowadays?' Betty, climbing ahead, looked down at him.

'Nobody ever told me.'

Betty opened the bedroom door, Perlman followed.

★　★　★

The pictures on the wall didn't bother him — the old black and white Celtic Lisbon Lions photograph, nor the framed 1967 Scotland v England programme, although these were arguably *juvenile* and didn't belong in a grown man's room — it was the general chaos that shamed him, the way everything rose up at him as if to accuse him of a lifetime of negligence: an abandonment of socks, shirts, trousers, a yellowing midden of old newspapers, the unmade bed, the bedside table where fag-ends had collected and disintegrated at the bottom of a glass filled long ago with water and now the shade of diseased urine.

He was dismayed. He saw the room through

37

Betty McLatchie's eyes, which made it all the more an indignity. He set the Hoover down and grunted.

'If we get the newspapers out first,' she said. She uttered no word of criticism this time, bless her heart.

He opened the window which overlooked the backyard. Ventilate, ventilate. Darkening air sloped into the room, bearing a damp green smell. A starling shot out of the drainpipe.

'In the future I fancy Zen,' he said. 'No chest of drawers, no wardrobe, no bed. A simple futon, some joss-sticks, who knows . . . ' He was babbling to cover his discomfort. A messy kitchen or a nightmare living room, somehow these were not as bad as a bedroom left to decay. The bedroom was the most intimate room in any house, and he'd allowed his to turn into a loveless slum. He'd had a few unsatisfyingly brief dalliances from time to time over the years, but never in his own bed. Only once, he remembered, had a woman slept in this bed. A lovely doomed junkie called Sadie, who he had rescued from her mental boyfriend, one Moon Riley. Even then, he hadn't slept with her despite her entreaties. But such a temptation. He'd lain awake on the couch for hours, hearing the bed creak upstairs as she turned this way and that in restless sleep. She left next morning before he woke. He'd never seen her since.

Betty was examining the stacks of newspapers. '*The Herald*, October 1998. *Scotland turns into a crime-fearing nation* . . . '

'Right, I must have kept it for that article,' he

38

said. A lie. Mibbe. He didn't remember. He scanned newspapers habitually, he just never got round to binning them.

'The Evening Times, January 1997. Christ, Lou. How far back do these go?'

'I don't know, but I know where they're going now.' He bent down quickly and grabbed a bundle and carried them outside to the top of the stairs. He dropped them, then went back inside the bedroom. He collected another pile, repeated the act. A cleansing process. He was energized by humiliation.

Betty began hauling papers as well. They had a rhythm going until they collided with each other in the bedroom doorway and she laughed and Perlman's stack slipped out of his arms and fell: the tumbling newspapers released a plastic zip-lock bag, which contained something black in a pool of grey fluid. Perlman couldn't remember any plastic baggie, unless it had contained food he'd brought upstairs one weary night, and he'd fallen asleep without eating it, and somehow it got buried under the dry dead weight of Heralds and Scotsmans.

He bent down to examine it, and immediately recoiled.

'What is it?' Betty asked.

'You don't want to know.' Perlman caught his breath and carefully picked up the baggie between tip of thumb and index finger and held it at arm's length. 'Oh dear Christ,' Betty said, and clasped the palm of one hand to her mouth.

7

In the lamplit car park of the Hilton, Dorcus stood with hands in the pockets of his hooded green duffle-coat. Rain slicked his glasses, and all the world was smudged.

Reuben Chuck held an umbrella which he kept to himself. 'I'm very satisfied with our arrangement. So far.'

Dorcus found Chuck menacing. He looked at people as if he intended to burn their sockets out with the force of his eyes.

'I'm assumin our partnership will be ongoin,' Chuck said.

'Ah y-yes ah of c-course indeed.' Dorcus was infuriated by his lifelong inability to communicate easily. Words came out of him like broken biscuits. He'd always been this way.

Reuben Chuck adjusted the brolly over his head. 'My clientele is elitist, worldly. They all love to spend.' He was beautifully dressed. His black hair was so richly gelled it reflected the lights in the windows of the Hilton. He wore long sideburns cut square, one in perfect alignment with the other.

Dorcus adored symmetry.

'Where there's a need, Reuben Chuck's the man to fill it. Happy customers.'

Chuck had very fine teeth, possibly expensive implants, but realistic.

'We all profit from this, Dorco.'

Dorco, nobody had ever called him Dorco before. 'Prof — well of c-course, I know, you . . . '

'Do I make you uneasy, Dorco?'

Dorcus smiled. He knew he looked gormless when he smiled. He *hated* his smile. He hated his whole face in fact, except when he had the surgical mask on. 'I don't ammm so-socialize much.'

Chuck dismissed this. 'You're an artist, Dorco. An artist has no social obligations. You don't have to doff your bunnet to any wanker. You remember that.'

Dorcus had never thought of himself this way. He was uplifted. It was the same feeling he'd had whenever his father directed a kind word at him, a very rare event. Judge Dysart, a permanently preoccupied man, had been miserly with praise.

Chuck asked, 'You'll have somethin for me day after the morra, eh?'

'Yes y-yes o — '

'I want to know I can count on you one hunnerd and one per cent.' Chuck squeezed Dorcus's shoulder tightly.

'Count on me, of course you can c-count on me.'

'Where did you say you'd trained, Dorco?'

'I'm . . . St Andrews.'

'St Andrews, aye. A man who graduates from a place like that is somebody special. Remember that.'

Dorcus pounced on some loose words like a cat on a bunch of baby rodents, and forced out a complete sentence. 'I have the assistance of a capable nurse, Ms Payne. She's a wonderful — '

Chuck interrupted. 'Good help's essential. A right hand, somebody you can trust. Where did Nurse Payne train?'

'Erm, the R-Royal Infirmary.'

'I had my tonsils whipped out there. Coincidence, you say? Coincidences are meant to *tell* us somethin.' Chuck winked, as if sharing a sly secret with Dorcus. 'They have purpose, Dorco. They have meanin. Don't you forget that.'

The hand squeezed Dorcus's shoulder harder. Dorcus felt his eyes water behind his glasses. Chuck grinned up close, and Dorcus could smell marzipan on his breath.

'I might come off as a hard-arsed business-man, but I have beliefs in other directions . . . ' Chuck looked mysterious and knowing, tapped into hidden sources of information. His slitty eyes became even more narrow. 'One day mibbe I'll tell you more.'

Chuck released him.

Dorcus had lost the thread somewhere around the word *coincidence*. His head had gone rambling. He worried about his house sitting empty and vulnerable. His two Dobermans, Allen and Glen, prowled the grounds in his absence, but dogs could be shot or thrown poisoned food. He had an alarm system protecting windows and doors, but he fully expected that one day the Slab People would scale the thirteen foot stone wall separating his property from the putrid wastelands of the towers. He'd strung razor wire along the top, but when the Slabbites were inebriated they didn't give a damn about personal safety, and once they'd climbed the wall they'd break a window and get inside the house and ignore the alarm, they didn't give a monkey's about anything.

Blood on the wire. Blood was currency to them. Scars were medals of courage.

Chuck said, 'Ahoy in there.'

'S-sorry I sometimes I d-drift — '

Reuben Chuck patted the side of Dorcus's face. 'Drift away, Dorco. Drift all you like. You're entitled.'

Dorcus took off his glasses, wiped them on his sleeve. It only made the lenses worse. It was a stupid thing to do. Just stupid. You ass. Rainwater on glass, glass on wet duffle, did you expect a successful outcome? Oh for God's sake Dorcus. He felt his skull tighten.

Reuben Chuck clamped Dorcus's shoulder again. 'I get the feelin you're hard on yourself, Dorco. Artists are their own worst critics. You know what your problem is? You don't know how to relax.'

'No, y-you're right, I . . . '

'It just so *happens* I know somebody who could help, Dorco. Beautiful girl. She's got ways of making the world go away. And don't you even think about openin your wallet. It's on the house.'

'But but.'

'Tcchhhh,' Chuck said. 'Consider it done.' He checked his Gucci SilverTone wrist-watch. 'Time and tide. I'm always under pressure. I'll send Glorianna over to you. She'll phone first.

Awright? She'll make you feel a whole new man
. . . And the next shipment. You remember where
to deliver it?'

'I d-do, yes.'

Reuben Chuck hurried to his parked car,
which had been running all this time. A very
large muscular man in a black leather coat had
been sitting behind the wheel, waiting and
watching. Chuck collapsed the umbrella and
tossed it in the rear seat, then he stepped into the
back of the car and gave a tiny flick of his head,
goodbye.

Dorcus waved. Nice car, a Jag-you-are.

Anxieties crowded him. Don't send me
anybody. Please. I don't need. I don't need a
woman —

I have Nurse Payne.

He made semaphore-like signals with his arms
upraised to catch Chuck's attention, but the Jag
was already roaring off into the blackening
arteries of Glasgow.

8

Inside the abandoned bowling-alley Reuben Chuck said to the blindfolded man, 'You haven't told me what I want to know, Danny.'

'Away tay fuck,' Turpie said.

'You're wastin my time, Danny.'

Chuck stood with his hands clasped behind his back. Some people love punishment, he thought. Turpie had been punched and kicked and mauled. His lips were split and his mouth leaked blood. Blood dripped from his skull and soaked his blindfold.

Chuck sighed, looking round at the assembly of his men who stood in shadows behind him. They were big men, some with shaven heads. They wore dark suits fashionably cut. Chuck knew they had handguns, knives, old-fashioned clasped razors, concealed in their clothing.

He turned to Turpie again. 'Say the numbers, son. All you have to do and you're out of here.'

'I telt you. I gave a vow to Stoker.'

'A vow to a dead man, come *on*, what's that worth?'

'Means something in my book,' Danny said. He was speaking with the difficulty of a battered prizefighter whose mouth was so numb it felt more like a protruding snout than a hollow where you placed food.

Struggling with impatience, Chuck surveyed the bowling-alley, rundown and drab. He'd acquired the property in the past week, thanks to the *putsch*, but hadn't decided if he'd keep or demolish it. The place smelled of bowling shoes worn by hundreds of different punters, the ancient jukebox was covered in dust, and some of the lanes were warped by damp.

He addressed his men. 'This guy has a death wish, boys. Karmic irresponsibility on his part.'

Danny Turpie said, 'You're talking pure shite.'

Chuck spoke slowly. 'Life's not precious to you, is it, Danny? You're throwin it away on account of a promise that has absolutely *no* value. In my book this is an affront to destiny.'

Danny Turpie said, 'Destiny my arse.'

Chuck was aware of his crew growing restless. These men failed to understand why he was still giving Danny Turpie a chance. They were stoked to rip Turpie's fucking head off his shoulders and put his corpse through a meat-grinder and never mind the bla-bla, the karmic babble.

'Numbers? I'll give ye a fucking number,' and Danny Turpie sang in a blood-thickened voice, *'Hallo Hallo we are the Billy Boys.'*

'A singer eh?' Chuck surveyed his gang. 'We've got ourselves a singer, boys.'

'Hallo hallo we are the Billy Boys. Up to our knees in Fenian —'

Chuck tuned out this sectarian trash. Some people didn't grow beyond the boundaries of their narrow-minded upbringing: football was a pagan form of worship, and stadia had become cathedrals of malice. 'Right, *right*, Turpie. Game's over. Chance after chance. And you're showin no respect for me.'

He nodded to his black-suited platoon.

The men quickly encircled Danny, grabbing him and throwing him down on the lane. He kept singing defiantly until somebody smacked him a few times in the mouth, and even then he managed to utter a few miserable phrases. Some of Chuck's men produced a rope, binding Turpie's hands behind his back, then tying hands to feet and pulling tightly. They positioned him facing the bowler's end of the lane. Danny struggled fiercely but pointlessly against the ropes. Chuck removed the blindfold without looking into Turpie's eyes. The men, having stewed too long in the adrenalin of delayed violence, hurried back to the top of the lane and picked up dusty old bowling balls from racks.

Chuck had done a lot of violence when he was a younger man, but he'd lost the appetite for it and, besides, there were problematic questions involved — when you hurt somebody for their stupid obstinacy, what were the repercussions in the greater scheme? For example: did you fuck up your own reincarnation?

I'm no comin back as a silkworm, no way.

He looked on. He had no choice. He couldn't show weakness in front of the big men. They were a cunning gang with predatory instincts, and if they caught a whiff of vulnerability in their Boss, they began to lose respect. He'd still be The Big Man, sure, but there would be noticeable differences — the men would be slightly less responsive in obeying orders, or they'd talk behind his back and clam up dead silent as soon as he approached.

Worst case, they might begin plotting against him.

So he was tough. Because he had to be.

He watched the black bowling balls thunder down the lane at great speed. They screamed toward Danny, and clattered into his face, skull, groin, knees. Danny shouted a couple of times. A few gutterballs missed him completely, small mercies. A second fusillade began. The balls racketed and vibrated and kept coming, ten, twenty, more, black cannon-balls. Danny's leather jacket was scarlet and blood puddled around him.

Chuck said, 'That's enough, boys.'

He walked to where Turpie lay and nudged him with his foot.

Turpie didn't move.

Chuck stared at the mass of flesh formerly Danny's head. Shattered nose, hair matted like red webbing, eyes shut, mouth wide. Danny was *deid*.

He glanced at his crew with a look of recrimination, then gazed back down at Turpie. How come Stoker, himself dead and buried, could maintain such loyalty from beyond the grave? You had to admire the fortitude of Danny Turpie's vow, if not his obstinacy. He wondered if any of his boys would do for him what Turpie had done for Stoker. He had his doubts.

'Clean and lock up before you leave, boys.' He walked away from Turpie and in frustration kicked the jukebox and it cranked into action. An old Lonnie Donegan tune played: 'Nobody's Child'. He kicked the jukebox again but the song wouldn't quit.

Somebody said, 'Mental wee cunt Turpie. Always a heidcase.'

Chuck stepped outside. The night rain had stopped and the air smelled clean. He thought about the access numbers to Bram Stoker's bank accounts, and how they'd died with Danny Turpie. Mibbe.

★　★　★

Ronnie Mathieson, tinted glasses, jaw as smooth as glass, drove Chuck in the Jaguar to The Number One Fitness Centre, situated in a small business park in Crossmyloof, south of the river. Chuck paused before he got out and turned to Mathieson.

'The bank's the Clydesdale, Ronnie,' he said. 'The branch on Buchanan Street. Find out who runs it.'

'Willdo.'

As Chuck climbed the steps to the aquamarine glass doors of the Fitness Centre he was struck by the realization of how many more interests he had than before. Apart from an upmarket bistro and a chain of health spas and a factory supplying bootleg Aberdeen Angus beef, all of which were in his possession before the deaths of Curdy and Stoker and their various underlings, he now found himself the owner of a fleet of buses equipped for the transportation of the handicapped, a squadron of taxis and minicabs, several brothels, a casino, an underground pharmaceutical concern geared to produce E and speed and assorted designer drugs, a textile company in need of reorganization, *plus* four boutique hotels scattered throughout Glasgow, three tenement blocks in Partick, two fish and chip shops, a dry-cleaning chain, one point nine acres of prime city-centre land licensed for commercial development — and, of course, the clapped out bowling-alley. He had his lawyers Roman, Glebe & Hack going twenty-four hours a day on all the paperwork, documents of ownership, deeds of exchange, the reassignment of which involved some serious diddlin and fiddlin — whatever it took. This wasn't the old days when you could just seize whatever took your fancy, today you had to make it appear legal, so you needed inventive suits who knew the score. More, you needed layers of suits, solicitors and clerks and an assortment of other figures who worked for lawyers, but whose affiliation with the law was not easy to define.

Chuck was blasted out of his thoughts by a sickening eye-scalding cloud of chlorine. Annoyed, he sought out Tommy Lombardo, who was in the ground floor gym training a muscular Romanian woman to lift weights.

Tommy was urging her on in his enthusiastic way. 'Concentrate, Slaca, concentrate, hold aw the air in yer lungs. That's my girl. Aw the air, keep it in. Know when to release it. Hang on.'

The woman sweated, trying hard to please Tommy. 'So deefycull, Tommy.'

'You'll get it.'

'Tommy,' Chuck said. 'A minute.'

Tommy Lombardo looked round. 'Mr Chuck, I didn't see — '

50

'I telt you to go easy on the chlorine. Explain to me why the first thin I notice as I come through the front door is the heavy stink of the stuff? This place is mingin.'

'I musta used too much.' Lombardo, who was six foot four inches tall, had gobbled enough steroids to make him the Muscle King of Glasgow. He also pumped iron every spare minute he had. Chuck was convinced the steroids had interfered with certain important cerebral connections, because Tommy was incapable of just about any task he was given — except that of attracting a certain clientele to the gym, gays who wanted *look-at-me-sweetie* muscle tone, butch lesbians who fancied themselves weightlifters, and assorted good-looking women who had nothing better to do than come down here and admire Tommy's musculature and even touch it. They were groupies, these women. They kept the member-ship high.

'That smell drives customers away, Tommy.' Chuck spoke slowly, as if to a child.

'I'm sorry, Mr Chuck.'

'And why is there nobody at the reception desk? I telt you, Tommy, make sure there's always somebody to sign in the customers. Remember?'

'It's Zondra's fault, Mr Chuck. She's always slipping out for a smoke.'

'Then deal with it, Tommy. Tell her don't smoke. This place is meant to promote *health*.'

'Right, I'll say to her. Don't smoke.'

Chuck patted one of Tommy Lombardo's

biceps. Hard as rock. Like his brain. 'I don't have time to be runnin round checkin on employees.'

Chuck walked away quickly. When people don't do the job you pay them for, if they don't follow orders . . . *Flashpoint. Business stress. Self-control wanted, Rube.* He gulped air that tasted of bleach. He walked through the reception area and climbed the stairs to the upper gymnasium where a half dozen people were working the machines. A white-haired overweight woman pounded the Lifestride treadmill, and an elderly guy, his expression one of stark fear at the idea of cardiac arrest, rode the Sportsart bike.

Chuck thought of this area as the Drop Dead Zone.

He found Glorianna in a private room at the back. She was lying on a lounger, earphones attached to her head and an iPod on her flat belly. She wore white shorts and a blue singlet with the logo Number One Fitness. Her hair was curled, black with blonde highlights. Her espresso-brown eyes were just a shade too wide for her slender face, but Chuck thought her straight nose perfect in all ways, the nostrils pleasingly symmetrical. He had a thing about noses.

He tapped a finger on one of the earphones and startled her.

'Rube, oh wow, you like scared me.' She affected American speech rhythms and expressions occasionally, because her ambition was to emigrate to California. Years ago, she'd been devoted to *Baywatch* and *Beverly Hills 90210*.

She dreamed cinema. She studied the gossip magazines, who was divorcing who, what star was being unfaithful to wife or husband. She took voice lessons and drama classes in preparation for the moment when she hit Tinseltown.

She removed her earphones and Chuck heard modern jazz issue from them.

'That Lombardo will be the death of me.'

'I know. It stinks down there, so I got Zondra to send for the Oxydoro guys, who'll be here within the hour and reduce the chlorine levels.'

'You're a star.' Chuck ruffled her hair.

She was quick and sharp and you didn't have to spell things out for her. She took action when it was needed. He'd given her control of all six Number One Fitness Centres, not just because he was very fond of her, and they shared an intense sexual history — because he trusted her more than anyone else in his tiny circle of intimates. Bottom line, she protected his interests.

She said, 'Tommy's so thick I bet he doesn't even recognize his own reflection in a mirror. I told him, one more fuck-up and you're on your bike.'

'He brings in the clients . . . Lissen, I need you to do somethin.'

'Tell me.'

'I have this guy I do some business with. He's a bit out there, very high strung.'

'The kinda guy who thinks Relax is something you take when you're constipated.'

'Right. I want you to call him.'

'And?' Glorianna took a tube of skin cream

53

from a box that contained dozens of similar cylinders. She opened it and worked the cream into her thighs. Chuck contemplated women and all their assorted creams. The whole lotion-skin relationship was a mystery to him.

He said, 'I'm thinkin mibbe one of your massages will do the trick.'

She looked at him with an expression of disbelief. He'd never asked her to do this kind of thing before. 'And if my massage doesn't work? You want me to *fuck* him, Chuck?'

'Now hang on a minute, sweetie. I'd *never* ask you to do anythin like that. Keep in mind I need his business, and I don't want to send him some rough tottie.'

'If he needs a great massage, Rube, that's what he'll get.'

'It's not like I'm pimpin you — '

But you're using me, she thought. 'I don't fuck strange men, Rube.'

'I hate when you swear, pet. Swearin coarsens you.' He took her hand and stroked it. He flicked a lock of hair from her cheek. She was in a sulk. He'd offended her, and hadn't meant to.

She said, 'I remember when you used to curse every second word.'

'People evolve. Baba says if you don't accept the possibility of change, you stagnate. And that's the death of the soul.'

Baba, Baba. Glorianna, who'd introduced Chuck to the guru nine months ago, still longed for the lapsed Catholic Rube used to be, hard-living, hard-drinking, meat-eating party beast and tireless lover. But that guy had vanished in Baba's domain. She'd imagined he might have been more sceptical about the guru's teachings. After the Catholic church had disappointed him, she guessed he'd been desperate to embrace a new system of beliefs — even if she didn't quite understand how he squared some of his business methods with the guru's words.

'Is it because I swear you don't *fuck* me any more, Rube?'

'No, no . . . it's . . . ' He drifted a moment. 'I'm searching for somethin. Somethin beyond all this.'

'Peace of mind. A world of harmony.' La-di-dah. *Babaspeak*.

'Aye right.'

She gazed at his face, which sometimes had an unexpected softness about it. *I could show you peace of mind*, she thought. Turn back the clock to the way things were. 'It's a tough road, Rube.'

'Anything of value is tough to attain.'

Echoes of Baba. She'd hung around the guru long enough to recognize his sayings. She'd been to his spiritual retreats, in a house near Loch Lomond, where he preached and his acolytes chanted. It was easy to fall into the guru's ways. Hadn't she done it herself? Been through the crystals, meditated, studied massage. She had a sensational Trigger Point technique. She read interviews with film stars who proclaimed their beliefs fearlessly: Gere had his Buddhism, Travolta and Cruise their Scientology. When she got to LA, she figured she'd better have something going for her beyond looks and talent and her massage skills — which Baba had suggested, in that persuasively quiet way of his, could be used for purposes of tranquility and relaxation, instead of sexual control and material gain.

Easy for him to say. Sometimes Baba was too idealistic for her. What was he suggesting — free massages? 'Somebody told me today I had a strong resemblance to Nicole Kidman.'

'By any chance was he carryin a white stick?'

She threw a towel at him. 'I got the name of an agent in Tinseltown. I sent off some photographs of myself.'

'You checked him out first?'

'You think I'd send them without doing background?'

Chuck said, 'Not you.'

She watched him for a time. 'You look tense, Rube. Take off your jacket and shirt. I'll massage you.'

He stripped to the waist. He lay face down on a towel she spread across the lounger and she kneaded the flesh beneath his shoulders in the way she'd always done. Then worked his lower spine, within reaching distance of his buttocks.

Chuck felt a familiar tingle. This celibate life had serious drawbacks.

She asked, 'You know how long it's been, Rube?'

He said nothing.

'Eight months. Four weeks after you first went to see Baba.'

That long. Chuck shut his eyes and heard an echo of 'Nobody's Child' inside his head.

9

At 9 p.m. Perlman's doorbell rang. He turned on the light in the hallway and opened the door. He was surprised to see Detective Superintendent Mary Gibson. 'A sight for sore eyes,' he said, and shook her hand. Her touch was light, her skin cool.

She held on to his grip. 'I heard about this 'discovery' of yours and I thought I'd drop in — it gives me a chance to say hello.'

'I'm delighted.' And he was. She'd always been sympathetic to him, and fair, even at times when they had disagreements, and she was obliged to pull rank. She had an open intelligent face, shrewd dark eyes, and a feature that always pleased Perlman — a trace of girlhood freckles. She was accompanied by a Detective Sergeant she introduced as Jock Tigge, a dour black-bearded man who looked at Perlman and grunted a kind of greeting.

Mary Gibson stepped inside the house. Jock Tigge, wide-shouldered as a wrestler, followed behind her. He had noticeably long arms. A baboon, Perlman thought.

'I like the new look, Lou,' Mary Gibson said.
'New look?'
'No specs. Contacts comfy?'
'They're fine.' Perlman fingered the slight ridges on either side of his nose. Sometimes he felt he was wearing phantom glasses and made to

57

adjust them, then remembered his schnozzle was gloriously naked. He escorted Mary Gibson into the living room, thankful that the place was shiny clean. Surreptitiously, he closed the door to the kitchen.

'How have you been?' she asked.

Perlman was preparing a catalogue of complaints, but she spoke before he could get a sentence out. 'Wait, don't answer. I know you, Lou.'

Perlman thought: *Kvetch* not. Grumbling was monotonous, and drained the spirit. Besides, he'd been diverted from self-absorption and pessimism by what Mary Gibson called the discovery. It was a discovery, all right, not one he enjoyed making, although it *did* provoke a welcome bafflement, a doorway into that world of perplexity and mystery he longed for. Forget the headless clown, he had *this* in his own house.

'So this found object is in the bedroom,' Mary Gibson said.

'Upstairs.'

'Somehow I never imagined you having a bed, Lou. I always thought you just flopped out on a sofa.'

'I'm a bundle of surprises,' he said.

Mary Gibson arched one eyebrow, and stepped across the living room. She was immaculate, lipstick perfect, hair just right. She dressed in soft colours, peaches and quiet tans, understated. She was elegant; she didn't look like a cop, didn't smell like one. She left in her wake a subdued perfume, an essence Perlman found captivating.

She surveyed the living room. 'Very tidy, Lou. I'm impressed.'

Be grateful she never saw it before it was Bettyized. He'd sent the pale-faced Betty McLatchie home. She might need to be interviewed at some point, he knew, but she said she was scunnered and would he mind if she came back tomorrow? Christ — he'd forgotten her missing son, blown out of his mind by the appearance of the baggie. Maybe Kirk would turn up, repentant and weary. Perlman hoped so.

At the foot of the stairs Mary Gibson paused. 'Lead the way, Lou.'

Perlman climbed past her on the narrow stairway. 'You'll need to step over these newspapers.'

'They have recycling places everywhere.'

'That's an urban myth,' Perlman said.

She glanced at a photograph on the wall. 'Your parents?'

Perlman said yes. A framed black and white, a studio shot, Etta and Ephraim and their two kids, circa 1953. Nobody was smiling. Ephraim wore the plain black suit he wore to *shul*, and Etta was dressed in a skirt and blouse — the blouse black and white striped, the skirt grey. They had the look of immigrants uncertain of their place in the world, assimilated only in the most superficial ways, but still and forever outsiders. Colin, six years old, a good-looking boy in a serge suit with short pants from the Cooperative, stood alongside his father. He was already a Glaswegian, already learning the ways of the Gorbals streets. And little Lou, in knee-length trousers and white shirt, stood next to Etta, frowning, peering suspiciously into the camera, an inquisitorial look even then.

'You're quite the tough-looking wee man, Lou. You have a slight resemblance to your mother,' Mary Gibson said. She continued to examine the portrait for a while. 'Your Dad doesn't look happy.'

'He was never at home here,' Perlman said.

No mention of Colin. Colin was erased, if not from the photograph then certainly from conversation. The bad penny. Perlman stopped on the threshold of the bedroom. 'In here,' he said. 'Excuse the state.'

'I promise, I'm not looking,' she said.

In Mary Gibson's presence the bedroom seemed even smaller than before, more tatty. Jock Tigge cleared his throat, as if suppressing a comment. Perlman knew he'd carry stories back to Pitt Street. You should see Perlman's bedroom, Christ, talk about a tip. The sheets haven't been changed since the year Dot. I've seen cleaner zoos.

He hated Tigge suddenly. Tigge wasn't on some trumped-up sick leave, Tigge could come and go at Pitt Street all he liked, Tigge could investigate and book miscreants, powers denied Perlman. How resentments expand until they fill the whole *heid*, Perlman thought. Clogging the noggin.

'We were in the process of cleaning up when we found the bag,' he said.

'We?' Mary Gibson asked.

'I have a nice woman in to help. Don't say high time.'

'The phrase never entered my mind.'

60

Perlman indicated the plastic bag, which he'd left on the floor.

Tigge produced a pair of latex gloves from his coat pocket and put them on, then bent to pick up the baggie. He held it in the air.

'It's a hand all right,' he said. He had a funny singsong rustic accent. Perlman thought Aberdeenshire. The accent annoyed him. He was doomed never to adore Tigge. The chemistry was pish.

Mary Gibson looked closely at the object.

Perlman said, 'It was stashed among the newspapers.'

'No rings,' Tigge said, eyeballing the hand. 'No obvious marks.'

'You can't see *shite* through the slime in the bag,' Perlman said impatiently.

Mary Gibson asked, 'No idea how it got here?'

'None.' Perlman was engrossed with the sight of the hand. The flesh was black, shrivelled.

'Have you had an intruder at any time?' Mary Gibson asked.

'Not that I know.'

'Do you ever leave the house unlocked, Lou?'

'Crazy? There are people here who'd take your false teeth while you slept. And I'm not talking teeth in an overnight glass, Mary. Right out your geggie.'

'Could somebody have broken in without you knowing it?'

'There are two doors, back and front, I bolt both from the inside at night. These are new since the shooting. When I go out, I lock them both, Chubb triple-action locks. I would've noticed if anybody had interfered with them, Mary.'

'Windows,' Mary Gibson said.

'Snibbed from the inside. You'd need to break glass to get a hand on the snib and release it. No glass is broken anywhere in the house. So what have we got? Houdini? A ghost? A being with special powers who can pass through glass and/or stone?'

Mary Gibson said, 'If you didn't have an intruder, and your house is a fortress — '

'I wouldn't go that far.'

'The question stays the same. How did the hand get here?'

Tigge smiled. 'A skinny dwarf came down the chimney.'

Perlman glared at Tigge. Who asked your opinion, Sergeant Simian?

Mary Gibson said, 'Take the bag to the car and wait for me, Tigge. We'll run it over to Sid Linklater.' Linklater was an owlish young forensics wizard. Scholarly Sid.

Tigge left, clumping on the staircase.

'Light on his feet,' Perlman said.

'Tigge only joined Force HQ from Elgin,' Mary Gibson said. 'Just so you know.'

'I'm to make allowances?'

Mary Gibson laughed. 'You don't know how.'

Perlman liked her laugh. It was low-pitched, and could even be bawdy after a few drinks. 'Maybe I did go out one day and I forgot to lock the door.'

'It's always possible — '

'Aye but it worries me.'

62

'We all have moments, Lou, forgetful, preoccupied — '

He feared the idea of mental decline. First you forget, then you drool. Halfway down the stairs he lit a cigarette and said, 'I wouldn't want to be within a mile of that bag when Sid opens it.'

'Young Sid is enchanted with all things morbid, Lou. The stench of putrefaction is pure cherry blossom to him.' They reached the living room where she scanned the music collection. 'I know what you're thinking. You have a proprietorial interest.'

'My bedroom. Finders keepers, Mary.'

'And you expect to be involved in an investigation.'

'I live in hope.'

'Lou.' She patted his arm.

'I'm about to hear your life's a disappointment speech.'

'Tay's not going to back you, Lou.'

'Oh Mary, it's fuck all to do with my wound. *I* know that. *You* know that. *You can't come back until your shoulder's truly mended.*' He walked round the living room, impersonating Tay's flat accent, and wagging a finger in the air. 'Translation: they want me out. It's all politics. I have a history down there of . . . saying what I think.'

'And doing what you like.'

'Feh, so I stepped on a few toes, crossed a few lines.'

'More than a few, Lou. This is *me* you're talking to. How long have we known each other?'

'I need back in, Mary. Talk to Tay.'

'He's a misogynist with a mind like an air-raid shelter. I'm a token in his eyes. And you broke a rule, so you're *persona non grata*. You always will be so long as Tay runs the show. But I'll try. Just prep yourself for a no.'

Perlman walked with her to the front door. He remembered she'd separated from her husband six months ago. 'How's the marital situation?'

'Larry doesn't want to be a cop's husband. I'm never home, he says. Which is true.'

'It's tough,' he said.

'It's damn sad . . . I'll get back to you, Lou.'

He opened the front door for her and watched her walk to a parked car and get in on the passenger side. He closed the door and returned to the living room.

Changes are in the air, he thought. It's *my* fucking hand.

10

First thing each morning Dorcus walked the inside of the stone wall that surrounded his property. Wearing thick rubber gloves, he raked up rubbish slung over from the towers. He often found wrinkled condoms, knickers, bras, shoes, lipstick tubes, punctured tyres, bicycle wheels, wads of used toilet paper. Once, he'd come across a set of false teeth, upper and lower. He shovelled all this stuff into plastic bin bags.

He'd written letters of complaint to the council about the junk, but nobody had ever come to offer advice, or suggest a remedy. Dorcus's old house was an anachronism and should have been knocked down when the estate first went up. Those Slabbites lived in another country, where the rule of law was a joke.

He finished clearing the rubbish and dragged the plastic bags to the bins outside his kitchen door just as the dogs erupted in a harsh chorus of barking and charged to the wall. A boy's face appeared in the leafy upper limb of a high oak that grew outside Dorcus's property, but branched several feet above the razor wire.

Dorcus looked up at the kid. He was eleven, twelve, and had a cigarette stuck between his lips. His hairstyle was one favoured by young Slabbites, skull shaved almost to the bone, leaving a faint fuzz.

'Hey you. Dysfart.' The kid tossed his cigarette

end at the dogs. 'My da says you're weird. He says you eat weans. Issat right?'

Dorcus stomped on the butt and glared at the boy. The dogs jumped at the wall, snarling. 'Your f-father's . . . t-talking stupid.'

'He says you're fuckn mental.'

Dorcus shouted back. 'He's the m-mental one.'

'He says you're a l-lassie, a j-jessie.'

Mocked by the kid's stutter, Dorcus tugged at his thin yellow hair, which grew almost to his shoulders. He quivered. Anger shook him.

Dorcus said, 'I'll set my dogs on you.'

'Oh aye, they magic dugs? Climb this wall, eh? Fuckn peddy. Arse-bandit.'

Dorcus knew he lacked a combative face. He'd never scare this kid.

'My Da says this hoose is hauntit, filt wi ghosts and aw that.'

'Your Da's a superstitious m-moron.'

'He is no.'

The boy hawked some phlegm and spat. It caught in leaves, and dangled. 'See, you're no even worth a spit, ya fuckn freak.'

Dorcus pictured laying the boy out on the surgical table and taking a scalpel with a number ten blade to his heart. Very slow incisions.

The boy lit a fresh cigarette. Then he changed his position on the branch and hung from it one-handed and made a jungle noise. '*Greoooo.* Me Tarzan, you Jane. Snort snort.'

The Dobermans launched themselves against the wall with renewed frenzy. They leaped and salivated, but they were six feet short of the boy.

Fall, you little bastard, fall, Dorcus thought. And just for a moment the kid slipped and looked like he would tumble, but he hauled himself back up into the thickness of leaves, adroitly evading the razor wire. Then he was gone and the branches vibrated a while after his departure.

Dorcus stared at the tree and thought: *I'll go out in the white van later.*

He stepped inside the house. His palms were sweaty. He dried them against his khaki trousers. He entered his father's study, where the old brown-tinted blinds were drawn. The Judge had bought this property in the early 1950s years before the Slabs came into being. The house was sandstone Victorian, with cupolas and sculpted ornamental fruits above the front door. There were more rooms than Dorcus could ever use. Some he never entered. He'd tossed curtains over chairs and sofas and wrapped his mother's piano in a dust cover. He tried to maintain the place on the money the Judge had left him, but the struggle against damp and decay was too demanding.

He sat in his father's cracked brown leather swivel chair. The Judge used to sit here night after night, law books open before him, and his big fountain pen in his hand. He scribbled notes in yellow legal pads. He often talked aloud to himself as he anguished over interpretations of the law. One bitter cold morning, Dorcus had come into the room hauling a bucket of coal to add to the dying fire. The Judge had taken off his glasses and set his pen down and asked, *How old are you now Dorcus?*

Nine, sir. Dorcus had thrown coal into the grate. His hands were black.

I never seem to remember birthdays, not even my son's, the Judge said, and stared at him in a forlorn way. *I live in the afterlife, Dorcus, which is my tragedy. And, unfortunately, yours. I have regrets.*

It was the only time in Dorcus's recollection that the Judge had ever spoken from his heart, and he'd done so uneasily, quickly. He'd replaced his spectacles and picked up his pen and resumed writing, dismissing the boy.

As a father, Judge Dysart was as distant, as cold, as the North Star.

Dorcus rose, left the room, shut the door. Why did he come in here anyway? What did he expect to discover — memories of warmth and affection?

He thought about the boy in the tree. That stupid-faced boy with his moronic taunts. Forget him. Forget them, all the Slabbites and their spawn.

Tonight he'd go out.

He left the study and climbed the stairs.

He usually moved past the cold spot quickly, but this time he paused when he heard a very faint conversation, voices at a distance. The sentences were splintered. And footsteps, always footsteps, but he could never tell where they came from. He smelled the essence of rose oil his mother used. He heard the tick of the thin gold wrist watch that had lain on her bedside table, a soft sound, like a fingernail against an eggshell.

He heard his mother's voice whispering in his

ear: *Dorcus, let me kiss you, my dear son* . . .

The chill on those anaemic lips, the smell of dying on her breath.

He thrust himself beyond the cold, reached the top of the stairs, looked back down.

There was nothing, there was never anything to see. It was as if he passed briefly through a zone where he didn't belong, a place where the dead, for arcane reasons of their own, assembled. A congregation of inchoate echoes, dissonant phrases, gutted sentences.

Hauntit.

Or it's my head, inside my head, all of it. He didn't want to think that. It never happened when Nurse Payne was here. She comforted him. They comforted each other. She'd been deep inside his heart where nobody had been before. Sometimes in her company he felt the world was populated only by him and her, and everyone else had perished in a catastrophe.

The telephone in his bedroom rang. He rushed to answer it. Maybe it was her. He threw himself on his narrow bed and stretched out for the receiver on the bedside table.

'H-Hello,' he said.

'Dorcus?' A woman's voice. Not Nurse Payne's.

'Yes.'

'My name's Glorianna and I've got plans for you. Wednesday night, say six-thirtyish, Dorcus?'

'W-wait . . .'

But she'd hung up.

11

Perlman had fallen asleep on the sofa and his body was stiff from lying in a confined space. He checked the room, a hangover-like blur. He'd taken out his contacts and couldn't remember where he'd left them. The pain in his shoulder throbbed, what an effort to get up. He opened a drawer in the sideboard and groped for his old Buddy Holly glasses and felt weird wearing them again, like a harness on his face. At least he could see. He walked to the front door in his red and black plaid dressing-gown. A few scraps of mail lay on the floor and as he bent to pick them up his spine creaked like the mast of a sailing-ship.

Junk mail. Dross. Nothing from the peripatetic Miriam.

A key turned in the lock and Betty McLatchie, looking drained, came into the hallway.

'Morning Lou, sleepless night?'

'Does it show?'

'A wee bit. I'll make coffee. I could use a gallon myself. Like the glasses. Will you sing 'Peggy Sue' for me?'

'Me? I've got a voice that would frighten children.'

He followed her into the kitchen. She set her bag on the table and she shook the kettle to check there was water inside. She turned on the gas and struck a match. The flame exploded

70

— whoosh, blue and yellow.

'I've only got instant guff,' he said. He opened a cabinet and found a jar of Maxwell House and two mugs, which he placed beside the stove.

'How do you take it?' she asked.

'No milk, no sugar. Straight and hot.'

She spooned coffee into the mugs. She took a cigarette from her bag. 'Sorry I had to leave yesterday.'

'How many times in your life do you see a severed hand?'

'Once is enough.'

He nodded at her cigarette packet on the table. 'You mind?'

'Help yourself.'

Perlman took one of her Benson and Hedges, and lit it from the flame on the stove. Betty poured two coffees. Perlman sat, reached for a mug and warmed his hands around it. He looked at Betty. She had dark circles under her eyes, and the eyes had shed their blue lustre.

She laid her cigarette in the ashtray in a tired manner, and blew on the surface of her coffee.

'No word from Kirk?' he asked.

'Not a thing.'

'I'll get on to it today.' He touched the back of Betty's hand, a gesture of comfort, something to say I'll do what I can.

She smiled at him uncertainly. 'I talked to a couple of his pals last night. They don't know where he is.'

Perlman sipped his coffee, tasteless shite. His shoulder pinged. He'd take a painkiller. 'Leave it with me. If I happen to need a photo of Kirk,

71

can you get one for me?'

She opened her purse. 'Here.'

She handed him a snapshot so quickly that Perlman was caught off guard, as if he'd been surprised by some dexterous sleight of hand. He hadn't expected her to be carrying a pic. He took it, studied Kirk's image. He wasn't handsome, he could be any face passing on the street, one you'd never look at twice. Where Betty's face was lively and open, Kirk's was a hard read. This was Betty's beloved son, this brown-haired, brown-eyed young man with a sullen air.

He said, 'I'm sure I won't need this.' Softening the edge of the situation. 'In case. Just in case. For my own use.'

'Right, I understand. I better get started on the kitchen now.' She finished her coffee, crushed out her cigarette, rinsed her cup in the sink.

'You sure you're up to working today?'

'I want to. I need to.'

He rose. Busy day ahead. He was quickened by the prospect of activity. As he got up he became uncomfortably aware of his pyjamas under the dressing-gown, a motif of horses' heads on a dark green background. What had prompted him to buy these ridiculous pyjamas — wait, a gift, that was it, something his Aunt Marlene had given him a couple of Chanukahs ago. She still thought he was a boy. Wee Louis. Here's a penny, go treat yerself to some toffee and watch the traffic. She was almost ninety and her mind often wandered in the distressed gardens of memory.

'I better get dressed,' he said. 'Who'd be seen dead in these?'

'They're not you, are they?'

'Definitely not.' He went upstairs to his bedroom, clambering over the newspaper stacks at the top of the stairs. He'd meant to bring them down, dump them. Slipped his mind. He needed to focus. He found a blue and white checked shirt in his wardrobe and a pair of blue trousers. The scuffed brown shoes he chose didn't go well with blue. He rummaged for a tie, gave up: I need a tie?

He entered the bathroom, saw his contacts on the edge of the bathtub — how did they get abandoned here? You leave things in places where you always forget them. How much of anyone's daily life is passed hunting contacts, glasses, other everyday things? He took off his glasses, inserted the contacts carefully, confronted his image. The treadmarks on his face. His life was inscribed in every whorl and wrinkle. This face had been punched, battered, shot at. He splashed soapy hot water over his cheeks and ran wet hands through his hair. To shave or not to? Forget it. He brushed his teeth quickly, spat. He picked up a roll of floss. He despised floss. He squeezed the roll as if to choke it. 'Who invented you, eh? What dickhead dentist with time on his hands came up with the idea of waxed thread to jerk between the gaps? You wee gum-bleeder monstrosity.'

He tossed the hateful floss into the waste paper basket.

Reconfigured Perlman, prepped for the day.

* * *

Downstairs, Betty was already scrubbing the surface of the gas stove. She worked energetically, sleeves rolled up. The skin round her elbows was glossy and cracked into little lines.

He hesitated in the doorway, juggling puzzles. Caffeine lit small brush-fires in the canyons. The hand. The missing son. Miriam. The clown. Such an accumulation of enigmas. His brain was warming up. Day one, new life, zoom.

'I'll be back whenever,' he said. 'If I hear anything, I'll call. And if you get hungry — '

'I'll know not to look in the fridge.'

Perlman smiled. 'Some people who opened that fridge were never seen again.'

'I brought a sandwich with me.'

'Foresight,' and he stepped into the hallway, grabbed his coat, left the house.

Halfway down Dalness Street, streaming along in his vermilion Ka, he realized he'd forgotten his painkiller.

* * *

He turned along Shettleston Road. A very cold sun hung in the sky and a chill wind cavorted between the tenements. There was a mean quality about this area, a desperation, a shabbiness. A few bleak bars, a bakery or two, a grocer, a fruit shop, everything rundown.

Break out the bright paint, Christ's sake. Get some fucking pride in your community. Perlman, civic booster. There was no energy here to

74

provide a makeover. Listlessness prevailed. A drugged girl in soiled clothes lay comatose in a filthy doorway. Weary teenage mothers, resigned to a future promising only more babies and little affection, wheeled prams along the pavement.

He passed a pool hall where a coven of hard men, pretending to be immune to the cold, stood bare-armed in the doorway, displaying their vivid blue tattoos. They sneered at Perlman. Their inbred radar scanned him: they knew he was polis.

His shoulder ached as if pinched in big crabclaws. On Duke Street, which connected the East End with the city centre, he looked for a chemist's. It was a long street of grey-brown tenements, rinkydink shops, stuttering buses blowing smoke. A sad anachronistic horse, blinkered and in obvious need of feelgood drugs — Perlman instantly bonded with the poor trudging animal — hauled a cart crammed with mismatched furniture held in place by crisscrossing ropes.

In new Glasgow, a daguerreotype of the old.

He parked on a double yellow line and jumped out, hurrying inside a chemist's, where he chanced his arm and asked if he could obtain some pethidine without prescription, a request sternly rejected by a pinched-mouth lady in a hairnet behind the counter. Perlman fumed under his breath and settled for Solpadeine with codeine and flamboyantly tossed two down his throat in front of the woman: fuck your scripts, hen, I don't need em.

He thought about stopping at Coia's café for

some decent coffee, changed his mind. The air from Tennant's Brewery, below the Necropolis where crosses and obelisks rose in the sky, was lushly bitter with the scent of hops. If the wind was right, you could get stewed on these fumes. The Great Eastern Hotel loomed up, once a famous flophouse, now a dark shell slated for conversion to flats. Old cigarette factories, abandoned churches, shutdown schools — they were all being converted to flats. Flats flats flats.

Glasgow was Flat City.

He drove past the blackened edifice of Royal Infirmary, where he'd been taken immediately after the shooting. He remembered waking hooked up to a drip, the excruciating pain, a sourpussed nurse miserly with the pethidine. Nurses, pharmacists — oh, he could get a nice wee rant going about how they hoarded all the good drugs, and doled out a few only when they were obligated.

He finally arrived in the area of Central Station and found a parking place in Wellington Street. He stuck a coin in a meter and walked, with the wind against him, a couple of blocks to the station. Scullion was waiting for him at the fruit and nut stand in the concourse. He had a bag of Trail Mix, which Lou considered a fancy-schmancy name for parakeet chow. Trail Mix, let's all hike this way in our big tackety boots, dudes.

Scullion had a look like a ruined crumpet. He stuck the bag of Trail Mix in his pocket. 'Why the fuck did you phone my house so late last night? Madeleine asks me what's the big urgency, why is Lou calling at 2 a.m.?'

'Two a.m. That late? I swear I didn't know the time, Sandy.'

'A 2 a.m. phone call unnerves my wife . . . I swear to fuck, Perlman, there are moments I'd like to throttle you. You never know the time. In all the years I've been associated with you, I've never seen you wear a watch or carry any kind of timepiece. You go through life not knowing the hour, and sometimes you don't even know what day it is.'

'Aye, well, I've got a genetic inner-clock malfunction,' Perlman said, trying to ease the hostility in Sandy's voice. He pictured Maddie waking, irked by the interruption. Scullion was angry because Maddie was angry. Probably the two kids and the fucking cat were angry because Maddie was angry.

'Everything is what you want when you want it.'

'You believe that?'

Scullion wandered off without answering. He was a few steps ahead of Perlman and crossing the concourse. People rushed to catch trains to places like Bogston, Williamswood. Places Out There, where Perlman never went. Beyond the pale. There was hurry, and the clatter of heels on platforms, loudspeaker announcements. The train now standing at Platform 4 is the Interplanetary Express to Mars . . .

'I could get scalped, Lou. You don't ever think about that, do you?'

'So you feel you're fraternizing with the enemy?'

'I've got a lot on my plate right now — '

'Plate? Aw, send in the clichés. Tell me the last thing you need is me becoming another turnip on this crowded plate of yours. Is this a preamble to a brush-off, Sandy?' He saw a look of fierce annoyance on Scullion's face and wished he could take back the words he'd just uttered. The instant leap into sarcasm — ah, he was pissed off with himself, pissed off with certain irrepressible elements in his own nature.

'Do you think I'd just drop you, Lou? I'm sorely tempted.'

Perlman made an extravagant gesture of appeasement. 'Forget what I said. I'm jumpy. Here, let me buy you a coffee, maybe a Danish, a peace-offering,' and he pushed open the door of a coffee shop, where rich espresso scents magnetized him, but Scullion kept moving away, striding toward the timetable boards.

Perlman shrugged, went after him. 'So coffee's out.'

'I don't feel like sitting.' Scullion stopped, leaned against one of the timetable boards. 'Mary Gibson had a meeting with Tay this morning about you.'

'And?'

'He doesn't want you back.'

Perlman tried to hide disappointment. 'Predictable. He was at the end of the fucking queue when they were handing out grey matter. By the time they got to Tay all they had left was pinhead oatmeal.' OK, he'd guessed it was coming, he'd foreseen Tay's response, but he'd elected to look on the positive side for once: hope makes you vulnerable, that's the drawback. 'That bastard Tay's barring me from the investigation of this hand, which incidentally I didn't have to report. This same hand God knows I should have kept to myself.'

'Kept to yourself? I've never heard anything so daft.'

'So I'm daft? Perlman: madman of Pitt Street.'

'Christ, you've been girning since you got here.' Scullion imitated a man playing a violin. 'One thing about you I always admired was your resilience.'

'OK, I had my hopes up.'

Scullion moved again like a man who wants to be alone to compose his feelings. He entered a chemist's, and Perlman followed. Scullion scrutinized the shampoos. Trying to be of some assistance, Perlman said, 'I recommend this,' and he indicated a bottle of coal tar.

Scullion ignored him, picked up Head & Shoulders and carried it to the cashier, paid for it, went back outside. 'Do you want to hear what I have to say?'

'If it's not about clocks.'

'Promise to keep a padlock on your tongue.'

'Scout's honour.'

'You were never a scout, Perlman.'

'I'll show you the badge I got for tracking stoats.'

'Stoats my arse. Where do you come up with stuff like that?'

'My brain's cursed.'

Scullion rolled his eyes. 'Sid Linklater's estimate, the hand was severed about two to three months ago. Neat cut by saw. A pro job.'

Perlman listened with the intensity of an eavesdropper even as he tried to imagine somebody entering his house and leaving the bag. Let's give Perlman a hand: hardyhar, a bad joke.

'What about fingerprints?'

'The bag's clean. Sid's working on the hand, which is in a serious state of decomposition, and impossible even to ascribe gender.'

Perlman considered this. No gender.

Scullion looked at his watch, making a big play of it, shoving back the sleeve of his coat and baring the watch. 'You fancy flying solo, don't you? Detective Sergeant Biggles, watch his jetstream. I know you.'

Perlman poker-faced Scullion.

'I can't condone it, Lou. But remember this — I don't want you keeping anything back that you might come across. And I don't want it known I'm feeding you. Clear?'

'Screw my head to a plank of wood and tweezer my toenails out, I'd say nothing.'

'One last thing. Don't you ever imagine I'm not on your side. But that's not a licence to call me in the dead of night.'

'I'll get a watch, I swear.' He thought, I'd only lose it.

'Why do you make everything so bloody difficult at times?'

'When was I ever difficult?'

'Every bloody chance you get.' He edged away from Lou just as a gang of travellers rushed past, scurrying for a train about to depart.

'You want to do dinner some night next week.'

'Dinner? You think Maddie will lay out the welcome mat?'

'She's always quick to forgive. And you know what we'll be eating, don't you?'

Perlman watched Scullion leave the station and go out into Gordon Street. He remained a while inside, listening to trains; he'd always loved trains as a kid, he'd enjoyed maps and wondered about the names of distant destinations, what were they like? York, Penzance, Bristol. And yet here he was, as he always was, embroiled in the complicated city of his birth.

He walked out into the cold sunlight. Skelped by the wind, he returned to his parked car. Flying solo, aye, wherever the journey took you.

★　★　★

Inside his car, he phoned Joe Adamski on his mobile. Adamski was a Detective Sergeant in E Division, which covered the east of the city.

Adamski asked, 'How's that bullet wound?'

'I'm getting over it,' Perlman said.

'Can't be easy. A bullet. I also hear you're not flavour of the month at Force HQ.'

'Try flavour of the year, George. Never mind that, the decade. They're calling it sick leave. I've got another name for it.'

'The cauld shoulder.'

'A very cauld shoulder. I can't step inside Force HQ even if I was in the vicinity and desperately needed a pish. Officially I'm unofficial.'

81

Adamski had a throaty voice, like the rasp of a hedge cutter. 'That's a raw deal.'

'That's what I think . . . Joe, I need a wee favour. I've got a missing person in your district. It's a personal thing. I promised somebody.'

Adamski said, 'Pen's in hand.'

Perlman took the photograph of Kirk McLatchie from his pocket. He gave Adamski a brief description, colour of eyes and hair, age and address.

'That address,' Adamski said. 'That's the badlands.'

'I know, I know. I'll be grateful if you can get me anything. Let me give you this mobile number, OK?' Perlman read it out.

'I'll get back to you if and when,' Adamski said.

Perlman thanked him, then sat for a time watching traffic on Wellington Street. He considered the decomposing hand: what had become of the rest of the body. Had it been cut into pieces and dumped somewhere? Or was the hand the only thing amputated? Keep an eye open for one-handed people.

12

Baba Ragada wore a white turban and an ankle-length white robe. His face was gaunt, skin stretched like papyrus over bone. He spoke in a deep monotone Reuben Chuck found hypnotic.

'Speak to me of your spiritual journey.'

Chuck, who squatted on the parquet flooring at the Temple of Personal Enlightenment, formerly a Salvation Army Hall, found Baba's seemingly simple questions heavily loaded. He might appear to be asking one thing, when really he was seeking an answer to something altogether different. The man had more layers than a sherry trifle.

'You're talkin about my karma?'

'Everything is a karmic matter. I am saying this. As your ship sails the ocean, your horizon changes. You see the curvature of this great planet alter every move you make on your epic journey. Does a passing cloud distract you from the horizon? Does an albatross in flight startle you? The great Gitavoga says we see eternity in the heart of the simple nettle, but must always be careful how we grasp it. I am saying, are you sailing in the true direction or do you allow thin winds to blow you off course.'

Reuben Chuck sniffed sandalwood incense. He liked it, found it restful. He pondered the Baba's words — how to answer the questions, there's the rub. Imagine you're a galleon on a wild sea. Aye, right. Wasn't easy. Wind in the sails. He dismissed a bunch of potential responses, none of which would have answered Baba. *I shifted seventeen ton of top-qual purloined Aberdeen Angus beef . . . I arranged for the murders of my enemies . . . I have further plans of a fiscal nature . . .*

Bigtime negative karmic acts, titanic.

He was aware of Baba Ragada staring at him, waiting. He had eyes that suggested numinous encounters with the true nature of things. All patience and quiet concentration, this Baba.

'I sent forty blind inner-city children to Ayr on one of my buses.' Chuck smiled a little. He was sure this generosity would delight Baba.

Baba listened, then said, 'On his deathbed Gitavoga's disciple Kativaka said, 'All my life is as a hummingbird's. I pass now into the cycle of rebirth and when I return I may not remember I had wings.' You understand me, Reuben?'

'Uh, all I was pointin out is I donated bus and driver.'

'I am saying this to you. Your actions along the journey may not result in spiritual advancement, nor in a rebirth of joy. Nobody has a guarantee.' Baba Ragada smiled, as if a mention of a guarantee was some kind of guru in-joke. He spoke so softly Chuck strained to hear. 'All generous acts are selfish.'

'Selfish? How?' Chuck was both surprised and offended but hid his reactions well.

'I am saying this. Krishna reminds us that a rich man with too many possessions may find no spiritual advancement in giving them away. What is the sacrifice involved when a man who is weighed down by material things gives away all his earthly goods, and yet remains in his heart attached to them and feels the pang of their loss? Even if this man becomes the most humble beggar, the act remains questionable as a true spiritual event in his life, unless he has realigned himself with cosmic truth. Perhaps not even then.'

Chuck hadn't read this Krishna stuff. He kept meaning to. It was such a fat book. But so was the Bible, and he'd ploughed through that. Most of it anyway. Some of it. Well, Genesis and Exodus, and one time, pissed out of his mind on rum and coke, he'd plunged into Revelations, which was a right old nightmare. 'Are you sayin I should have driven the blind kids myself.'

Knock off point. Karmic wheel grinds into reverse, squawk.

Baba sighed softly. 'When you have divested yourself not only of material objects but have also cleansed your soul of resentments and grudges and demands of the flesh, only when the heart is as unsullied as new-fallen snow — only then can you be certain you are acting from unconditional love.'

Reuben Chuck struggled with this concept. In his world, everything was conditional. How you behaved. How you ran your businesses. Was he supposed to have loved his enemies and allowed them to flourish? Oh aye. And how would that have gone down? Mr Reuben Softee, that's how. The gaffer's gone all funny on us. He disny even eat meat for fuckzake. He has sprouts and goat's

85

milk, by Christ. Also he quit the bevvy. Let's depose him. Let's kick shite out of him. Kill the king.

As for his possessions, how could he give up his penthouse?

He looked at Baba and saw the long eyelashes quiver. Baba did his spooky eye routine. He drew the irises up into his head somehow and all you saw were the whites, blank and terrible. It gave Chuck the creeps first time, but he was used to it now.

'Understand,' Baba said. 'Forty blind children taken to enjoy some sea air, this is not a sin.'

'Plus as much ice-cream as they could eat. Also free rides at the local carnival. *And* they walked along the promenade to enjoy fresh sea air on their wee faces.'

Baba Ragada seemed not to hear this. 'The intention is good in itself. The *execution* is the problem in universal terms. You must listen to your heart's voice.'

And whit was the heart's voice exactly? Pondering this, Chuck gazed slowly round the room. He'd always imagined most gurus led simple lives when it came to ornaments, but Baba had been accumulating over the months many items that were clearly of value — large oriental tapestries, handmade from silk, hung on the walls. Intricate panoramas, depicting exotic trees and half-moons and stages in the Krishna's journey. There were also a couple of large carved-wood statues of the Buddha, one of which showed him surrounded by snakes. Several antique Tibetan handbells stood against the wall. He wondered how much of his own monthly donations had gone into the acquisition of this stuff. He knew he'd paid for the expensive parquet flooring, because he was the one who'd suggested it, and probably the fat embroidered silk pillows Baba sat on. The stained-glass windows, which showed mostly lambs and shepherds and a Christ with an eye recently vandalized, had obviously been the property of the Sally Ann before the Temple took over.

In one corner he noticed a galvanized bucket which was placed directly below a rain mark in the suspended ceiling. Get in a roofer, he thought, win some points in the circle of life and rebirth. Call in a glass repairman and have Christ's eye fixed. Yo ho *score*. He'd also jack up his monthly contributions which were presently running about three grand. And why not? When he'd been a Catholic he'd lashed out dosh with frenetic energy, money for a new church organ, a marble pulpit, and a sporty wee car for Father Skelton.

There was a piece of work, that Father Skelton, paedophile. Boys here, boys there, in the bushes, in toilets, the *confessional* even. About fifty of the abused came forward when Skelton was arrested and shamed. Skelton fled the country the minute he was bailed and was last heard doing missionary work in Calcutta.

Rome took care of its own.

Chuck left the church in disgust. His soul needed another kind of infusion. If he feared anything more than the loss of respect, it was the prospect of damnation. OK, so there was no actual *hell* in this Enlightenment culture, but there was always that other threat, reincarnation in a form you didn't want. Somethin disgustin.

Like plankton. Life span three seconds. But here was the problem: if you came back as plankton or anythin else, how did you ever know? It wasn't as if plankton floatin in the deeps had a memory of being Reuben Chuck, right?

And Chuck had no recollections of ever being anybody or anything else. So this was tricky.

Some kind of amnesia had to be involved in the reincarnation process.

'The heart's voice speaks in the language of charity,' Baba said. He lifted one emaciated hand and pointed at Chuck.

'Charity,' Chuck said.

'Free yourself!'

Penny dropped. 'I donate that bus to the blind society, do you mean?'

Baba went into white-eye mode again, as if receiving reams of data from an infinite source of wisdom. 'There is another blindness beyond the physical, Reuben. Blindness of the spirit, which affects many souls.'

A firework exploded in Chuck's head. 'I'll give you the bus, no strings.'

Baba's eyes swivelled back into place. 'The Temple cannot accept such a donation.'

'It's in fine condition. And you could make good use of it, travellin to spiritual conventions or whatever. Take it, Baba. Don't refuse it.'

Baba looked thoughtful. 'Our transportation is often uncertain, I know . . . '

'I'll throw in any refurbishment you need, a complete mechanical check, and a paint job.'

Baba Ragada said, 'Your heart is generous, Reuben.' He reached out and clasped Chuck's hand. Chuck had never touched Baba's skin before. It was cold and you could feel the bones. Did he ever eat? His hand was as heavy as a sparrow's body.

'There is one small matter,' Baba said. 'I understand you need to assign legal documents of ownership. Is this so?'

'A mere detail,' Chuck said dismissively. 'My lawyers will deal with any paperwork.'

'I am moved, Reuben. Truly moved. You are beginning to understand the cycles.'

Reuben Chuck experienced a flame of elation. Blessed by Baba. He'd jumped a notch on the wheel. Lookin good. Lookin peachy. And all it had cost him was a bus, but that was a gift, therefore a tax deduction, and why did he need another bus anyway? Scarfin diesel like a drunk on wine. He had plenty of buses, a fleet.

Baba Ragada stood up slowly. 'It is time now for my hour of meditation. May your dreams be scented with flowers.'

Chuck bowed his head. He always did when Baba took his leave. When he raised his face again, Baba had disappeared behind a saffron-coloured curtain beyond the heap of pillows, as if by divine magic.

Chuck walked out of the Temple. Mathieson was parked in the Jag whistling 'All the Nice Girls Love a Sailor'. He opened the rear door and Chuck climbed in.

'Everything OK, Mr Chuck?'

'The berries,' Reuben Chuck said. 'Call Willie Farl. Tell him the Temple needs some roof work. Today. Also contact that glazier who did the tinted windows in my penthouse and tell him to fix some stained glass on the double. What's his name?'

'Robbie Robertson. Willdo. By the way, you got a phone message, Mr Chuck. An Inspector Scullion.'

Scullion, he knew Scullion. Chuck relaxed, laid his palms on his knees.

Scullion could wait.

13

Mid-afternoon in moribund Govan: Perlman drove down a side-street, his progress instantly stalled by a gang of kids in hooded jackets and tracksuit pants. They kicked a ball around and they weren't moving for *anything*. He tooted his horn, a brisk little sound. The kids ignored it. Glasgow defiance. *Bloody hell*. Perlman parked the Ka and got out. The ball bounced toward him and he trapped it with an elegance that surprised him. *I could've been a player. Nightclubbing and stoating lassies hanging on my arm. Suits by Armani, no sweat.*

The kids stared at him, waiting. He kicked the ball back to them, using the outside of his foot to impart spin, an intention that failed. The hooded kids hooted — *ya ya* — and went on with their game. Street football, goalposts chalked on a wall.

Perlman locked his car outside a fire-scorched tenement that was scheduled for demolition. He took a deep breath before he entered the building, edging past a bent sheet of steel meant to discourage trespassers, but this had been battered and hammered so many times that any security function it might once have served was a bad joke. Discoloured whitewash hung in sheets from the walls. The smell of sewage flowed from a burst pipe somewhere out back.

The alpha scent was charred wood.

He stepped along the passageway carefully,

wary of broken glass and excrement and the possible hazard of used needles that might lie concealed underneath. He approached the stairway, looked up through the gloom. No sun ever reached in here. The only thing that bloomed was a parasitic blue mould visible through plaster cracks, like varicose veins.

He climbed to the first landing. Flakes of brown plaster fell from the uppermost ceiling, concealed in dimness way overhead. The window on the landing had been replaced by plywood: there was no opening where any breathable air might enter. Perennially sour twilight. I should turn and piss off back down the stairs before I choke from ash and effluence.

Polisman found deid in horror tenement.

He climbed the second flight. He was faced by three doors, three separate flats. Two of the doors were buried behind steel. These *verboten* flats were probably used as squats or shooting galleries, dopers and drifters sneaking in and out. Perlman wafted the offensive air in front of his face: *feh*. The places I go. The environment was depressing, but it wasn't despondency he felt — in fact he was zapped by the bee-sting of purpose and anticipation. On the move again, ransacking the stockroom of his experience, coming here and playing a long shot.

He knocked on the one door that wasn't hidden behind steel. Nobody answered. He rapped his knuckles again. No response. He waited, then banged a fist against the wood.

A voice came from the other side of the door. 'Who is it?'

'Perlman. Let me in.'

'I've got nothing to say to you.'

'Open the fucking door, *schlemiel*,' Perlman said.

The door cracked a slit, a huge beard appeared. 'You on your own?'

'You kidding? I brought Tonto *and* The Lone Fucking Ranger.'

'Come in, come in quick.'

Perlman entered a tiny one-room flat. The man who'd opened the door, Tartakower, seventy-eight years old, was hunched, dressed in a singlet and a pair of old black trousers four or five sizes too big for him. He shuffled into the kitchen, Perlman followed. Plywood had been bolted over the window here as well. A paraffin lamp glowed on a table, throwing a parsimonious light that illuminated cheap bits and pieces of furniture. An animal of some kind — dog, cat, ferret, who could say in this pervasive gloaming? — lay huddled in a cardboard box.

Tartakower bent over the table for a battered tin teapot. 'You want tea, Perlman?'

Perlman didn't want anything except to ask a couple of questions and then be gone. He saw the silver hairs in Tartakower's huge beard gleam. A mass of chest hair grew over the collar of his singlet, and tangled with the vast bush of his beard. Where one began and the other left off was anybody's guess.

'How is it I have come to this,' Tartakower said. 'The firemen, they should've let this place burn to the ground.'

'Second that motion.'

Tartakower poured strong tea with a trembling hand. The animal in the cardboard box stirred listlessly. Tartakower raised his face and his eyes glistened as he looked at Perlman. 'At least this poor creature gives me loyalty. As for the rest of my life, ah . . . '

Perlman thought no, I don't want the epic tragedy of Ben Tartakower's existence. I don't want his *tsuras*. He'd heard it already how many times. 'I need to ask you a question.'

Tartakower rolled over Perlman's remark, his deep voice rumbling out of hairy sources. 'I don't have my music even. Some *gonif* stole the record-player and took the LPs. My Mendelssohn, my Bach, Schumann, gone. Who says Jews have all the luck? I go out, they break my door, steal from me. I'm a prisoner. And the *untermenschen* in this building, they threaten my life. Knives, guns, knuckledusters, swords even, you name it.'

'You have family, they'd help you.'

'Family? They call me *schnorrer*. Don't talk to me family.'

Perlman felt it coming, the story of Tartakower's rise and fall: a fine surgeon once, also an accomplished cellist, the wife he never loved fucks some goy fancydan, steals his money, leaves him, he tries suicide, the pills fail, this should surprise him? He loses his surgeon's licence, he's so blocked he can't play his beloved cello, life's a ladder and he's heading to the bottom but before he hits it he borrows money from a rich cousin — never repaid — and rents a big house in a backstreet in Langside which he operates as an unlicensed private clinic, a chop-shop, running a string of young surgical assistants to help him through cut-price operations, abortions, removal of bullets from wounded crims no questions asked, the occasional crazy foray into plastic surgery, a woman dies on the operating table . . . and he, the great Tartakower, surgeon and professor, gets busted. Four years in the nick for practising medicine without a licence, a sob story, a soap.

Perlman couldn't bear to hear this yarn again. A pre-emptive strike was needed. 'You could get out of this dump. Social services, go see them.'

'Social services. You think it's easy, ask for a handout? How would you know?' Tartakower swatted the air with a skinny hand. 'Your job, a pension, my heart doesn't ache for you. What do you want anyway? I don't see you in years, and you turn up and tell me you have a question.' He slurped his tea then stared into his cup. 'You put me in jail, Perlman. A fellow Jew, you put me in jail, I do my time, I walk out a free man and my debt to society is paid and look around you, call this freedom? This is living? I'd be better dead.'

Perlman held up a hand to stop Tartakower's flow. 'They moved you to the open prison at Noranside after eighteen months in Barlinnie, in case you'd forgotten. With you it's always selective memory. Let me ask what I came to ask, so I can get out of here.'

Tartakower had the face you saw on one of life's victims, the expression that suggests there might be a deep pleasure in the ache of sorrow; the supplicant angle of head that invites all the blows of misfortune. He was a man waiting for a bus to hit him.

'When you were operating your unlicensed surgery — '

'Don't overlook I did some good work there, Perlman. People on waiting lists for a bed in some germ-infested NHS hospital, I helped them, you wouldn't believe how many — '

'Including the woman you killed.'

'An accident. Tell me they don't happen.'

'They happen more often when you're strung out on amyl nitrate or ether.'

'This tragedy you need to remind me? I was weak-willed, too much pressure, I had a habit. So? Now I'm clean.'

Perlman said, 'Back to the question I came to ask. Did you ever run any talented young student surgeons through the place?'

'I had eager students looking for hands-on experience they couldn't get quick enough in universities. Why are you asking, why are you digging up old graves? Some of these kids went on to eminence.'

'Did any of them — how do I put this — did any of them strike you as *wrong*? They were in medicine for the wrong reasons?' No, this wasn't it, not quite. Perlman tried to rephrase it, but Tartakower spoke first.

'What are you fishing? Do you mean criminal types?'

'Mibbe. More like a guy who wasn't glued together the right way. Somebody whose laces were loose.'

'Is it a psycho you're looking for?'

'Could be.'

Tartakower scratched his beard. Flakes of dried food drifted out of the massive tangle. 'This I need to ponder, Perlman.'

'How much ponder and how much money?'

Tartakower pulled out his empty pockets. 'Remind me what money is.'

'The man I'm looking for is skilled. I'm not talking any old bonechopper, Ben, you understand? I'm looking for somebody gifted.'

'And *meshugane*. With thoughts you don't want to hear and questions you don't want to answer. I need time to think.'

'You don't have time.'

'Oh I should be in a hurry to do Perlman a favour, the man who incarcerated me? What is this individual alleged to have done?'

'He cut off somebody's hand. A clean cut.'

'Why come to me? There are skilled cutters all over this city of damned souls. There are Muslim butchers and kosher butchers and abattoir butchers and butchers who churn out T-bone steaks and lamb chops. What makes you think was somebody who worked for me?'

'Because you know more bonecutters than anybody I can think of. Why shouldn't I come to you? How many kids assisted you?'

'Who knows, thirty, forty. More.'

'At your trial I remember the prosecutor claimed at least a hundred, low estimate. You had a crowd coming and going.'

'Such a gift for exaggeration that *shmendrik*. Only to make me seem more a monster and win for himself a bigger sentence, bigger headlines.'

'I'll give you fifty pounds for a name.'

'Pah. Fifty doesn't go far. I have Issy, this sorry creature, to feed. Admittedly my own needs are tiny. Tea, bread, a little margarine.'

'OK, sixty.'

'A hundred.'

'You're crazy. Seventy-five.'

'Eighty.'

'Done.'

'Plus one for Issy.'

'What is that animal anyway?'

'Issy is more than an animal, Perlman.'

Perlman didn't ask. Tartakower was fond of riddles.

Perlman took his wallet from his back pocket. 'I want the name now.'

'My brain, my poor memory, sometimes fuzzy . . . also keep in mind many of these boys came with made-up names, they didn't want to work under their own identities, who can blame them? I had a Donald Duck working for me. A Mahatma Ghandi also.'

'Come to the point,' Perlman said.

Tartakower shrugged.

'You push me, Perlman. I could get into mounds of shite helping you. Giving out information, these kids don't want to be remembered — '

Perlman made to stick his wallet back, and Tartakower said, 'Jackie Ace, he comes first to mind.'

'Not his real name, I assume?'

'What do you think? A flash boy with fingers, a sweetheart cutter. With a surgical saw, he cut like

98

a dream. This is natural, this you don't learn. But something wrong.' Tartakower tapped his chest and frowned. 'Something you sense.'

'Sense, like how?'

'Off, Perlman. Something off. How more explicit you want?'

Perlman shrugged. 'An example of strange behaviour would be a start.'

'They were all strange in their own ways, these boys.'

'You any idea where he lives?'

'I look to you a street directory?'

'What else do you remember about him?'

'Jackie Ace made friends easily. Played cards, took some of the other boys for a bundle. Poker, brag, always a winner. Did he cheat? Sure, but who could accuse him? Hands like his could've plucked a feather off a goose and the goose wouldn't blink. Also he did card magic.'

'What does he look like?'

'What is this — Mastermind?'

Perlman laid money on the table, hoping the sight of green would encourage Tartakower, who squeezed his eyes in an act of remembering. He looked constipated. 'What else you need to know? He's got red hair and green eyes? He's eight feet tall humpbacked? If it was me searching for Jackie, I'd go where people gamble on cards.'

'Casinos.'

'Fast as a rabbit fucking, Perlman.'

'Fastern,' Perlman said. Jackie Ace, he thought. You start somewhere. The detection of every crime has a point of origin, that uncertain

99

place where you have the first flutter. It pays off sometimes. Most times not.

Tartakower picked up the money, stuffed it into his pockets. 'So call again. We'll have strawberry blintzes and cream, you give me notice.'

Tartakower rose. Perlman stepped out of the flat. Just before Tartakower bolted the door, he said, 'You'll know when you see Ace, Perlman.'

'What's that supposed to mean?'

Tartakower didn't embellish. The door was closed and bolted.

'Hey,' Perlman said. He knocked on the door, heard only silence from within. Tartakower wasn't going to open up again. He'd already be sitting at the table counting his cash, then stashing it here and there inside his room. He probably worried about Perlman changing his mind and wanting the gelt back. He lived in a state of hermetic paranoia, everybody stole from him, everybody had it in for him. Plus he'd been cheated out of his life — so why open the door again to the man who'd sent him to hell in the first place?

Perlman descended to the street. No kids were around now. He walked to his car. His wing mirrors had been thieved. *Fuckety fuck fuck.* Pissed off, he did a little dance of rage and kicked his tires a couple of times ferociously, then he calmed when he realized he'd been let off lightly. His wheels might have been stolen, his windows smashed. The whole car might have been seized and driven off to some yard and stripped down for parts.

He unlocked the car. When he'd driven as far as Govan Town Hall, he pulled to the side of the road and took his mobile from his pocket. Still irked by the loss of his wing mirrors, and the fact his coat stank of burned timber, he punched in a number he rarely used.

'Hello.' A frail voice, cracked a little.

'Aunt Hilda,' he said.

'Louis? The same Louis used to be my favourite nephew? The same Louis who goes to live in Egypt, forgets family, and phones once in a blue?'

'OK I'm ashamed,' he said. He pictured Hilda's face, florid from high blood pressure, eyes that were magnified behind thick lenses. She was his mother's younger sister. At the age of ten she'd followed in the footsteps of Ettie and Ephraim, escaping Germany a year before Hitler's war, aided by a Jewish action group that smuggled both her and Marlene into Switzerland. How they made the trip from Geneva to Glasgow was a story neither woman ever told.

'When do we see you?'

'Soon. I promise.' Perlman felt guilty.

What the hell would it cost him to go eat some homebaked biscuits that had the heft of landmines, and swill Hilda's watery green tea and stay an hour or so? But he hadn't gone in how long, not even with all the hours that hung so heavily on him during this 'sick leave'. It was no great trek to the deep south of the city. He'd been devoured by the job too long, compelled by the need to go out day after day and night after night to check the city's crime barometer. He'd

101

turned into a meteorologist of the seamy side, cut off from clan, and lived a life of self-imposed exile.

'I'm a million miles away Lou? Aunt Marlene also would enjoy seeing you. Your poor mother, you think she'd be happy she knew you never came to visit her own sisters?'

He pictured the two old women in their somnolent parlour. Clay geese nailed to a wall, a grandfather clock with an inexorable tick that would stop only on doomsday, Marlene's arthritic china-white hands twisted in her lap.

'Have you heard anything from Miriam?'

'*Miriam*. So *this* is the real reason you phone me? I may be old, but nobody's fool, Louis.'

He knew he was blushing. 'I was wondering about her.'

'She doesn't write you?'

'One postcard from Florence, then another from Copenhagen.'

'Me, I was privileged to get one from Amsterdam I don't know when. Weeks.'

'Did she drop a hint she might come home?'

'What home? Miriam, a global lady.'

Perlman didn't want to think Miriam would stay away. 'I'll visit soon. Promise.'

'Give me notice, I'll bake. So how is Betty working out for you?'

'She's a genius.'

'And not so bad to look at, nu?'

'No, not bad at all.'

Perlman said goodbye, closed the connection. Hilda was always trying to matchmake. To her it was a travesty that Lou should be a bachelor, and as for that hopeless love he carried around like a precious picture in a wallet, did he really believe it was leading to the altar?

He speeded away.

My peripatetic Miriam, he thought. Amsterdam. Florence. Copenhagen. And men, she'd draw them to her naturally, a lovely woman drinking coffee alone on some hotel terrace overlooking a lake. With gulls. Men would lust after her. He saw hotel rooms in the afternoon, blinds drawn, Miriam giving herself with spread thighs to a dark-eyed romancer, a man sophisticated in the ways of loving women. They'd speak Italian together, Miriam and this *gigolo*, and drink wine in bed and he'd lick spilled drops from her nipples and later they'd talk about Michelangelo and Leonardo. This sickening intimacy . . .

Loverboy would be called Mario or something like. He'd be an expert in a kitchen too, knowing a secret ingredient that brought *putanesca* to life, and just how to chop garlic for maximum flavour, and the precise time to pluck fresh oregano.

Lou couldn't bear it, hated this fucker Mario.

14

Samuel Montague gazed up into his wife's eyes. Strands of black hair fell across her forehead and she had a look of euphoric abandon. He was transported by her, by the intensity of lovemaking and the words she spoke *fuck me, fuck me hard and hard deeper into my cunt Sammy oh*. Sweat created a film between their bodies. It dripped from her face and landed on his lips and he tasted its wonderful saltiness.

Straddling him, she rose and fell, her hands splayed on his shoulders, her nails digging his flesh as if she was determined to contain as much of him as she could at this crucial moment. He thought the same thought every time: this is the most exciting thing ever. His coming was a pure fire. He shouted her name and felt her shudder and she threw her head back in blissed release, and screamed even as he pushed himself up from the floor to penetrate her as deeply as he might. They were bonded, locked, devouring.

She laid her face against his and for a while they both breathed very hard. Their hearts roared. Neither of them was ever able to speak coherently for a time afterwards, but they made sounds, sighing, purring, intimate little half-words that would mean nothing to anyone else.

'Hey, take a gander at this, boys,' a man said.

'A porn film, intit,' somebody else said.

Shocked, Samuel Montague turned his face to the bedroom door.

Three men, masked in scarves, looked down at him. He saw only their eyes. He instinctively reached for something to pull over the naked bodies of his wife and himself, and found the edge of the sheet on the bed above them, which he dragged downward, but one of the men stamped on his hand and said, 'Naw, don't deprive us of the view.'

The pain caused Montague to groan.

'Jesus Christ,' Meg said. She scrambled for the sheet but one of the men kicked her in the shoulder and she slid away from Sammy, who tried to rise, defend himself, his wife, his home.

Montague said, 'Please, Christ, don't hurt her.'

'That's up to you, Sammy.'

'If you want money just help yourself, there's a couple of hundred pounds in my desk and my wife's jewellery is in a room at the end of the hall and take the car if you want it, leave us alone.'

'We want none o that crap,' one of the men said. He wore white latex gloves. Montague noticed that they all wore them.

A shotgun was pressed into his forehead. He'd never felt such deadening fear in his life. This was the stuff of newspaper headlines, the kind you read and never imagine would happen to you. *Suburban couple's home invaded by gunmen*.

'That's the gemme, be very still,' the man with the shotgun said.

Another of the trio, this one small and cocky,

said, 'Lookit they pictures on the walls. It's a brothel in here, widdye believe what respectable people get up to in Bearsden, eh?' He examined the Kama Sutra prints and the explicit lithographs Samuel and Meg had purchased during a trip to India.

The man bent down and picked up Meg's discarded panties, brief and red silk, and he sniffed them. 'Oh oh, I'm feeling something here, boys.' And he grabbed his crotch.

Sam Montague said, 'Just tell us what the fuck you want.'

The man still holding Meg's panties pulled open a wardrobe door. 'Widye look at this, boys? Here's a wee kilt and a schoolgirl's blazer and a nice short black leather skirt and what's this, leather straps? Red silky rope? And look at this — '

'Please stop,' Meg said.

The wee man ignored her. 'Here, sweetie, put this on.' He tossed a transparent negligee to Meg who turned away, pulling the garment over her shoulders quickly.

The big man with the shotgun jabbed Montague's neck. Montague felt the blunt pain but this time made no sound. His left hand was a knot of agony. He reached with his right for Meg, who had her arms folded over her breasts.

'Just tell me what you want,' Montague said.

The third man, who'd been wandering the room, saw fit to kick in the glass cabinet that contained the Montague's collection of wedding photographs. Glass flew all around, photographs slipped from shattered frames. 'I hate fucking wedding photies,' the man said.

Montague said, 'If it's not money and it's not stuff — '

The wee man who'd rifled the closet said, 'Talking of stuff, your wife's a tasty-looking bird.'

The lascivious way the wee man said this set off a loud clock ticking in Montague's head. It was wired to an explosive. If this little bastard touched Meg . . . He edged closer to his wife, who was staring at the intruders with a noticeable defiance. She was no weakling: she had a core of fortitude. 'Big shots,' she said. 'Guns and destroying things and scaring people, oh such big shots — '

'Shut yer fuckin gob.' The man who'd smashed the cabinet reached down and grabbed Meg's long hair and twisted it back, so that her small pretty face was forcibly angled upward. 'I canny stand a whining cunt.'

The wee man suddenly crossed the room, unzipped himself, flashing his stubby purple-headed cock and spraying urine at Meg, who averted her face but not before she'd been doused with piss. She made a gagging sound. Her negligee was soaked.

Enraged, Montague tried to rise but he was slammed in the gut with the shotgun and the blow blasted all air out of his lungs. Dizzy, he doubled over, face pressed into the carpet.

The big man said, 'My wee friend has no fucking control over his bodily urges. If he fancied it, he'd shite on your nice rug. In fact he'd shite in your wife's mouth if the mood came over him.'

Meg said, 'Disgusting bastard.'

The wee man zipped himself up and snorted and hee-hawed. 'Speak dirty to me, gonny?'

'Say what it is you want,' Montague pleaded.

The big man bent down beside Montague and shoved the barrel of his gun into Montague's cheek. 'Love your wife, do you?'

'Yes yes I love her.'

'Awfy pretty girl, Mr Montague. Awfy pretty.'

The wee man said, 'Turns me on something terrible, so she does. Oooh. Where did I put those knickers? I want another sniff.'

'Getting the snapshot, Monty?'

Montague raised his head, glanced at Meg. Her nipples were visible under the fouled garment. Dearest Meg. He'd do anything to keep her from harm. These pigs had no scruples. They were slime.

'I'm getting it,' he said.

'Fine,' the big man said. 'Then here's the deal.' He helped Montague to his feet and led him to the bedroom door, and Meg tried to follow, but the other two grabbed her, holding her back.

'My wife,' Montague said, and turned from the doorway with a look of fear.

'She'll be fine,' the big man said. 'You and me need privacy.'

Meg said, 'No.'

The wee man said, 'Shut your cakehole, hen. And fucking behave.'

15

Perlman drove through the southern part of the city centre. Layers of grey clouds hung low: seasonal cruelties would soon rage. The heater of his small car churned and the radio was tuned to one of the Beeb's stations, where a man was interviewing an author of ghost stories. *I suppose everybody asks you this, how do you get your ideas?* The writer answered with a heavy Glasgow accent. *I have a verrrry close relationship with the Devil.*

A relationship with the Devil. That's what I need, Lou thought: Me and Lucifer attuned, clues from occult sources, signs inscribed in flame or the fire of dragons. Who held the blade? Who cut the hand and left it? A storm rumbled through his brain. He drove along Argyle Street, passing under the glass-walled railway bridge known as The Hielanman's Umbrella.

He wasn't far from Virginia Street, where Miriam's loft was situated in a building that had once been a tobacco warehouse in the days of Glasgow's flourishing. He'd thought of going there a couple of times before, but never had . . . Look, see. Who knows what?

He turned the Ka into Virginia Street and parked as close to Miriam's building as he could. He got out, blowing into his hands for warmth as he paused to look at the buzzers at the side of the door. He rang Miriam's, even though he

109

knew nobody would answer.

He waited, then rang the caretaker's bell.

A woman with her head in a scarf appeared behind the glass door of the entranceway. She had a flustered look and a paintbrush in her hand.

Her face and scarf were spotted with white drips.

Perlman showed his ID, pressing it to the glass.

She undid the lock. 'What can I do for you?'

'Sorry, I'm interrupting you,' Perlman said.

'I hate painting walls anyway. Louis Perlman? . . . are you a relative of Miriam's?'

Perlman entered. 'She's my sister-in-law.'

'Oh. OK. Nice lady, Miriam. I haven't seen her around for a while.'

'I'd like to take a look inside her loft,' Perlman said. He had explanations ready if she asked — he'd left something behind, or she'd asked him to change the heat-settings, but no question came.

The woman simply said, 'No problem.' She had a clutch of keys attached to her belt and she slipped one off, and gave it to him. 'Drop the key in my letter box before you leave.'

He thanked her and moved toward the stairs. The lift was out of order. In the few times he'd come here, it had never worked. The same Do Not Use sign was still taped to the lift door. The loft was way at the top, the fourth floor.

He tightened his fist around the key as he went up. Strange to be here again: how many months had passed since the night he'd lain with

110

Miriam and a seagull had flown blindly into the skylight? At the time he'd wondered if it was some kind of omen. Bad or good, he hadn't been able to decide. Now he knew, given Miriam's unannounced odyssey, that gulls crashing into skylights were not harbingers of love requited.

He turned the key in the lock, went in.

The air was stale, atmosphere dead. The long loft was shadowy, but he could see her paintings on the wall, and her easel stood where it always did. A sadness gatecrashed him. He'd hoped that night she'd tell him they had a future together, but he couldn't remember exactly what words had passed between them. Painkillers he'd taken for his gunshot wound had made him dreamy at the time, and his recollection had an hallucinatory feel.

He ran his hand along the back of the sofa where they'd fallen asleep together in a chaste embrace. Oh Jesus, how he'd wanted her. And he'd thought at the time: this is going somewhere lovely.

He ambled past her paintings, small intricate canvasses, colourful abstracts. What the hell did I ever think we'd have in common, her a painter and lecturer at the Art School, me a cop? Reaching too far, too hard. She could speak about culture, and schools of painting, the history of art. What could he offer her in return except news from the criminal side of the city, arrests he'd made, villains encountered, or the savage politics of Pitt Street?

He entered the kitchen, looked inside the refrigerator. Mouldy sauces in jars, tubs of yoghurt long outdated, a gnarled thing that might have been a knot of ginger. He shut the door. The dishwasher was empty. He checked the phone. No tone. He opened the bedroom door.

A room he'd never been in before.

The bed was made. The quilt was a splashy lime colour. A dressing-table stood in the corner. He scanned the things that lay there. A lacquered box, lid open, an assortment of brooches and bracelets. A gifted psychic could touch these items and say *She's in Latvia, Albania, wherever*. Perlman was bereft of such ability. He picked out a string of pearls and dangled it from the palm of his hand but he received nothing, not a picture, not a ghost shimmering in his mind.

Such desperate endeavours.

He returned the necklace to the box and wondered: why did she go without taking the jewels? Because she had others, obviously. And if she was planning to go for a protracted length of time, why hadn't she cleared that stuff out of the fridge? And the phone, had she asked for that to be cut off or had the company snipped it for non-payment? He'd check, it was easy to do.

Miriam, My Lady of the Mysteries.

He peered inside a wardrobe. Dresses and blouses and pants, all neatly hung. Beneath them lay an array of shoes. So what *did* she take with her when she left? I come here like the grieving husband, a widower, and I sift the forsaken remains. She'd gone without a word of farewell, not to him, nor to the aunts.

112

The last time he talked to her, by telephone, she'd made no reference to a trip. That was during the infamous *I need some time, Lou* conversation. The first thing he knew of her journey was a postcard from Florence ten weeks ago, with the message *Lovely place, M*, followed by the 'fond' one three weeks later from Copenhagen. She knew she was going away, except she hadn't deemed him worthy enough to be told of her intentions.

He shut the wardrobe door, sat on the edge of her bed. There was a silent alarm clock on the bedside table — and there, placed beside the alarm, something that shocked, caused a ricochet of feelings. Why would she have kept *this*, and why have it here in the bedroom of all places? He reached for it, picked it up carefully: a photograph in a thin silver frame.

It depicted Colin and Miriam in another time — five years ago, he guessed — Colin prosperous and sleekly handsome in tuxedo, Miriam heartachingly beautiful in a simple black dress. They had their arms linked and they were gazing at each other, faces turned away from the camera: two people in love.

Two people *crazy* in love.

Or was this a show for the camera, an illusion of devotion?

He wanted to think the latter. He needed to think that. But why did she keep it, given the tumultuous history of her life with Colin?

He set the photograph down and his hand trembled and the frame slipped its fragile moorings. The photograph, as well as the cardboard backing, slid out. He cursed his clumsiness. Detective Thumbs. Why didn't they make solid frames that stayed in place instead of these shaky constructions? It wasn't exactly difficult technology.

He tried to slide the picture back inside the frame, a fiddly job. He saw Miriam's handwriting on the back of the photo. Her penmanship, showy and confident, was unmistakable. *On our Anniversary, our love shines through, Miriam.* When did she write that, what anniversary?

And if she kept it near her bed, what did that signify? She still loved her late husband, needed his image close to her, hadn't ever got over him?

No, he wouldn't entertain that. He looked at his brother. The charmer, gifted with easy social graces. *Colin, you fucked up. You cheated, stole money, broke hearts.* He pressed the photograph back inside the frame but he couldn't get it to close and when he heard the floor creak in the studio, the sound of somebody's coat brushing against a wall, he hurriedly shoved the frame, photo and cardboard inside his coat pocket.

He stood up, tense, big heartbeat. Miriam coming home, his first thought, sneaking back into Glasgow. She'd wonder what he was doing in her bedroom. He felt like a snooper, a perve. Then he heard a cough, and knew at once it wasn't her. The cough was deep, masculine. He walked out of the bedroom and into the studio.

Inspector George Latta was standing in the middle of the floor, grinning at him. Latta brought back a tidal rush of bad memories. The last time he'd seen the Inspector here was the night of Miriam's arrest. He'd punched Latta on that occasion and the memory was still vibrant, still sour.

'You never got your teeth fixed, I see,' Perlman said.

'Too busy to sit in a dentist's chair,' Latta said. He wore his customary brown felt hat and a crumpled blue gabardine coat and big sturdy black shoes as solid as ocean-going boats. He had hairy hands, like a Yeti's.

'Worst choppers on the force,' Perlman said.

'Strong bite, though. I could sink them in your neck and you'd be powerless.'

Vampire man. Latta's aggressive manner and his smarmy air angered Perlman. The swaggering way he strolled past Miriam's paintings was a provocation. He leaned close to the artwork and sniffed, as if he detected a bad smell. He picked up one of Miriam's brushes and looked at it, then disdainfully he tossed it down again.

'So where did the cunt go, Perlman?'

The word cunt offended Perlman. 'How would I know?'

'You're not planning to meet her some day and divvy up the money, eh?'

'Can't shake that old obsession, Latta, can you?'

'Call it a lust for justice.' Latta continued to peer at the paintings. 'Crap. Unambitious. Tiny. Nothing of interest here.'

Quietly Perlman said to himself, 'Inspector Fuckedteeth's an art critic suddenly.'

Latta whipped round. 'I didn't hear that.'

'I was mumbling. I do that. I'm a mumbler.'

Perlman wasn't going to be drawn into an argument about Miriam's work. He clenched his pocketed hands. 'Have you been following me?'

Latta looked pleased with himself. 'I have a pecuniary arrangement with the caretaker. Anybody asking to see this loft, she phones me. And here I am. I've been wondering when you'd come around. What took you so long?'

The caretaker, seemingly so concerned about Miriam, was Latta's in-house spy. So. It was Latta's sneaky way. He corrupted people.

'Empty lofts trouble me,' Perlman said.

'When your lover has gone. Aw, Lou, you sad bastard, is that what it is? Missing the thieving cunt so bad you can hardly visit her old lair?'

Perlman had a jet of blood to his head. 'You have a delicate way with language. You're a poet, Latta.'

Latta looked at Perlman in a confrontational manner, chin forward, eyes narrow. 'I would've thought she'd have left you a clue where to find her. Maybe something hidden in this loft. Something only you'd understand. So you could meet her and count the dosh — '

'Find a new tune, Latta. She was innocent. Or were you not in court that day?'

'Of course I was in the bloody court and what I saw was a fucking disgrace.'

'The jury believed the money was rightfully hers — '

'The jury were eejits. She put on quite a show, have to say. The mourning widow, unhappy marriage, years of anguish, husband an unfaithful beast, bippety-boo, pass me a hankie. The money was never hers. You know it, I know it, it was cash your dear departed brother embezzled. And now she's done a runner with it. Wait . . . has she shafted you right up the arse with a pointy stick? Has she fucked you *over*, Perlman?'

Latta laughed. It was a scornful sound and Perlman laboured to keep control of himself. How long could he stand this. A shadow passed quickly across the skylight and he looked up to check its source and saw a cloud blown by a strong gust of wind above the chimney-line. Miriam had said *poor bird* the night the seabird had struck the glass roof and he remembered clearly now — the bird had struck the glass so hard it snapped its neck and slid down the slope of the skylight's angle, wings folded. And he recalled the terrible pain of his gunshot wound, and how solicitously Miriam had dressed it. She'd even cleaned his glasses, a touching little gesture.

OK, so the relationship was withering, a paralyzed limb, even if he continued in his dumb romantic way to deny the fact, and nurture a fool's hope for a sign of encouragement. But there were memories, good or bad didn't matter, and this place, rich with the ghost of her presence, meant something to him.

And now the loathsome Latta comes strutting in and sullies the loft with his sneering accusations.

'You've been fucked, Perlman. She's pulled the wool over your eyes, am I right? Wait, make that a sack of wool. She promised you a share of the loot — '

'The *fuck* she did — '

'Plus nooky on a regular basis — '

Perlman took his hands from his pockets.

'In return for your testimony that she'd been wronged by your beloved brother, and that she was honest as the day was long. You were good in court as well, have to say. Although you did yourself no fucking favours in the Force, did you? And the newspapers ate up the story like a goose at Christmas. Detective defends sister-in-law's virtue. Virtue my arse! Now she's fucked off and you'll never see a penny. Excuse me if I find fucking *big* merriment in this — '

This big merriment extended to Pitt Street HQ, to Tay's rookery where the carrion-feeders gathered, waiting for their bloody lunch: Perlman raw.

He remembered Tay's fury on their last encounter. *You can't speak on behalf of the accused, I don't care if you've been cited by the defence, it's a bloody travesty.* In that moment Tay had decided Lou's leave was going to be much longer than Perlman could ever have anticipated, although he'd never said so to his face. Tay worked the secret crevices and passageways, always grey-faced and deceptively bland, and when he acted he did so with the quiet stealth of a cobra. Slash of a pen, check a box on a form, a career demolished.

Latta quit laughing. 'I heard about a hand in a baggie.'

'What about it?' Lou was defensive. Another strand of his world exposed for Latta's rabid attention.

'Suppose you tell me.'

'Tell you what?'

'Like how did it get there?'

'I don't know.'

'Aw come on, how could you not *know*?'

'Are you insinuating something, Latta?'

Latta laughed. 'Who needs insinuation? Your life's one big fuck of a mess, Perlman. Banned from HQ. Your sweetheart buggers off with the loot. Your brother was a crook. And now there's this severed thing in your bedroom. You're a fucking shite-magnet.'

Perlman shoved him back against the wall and grabbed him by the lapels of his coat.

Latta placed his hands over Perlman's and tried to pull them away. 'This isn't the smart thing to do, Perlman.'

Perlman moved in close, drew a hand back, held it there a second in mid-air and looked into Latta's eyes, where he saw a light of apprehension and a suggestion of encouragement. Latta wanted to be struck, because it meant another black mark in the Big Book of Perlman's transgressions, but at the same time didn't welcome the pain.

It was madness, Perlman knew, but the rhythms in his brain had become a constant voodoo drumming,

He released the punch, a short right-handed blow that cracked against Latta's lips and teeth. Latta slid to the floor, and shook his head. Blood flowed from his mouth.

'Last time I was here you hit me,' Latta said. He groaned, and his voice was cracked when he spoke. 'It's getting to be a habit.'

'I remember.' A swinging backhand that hit Latta in almost the same place as he'd struck him now. 'Also I remember loving it.'

Latta put his fingertips to his mouth and looked at his blood. 'I bled the last time as well,' he said.

'I loved that too.'

'You won't love the consequences nearly so much, Perlman. When I report this assault to the right people at HQ — '

'Report anything you fucking like.' Perlman drove his foot hard as he could into Latta's thigh, and Latta moaned, clutching the place where he'd been booted.

Lou took a few paces back. He knew he'd hit Latta again unless he created some distance. 'I've searched for a saving grace in you, Latta, and I always come up empty-handed. As a human being you're a pisspot.'

He walked to the door. He opened it, took a step toward the stairs.

'You're in deep,' Latta said.

Perlman ignored this, and continued to descend.

Latta shouted after him, his voice liquefied by blood. 'Oh I am grinning widely now. A hand in a plastic baggie! God just keeps sending me gifts!'

'What mad God is that?' Perlman called out as he went down the stairs and out, seeking the sanity of the street. He walked to his car and sat behind the wheel and smoked a cigarette. He'd surrendered to rage, and that was that. You can't go back and alter things. He thought about Latta's deranged pursuit of a folly, his warped conviction that Perlman and Miriam were associates in a crime.

And now the hand was planted in Latta's head as well.

Too many years in Fraud Squad had buckled George Latta's brain.

Perlman smoked his cigarette down to the filter. Look on the bright side — maybe he'd helped Latta's miserable dental situation by realigning a couple of those lopsided teeth with his fist.

Then the photograph in his coat pocket came back to annoy him.

16

He stashed the photograph on the floor behind the passenger seat and drove until he came to a pub. He rarely used pubs. He went in, ordered a Cutty Sark. He'd drink the taste of Latta out of his mouth, gargle, swallow. That fucker, was there no end to his prying, his relentlessness, his twisty mind? The Cutty was neat and sharp and fired his blood but it didn't cause Latta to evaporate.

He scanned the clientele around him, mixed crew. Some wore business suits and stood in cheerful huddles. Others, like himself, were solitary, sitting hunched at the bar, reading newspapers or staring into their drinks like fortune-tellers crystal-gazing. He recognized the raucous wee man who sold *The Evening Times* outside Buchanan Street Station.

Suddenly ravenous, he surveyed the sand-wiches in the display case, and asked the girl behind the bar for egg and tomato on brown bread. He munched it down before it had time to activate his taste buds. Then he sipped the dregs of his Cutty, contemplated a repeat, decided against it. He was a weakling, booze went like an express train to his head.

He needed some clarity.

Did Latta often visit the loft on his own? Did he sit on Miriam's bed, or search her clothes, open her mail, plunder her drawers and cabinets, forever hunting the one significant clue he needed to nail both her and Perlman? Maybe he saw private messages in the canvasses. He was a victim of his own mania. Who knows, maybe on one of his ransackings he'd found that picture of Miriam and Colin and set it beside the bed, guessing Perlman would be drawn inexorably back to the loft and find it. A taunt, an act of malice. See, your wonderful Miriam still yearns for her late husband. *Can't fight a memory, Lou.*

I'm fucking glad I hit him.

He ate another sandwich. The businessmen roared with laughter at some joke whose punch-line Lou eavesdropped. *You ask me if I knew Pancho Villa? I had lunch with him.* An old joke, but the preamble to the pay-off eluded him.

He took out his mobile phone and dialled a number.

The voice that answered was slurred.

'You been on the piss, Pickler?'

'Mr Perlman? I've been on the bevvy aw day, man. Slambam. Ridin that train, ridin that train.'

'You'll kill yourself.'

'Aye but what a way to go, eh? Up and up like a fucking kite. Wheeee. That's the gemme.'

'You sobre enough to answer a question?'

'Is it about that beheided clown? Christ, Mr Perlman, you set some toughies. Millerston, fuck me, it's a graveyard with two pubs. The people out there remind me of *The Night of the Living Deid.* Nobody's talking.' The Pickler laughed uproariously. 'Sorry, Mr Perlman. A clown with no heid. I find that fucking funny. Ho ho, it's a riot, so it is.' And off he went again, laughing like one of those showground sailor dolls in glass cases that rocked with Jack-tar glee if you shoved a penny in a slot. Perlman held the handset away from his ear while The Pickler tired himself out.

Perlman said, 'Forget the clown. OK?'

'As you wish, Mr Perlman. Case closed. Ask me anything, the Pickler never lets you down.'

Untrue. Sometimes his information was worthless and led you into a maze of mistakes. But he came right about fifty per cent of the time, and Perlman had never known any informant to be much more accurate than that. He'd never visited The Pickler's residence, but he imagined it — a bare mattress in a two-room flat in Ibrox, a squalid box of a place that would make the house in Egypt seem like a pristine parsonage. Empty beer cans and the crusts of old mutton pies and pizzas with mould which The Pickler probably ate when he was too drunk to notice fungal activity.

'Concentrate. I'm trying to locate a certain Jackie Ace.'

'Jackie Ace . . . ' The Pickler burped joyfully. 'Sorry about that.'

'At least I wasn't forced to smell it.'

The Pickler guffawed. 'Jackie Ace Jackie Ace. There used to be a country singer called Johnny Ace. Remember him? *Forever my darlin I love only you* . . . How did the rest of that go?' Pickler's singing voice was like the panicky sound of a toad trapped in a knotted condom.

'Never mind Johnny Ace, I'm looking for Jackie.'

'Try The Triangle Club, Mr Perlman. Ace is a dealer down there.'

'Cadzow Street?'

'You know your Glesca, don't you?'

'Some days I wonder.' Perlman severed the connection.

He left the pub. As he stepped back inside his Ka his stomach growled like a man in a soup kitchen happy to have received his first sustenance in a long time.

★   ★   ★

In Cadzow Street he parked close to the entrance to The Triangle Club. The sign outside was made from distended neon letters that changed colour, red to pink to blue and back again. The front door was painted with a big glossy Queen of Clubs. Perlman opened it and entered a bright reception area with a multitude of mirrors and hanging disco balls. A girl in a short red skirt and white blouse greeted him as if he was a welcome regular. Above the right breast of her blouse was a monogram — TriClub surrounded by a small Queen of Clubs.

'Hi, I'm Rhoda,' she said, wide happy smile.

No denying it, Perlman enjoyed the smiles of young women. 'Lou Perlman.'

'Are you a member, Mr Perlman?'

'Of the Strathclyde Police.' He showed his badge.

The girl kept the smile going. He wondered if she ever allowed herself a moment of gloomy self-examination. 'Do you need to check the premises, sir?'

'Check the premises?'

'Make sure we're complying with the Gaming Laws?' she said, as if the existence of such ordinances were a joke she shared privately with him.

'Nothing like that, love. I'm here to see Jackie Ace.'

'If you pop through that beaded curtain, you'll find Jackie at one of our poker tables. Is there anything else I can do? Will you be wanting a complimentary cocktail?'

'I don't think so.'

'Can't tempt you with one of our Triangle Troubadours, a shot of vodka, a touch of *crème de menthe*?'

'I'll pass, love.'

'You don't know what you're missing. Take your coat?'

She already had a hand on his shoulder and was stepping behind him to unburden him of the garment. He liked the touch of her hand and the scent of her perfume and that small happy-to-please face of hers. Take my coat, please.

'I think I'll keep the coat on.'

'OKdoke. Anything you need, Mr Perlman, remember my name.'

'You're not the forgettable type.' He pressed a five pound note into her hand and she took it.

'You don't have to.'

'There's a lot of things I don't have to do,' he remarked, smiling brightly.

'Enjoy,' she said.

She pushed the curtain aside for him, and he

entered a huge room beyond. It was glitz and silvery lightstrips and more pert short-skirted girls carrying trays of brightly coloured booze from table to table. The place was crowded, yet hushed with the ecclesiastical atmosphere of serious gambling. Perlman wandered between the tables, listened to the flip of cards, the quiet plastic chink of chips, an occasional exasperated sigh. The dealers were mainly young and good-looking and attentive. A roulette wheel turned, and a couple of slot-machines placed well away from the tables whirred.

Perlman lit a cigarette and counted ten blackjack tables and six poker, where the games were high-stake and serious. He walked to the back of the room. He watched a glamorous dealer, dressed in shiny blue jacket and ruffled blouse and tight blue pants, shuffle a deck and float cards to each player with light-fingered ease of movement.

Good hands, delicate fingers, long nails perfectly lacquered deep red.

Perlman moved closer. The dealer glanced at him, then she continued to distribute cards. The punters picked them up, examined them, fidgeted, tapped fingertips on baize. Heavy casino action sometimes put Perlman in mind of a wake where nobody knew how to break the ice. There was some bluff and bluster, and cards were tossed aside until only two players remained. The pot was eventually scooped by a guy in a grey Armani jacket.

'I'm on a nice wee roll,' the winner said, dragging chips toward his pile.

The dealer lightly flicked a fallen lock of blonde hair from her eyes. A sexy gesture, Lou thought. 'Your luck's in, Stan.'

'Right enough, Jackie,' the man called Stan said.

Jackie.

Perlman couldn't take his eyes from her. Conscious of his stare, she gave him a quick look, then dealt a new round. He was transfixed: a stunning woman. When she glanced at him again, he turned his face away a moment before looking back. She continued to deal. The cards floated baizeward, seeming to hang just a second too long in the air. She had the touch, the deft magic.

When the play was finished, Jackie Ace stepped from the table and approached Perlman. 'You're staring at me.'

'I wasn't aware, sorry,' Perlman said.

'It becomes a little unsettling.'

'I didn't mean to upset you.'

'Is there something you're looking for?'

'You *are* Jackie Ace?' Perlman's throat was dry. The air in here.

'Got it in one.'

'I need a minute of your time is all.'

'I'm due a five minute cigarette break, even though I don't smoke.' She walked away from him, and he followed behind the slots and through a doorway into a dimly lit room where busted machines had been gutted for repair and the air smelled of solvents.

'You're a cop.'

'It shows?'

'Just a touch. It's like a whistle only dogs hear. I'm not saying I'm a *dog*, mind you.'

'Far from it.' Perlman smiled, drawn into Jackie Ace's eyes which, surrounded by sparkle and long false eyelashes, were sharp and intelligent.

'Compliments always welcome . . . OK, I've only got five minutes.'

'My name's Perlman, by the way. Detective Sergeant.' He reached in his pocket for a smoke. Empty packet. He felt the strong pinch of a nicotine need. He took out the packet and squeezed it. A prisoner of unhealthy needs.

He cleared his throat and said, 'This is out of the blue. I was talking to Ben Tartakower, who tells me you're impressive with a blade.'

She looked into his eyes, checking him out. 'I haven't thought of old Tarty in donkeys. It's another lifetime — '

'But you remember the abortions, the illegal — '

'Stop there. Are you here to pin any of that on me?'

'Christ no. That's past and dead as far as I'm concerned.'

'Good. I have absolutely no interest in going back to that period of my life.'

'Fair enough.' Perlman watched for a sign, some little tell in Ace's painted features that would suggest a lie, a swerve. But he felt no blip of menace, no sense of anything hidden. Tartakower had said: *something wrong, something you sense.* Yes. But not the way I understood you, Tarty. I wasn't expecting a transvestite who emitted glamour and sex appeal in palpable waves — and whose sexuality was revealed only by a certain slight protrusion of brow, and a tiny Adam's apple barely noticeable.

'You still haven't told me why you're here,' Ace remarked. 'You're not just trawling ancient history because you're at a loose end.'

'I'm working a case at the moment. Looking for somebody who severed a hand.'

'Don't tell me Tarty suggested *I* might have done this?'

'No, no, nothing like that.'

'I bet he said I was fast but I had the wrong attitude.'

'That's the gist.'

'He's a grumbling old git.'

'Hasn't changed.'

'He used to think of me as his assistant. He was on amyl a lot of the time.'

'I heard that — '

'So he needed somebody to prop him up. He resented the fact he had to rely on anyone, especially me — with my obvious predilections. I managed to get out before the roof caved in, and I don't think he was a happy camper when he was the only one who went to jail.' She laughed quietly. 'I cut decks for a living, Mr Perlman, not human flesh.'

Perlman shrugged. This wasn't the first pointless pursuit of his career, and it wouldn't be the last. Fuck you, Ben, for the goose-chase. Are you sitting in your hovel smirking?

Perlman asked, 'Why give up a surgical career?'

130

'I got tired of bodies, Sergeant. You know the feeling.'

'I know it all right . . . If you remember anything you might have forgotten, call me. Anything at all. Names of the other students, whatever, it might be important . . . ' He took a card out of his wallet and wrote his home phone number on it. 'Here.'

Jackie Ace laughed. 'You know, I can hardly *believe* those times existed. Sometimes I think I dreamed them. You'll have to excuse me, work to do, cards to deal. Nice to meet you.' Ace walked away, stopped, looked round. 'You saw through me, didn't you? A lot of the punters don't. How long did it take?'

'I'm not sure,' Perlman said.

'Ah, but you had an unfair advantage. Tartakower gave you my name — but I bet he didn't tell you what to expect, did he?'

'No, he didn't say.'

'What if you hadn't known my name?'

'Then I'd never have guessed,' Perlman said.

'You're sweet,' she said.

She walked out of the room, leaving Perlman alone with the stripped slots and his nicotine cravings. He left the casino the way he came in, through the beaded curtain.

Rhoda popped up like a sudden rainbow. 'Leaving so soon?'

'No reflection on your casino, love.'

'We like to think we run the best in the city. The others are all a bit naf, past their sell-by. We like to keep the clientele in a good mood. We Try — that's our motto.'

'Mission accomplished,' he said.

Outside, darkness, street lamps glowing. *Cauld*. He walked back to where he'd left his car. He unlocked it, got inside, scavenged a cigarette-end from the ashtray and lit it, almost singeing his nose. Two puffs, deid.

Fag end of a lost day, he thought.

Tartakower's joke. You give me the name of a guy who likes to dress as a woman. And you don't tell me. So egg on my face.

He rubbed the knuckles of the hand he'd used to fell Latta. They were red, and they ached. Inflict pain, you always get some of it back.

17

Because the battery of his mobie was almost flat, Perlman made a call from a public telephone outside a twenty-four-hour petrol station in Alexandra Parade. Madeleine answered. Perlman offered a profuse apology about the unholy hour of his previous call: he was notorious, ha ha, for failing to keep track of time. He told her he was so absent-minded he'd probably forget to show for his own funeral.

She was never annoyed with Perlman for long. She found his stories of clueless criminals and their vainglorious plans intriguing, because they were her only link with her husband's work. Sandy dumped his professional life outside the house, as if he were removing objectionably muddy wellington boots. She began to tell Lou about her latest discovery on the Internet — she'd found a Porteous McNiven who'd emigrated from Dundee to New Zealand in 1856. Lou listened, tapping fingertips on the coinbox: *here she goes.* She was genuinely excited by this discovery. She'd been tracking her family name for years.

'And this character's important?' Perlman asked. He found the roots business a bore, and hoped Maddie wouldn't relate the life and times of Porteous McNiven to him. But she did, long arduous trip and hostile Maoris and a shipwreck, all you could ask for. He was fond of Maddie, and enjoyed her company hugely, but Jesus she could be longwinded when she got on to the subject of her genealogy.

' . . . I've only tracked him as far as Dunedin,' she was saying.

'Maddie my dear, I need to talk to your inferior half if he's there.'

'He's slumped in front of the telly. Hang on.'

Perlman heard Scullion's voice in the background, then the phone was picked up. 'In search of updates?'

'I was hoping for some.'

'You saved me a call,' Scullion said. He was quiet a moment, presumably waiting for Maddie to move out of earshot. Perlman picked at a wart of chewing-gum stuck to the wall of the phonebox, then drew his hand away when he considered health threats. 'It seems the victim was alive when the cut was made, Lou.'

'Sid's *sure*?'

'Positive. There was evidence of bruising, and that apparently only happens in the living.'

Perlman shut his eyes because the neon sign at the edge of the concourse was suddenly too bright. 'I can only hope this poor fucker was drugged to the moon.'

'Even if he wasn't unconscious, he'd pass out from the pain.'

'And he wakes up and then what? Bleeds to death? I doubt if the stump was cauterized properly. This isn't some routine hospital operation — unless its NHS policy to dump amputated limbs in people's houses. I know they're in a fuck of a mess, but even so — '

'Sid's still waiting on the DNA test result to establish gender, which I'll pass along as soon as I know anything. I can't push him, because this isn't my case.'

'Whose case is it?'

Scullion hesitated. 'Tigge's.'

Perlman had an effervescent burst of rage. 'How the fuck did that bearded plodder get it?'

'Tigge is Tay's wife's cousin.'

'Nepotism,' Perlman said. He watched a hooker get out of a taxi. She was all spangles and fishnet stockings. She sashayed inside the station. This interest in girls, what was happening to him: resuscitated adolescence, a new influx of randy born-again hormones?

'Don't tell me you believed it was all a meritocracy, Lou?'

'I had moments of delusion.' A cousin of Tay's wife. He'd never heard of Tay *having* a wife. He caught himself picturing Tay in an act of intimacy, that small clam of a mouth sucking on his wife's tits, and his rotund white arse exposed as a duvet slid from the conjugal bed.

The hooker came out of the station with a packet of cigarettes. She smiled at him as she undid the cellophane with her teeth, and then got back into the taxi.

'Another thing . . . Why did you beat up George Latta?'

'One quick punch, that's all.'

'And a kick.'

'Oh aye, I forgot the kick. He was insulting. He's calling Miriam names and accusing me of that old alleged scam to share her embezzled

135

loot, so-called. Latta's an evil bastard.'

'Evil or not, he'll talk to Tay. Count on it. And these guys are not your friends.'

Perlman was defiant. 'You know how fucking good it felt to smack that arsehole?'

'I can only imagine.'

'He also brings up the hand, like he's holding me responsible for it.'

'How?'

'Who knows what goes on inside the hall of mirrors he calls a brain? What are they saying about this hand at HQ, Sandy?'

'The buzz is the buzz. Inconclusive, wild. A practical joke just to keep you occupied and out of Pitt Street — '

'I'm laughing.'

'Somebody else suggested it was probably evidence from some long-ago case you'd taken home with you and forgot to return.'

'A gem.'

'Another theory is that it was planted there to implicate you in an unspecified crime. A set-up.'

'Sinister. And what crime is that supposed to be?'

'Who knows.'

A set-up. A crime. It's all gossip, gossip, reams of yack. Jesus, they were like crones down there at HQ, clacking in the corridors, whispering in their offices, chuckling over the Case of Perlman's Hand.

'Maddie would like another word with you, Lou.'

Madeleine came on the line. 'How about dinner next week, Lou. Thursday, seven-thirty for eight. Sound OK for you?'

'Sounds just fine.'

'You don't have to dress up or anything.'

Dress up as what, Perlman wondered. 'I'll leave the tux at the cleaners. What's on the menu?'

'I'll surprise you.'

He replaced the handset and wandered across the forecourt of the station and sat for a time in his car, smoking butts until there were none left. His mind drifted through recent encounters and occurrences — Tartakower, Jackie Ace, Betty McLatchie's lost son, Aunt Hilda making him feel guilt, and now, so help me, *Latta* — baggage that had gathered on his trolley all at once. And the hand, cut from a living human being. He felt like a man sifting dry crematory ashes in the hope of finding something useful, something *intact*, that he might retrieve from the furnace.

Like news of his heart's condition.

★　★　★

He was still niggled by resentment of Tigge, and carrying the incubus Latta on his back, when he parked outside his house. Lights were lit in all the windows, a warming effect. He normally came home to darkness. He'd unlock the front door, reach for the light switch in the hallway, and the illumination of that solitary bulb would direct him into the unwelcoming recesses of other empty rooms.

He heard music, an ancient Kingston Trio album he'd forgotten he owned. The things you gather only to forsake. *You pass me by, and all the folks all turn and stare, they wonder why* . . . Betty McLatchie was singing along to it. She had a high sweet voice. He took off his coat and hung it on a peg, then stopped on the threshold of the living room and watched her. She was on her knees, scrubbing old stains out of the carpet. Unaware of his entrance, she didn't look up. She was lost in the song.

Oh heart of stone, you pass me by . . .

He cleared his throat. She raised her face, stopped singing.

'Took me by surprise,' she said.

'I'm Fred Astaire, light on my feet.' He demonstrated, did a little two-footed circular shuffle, pretended Ginger was hanging on his coat-tails. Me and my shadow.

'Needs work, but I see the raw talent right enough.' She raised herself to a kneeling position and studied the carpet. 'Some of these stains go back years.'

'And every one of them has a history.'

'I wouldn't be surprised.'

Perlman was more aware than ever of renewal all about him. Not only the smells he'd encountered before, the air freshener and the pine-scented polish, not only the sight of shining wood and the dearth of dust and spider's webs, now there was the deep-perfumed foam of carpet shampoo and a couple of chocolate-scented candles burning on the window-sill. The angle of his TV was altered slightly, and so was the position of his favourite old velvet armchair. Betty had also moved the sofa a couple of feet, creating a kind of triangular viewing centre. Rearranging his life, a little comfort. He was pleased.

He asked, 'You always work this late?'

'Keeps me busy, Lou. I don't mind cleaning anyway. You put in the work, you see instant results.'

'What cop can say that?'

She smiled and began to rise. He took her hand and helped her up. Her skin was hot. He had a spontaneous urge to put his arms around her, as if to prolong the unexpected illusion of domesticity, which he found touching, an intriguing novelty. I've been alone too long, far too long. Their faces came close together a moment, within kissing distance. He took a step back. Come on, did the idea of a kiss really cross his mind? Maybe the unfamiliar intimacy of the situation affected him, and he felt moved to express gratitude, or it was some simple need for the touch of another person. Homecoming, Betty's presence, a clean well-lit house. *Sweetheart, lemme tell you what a day I had at the office.*

She lit a cigarette and Perlman, who'd forgotten to buy any, cadged one from her. She held her lighter toward him.

'You deserve a medal, Betty.'

'I was worried you'd think I'd taken liberties. What about the candles?'

'I don't think I've ever had candles in this house. Never scented ones anyway. Are they edible? I could make one into a sandwich, if I had bread.'

'Just remember to blow them out before you go to bed.'

The music stopped. Perlman smoked in silence and watched Betty gaze at pools of foam drying on the carpet. She was lingering, he knew that. She didn't want to leave before asking about her son — but she didn't want to appear pushy.

If he told her he had no new information, would that increase her worries or elevate her hopes? No news is . . . whatever they say it is. He stubbed his cigarette in the ashtray on the sideboard and felt the acuteness of her uncertainty. He wished he had some means of reassuring her. How? He wasn't about to spout an easy fiction or mutter a mealy palliative that might still her anxiety for a brief period.

'This place feels like a home,' he said quietly. He felt the tips of his ears heat. Was he blushing, please no. 'I don't feel ashamed of it any more, Betty. I thank you for that.'

'Isn't that what life is all about? Making people feel a little better about themselves and their environment?'

What a pleasing outlook, he thought. She moved a couple of steps toward him. He noticed she'd pinned back her unruly hair with wine-red plastic barrettes that made her look younger. The zodiac jeans had been swapped for a pair of black Levis which she wore with the cuffs turned up. One time she must have been cheeky and funny and sexy — she still was.

'Isn't it all about *kindness*, Lou?'

'In an ideal world.' He imagined her cavorting

140

in Woodstock mud. Life was all in the now. Later, there would be a one-night stand and a fatherless kid gone missing and a great tide of fear inside her. Who in their right mind would want to know what the future held?

Without warning, she wept explosively, and pressed her face against his shoulder. He stroked her hair. He was connected to the depths of her pain, its savage cut, the force of it.

'Betty, listen to me, never give up hope, always hang on. You understand?'

She tried to speak through her tears. He didn't catch a word. She simply wanted to be held.

'Cry all you want, cry . . . '

'I'm falling to fucking pieces, Lou.'

'I'm here, I'll catch you.'

She pulled back from him, rubbing her eyes, trying to force a smile that didn't quite work. 'You're a nice man, Lou.'

'For a polisman.'

'A nice man full stop.'

Perlman placed his hand under her chin. 'I've got some old wine somewhere. Fancy a wee medicinal glass?'

She drew her sleeve across her face. She trailed a thin line of pale mucus across the back of her hand and looked embarrassed. 'I'm sorry.'

'For what? Let me get the vino. I'm not claiming it's drinkable. It might be complete piss. If I can find it.' He turned toward the kitchen door.

'Third shelf in the pantry. Above the sauce bottles.'

'I've got sauce bottles? I never knew.'

'Some from companies that went out of biz years ago.'

'Amazing. You sit down. I'll be right back.'

'You'll find clean glasses in the cabinet.'

'One day give me a guided tour of this house.'

She struggled to smile again. 'It's a date.'

He walked into the kitchen. The room gleamed. He took the pic of Colin and Miriam from his coat and stuck it into a drawer, then he found the wine and the glasses where Betty said they'd be, and as he turned back toward the living room — brimming with sympathy and the need to comfort her — his half-dead mobile phone rang weakly in his jacket pocket. Not now, not now . . . He dragged the phone out and heard Adamski's voice, a croak from the reaches of dead space.

'I think we might have your missing person, Lou.'

18

All night Dorcus Dysart drove his white van around the city. He'd checked the hookers on the edges of the city centre, but they were high-risk, these girls in their hiked-up skirts and stark powdered faces. They were likely to be diseased, drug-ridden, probably both. Impurities flowed in their blood, toxifying their organs.

He travelled south of the Clyde and into the silent gritty streets that branched off Paisley Road West. Yellow street lamps, some of them shattered, and nobody moving except some late-night drunks singing *Ah'm no Hairy Mary ah'm yer maw.*

Solitary pedestrians were difficult to find. People tended to move in pairs, or three- and foursomes. They read the papers, saw the news. Bodies had been found. Somebody in this city was doing 'spare-part surgery'. Quote unquote.

Circumstances had to be perfect — a person walking alone under dim lights. Weight mattered, and accessibility.

He drove deeper into the territory. Pollokshields, Shawlands. Locked shops, shuttered restaurants, dark tenements: he might have been driving the streets of an abandoned city. Sometimes a desperation overcame him: he'd never find anybody ever again, and then what? What would he do for money? And then he began to obsess about this Glorianna who'd telephoned him, Mr Chuck's friend. She was coming to his house, he'd never had a woman there.

Except Nurse Payne.

She was sacred to him, a love so constant he sometimes wondered if she was somebody he'd dreamed. He pictured her face. That intelligence in the eye.

Now this Glorianna was coming too . . .

What would he say to her. What would he. How would he say. Look I don't want but thanks anyway, don't think I'm ungrateful. He'd phone Mr Chuck and say, don't send the girl, I'm too busy working, but he had the feeling Reuben Chuck was a man who didn't like his gifts rejected.

At 2.30 a.m. he changed direction and went back across the river and up into the area around the University. The thoroughfares were empty. This was Studentland but where were the inhabitants, where were the party people? He pulled over, cleaned his glasses with a special little chamois cloth he kept in the glovebox.

On Byres Road, he saw a few groups of late loiterers. Then side-streets — Dowanside, Havelock, White Street, Caird Drive. Up and down and round and round. He went back the way he'd come, prowling. Along Woodlands Road a few taxis cruised, a couple of cars passed. He slid a hand under his glasses and rubbed his tired eyelids.

An unfulfilled night. No, no, you have a deal with Mr Chuck.

Mr Chuck who likes you, calls you Dorco.

144

Says you're an artist, looks up to you, wants your skills, pays highly for them.

Halfway down West End Park Street he saw the girl come round a corner, trying to hurry on wobbly high heels. She was short, trim, lightweight.

Slowing his van, he followed her a little way.

If she made it to the main crossroad, Woodlands Road, opportunity might be lost to him in a sudden burst of traffic, or more pedestrians. He pulled his van into the curb alongside her and slid open his door.

'Excuse me,' he said.

She didn't look, kept walking. Same pace, didn't want to appear frightened.

He edged the van forward to keep up with her. 'Sorry to t-trouble you.'

She turned now. Her face in the headlights was plain, mouth a mournful downturned slash. Her eyes were red from crying. She was upset. He wondered why — perhaps heartache, broken promises.

People in love were vulnerable. Often they trusted their hearts to shits.

He felt sorry for the girl.

'What the *fuck* do you want?' The expression on her face was shaped by years of urban fear: *don't talk to strangers, don't take sweeties from men you don't know, stay away from bushes.* In her emotional state she'd overlooked her own rule. Or forgotten it.

He braked, gazed down at her. He knew he had a certain awkward innocence about him. He projected harmlessness. People saw the benign face and the thick frames of his glasses and they heard the quietly hesitant way he spoke and the stutter and they felt sorry for him. They might wonder about the long hair, but they thought they divined his nature easily enough: kindly, no hidden threats, a nice guy but just a little out there. Nurse Payne always said he could knock on any door and be given shelter for the night.

'I'm l-lost and looking for . . . uh, G-Great Western Road.'

'You're not far,' she said.

'Excuse me, are you all right,' he said.

'What you mean am I *all right*?'

'You look a wee bit d-down.'

'That's my problem intit?'

A defensive moment. Dorcus felt she could easily slip away if he wasn't careful. 'I'm not b-butting in, excuse me. I only wanted . . . '

'Great Western, you said. Go to the end here, that's Woodlands Road. Take a right on Park Road and you'll come to Great Western, OK?'

She turned away from him, walking quicker now, but wobbling more. He jumped down from the van, landed quietly on his rubber-soled trainers. He had the chloroform out of the bottle and into a hankie in one slick well-rehearsed movement, and he grabbed her from behind and she shouted '*What the hell do you think you're*,' just before he crammed the hankie over her mouth. The inside of his head vibrated like a struck drum. This is always the bad time. This is where anything can go wrong, she can break loose, fight, or the chloro isn't strong enough to bring her down, or worse, the chloro is too strong.

146

She moaned, struggled against him, tried to bite his hand, kicked, then abruptly buckled as if life had just drained out of her, and she slid downward against his legs and slumped on the pavement.

He stuffed the hankie into his pocket and dragged the girl to the back of his van, opened the door, picked her up and laid her carefully inside. He got in beside her and tied her limp hands with straps of leather, then bound her legs with a long chain welded to an interior panel. He padlocked the chain, then he placed an old burlap sack, in which he'd scissored two holes for breathing, over her head, and he knotted the drawstring under her jaw.

He slid into the driver's seat and travelled until he was in the east of the city, moving along Edinburgh Road toward home. He checked his mirrors time and again for police vehicles. If he was stopped he'd have to explain his passenger — don't think that way, do not. Outside his house he unlocked the high metal gates and drove through quickly.

He heard the Dobermans: dogs of war.

He drove the van into the garage and the door closed automatically behind him. He lifted the girl out and carried her into the house, calling 'Nurse Payne Nurse Payne, is everything ready,' as he ascended to his surgery at the top of the stairs, passing, the way he always did, through the ghost zone, the mist of ice.

19

Five a.m. in the morgue, and Perlman had no desire to sleep, no chance of getting any even if he wanted: the idea was like voyaging to a country too far to reach. Death had a magnetic energy field, and it kept him hyped, edgy. He drank cup after cardboard cup of bad black coffee from a vending machine.

Now and again he was drawn back to the bed where Kirk McLatchie lay exposed for the purpose of examination, illuminated by a cruel overhead light. A sorry end. No privacy, less dignity.

Adamski was standing a few feet from the body. Burnt-out, he massaged his beefy eyelids continually and sighed time and again — regret, sadness, maybe disgust with the ways of the city he'd served for years. This corpse had been found by two lovers walking in woodland near the Clyde where it flowed close to Cambuslang Road. What a memorable date that turned out to be.

Perlman's mind kept going back to Betty, and the glass of wine she was destined never to taste. How had he broken the news to her? *About Kirk, I'm sorry to tell you they've found your son . . .* He had no specific details to give her at that point, just news of Kirk's discovery. She sat motionless, as if paralyzed by a stroke. She shrunk in front of his eyes, diminished by pain. She didn't go through the predictable phases of

148

denial — no, it can't be my son, it can't be Kirk — as if she'd known that the life of her missing kid would end badly all along. She'd tried to light a cigarette and it slipped from her hands and she made no move to pick it up. He saw terror build inside her. She began to shake so badly he knew he couldn't ask her to go to the morgue to identify the boy.

He gave her two sleeping-pills he found in his bathroom cabinet and hoped they'd knock her out. He covered her with a blanket and sat for a long time beside her as she curled up, mute and tiny, on his sofa. Once or twice he'd stroked the side of her face or her arm, and murmured words of condolence, but she seemed neither to feel his touch nor hear his voice.

Sooner or later, she'd have to make an identification, unless Kirk's wife Deborah could be found first — but the phone rang unanswered in Deborah's flat when he'd tried the number, and she didn't respond to the two patrol cops who'd been sent from E-Division to knock at her door. Gone AWOL, a late-nighter, a petty little jab of vengeance at her errant husband maybe. Bad timing.

He watched the medical examiner scratch the tip of his nose. He was a tall stately man with grey hair that overhung the collar of his white coat. He was fastidious, solemn. Perlman had run into coroners who were jokers, comics lightening the gloom of their profession. *Dead end job this, chuckle. Nothing but grave prospects here, ho ho.* Harry Whelan was no stand-up act. He worked in silence, and when he had to record his observations into a microphone he spoke softly.

Perlman wanted cold fresh air, away from the confines of this place. But he had a responsibility as a substitute for the boy's mother.

Harry Whelan switched off his recorder. 'Long night,' he said.

'You're telling me,' Adamski said.

'You'll get my written report in time, gentlemen, but I imagine you already know roughly what I'm going to say in it . . . you've been listening to me talk long enough, after all.' He gazed at the silver instruments of his trade lying in a bloodstained tray beside the bed.

Perlman felt light-headed. He crossed his arms and leaned against the wall. Christ, all his professional life he'd dealt with the violent dead, stab and gunshot victims, the strangulated, the ledge-jumpers. Had he reached that point where he'd become too thin-skinned to cope with the faces and bodies of corpses? It happens, cops lose their objectivity, they grow sick and jaded, and every morning shades seamlessly into the one before. The grim sameness of things. Other polis developed a shell of indifference: dead meat on a slab, too bad, another stat. Or was it because he knew Kirk's mother that he was more sensitive than before? Knew her, *liked* her. When he thought about it he realized he'd liked her from that first meeting, her candour, the honest way she looked you straight in the eye.

He wanted to hurry back to his house: if the pills had worked, they'd wear off soon enough, and he didn't want her waking alone. And then

150

he had the dilemma of how to break *this* news to her — the manner in which Kirk's life had been ended.

Harry Whelan, who'd undone the stitches on Kirk's body to perform the internal examination, and then carefully closed the corpse up again, said, 'Both kidneys removed. Also the liver. And the heart. The surgery was good, economical. Somebody with experience. No question.'

Perlman's thoughts immediately rushed to Jackie Ace. He'd found him convincing. Maybe a second interview would reveal something else, but he didn't expect wild revelations. *I got tired of bodies, Sergeant.* It was a simple, credible reason for giving up surgery. No matter, Perlman would make a point of talking to him again.

Whelan said, 'Organs. Lucrative business, sadly.'

Perlman asked, 'Why go to the trouble of plundering the organs and then stitching up the body again? Why not just dump the corpse as is?'

'A compulsion. Likes to do a tidy job, feels an obligation to finish. Who knows?'

'I don't mean to sound callous,' Adamski said, 'but if it was me I'd just toss the remains. I wouldn't waste time sewing, especially if time's a factor. You've got what you want, why bother with needlework?'

Whelan shrugged. He drew a sheet across Kirk McLatchie, glancing at Lou. 'We still need somebody connected to the family to come down and identify him. Meantime, gents, thanks for the company. It can get lonely here at four in the morning.'

The silent company of the dead, Perlman

thought. You bet it's fucking lonely. *Betty's going to be lonely*. He walked out of the room into the corridor.

Adamski followed him. 'Sorry it turned out this way, Lou.'

'I asked for help. You gave it. I'm grateful.'

Adamski looked balefully at the lights along the corridor. 'The older I get the more I want happy endings. What does that make me? A sentimental fool?'

'A human being.' Perlman clapped a hand on Adamski's shoulder. 'You have a smoke I can borrow?'

'I quit last year.'

'Smart move.' Perlman stepped into the street. The clear night air was starry and cold.

Adamski said, 'I'll keep you up to snuff with developments.'

'And anything I can do,' Perlman said. 'Just ask.'

Lou walked to his car and turned once to wave at Adamski.

* * *

He drove back to Egypt.

Betty McLatchie was lying on the sofa where he'd left her, buried by the blanket. Her breathing was so light he had to lean close to her to hear it. He watched her for a while. Soon she'd wake, and crash straight into the truth she was escaping from in deep drugged sleep.

He walked the room in slow steps, waiting. The two brown candles on the window-sill were out.

20

Reuben Chuck woke in his penthouse bedroom to find Sandy Scullion sitting in the raffia chair by the balcony door. Chuck never needed time to drag himself out of sleep: instantly alert, always. He sat up in bed, looked at Scullion and said, 'New hairstyle, *and* moustache. Makes you look — what's the word? Mature. Man about town.'

'I don't need a scumbag's opinion.'

'Scumbag? My oh my. Strong stuff. And I thought you'd just broken in for a wee chat.' Chuck stepped out of bed. He wore black silk pyjamas. He slipped his feet into a pair of kidskin slippers, and strolled to the balcony window where he yanked the curtain all the way open. 'What a view. Stunnin, intit?'

Scullion said, 'I'm not in a view mood.'

'Suit yourself.' Chuck stared out across the river. The day was standard Glasgow issue, dour and unpromising, but the vista enthralled him. He could see all the way beyond the south bank and past the new Gorbals and King's Park and Cathcart as far as Castlemilk, where the Cathkin Braes rose, a great sweep of this fractious profitable city.

'I phoned, you never got back to me,' Scullion said.

'Couldn't find a spare moment. How did you get in?'

'Your doorman's frightened of cops. I threatened him.'

153

'He's a wee nyaff. I could have him fired.'

'But in your infinite compassion you won't.' Scullion rose, the wicker creaked. He strolled the room, ducking under hanging crystals. He touched one and it twisted, turned like a wandering glass eye. 'What's with all the beads, Chuck?'

'Crystals,' Chuck said.

'Crystals, oh, excuse me.'

'I'm on a certain path.'

'Damnation alley?'

Chuck smiled. He had a smile that could freeze a budgie from twenty feet. 'I don't think you're in tune, Scullion.'

'Let me guess. You're a New Ager all of a sudden?'

'Foo, simplistic label.'

'You're seeking what . . . enlightenment? Is that the word *du jour*?'

Chuck said, 'I could talk my arse off and you still wouldn't get it.' He picked up the red robe that matched his pyjamas and put it on. Silk made him feel good. He wondered how many worms did it take to make this ensemble, and how many Chinamen. And how many of these worms were reincarnations.

'What's the story, Scullion? Polisman breaks into exclusive high-rise apartment. I don't 'spose you happen to have anythin like authorization, a piece of paper, a warrant.'

'A what?'

'Thought so. It's funny seein you on your own. You look a wee bit lost. Where's your sidekick anyway?'

154

'Sick leave.'

'Oh aye, the gunshot. Unfortunate matter. You must miss him.'

'Forget Perlman, Chuck. Your main worry right now is *me*.'

Tough guy act. Unconvincing. Reuben Chuck had always thought Perlman was the one who gave the partnership its *sting*. Scullion was heavy-fistit. It was the Jew you had to be wary of. He had a cheeky habit of provoking your anger — and anger wasn't cool, because it meant you'd transferred your power to somebody else.

''Spose you tell me why I should be worried about anythin, Scullion.'

'Start with your dead competitors.'

Chuck shook his head in feigned disappointment. 'Aw, you're goin about this the wrong way, Scullion. Perlman wouldn't come out and say anythin as obvious as that. He'd shadow-box, this way that way, mibbe throw out a puzzlin wee remark to draw you in, then he'd come up with a punch you never saw. Confrontational approach gets you nothin.'

'I'm not here to discuss Perlman's fucking technique, Chuck. Let me recite the roll-call of the dead to refresh your memory. Jimmy Stoker. Plus Stoker's muscle, the brothers Jack and Tony McAlpine. Gordy Curdy. And Curdy's wife. And no doubt we'll dig up a few more bodies along the way.' Scullion flicked another crystal and it swayed up and back.

'And what has all this got to do with me precisely?'

'You're a vicious hungry bastard and you

155

reached out and grabbed this territory and that, and in the process you left a lot of blood — '

'Hang on, sonny boy. *I* left a lot of blood? Where and when? You want me to account for my movements at specific times? Go ahead. Ask me. Any day. Any time. Go ahead — '

'We both know that would be a total waste of effort, Chuck.'

'You're makin a serious accusation here, if I understand you.'

'And I want you to know it.'

'You're awfy lucky I'm not the kind of man who goes runnin to his lawyer every time some polisman makes a blunderin arse of himself.'

Scullion pointed a finger. 'Lawyers don't bother me. You'll fuck up with or without one. Somebody close to you will say the wrong thing in the wrong place. Somebody you trust will speak out of turn. A ned with a grievance, a drunk in a pub shooting his fat mouth off. You scum are all so fucking predictable I can sit back and wait for it to happen, then I pounce. Today, tomorrow, next month. Doesn't matter. I'm a patient man. All the time in the world.'

'And this is what — a wee warnin?'

'Call it anything you like.'

'You're pissin into a force nine gale, pal.'

'Not me. I don't like splashback.' Scullion reached up and stilled a swinging crystal, holding it in his fist.

Chuck thought: I'd like to shove that crystal up your jaxie.

Scullion said, 'The lines are drawn.'

Lines are drawn, my arse. Only in your heid,

Scullion. 'You fancy a cappuccino? I bought this new Italian machine. It's a doddle. Froths milk, a wean could work it. Here,' and he went into the kitchen, Italian marble floor, slatted granite-grey blinds, stainless steel appliances. He indicated a Gaggia de Luxe. 'Top of the range, that one. I'll brew you a cup.'

'I'll pass.' Scullion looked around. 'Nice kitchen.'

'Costa fortune.'

'You're doing well.'

'Keepin my heid above water. It's a hard world. Lissen, do yourself a favour and come to my bistro some night. The Potted Calf, Broomhill Road. Chef's a French-trained Korean. Top man, cooked all over Europe. He does a terrific pork *gitane* and his *fegato Venezia's* out of this world, although I don't eat meat myself. Keep your wallet in your pocket if you come.'

'A bribe, Chuck.'

'You've got a suspicious turn of mind. Your Superintendent Tay's been known to sup at the Calf, and some of his pals. They always leave happy.'

'And do they pay?'

'I'm not runnin a soup kitchen. They pay through the fuckin nose. But I always throw in a free sambuca. They're top brass, they expect somethin extra. You know how it is.'

'I'm not sure I do.'

'The way I look at it . . . ' Chuck unscrewed the coffee-basket, and measured dark brown oily grounds into it, sniffed the aroma with a smile of anticipation, then slotted the basket back in

157

place. 'What's a free after-dinner drink anyway? It makes the customers happy. I try to spread a little cheer as I pass through my journey, Scullion. And this is only one level.'

'Don't tell me there are others?'

'For those of us who follow the path.'

'Tell me more about this path.'

'It's the true way of the Baba.'

'The *who?*'

'Baba Ragada. Here, you might give him a shot yourself. Helps you relax, offers you new insights. Ask me, you're too tense.'

Scullion smiled. 'Three pints of Tennants soothes all my pains.'

'Joke and smirk, pal. Booze is a poison. The Baba offers another way.'

'I'm sure he does.' Scullion moved toward the door.

'You leavin already?'

'Very heavy schedule. An appointment with my hair stylist, then my harpsichord lesson after that, followed by my pastry class. We're doing choux today.'

'If the choux fits,' Chuck said. 'You see Lou, give him my best.'

'That'll brighten his day.'

Chuck heard the door close. He flipped a switch on the Gaggia, and made himself a small shot of espresso which he carried to the kitchen banquette. One sip, a quick poke to the system.

OK what have we got here. Scullion comes to dust me with menace, so he thinks. The polis has its eye on me. I am under observation. They're watchin, they're waitin. Somebody will slip up.

Bang. A *shiver* runs through me. I'm scared shiteless.

Scullion's a one-legged man without Perlman.

He stuck a sugar cube in his mouth and wondered if Farl the roofer had gone to fix the leak at the Temple, and if the cracked Jesus eye had been replaced. Then he picked up the phone and called Ronnie Mathieson and said, 'Your lot moved yet?'

21

Samuel Montague was at his desk by 9 a.m. He tapped the keyboard of his computer with fingers that were stiff and ached, and scanned the financial news, watching ever-changing yellow figures scroll across the screen. Usually he absorbed them in microseconds. He had a slick brain. But the numbers were Aramaic to him today.

His secretary came in, laid his post on the desk. 'Good morning Mr Montague,' she said. A wide-hipped woman of forty-three, Mrs Liddle was cheerful, anxious to please. She'd been with the Bank all her adult life. She thought Montague seemed distant this morning. Also a little pale, weathered. Usually he was warm and smiling.

'Fair amount of post,' she said.

'I see that, Mrs Liddle.'

'Call me when you want to dictate.'

'I may have to go out of the office for an hour or so,' he said. 'Family matter.'

'Is everything OK, Mr Montague?'

'Everything is just fine, Mrs Liddle.'

Mrs Liddle lingered, unconvinced. She waited for Montague to elaborate on this family matter he'd mentioned, but he didn't. Something was just not right. She was very fond of Montague, she knew his expressions and moods. And today he was not himself, although it was difficult to put a finger on it precisely. His pallor suggested ill health, a cold coming on. Or maybe his wife was unwell, and he was worrying about her.

She'd worked for some skinflint miseryguts in her time at the Bank. Mr Montague was different. He gave generously for staff birthday presents, and when somebody was sick he was head of the line to send flowers or a basket of fruit. When he'd married about a year ago he'd invited everybody in the Bank to his wedding at the St Andrews Scottish Episcopal Church in Milngavie. She'd never seen him so happy before, nor indeed so handsome. He looked filmstarry in a grey morning suit with a dark cravat. And his bride, Meg, what a joyous girl, everybody commented on her beauty and grace, and the gift she had for putting people at ease. They were a perfect match, universally agreed.

They honeymooned in Barbados at a Five Star resort. The younger tellers went around looking dreamy-eyed for a whole week, exchanging fairytales about what it would be like to be Mrs Meg Montague, canoodling in the Caribbean. In the canteen one day, Mrs Liddle overheard Joyce McMillan say to Emma McCall, 'They probably spend all day in bed.'

Emma McCall, bony-faced, huge glasses, said, 'I bet they're hot together.'

Joyce McMillan looked up from her copy of *Elle*. 'Oh hot, of course they are. You only have to look at his brown eyes and you can tell. And she's definitely all fire underneath those lovely manners. Hot? Scalding, you ask me.' She blew on her fingertips and said, 'Whoooo.'

161

'When he's not a banker, he's a bonker,' Emma said, and giggled.

'Chatter chatter.' Mrs Liddle tut-tutted the girls as she passed, but found herself thinking of moonlight, palm trees, two newly-weds leaving footprints along a beach, passion in a bamboo bed, the whole tourist brochure.

Montague said, 'I'll buzz you if I need you, Mrs Liddle.'

Startled from her reverie, Mrs Liddle said, 'Yes, of course.'

The frosted glass panel of Montague's office door caught a flash of light as it shut behind her. He checked his watch, a birthday present from Meg. Then he tapped his keyboard and entered the personal files of his customers. He found the name he needed, then wrote the number of a safe-deposit box on a notepad, ripped the sheet off, folded it and placed it in the right-hand pocket of his trousers.

If you don't come through, your wife's gonny be deid by ten thirty sharp, Monty. After she's been shagged stewpit, that is.

He shut his eyes, trying to ignore the ache in his gut, where he was bruised. He'd worked hard for his present position. Before marriage, the Bank was everything to him, his favourite Uncle, his future, his retirement. Had it not provided him with a generous mortgage for his house in Bearsden? And had it not loaned him, at preferential rates, funds to purchase the BMW of which he was very fond?

He owed the Bank. OK. But it was piss compared to what he owed Meg. Meg was his world. Before Meg, life had been acceptable but dull. And then came lightning, and his heart was liberated. He loved her beyond anything or anyone. He was stunned by love.

He looked at his watch again. Nine oh eight. White latex gloves. He kept seeing them.

No, the Bank didn't matter a damn. Anyway, it was unlikely the Bank would ever know what he'd done, unless he confessed. And he wouldn't, because it meant having to reveal the sordid details of the despicable way his wife had been treated. He remembered with deep disgust the man urinating on her, the stains on her negligee, and the strong hop-like after-scent of his pee.

She'd been humiliated.

Dangerous men, all three of them. Animals.

And they were still in his house.

All night long he'd been separated from her, locked in a small storage room — but where were they keeping Meg? He listened hard, ear pressed to storage-room door, but he'd heard no sound of her. Once or twice there were noises from downstairs, men clumping and thumping around, going from room to room, laughing and cursing as they broke into the drinks cabinet.

But nothing from Meg.

Was she in the bedroom, miserable and alone?

Was somebody with her, guarding her, making sure she didn't try any desperate moves? The fact he had no idea escalated him to a new scary high of anxiety. He shouted aloud a few times, called her name, but the only response he got was when one of the men climbed the stairs and struck the

163

door with what might have been a hammer and screamed at him to shut the fuck up and if he didn't, if another peep was heard out of him, if if — the man didn't spell out the consequences.

Montague had listened to the footsteps fade and then more clattering noises from below. He'd sat hunched in the tiny box of a room, tense and miserable hour after hour, plans rushing through his mind only to be discarded: escape the windowless storage room — but how? Rescue Meg — but only if he could free himself from his prison. Nothing came to him, and his nerves grew all the more taut. Meg, where was she? What were they doing to her?

In quieter moments, when he managed to think with any kind of lucidity, he understood the policy — separate and conquer, keep them apart and Montague would be all the more malleable and ready to meet their demand.

He rose from his desk, walked out of his office. He didn't look at the staff. He wondered if anyone was watching him. One of the gang, say. Sent here to keep an eye on him. Fine with him, he was being obedient, he wasn't doing anything stupid like secretly calling the police, he'd never jeopardize Meg. He thought of her now as he entered the locked vault where the safe-deposit boxes were stored. He'd asked to see her, just to check on her before he'd left the house that morning, and all he received was a shotgun thrust into his chest. *Do the business, you'll see her then . . .*

The air in the safe-deposit vault was filtered but still stuffy. In and out, quickly. Even if he gave these animals what they wanted, he had no absolute guarantee of Meg's safety. Were they the kind of men who'd keep their word?

Fat chance, but one he had to take.

He used his emergency pass-keys to open a safe-deposit box, which he carried to a private cubicle. Inside the box he found an envelope, ordinary, brown. This everyday envelope was worth his wife's life. He had an urge to open it. He checked the seal, slipped his finger beneath it, tested the strength of the gum. He could slit this open and reseal it without anyone ever knowing.

He eased the flap open very carefully.

It contained a single sheet of paper with the typewritten words: *The Azteca Bank of Aruba. Account: 957 8671-045. Password: count-dracula.* He placed the paper back in the envelope, licked what little gum remained on the flap, resealed the envelope and pressed it tight with the fingertips of his good hand. He put the envelope in the inside pocket of his jacket and stepped out of the cubicle, then returned the box to its place among all the other safe-deposit boxes.

Done.

He left the Bank, conscious of Mrs Liddle watching him from behind her desk, and he walked up Buchanan Street. He was a tangled knot of aches and pains and nerves. On St Vincent Street he headed west. *Somebody will meet you*: that was what he'd been told. *You'll hand over what you took from the Bank and go back to your office until we call you.*

Keep walking along St Vincent. How far, he didn't know. He reached the corner of Hope Street.

Hope Street: remind me of irony.

He wondered again if he was being watched. Perhaps a member of the gang had been detailed to track his movements. Or maybe there were more than three men involved, a fourth member whose task it was to make sure he did what he'd been told. He knew nothing about how gangs were structured. All he knew was that this vicious trio dictated his future. Christ, he felt such a loathing, such a burden of anxiety.

He was so absorbed by his feelings he didn't see the man who appeared at his side.

'You got something for me?'

Montague turned. The man wore a navy blue scarf that covered his jaw and mouth. His sunglasses were impenetrable. The scarf muffled his voice. A slit allowed Montague to see that the man's cheeks were volcanoed with the pockmarks of old acne. They looked like small asteroids that had been bombarded by space debris.

'Hand it over fast.'

It was suddenly of enormous importance to Montague to have reassurances. 'I want to know you haven't harmed my wife.'

'She's shipshape.'

'How can I believe you?'

'Because I'm fuckn telling ye.'

'That's not good enough. I'm supposed to accept your word — '

'Pal, it's a matter of choices. You give me what

166

you've got for me, OK, your wife will be waiting when you get home. Intact, if you get my drift. You act in any other way, you go home to an empty house.' The man slipped a hand menacingly into his coat pocket. 'Another choice is I fuckin chiv you right here in the street, mate. Nay problem. And then you've got nothing but a big bad bleeding wound, likely fatal. And the only home you'll go to then is a funeral one.'

He imagined Meg being harmed. Or worse, made to disappear. He imagined dying in a city street, a knife in his ribs. The images ripped him apart.

He took the envelope out, and gave it to the man who glanced at it before pocketing it, and then he was gone quickly, overcoat flapping, down Hope Street in the direction of Sauchiehall and God knows where after that.

Montague walked back to the Bank. In his office he shut the door and thought, I could have tackled the man, grabbed him, dragged him to the police. In whose dreams? He'd wait until 5 p.m., then leave. He wondered why these villains needed — and here he checked his watch — another seven hours? What did they propose to do with all that time?

Of course, it might take them hours to make sure the paper was authentic. Phone calls to make, people to confer with. They might have to wait until the Azteca Bank in Aruba opened before they knew for sure that they had the genuine article. He'd never heard of the Azteca Bank. He didn't know their hours of operation. Complicated time zones might be a factor. He

167

tapped his keyboard. The Azteca Bank had a gaudy website, all blue and gold and palm trees. He scanned it quickly.

The Azteca Bank, founded in 1987, has deposits of 13 billion dollars. Our aim is customer satisfaction, complete confidentiality, and discretion. We offer investment counselling, and professional advice on legal matters, among many other services. Contact: azteca@aruba/14.com.

It's a money-laundering outfit, Montague thought. No phone number, no address, no opening hours.

He swallowed an aspirin and thought of Meg. He needed to hear her voice. Nobody had told him he couldn't phone the house if he wanted. He punched in six of the seven digits, then replaced the handset. If he called, he might upset these gangsters.

But Meg. God, he needed to know she was all right, if being all right was even possible in the circumstances.

He fingertipped the numbers slowly. The phone rang for a long time. What was happening in his house, what was Meg doing, what were the gangsters —

He heard Meg's voice. 'Hello.'

'Meg,' he said, relieved. 'Are you free to speak?'

'Yes, Sammy.'

'How are you darling?'

'Fine, I'm fine.'

Fine, how could she be? 'Those men, what are they doing?'

168

'They've been different this morning,' she said.

'Different?' Did he hear somebody breathing on the extension? He wasn't sure.

'Not like yesterday.'

'I got what they wanted,' he said.

'That's why they're pleased.'

Montague was appeased somewhat. But still unhappy. 'They haven't hurt you, have they?'

She said, 'No, nothing like that. They'll be gone before you get home.'

'And you . . . you're comfortable with the situation?'

'Comfortable? How could I be *comfortable?* It's better than it was yesterday, that's not saying much.'

There. He heard a tiny note of stress in her voice. Why wouldn't she be stressed in this situation, for heaven's sake?

'When you come home, all this will be behind us. And we'll forget, won't we?'

'We will, I promise. We'll go away for a few days. Somewhere nice.' He adored her. 'I love — '

The connection was cut. He imagined a man's hand tugging the wire from the wall.

He took another aspirin. Seven hours, counting down.

22

Perlman napped fitfully in the armchair, and opened his eyes only when Betty shook his shoulders.

'I've been up for ages,' she said. She had a blanket draped over her shoulders. 'It was my place to go to the morgue, not yours. I didn't have the courage. I couldn't look at him.'

'Courage doesn't come into it.' His mouth was dry. Betty followed him inside the kitchen where he filled a glass from the tap and drank it in one long swallow.

'I backed out. I was a coward. You saw him. Now it's my turn. A mother should see her son.' She lit a cigarette.

Maybe not, Perlman thought, and drew a second glass of water. 'They're going to need a family member to make the formal identification. I tried getting in touch with Kirk's wife, but I couldn't track her down — '

'No, I don't want *her* to go before me. Kirk never loved her.'

'If that's what you want.'

'It's what I *need*, Lou.' She made a flustered gesture with her hands, as if fumbling for something in the air. Cigarette smoke wafted into her eyes and stung. 'Fuck. *Fuck*.' She leaned over the sink and splashed water into her eyes then dried her face with a paper towel.

Perlman listened to the squeak of the old tap

and wondered how he could prepare Betty for the morgue. This was once your wee boy, Betty. Now he's skin and bone, opened up and restitched, in a cold box.

'I'll come with you,' he said.

'I'm grateful, Lou, but I need to do this on my own.'

A mother looks at her dead son and indescribable emotions churn through her — feelings beyond Perlman's experience. He didn't have the biological equipment, he hadn't carried a child, hadn't established that bond, he wasn't even a *father*.

This was more than a dead son, this was a butchered carcass.

'Let me drive you there,' he said.

'No, I'll take my own car.'

You couldn't break down her obstinacy if she'd made her mind up. He realized that much about her. 'I could call you a taxi.'

'I'll drive myself, Lou.'

He held her a moment, then he walked with her to the front door. He needed to prepare her. There was no way he'd let her leave, not knowing. She opened the front door.

'Wait, Betty. Just wait. Before you go.' He put his hands on her shoulders and looked directly at her.

'Tell me what it is, Lou,' she said.

He tried to pick his words. *You're not going to find him as you might expect, Betty. He was cut —*

She interrupted. 'He was stabbed, is that what you mean?'

171

'No, it's more than that — '

'How more? They cut his face?'

Perlman shook his head. There was no simple way to say it aloud. He fumbled to make a compassionate sentence out of words that had no mercy. He heard himself speak as if novocained.

She buckled, and Perlman caught her, held her against his body. 'Oh dear God, oh dear God, no, no . . . '

'I'll come with you, Betty.'

She pushed him away fiercely, as if to say she could stand on her own two feet, she didn't need anyone else to do things for her. She looked stricken and lost and yet utterly determined to maintain one small space inside her that was intact — even if it was already beginning to crumble. She ran toward her car, an old brown Mini with a faded gold racing-stripe. He went after her, calling out her name, but she didn't turn back. He waited until she'd driven out of sight before he shut the front door and listlessly gathered the few items of mail that lay on the floor. An electricity bill. A TV licence reminder. A credit card statement. He tossed the post back on the floor.

His phone rang, and he went into the living room to answer it.

'Meet me,' Scullion said.

'Where and when.'

'I've got a quiet place in mind.'

23

Perlman had never been inside Glasgow Cathedral. He'd passed it almost every day of his life, but he'd never entered it. Some hangover from childhood. Good Christian Germans had murdered his relatives in camps — Ephraim never quit drumming the holocaust into him. He looked up at the spire, idling before he went inside. A morning of rare sunshine gave the dark grey steeple a bright clarity. He pictured monks wandering around here through the centuries, chanting, praying, growing things — whatever else monks did.

Maybe he needed a church today. Maybe he'd find some form of uplift. He never prayed, but perhaps he could find it in himself to offer up a few silent thoughts about Betty.

Inside, the cathedral was as huge and hushed as a god's heart. No city traffic could be heard. The long stained-glass windows, etched in rich colour, magnetized him. In the nave, his eye followed a line of stone arches which supported a second arched storey. Higher, there was a vaulted ceiling that suggested impenetrable mysteries. He was surprised: in the centre of this rowdy city a lovely sanctuary of tranquillity he'd never known.

He felt like a tourist in his own Glasgow.

There was no sign of Scullion, so Perlman wandered, half-expecting at any moment to be stopped and questioned by a Cathedral security guard — but there were none. How about that. He was free to set aside his paranoia, and roam.

He found a plaque on a wall, inscribed to the memory of a certain Lieutenant John Sterling, twenty-three, of the Bombay Army attached to the cavalry of His Highness of Nizam. Sterling 'fell while gallantly leading an assault against the fort of Dunahooree. MDCCCX XVIII.'

Fighting for Empire, slaughtered, and commemorated in a cathedral. Perlman thought: Imperialism, death, and God — human history, capsule form.

Scullion tapped his shoulder from behind.

Perlman jumped, turned. 'Oh it's you.'

'Who were you expecting?'

'God mibbe. It's that kind of place.'

Scullion smiled and sat down on one of the wicker chairs that were placed here and there. Perlman sat beside him, deeply relaxed by the serene almost liquid quality of light.

Scullion said, 'Let's talk about this hand of yours.'

'All ears.'

'No *prints*.'

'No what?'

'Burned off. Sid says a blowtorch might have been used. Lysergic acid hurried the process. The serious decomposition is a hindrance.'

Somebody began playing scales on an organ hidden somewhere. Hands on keys, hands in ziploc baggies. Perlman looked down at his own hands, studying the fine hair on the backs of his fingers. He remembered Latta's wolfman hands, hairy horrors. *Polisman haunted by hands. Checks into rest home.*

'What the hell is Tigge doing, Sandy?'

'Head stuck in a computer, scanning missing persons lists. I don't think he likes leaving the office and hitting the streets.'

'He's a *teuchter*, he doesn't *know* the streets. He hasn't bothered his arse to interview me. Odd, considering where the damned thing was found.'

'Skip Tigge, what have *you* been doing?'

'Outsky aboutsky. Poking my nose in here and there.'

'Knocking on some funny doors, eh? Hanging out with scruff, tap-dancing in shady lanes?'

'These arc a few of my favourite things.'

'You're a secretive bugger, Lou.'

'Born furtive.'

'Grapevine chatter is you had the sorry task of ID-ing your cleaning lady's son.'

'She's more like a friend who wants to put my house in order.' A friend. He'd promoted her already.

'She'll need your shoulder to lean on. Her kid's victim number three in the last two weeks. Nouveau-riche Chinese capitalists are crying out for new organs.'

'I'm never sorry for rich capitalist pigs, Chinese or otherwise.'

'I talked to an old acquaintance of yours. Reuben Chuck. He thinks the world of you.'

'It's not a mutual appreciation. I haven't seen Chuck in, oh, two years, George Square, Christmas insanity. We exchanged some chitchat.

Bred any good crooks lately bla bla?'

'A killer routine, Lou.'

'Here, Stanley Baxter used to steal my stuff. What struck me most was the woman with him. Glorianna . . . I didn't get her last name. Easy on the eye, articulate, not your standard crimcrumpet. She was loaded down with Armani bags, aye, but I don't think she was fluff along with Chuck for the material ride.' Perlman remembered her eyes the colour of drinking chocolate, and black hair suffused with small blonde touches. She'd worn a full-length fur coat that didn't conceal the slimness of figure. 'If Chuck's on your score-sheet, Sandy, nail the bastard.'

'You tried a few times.'

'He's slippery as a rat in a drainpipe.'

'You should see his digs. Penthouse luxury. He invited me for dinner at his upmarket bistro. And oh — check this: he's got himself a guru, a certain Baba Ragada.'

'Guru.' Perlman emitted an involuntary scoff at the word.

'Chuck seems to rate him.'

'He's probably donating a bunch of money. Thinks he can buy anything, enlightenment included.'

'If I drilled his head to a wall with a twelve inch nail that might enlighten him quick.'

'It would get his attention.'

The organist played 'Abide With Me' and then struck a bum chord, at which point he segued into a couple of Jerry Lee Lewis boogie riffs before he stopped, leaving a silence that vibrated.

'Cool,' Perlman said. 'Whole Lotta Shakin.

God allows rock in his house. I like this place.'

'I don't think God heard. Since we're talking about Chuck, here's a sad wee story for you.'

'Och, gimme something to cheer me up,' Perlman said.

'I'd like to, believe me. Guy called Samuel Montague, bank manager, was brought into Pitt Street earlier this morning. His house in Bearsden was invaded yesterday by a gang of three Neanderthals breaking stuff, abusing his wife. They wanted a favour.'

'Funny way of asking,' Perlman said.

'Brutal. In return for his wife's safety, he was obliged to provide the password to a bank account in Aruba. Montague's understandably desperate, steals the info, then goes home expecting to find his wife safe and free . . . ' Sandy Scullion paused.

'Do I want to hear this, Sandy?'

'You're going to. The poor bastard finds her naked, hanging by a black leather strap in the attic. He's hysterical, out of control, calls the local cops who can't get a coherent statement out of him. Paramedics shoot Montague with enough dope to fell a giraffe. When he comes round hours later, he's still disoriented, so they shunt him over to HQ. They assume we're better equipped to handle him.'

'Where does Chuck come in?'

'Getting to that. Montague supplied these intruders with the password to a bank account in Aruba which was the property of the recently dead Jimmy Bram Stoker. Now who'd want access to Bram Stoker's money?'

A penny rolled swiftly down a chute in Perlman's head. 'Whoever seized the badlands and couldn't find Stoker's stash.'

'Could be Chuck.'

'Lots of luck proving it.' Perlman tipped his chair back to the wall. 'That rumour about Stoker's hidden zillions has gone round Glasgow so many times it's developed a serious case of vertigo. The tax gestapo had a season ticket to Jimmy's anus, and they were up there regularly with microscopes, but even *they* couldn't find it.'

'Well somebody's trying to find it now, and I'm praying Montague remembers some little detail. Maybe a name, or a peculiar accent. Or he might just recognize somebody when he's rational enough to go through the mug shots — although these bastards wore scarves over their faces. But they might have left something behind. They usually overlook a little thing.'

'Or we'd never catch them,' Perlman said.

Scullion glanced at his watch. 'I need to get back.'

Perlman accompanied him out of the cathedral, where clouds had begun to drift across the formerly clear blue sky. Glasgow darkening: rain by noon. Count on it.

'Bram the bampot,' he said, and stuck his hands in his pockets, swaying a little on his heels as he stared back up at the spire. 'He had a thousand mourners at his funeral. All those thicknecked thugs and their stout wives in black gear *weeping* for this piece of human *schmatta*.'

Scullion said, 'Gangster glamour.'

'Is that what you call it?'

Perlman shook his head in despair. A thousand mourners for a monster. In this disaffected world, criminals attained the status of superstars and developed an obedient following. Jimmy Stoker might have been a minor pope, for all the pomp and grief of his burial. Pope Bram the First.

Scullion walked to his car. 'I'll be in touch.'

'What made you want to meet here?'

Scullion smiled a little. 'Faith, Lou. I'm in constant danger of losing mine, and I need a reminder every now and again.'

'What faith?'

'A simple one. That there's an order in the world.'

'And you get that here?'

'You'd be surprised.'

Perlman watched him drive away.

Scullion's faith: in all the years he'd known the man, it was the first time he'd ever heard Sandy mention any. The things you don't know about the people close to you. He studied the spire for a while and wondered about the faith of the men who'd built it. The higher you rose, the closer you got to God.

It must have seemed a good idea at the time.

24

Treading water at the deep end of his glass-walled rooftop pool, Reuben Chuck said, 'Run that again. The woman's what?'

Ronnie Mathieson, who stood at the edge of the pool in a black suit, spoke quietly. 'Dead, Mr Chuck. Hung herself.'

Reuben Chuck stared through his streaky goggles. 'Hung herself by the neck, is this what you're sayin?'

'Big Rooney says she was going round in her nightie, flashing her tits, groping the lads.'

'Are you tellin me this bird was actin the hoor? This was a respectable woman, a banker's wife, not some five quid bint workin a street corner.'

Mathieson looked unhappy. 'Yeh, but she was making herself available so ah . . . so they sort of took turns at her. More than once.'

'She screwed the crew, eh? And why do you suppose she hung herself, Mathieson?'

Mathieson shrugged. 'Guilt. Shame. I'm guessing, Mr Chuck.'

Chuck dismissed this. 'What I think is they gang-banged her stupid and then hoisted her themselves so she can never tell anybody what we did. A buncha gorillas would've behaved better.'

Mathieson said, 'I'm only the messenger, Mr Chuck.'

'I laid down the law on this one. I was specific.'

'I gave them your instructions word for word, Mr Chuck.'

Chuck snapped off his goggles and stared at Mathieson. It was the killer stare, the one nobody liked to see. 'I count on you, Mathieson.'

'I wasn't at the scene to prevent this.'

'Mibbe closer attention to these vermin and this wouldn't have happened.'

'I can't be everywhere at once, Mr Chuck.'

Chuck scratched his wet hairy chest. Mathieson was loyal insofar as you could ever be certain about any man's fidelity. But he'd taken his eye off the ball, that's what he'd done. He sent the wrong crew. When it called for a modicum of finesse, he'd sent brainless hooligans who couldn't follow instructions even if they'd been written in bold crayon by five-year-old kids.

Chuck's fingernails dug the flesh of his palms. Disobedience was first cousin to disloyalty. He'd been very specific, no more blood. Don't lay a finger on anybody unless *absolutely essential*. No more polis fuel. Possible ammunition for the polis, even if Chuck didn't fear them, was not a bright idea. He wanted at least a semblance of calm after all the blood that had been spilled. One day he wanted to open a newspaper that didn't have the word Gangland in it. Let me sail my boat in quiet waters and enjoy this life.

'Big Rooney — and who else was on the team?'

'Stipp and wee Vic.'

'Wee Vic? He's a *perv*. He'd stick his willie into a cup of maggots. Why did you send him?'

'I let Rooney choose the team.'

181

'Why did you let that scrote choose? He's a stick of gelly waitin for a match. Your judgement's out the window, Ronnie. I telt you, pick men you can rely on. Do I have to do everythin myself? Do I?'

Mathieson had the pale look of a man whose parachute remained stubbornly closed at five thousand feet and dropping.

'And where's the husband, Ronnie?'

Mathieson stroked his chin with an unsteady hand. 'I hear he's in polis custody, Mr Chuck.'

'Answerin questions, is he?'

'He can't identify anyone.'

'How do you know that? How can you be *sure* of that?'

Mathieson was silent, chewing the inside of his mouth. He looked down into the pool where water was disturbed, foamed by Chuck's movements. He took a few steps back from the edge. Because he was a non-swimmer, pools made him wary. And the fact that Glorianna, stretched out on a lounger at the shallow end and hearing Chuck's anger, added to his discomfort.

Now Chuck fell into a fulminating silence, and looked past Mathieson at Glorianna, whose face was hidden behind a magazine. She wore a cream bikini and a gold bracelet, and she had one leg raised, angled suggestively.

I remember when we were at each other like two cats in heat, Chuck thought. He had a surprise underwater erection, hard as Rothesay rock. Auld Lang Syne. He hadn't felt this desire in a while. Celibacy was a killer.

182

'Should you not be on your way somewhere, Glori?' he asked.

'Is it that time already?'

'Close enough,' Chuck said. 'You know the address?'

'Welded to my memory.'

'You'll need to take a taxi, doll. Charge it to the Fitness account.'

'I thought Ronnie would drive me — '

'I'm no finished talkin to Ronnie yet.'

She'd been looking forward to travelling in the Jag. It was the least Chuck could provide, considering she was setting out to do business on his behalf. But no, she was dismissed, get yourself a cab, charge it. Thank you Reuben. Oh thank you for making me feel like just another employee on the Big Man's payroll.

She rose from the lounger and padded barefoot along the tiles. She took her magazine with her. She'd been reading an article entitled Five Sexiest Couples in Hollywood.

'See you later,' Chuck called out to her.

She snubbed him, didn't look back to answer. She left the pool area and began to dress in Chuck's spare bedroom where an ornately framed photo of Baba sat on the dressing-table surrounded by a few rose petals and some quartz crystals. A wee shrine to the guru: what's *happened* to you, Reuben Chuck?

She put on her panties, then a black skirt and a pale blue blouse. She slipped her feet into low-heeled black shoes, applied a little make-up, brushed her hair. She reached for her black cashmere overcoat, tied the belt loosely. She checked her bag to make sure she had massage oils and scented candles.

She could hear Chuck continue to read the riot act to Mathieson. *Somebody lets me down they hardly ever get a second chance, Ronnie. I wipe my arse with them*. She hadn't heard him so angry in a long time. Losing the plot, she thought. Remember the Baba's teachings, Chuck.

Poor Ronnie, he always did his best. He deserved better treatment. He'd resent being made to feel like an eejit in her presence.

Sure, he'd survive because Chuck needed him, passably competent people were rare. But she wouldn't bet money on the life spans of the three goons who'd done the banker's wife.

25

She took the lift to the lobby. The uniformed doorman smiled at her as he held the front glass door. She blew him a kiss as she passed through and headed for the curb where a taxi was waiting. The cabbie, a man with a face like a red cabbage, smiled at her too. All men did. She could bring cheer to pallbearers shouldering a corpse.

She gave the driver the address and settled back to watch Glasgow flick past in a gallery of café lights, bars, small corner shops, the sullen bastions of the tenements. Out of the city, the taxi travelled close to the eastern housing schemes. Here was Cranhill, and beyond the yellow chemical lump of the Sugarolly Mountain lay the streets of Ruchazie. She'd been brought up in Drumchapel, and what she remembered most about The Drum was boredom, the endless grind of life, the drudgery of unemployment, the alkies who hung out on street corners and fell down drunk wherever they fancied.

It wasn't life as she wanted it to be.

She was nineteen when she met Reuben Chuck in a city bar called Arta. She had a boyfriend at the time, naïve and sweet, a long way behind her in ambition. Chuck came on like a blast of gelignite, and tilted the axis of her world. He was the first man she'd ever met with the power to click his fingers and bring waiters scurrying. He got the best tables in restaurants, even when he hadn't booked. He wore designer suits and shoes as soft as gloves and he moved through Glasgow as if it was a property he was thinking of buying. She learned to ignore the entourage of minders that always discreetly accompanied him: they became background, wallpaper. She hadn't been entirely sure what Chuck did for a living, but she was sharp enough to realize quickly that his activities were on the opposite side of the street from legal.

He escorted her to parties in flash houses belonging to loud self-satisfied men like Stoker and Curdy whose wives and mistresses wore tons of tacky jewels and tight sequined dresses. Splashy Botox-browed burdz with big mombassas and bagza glossy lipstick and shiny helmetlike hairdos and gutter Glesca accents. Chuck never gave Glorianna anything ostentatious. All his gifts were thoughtful, stylish. He took her to the opera, presented her with a cashmere stole and a small Celtic cross, and piloted her for romantic trips in his four-seater Cessna — Skye, the Highlands, London, Paris.

And the sex — oh, it was all thunder and lightning. He made her weak-kneed. They couldn't get enough of each other. He made her feel she was important in his life, not just some young crumpet he was doing.

And now he was Captain Celibacy, keeping his pecker in his pants, and eating muesli and organic figs. Now she was told to grab a cab instead of his cock. She felt neglected. OK, she owed her rise in the world to Chuck, and he'd always treated her with respect and tenderness in the five years of their relationship, and he'd listened carefully to her dreams — *Go for them,* he'd say. *Reach out and you'll grasp them.*

But she was still pissed off with him.

At times she wished he hadn't been so encouraging, that he'd asked her to stay in Glasgow with him and forget this LA stuff . . . but he hadn't.

Maybe he would. And then what?

She'd want her own Jag and chauffeur before she'd even think of staying. She was worth at least that.

★ ★ ★

'Here we are,' the driver said. 'Spooky intit. Rather you than me.'

She peered through the window at a high grey brick wall surrounding an old house that looked like a manse. It was incongruous against a background of the four- and five-storey towers of a housing scheme. She gave the driver the Fitness Centre's account number, signed a receipt to which she added a generous tip, then stepped out.

She heard ear-cracking music from the towers, boomboxes reverberating. A shotgun was fired, a single burst that echoed between the buildings. And something was on fire back there. Flames rose, and sparks scattered. She caught an oily stench in the air. A car aflame, maybe. Kids at their regular play. Let's torch this jalopy. Let's shoot a gun.

I should just have said no. Find yourself another girl for this *fucking* job, Mister Chuck.

She walked to a set of tall spiked metal gates cemented into the stone wall. A bell-button was buried in brickwork. She pressed it, waited. Nobody came. Dogs barked with savage intent. She hoped they were securely locked up.

She looked the length of the street. Dusk, a few lamps were lit, others broken. There was always a latent tension in this kind of neighbourhood, that persistent thud of music, the fire illuminating the cheerless façades of the towers, the proximity of guns, but no sign of anyone — although she suspected that danger-ous figures, muggers, louts and the genetically violent, could materialize menacingly out of the shrubbery.

She pressed the bell again, holding her finger on it for about a minute. Hurry hurry up. She stared up the long driveway at the house. Time passed, nothing happened. She rang the bell again in short bursts — *I'm leaving if he doesn't come.*

A porch light went on to reveal a man coming out of the house. He wore his long hair tied back in a ponytail.

'Forget I was coming?' she called as he approached. She used her good voice, like an actress enunciating her lines clearly in an accent that belonged to no particular geographical location. In the role, she thought. *Masseuse* extraordinaire.

The man looked at his watch and shook his head as he reached the gates. He took a big key

188

from his pocket, unlocked one gate.

'Dorcus, right?' she asked.

'Y-yes,' he said. 'But you're early. You s-said seven-thirty. It's only about six-thirty.' He locked the gates behind her, slipped the key in his right pocket.

'No, I believe I said six-thirty.'

'W-well that's not how I r-remember it.'

She heard the dogs again. 'I can go away, come back again.'

'No, you don't have to do that.'

The client is always right. She said, 'Dorcus is an unusual name.'

'Some people s-say so.'

She assessed him fast as they walked up the drive. Weedy, bookish, coy. Easily flustered — as he was now. The glasses made him look glaikit. He wore silly brown corduroy trousers and a long-sleeved navy blue shirt, the kind you buy in Army & Navy stores. He was angular, and had a tentative quality in his movements. He couldn't bring himself to maintain eye contact for more than a few seconds. He gave off a potent chemical smell, as if he'd just come straight from swimming in a pool of industrial-strength disinfectant and tried to disguise this stench with a spray of cheap deodorant. She thought that if he put a lot of work into himself — did something cool with his hair, got himself some modern specs, wore decent clothes, and didn't smell like he'd fallen in a vat of undiluted Dettol — he'd be OK, and passably pleasing to look at. But he had a long way to go.

'Come in, f-follow me.'

189

He led her into a hallway. The air smelled like wet laundry drying slowly. An antique crystal chandelier with two functioning bulbs was the only light source. It illuminated a huge green patch of damp on the wall and a series of intricate cracks that rose to the decaying cornice-work. She looked up, saw dragonflies and flakes of fallen plaster trapped in intricate strands of a great webdrift. Whole place was falling down. One mighty storm would flatten it. Who'd want an old mansion next to Boombox Bay?

She noticed a couple of oil-paintings on the wall, one of a sombre man in judicial robes, the other a pale woman with a fragile consumptive look. Neither face smiled.

'Who are they, Dorcus?' she asked.

'Parents.'

'They live here?'

'Oh no, they're . . . they're dead. I'm on m-my own.'

He led her to the foot of a staircase, then stopped. He didn't move for a while. What's he listening for? His smell was stronger when he stood still. She took a step away.

'What time's the bus, Dorcus?'

'The bus?'

'I assume we're standing here waiting for something.'

No wee smile, no nod of recognition at her little joke. Humour just wasn't his thing, she could see that. He stared over her shoulder and she turned to see what had absorbed his attention. She followed the line of his eye into a room where dust-sheets covered furniture. She made out the shape of a piano in the gloom, and a wingback chair that, with a sheet covering it, suggested the figure of somebody sitting there in a shroud.

She asked, 'Do you play?'

'Play . . . what?'

'The johanna.'

'Me? N-no never. It was uh my mother's and she played a long time ago . . . y-years.' He sprayed saliva with some words, and choked back others.

He led her from the bottom of the staircase and down a corridor, away from the room with the piano. Corridors went this way, that way: the house had an abundance of passages, a maze.

'Rube says you work with him.' She couldn't imagine what this hesitant stooky of a man had in common with Reuben Chuck.

'Mr Chuck, I don't c-call him . . . '

He was never going to finish the sentence. 'What is it you do exactly?'

Dorcus opened a door and showed her inside a room with a long black leather couch and a shelf of leatherbound books. An old black Bakelite phone sat on a table. The curtains at the window were covered with cartoon characters from old DC Thomson comics. Desperate Dan. Lord Snooty. Christ, she hadn't seen these in years.

'I provide him w-with office supplies,' he said. He shut the door.

'Really?'

'Paper and printer c-cartridges and that sort of . . . '

Glorianna took off her coat, slung it across a chair. She sat on the couch. It squeaked under her. The only office supplier she knew in connection with Chuck's businesses was Grimmond & Company of Finnieston, who provided invoice books, business cards, and stationery to the Fitness Centre. But then she didn't know everything about Chuck's affairs, and didn't want to.

Too much knowledge — you know what they say.

Now she heard what seemed like the sound of footsteps very far away, muffled, the slop-flop an old man might make as he shuffled along a track of threadbare carpet in brokenbacked slippers. Dorcus, who'd drawn the curtains and turned on a lamp, began flexing and unflexing his hands nervously. Outside, the dogs roared as if they'd found a couple of newborn babies, perfect aperitifs.

She was cold. A draught blew at her. She couldn't locate its source, it was erratic and swirled around her, carrying a hint of perfume reminiscent of — what? She wasn't sure. Flowers, but what kind? OK, maybe one of those little scented Airwick things in a bottle tucked in a corner. But where was the draught coming from? The door was closed, the curtains drawn.

Dorcus appeared to be listening for something, head tipped to one side.

'Are you sure you don't have a lodger, a room-mate?'

'Yes, nobody, n-none.'

Fine. I'm the one hearing stuff. Maybe it

wasn't anyone walking, just the rising and settling of ancient floorboards. Old houses had arthritic tics of their own. And that odd draught was just . . . air rushing through the gaps in warped window frames, blowing down old chimneys, and joining in a shimmy of wind.

She heard the erratic clink of piano keys.

'Mice,' Dorcus said. 'It's an old . . . '

An old house, yes sweetie, I clocked that instantly, it's rotting away, honeycombed with rodent runs. *Gross*: she wasn't enthralled with the rodents running up and down the keys of the piano. She didn't like mice. They creeped her. Their whiskers, their cunning eyes and furtive movements. She was about to suggest traps or an exterminator, but what business was it of hers? And she wasn't warming to the prospect of laying hands on Dorcus. But she'd do what Chuck asked, she'd do it as quickly as she could, and then get the hell out.

The piano keys rattled again. 'That good old rodent rock,' she said. 'You think it's a special night for them? Somebody's twenty-first?'

No response, no wee smile.

'Come here,' and she reached out for his sweating hand. She felt resistance. His body was unyielding, his expression stricken. 'Sit beside me, Dorcus. Come on.'

She tugged his hand, but still he didn't move. *Reuben, you have some serious fuds for associates. This guy's been double-dipped in a cryonic substance.* 'Let me massage your shoulders. You'll feel better.'

Dorcus lowered himself tentatively to the edge

of the couch, keeping a safe distance from her. She opened her bag, took out a vanilla-scented candle, lit it: it helped defuse offensive odours. She uncorked a bottle, and tipped massage oil into her hands. She rubbed the backs of his hands, stroking them, noticing the ragged fingernails.

'What's that smell?'

'Lavender and almond-honey. Feeling better, Dorcus?'

'Uh . . . '

'Tell the truth. You're unwinding. I know you are.'

'A wee . . . little, yes.'

He was lying. 'You got anything to drink? Scotch? Vodka?'

'I might have some wine . . . '

'Why don't you pour a couple of glasses?'

He got up quickly and left the room. She wandered idly. She glanced at the bookshelves. The big leatherbound volumes were medical textbooks. *Surgical Physiology. Complications in Surgery. The Anaesthesiologist's Manual of Surgical Procedures* . . . There had to be a hundred such books, more. Tucked at the end of a shelf she found a batch of medical supply catalogues. She flicked some pages.

Operating scissors. Haemostatic forceps. Surgical blades. Drainable Fecal collectors.

Drainable fecal . . . ? Vomitarium reading material.

She stuck the catalogues back in place.

Dorcus returned with two thick glass tumblers half-filled with wine.

She took one. 'Cheers,' and she sipped. It was plonk, truly vile. Chateau Oxter-Rot. It left a taste of vinegar at the back of her throat. She felt like spitting it out. Dorcus took one niggardly sip, then set his glass down beside the phone.

'Mmm,' she said and put her glass alongside his.

'The wine's b-been here oh a long time.'

'Old wines are always the best . . . I was checking your books. You're a medical student?'

'*Student?*' He uttered a derisory laugh. 'I'm fully qualified . . . '

'You're *Dr* Dorcus then?'

'Yes I am.'

'But you also sell office supplies?'

'Well . . . this house is . . . I need extra income.'

The qualified physician flogging reams of Xerox paper. 'You work two jobs.'

'I'm kept b-busy,' and he gestured vaguely.

OK. Whatever. She patted the couch. 'Take your shirt off and sit beside me.'

He stared at her as if this request was an attack on his personal morality.

'Look, I need your skin, Dorcus. I'm *very* good at this. Trust me. Do you find it hard to trust people?'

'No no, n-not really, I don't know . . . '

He unbuttoned slowly. He didn't take the shirt all the way off. He exposed his white bony chest. She thought of a turkey at Christmas, gorged, denuded, a yawning white carcass.

He sat down. She tipped more cream into her palms and reached out, feathering the back of his hand with her fingertips. 'You don't have to be nervous. I guarantee pleasant relaxation.'

'I'm not n-nervous.'

'You just bite your nails for nutritional reasons?'

'There's no nutrit — oh, you're having a j-joke.'

'A small joke,' she said and drew closer to him. That wine came back up into her mouth. *Gut rejection*. She slid the shirt off him. She touched his nipples, felt the ridges of his ribcage. Did he ever eat? Maybe he was a vegan, a bean-muncher, the way Chuck had become. Chuck, bloody Chuck, why couldn't he have stayed the way he was instead of turning into a Temple devotee? Fun had gone out of his life, plus I *miss* all the great fucking we had. I thought it was love, I truly did, romantic me.

Teasing, she slipped off Dorcus's glasses and peered through them, oh God, the room became an instant fog, she could see nothing but blur.

'P-please give me my glasses back,' he said.

'Blind without them?' She popped them on his nose.

'My eyesight's not too good,' he said.

She moved closer to him, kneaded his right arm slowly, then the left. He was rigid. She couldn't unlock the knotted muscles. His hands were clenched against his knees so tightly that no circulation was reaching his knuckles, which were sharp white stones.

'Lie back,' she said. 'Shut your eyes.'

He slumped backwards but didn't close his eyes. His lips were tight-shut in resistance. She

196

worked up to his shoulders with her fingertips.

'Feel the warmth coming out of my fingers, Dorcus? Think of your body as a slow moving river, it's flowing gently, very gently, the water is clear. You're weightless. You're floating in a womb, it's very silent, nothing can harm you . . . '

He was motionless, a plank. A pained look creased his face. OK, he's over-anxious, he's never been massaged before, and for all she knew he'd never been touched by a woman. She ran the flats of her hands down his chest toward his navel, then rippled them back up again. Again, again. Energy was streaming out of her — but failed to penetrate him.

'Feeling it, Dorcus? Are you letting go?'

'I don't . . . no, I don't . . . '

'You won't sink. The water will keep you afloat.' Hard damn labour this. She took a towel from her bag, dried her hands, and poured a little Green Tea soothing cream on to her palms. She worked him all angles, kneading and stroking and then, having asked him to turn over, she pummelled him close to the spine. She counted the pimples on his back, noticing a small mole under his shoulder-blade.

She stopped, sighed. 'You're not getting anything out of this, are you?'

Dorcus said nothing. She couldn't see his expression because he had his face hidden in a cushion, but she guessed he had the look of a man eager for an ordeal to end.

'OK. Let's try something else. I need you to take your trousers off and lie face down again.'

'My t-trousers?'

'I'll look away if it makes you feel more comfy. Remember, I'm a professional. I do a lot of massage. You're a client, as far as I'm concerned. I don't see you as a *man*. No offence.'

'I . . . I find th-this difficult.'

She turned her face aside. 'See? Not peeking, am I?'

She heard him unbutton his trousers, then the sound of them sliding down his legs to the floor. The couch creaked as she turned to look at him. He was naked except for his thick slack white socks, and his tartan boxers. He had pale skinny legs covered with very fine hair.

'Face down,' she said.

He slid on to the couch, buried his face. She bent, pressed the base of his spine. She made rippling circles with her fingertips, digging them into the skin above his buttocks. She was forceful at times, at other times gentle.

Dorcus was a locked dungeon. *Fucking useless.*

Chuck used to get hard as soon as she touched him in this area. Wowee, like *that*.

Take a taxi, Glori.

Up yours, Reuben.

She heard no change in Dorcus's breathing. She wondered if he had a lover, and what tricks this woman might use to warm up Dorcus and bring him to life. *How did she get his little sentryman to rise?*

'Dorcus, I need to lower your shorts, but only a little. Are you OK with that?'

'I d-don't, ah, well . . . if you . . . '

198

She drew the tartan boxers down an inch and rolled her fingertips through the scrawny muscles of the upper buttocks. He had no arse to speak of. She pushed, and strained, then she let herself relax a moment. Her finger joints ached. She began again, working her hands under the boxers. It was exhausting and after twenty minutes of pushing, kneading, pulling and stroking, she understood that she had a dead man on her hands, the ultimate hypertensive.

She dropped her hands away from him and sighed. 'Dorcus, I hate to say this, but our stars are in different quadrants. Maybe this just isn't a good time for us. You won't be offended if I call it a day, will you? It'll be like I never came to see you in the first place. That suit you? I'll tell Mr Chuck it didn't work out — '

'No, no, d-don't tell him that. I like Mr Chuck. D-don't tell him that . . . '

'OK. What if I say . . . it was the best massage I ever gave and you loved it?'

'Yes, tell him that, s-say that to him.'

She heard the piano again. A whole army of mice had to be running across those keys. They scampered over the bass notes boomp boomp boomp. She repressed a shudder. Fur on the ivories. She got up from the couch. Dorcus was sweating. He reminded her of a geeky kid who'd never quite become adult, and so goddam *tense* his guts had to be twisted up inside like bad macramé.

She shrugged, picked up her coat and took her mobile phone from her coat pocket.

'Who are you c-calling? Mr Chuck?'

'Well, Dorcus, I can hardly *walk* all the way back across Glasgow. And no, I'm not calling Mr Chuck.' She began to tap in the numbers of her regular taxi company when Dorcus made a swift unexpected move toward her and chopped the mobile out of her fingers. She was astounded by his action, the suddenness, the shock of it. What the fuck.

'I'm sorry so s-sorry,' he said. He went down on his knees, picked the phone up, stuttering apologetically. 'I d-don't k-know w-what came over me — '

'Forget it, Dorcus.' Brush it off, make out it's only some weird spontaneous discharge of energy, who could say? But it disturbed her on a level where she didn't want disturbances. He handed her the phone. The little plastic screen was cracked. When she tried to make a call the line was dead. The force of the phone striking the floor had either dislodged the battery or busted the circuits.

'*This* is a bloody nuisance,' she said.

'I d-didn't mean, h-honest I just had this fla . . . '

'I know you didn't mean it,' she said. 'Fact is, you did it anyway. And look — I'm left with one very dead phone.' She shook it as if this might accomplish a rearrangement of the circuitry, which was like kicking a flat tyre in the hope it would reinflate.

She nodded at the old Bakelite phone on the table. 'Can I use that?'

'Doesn't work,' he said. He turned away from her and pulled up his trousers and buttoned them.

'You must have a phone in the house that *does*, right?'

She wanted to go, had to. Dorcus wasn't the kind of person she longed to spend any more time with. Forty minutes in his company already, and what? — one bolted-down gulp of execrably bad vino, none of her techniques had worked on him, *plus* the broken phone. It wasn't a cheerful list.

She wasn't at all happy about the way he'd lost control and just whacked her mobie out of her hand — what was he? An epileptic? a guy with uncontrollable fits and seizures? And if he was a doctor why didn't he prescribe himself some medication for the condition?

It's none of my business. She put on her coat. She saw a bunch of his tartan boxers spill from the badly buttoned fly. It was funny, but she knew that if she laughed he'd take it the wrong way.

'D-don't tell Mr Chuck what hap-hap . . . '

'I already promised you. Now show me a phone I can — '

Dorcus swallowed hard, as if choking, then turned pale and stuck a hand across his mouth. He rushed out of the room so suddenly he was gone before she could finish her sentence. She heard him climb the staircase rapidly.

Dorcus in stricken flight — why?

She went into the corridor. She could hear him run along a passageway overhead. Then, from above, the sound of a door slamming.

She walked to the foot of the stairs.

She needed a phone to call a taxi, and a key

from Dorcus to open the front gates. If she hadn't needed either, she'd have split already. In fact, she'd settle for the key *alone*, and take her chances finding a taxi cruising along.

She climbed halfway up the staircase. The air became bitter cold all around her; she'd entered a space where for no apparent reason the temperature plunged. Shivering, she hurriedly climbed the second flight. The cold that had clung to her dispersed as quickly as it had occurred.

Inexplicable draughts, distant footsteps, a chill zone — *wooooeeee.* She didn't believe in occult happenings. It was easier for her to believe that crystology was a genuine science than in any spooky supernatural stuff.

She reached the upper hall, which stretched away in a series of closed doors. She walked slowly. 'Dorcus? *Dorcus?'*

She heard the sound of somebody vomit — an outrageously powerful upchuck, the thick splatter of undigested foodstuffs barfed at velocity. Expressboke.

Behind which door was his *chambre du vom?*

She listened. Silence. She felt sorry for him. He was a complete *numpty*, like the wee boy with the beaky pigeon-like face who always sat cross-legged in the front row of a class photo. Usually called Archie or Angus. The kind that would never be able to cope with the world. They went through their allotted span with nervy eyes and sometimes a twitch and often some anti-social affliction they couldn't kick, like bedwetting, or snotterynose.

She wandered along the hallway. 'Dorcus? Are you OK? Dorcus? Talk to me, Doc . . . '

She heard him throw up again, a vigorous release, followed by a groan. Now what room was that? She paused outside a door, pressed her ear to the wood. 'Dorcus?' She tapped lightly. 'I need your key to get out of this gaff. Come on, Dorcus. Open up. Let me out.'

She heard movement from inside, she wasn't sure what. She turned the handle slowly, pushed the door open a little way, an inch, two inches. She was struck at once by the force of that brutal disinfectant pong Dorcus dragged round with him as if it had been injected into his sweat-glands. She could even smell traces of it on herself.

She took a half-step inside the room, which was hard underfoot, uncarpeted. Tiles, white tiles. A soft light burned above a steel sink, where hot water ran slowly and quietly from a tap. Steam fogged the air. This vapour clouded a long-haired figure standing naked at the sink, spine turned toward Glorianna, face hidden by a towel. The figure turned very slightly, revealing a glimpse of breast.

Glorianna watched her turn and saw the towel fall from the woman's hands to the floor — slowly, like a wounded game-bird in a dying fall. She saw the figure's darkened pubic region exposed by an eye of light, and she gasped, pulling the door shut on the steam and the falling towel, and the way the shadow of the figure was thrown halfway across the room to a bed — and although all this was misted, and lacked clarity, Glorianna knew what she saw.

Or thought she knew.

She moved quickly along the hallway. She didn't look back when she heard a door open. She thought, sometimes you see things in mist that aren't there.

She heard voices behind. One belonged to Dorcus.

The other was unfamiliar.

The voices rose and fell, angry, accusatory, defensive, reproachful. She couldn't catch what was being said, only the alterations in tone. Strident cry, a lament, the crack of a reproach. She kept going down and the steps creaked under her and she wondered what she'd do if she made it outside the house and into the garden and reached the gate.

At the bottom of the stairs she turned right, realized in a panic she was lost, couldn't remember the way to the front door. She'd entered the house directly into a hallway with the two dark portraits on the wall and a chandelier. Now what?

Confused, she entered the room with the wingback chair and the piano. A lamp glowed in the corner — had this room been lit the first time she saw it? Couldn't remember. The light was dim, twenty-watt. She thought somebody sat in the wingback chair, a man with his face turned away from her. An outline, an impression — and yet she imagined the head turning, a crick of ossified bone, the face seeking her out.

The mice plink-planked on the keyboard. Their small rounded outlines squirmed under the dust cover. One emerged from concealment and fell to the floor and ran blindly toward her feet. She restrained a scream, backed out of the room just as the lamp popped, plummeting her into a darkness that would have been total except for the sliver of light from the top of the stairway she'd just descended. She heard the rodent scamper somewhere and the keyboards played on discordantly. The mice had a maddening repertoire.

She turned another way and saw the chandelier and the stretch of hallway leading to the front door. Familiarity. She couldn't remember seeing Dorcus lock this door when she'd arrived. Maybe he did, probably he did. She'd kick the door down if she had to. She wanted out of this house and away from Dorcus, and the dim image of a man rising from a wingback chair, and the long-haired figure dropping the towel in that room with the white tiles, and all the rest she didn't want to think —

Chuck, oh you bastard, thank you for sending me to Horror House. You didn't know what this Dorcus was like? Didn't even suspect he was a fuck-up in all departments? Did you even give a thought to my safety?

The front door. A key was in the lock. She twisted it, pulled the door back, the night air was chilly and the only light in front of her came from the miserly bulbs in the chandelier, and that reach of illumination was short, maybe a few yards, then nothing, she'd be out there practically sightless —

Now she heard dogs bark nearby. Were they

loose? She hoped not, they sounded monstrous, but why should that surprise her? Everything here was monstrous — she'd expected this to be a simple brisk business transaction, good massage, blissed-out client, cheerio, Chuck will be happy with you. But it had collapsed entirely and she kept hearing her heel on the tiles and the figure at the sink and whatever else —

She ran, following the light until it faded close to the driveway. If she continued down the drive she'd reach the locked gates. How high were they? She had no idea. She stumbled when she reached the drive. She kicked her fucking *useless* shoes off. She felt gravel under her feet. Ow Jesus. An outreached arm of shrubbery brushed her face and she screamed aloud because for a second she thought it was Dorcus who'd come after her, and any moment she'd feel his arm tighten round her throat, or maybe it was the dread figure she'd seen getting out of the wingback chair —

Just a shrub, a branch, something.

She spotted a second light now, a street lamp on the other side of the wall. It was thirty yards away or so and its yellow glow too thin to be of much use. She lunged forward into the path of this illumination, but where was the driveway? She'd wandered from it. She felt grass under her feet instead of stones, and she reoriented herself by looking back at the house where the front doorway lay open. The dogs roared. Chains rattled. Maybe Dorcus would come down any moment and free them and they'd hunt her down in the darkness and eat her throat out, rip her to ragged strips of flesh with their fangs.

She punched her way through more shrub-bery, then saw the driveway again as a car passed quickly along the street, its lamps shining a second on the gates. Now she had a sense of direction, all she needed were grappling irons and some climbing boots —

'*Stop p-please I n-need to talk to you!*'

Jesus he was coming to look for her.

'*I'll g-give you the key, just stop!*'

You'll give me the key. *Aye, right, Dorc.*

The gates, just get to the gates, see what it takes to get over. She lurched down the driveway. Gravel nicked the soles of her feet and she had to hop, redistributing her weight because of the pain. In a few hours her soles would look like blisterpack.

She made it to the gates, gripped them, shook fiercely. They rattled, but they were never going to yield. Too solid, embedded too deeply in the brick wall. What now?

'*Come back, c-come b-back I'm n-not going to hurt you!*'

She grabbed the gates and hoisted herself a couple of feet, but she was scrabbling, she'd never make the top.

'*You want oot?*'

She was astonished by the appearance of a small boy on the other side.

He was smoking a cigarette. 'It'll cost.'

'Just get me out — '

A group of other kids materialized. A rope came over the top of the gates. She gripped it hard and the kids began to pull.

'*Quick Missus!*'

God knows how many kids were out there, five, half a dozen, more. They were a blob of small shapes, straining away at the other end of the rope. She felt the rope burn her palms, but she was fucked if she'd let go. When she reached the top she heard Dorcus call. '*We c-can talk this over, wait* — '

He was what — oh god, six feet behind her? He could leap, lunge, grab an ankle, bring her down —

'Dreep!' a boy shouted.

'I'm *dreepin*,' and she slid down the rough rope, feeling its friction against the front of her body. She hit the ground and the kids told her to run like fuck. And she ran, she *ran*, feet aching, stomach lurching, following the kids around the wall and into the scheme where the car still burned, and sparks fever-spotted the sky, and TVs and boomboxes played loud enough to waken long-slumbering demons.

She stopped running when she realized the soles of her feet were murdering her and she had no breath left. She noticed the kids all had blackened faces and dark gloves. Night operations, mini-marines. They clustered around her. 'Pay up missus.'

'How much do you want?'

'Whatja got?'

She reached in the pocket of her coat and fingered some crumpled notes. Shaking, she couldn't stop shaking. If she gave them all her cash how was she going to get back home, which was miles from here?

One of kids held open a plastic bag from which an intolerable stench arose. 'We were plannin to pyzen his dugs wi this. It's spiled meat wi bleach and stuff in it. Think they'd eat it?'

She took a step back. No dog would ever go near this noxious mix of rancid meat and chlorine.

The kid with the bag said, 'We're sick o him and his hauntit hoose.'

A haunted house? No, she didn't have time to think about haunted houses. 'I'll pay you if you can tell me where to find a taxi.'

'That wisny part o the deal missus.'

'It is now.'

The kids complained, then whispered among themselves. Finally one of them said, 'We'll take you to a guy who might drive you. If he's sober.'

She limped after them down a dark street between a row of towers. Noise all around, guys and girls on corners, idling, laughing. She smelled hashish. She flinched at the sudden crack of fireworks, rockets that rose flashing skyward and burst in an array of bright colours.

One of the kids went inside a building and came out minutes later with a bare-chested fat man whose trousers hung loosely from his hips and his braces dangled.

'Rightyo who needs a taxi?' he asked.

'Me,' she said.

The man wasn't altogether sober. Obviously numb to the cold, he swayed as he came toward her, passing under a street lamp that revealed a great tattoo of a shamrock in the middle of his chest. The image was crushed between his flabby breasts. 'Where you gaun?'

'West End.'

The man thought about this a minute. 'Twenty-five pounds in ma haun.'

She agreed.

'Rightyo, get in the car.'

'That's your taxi?' She saw him point to an old black hearse.

'Aye. Take it or leave it.'

She didn't have to answer. He unlocked the passenger door, and she climbed in. The kids clustered around for their pay-off. She counted her money quickly. She had fifty-four pounds — two twenties, a ten and four coins. She gave the kids one of the twenties.

'Is this aw we get?'

'It's all I have.'

There was some grumbling and dissent. The driver got in behind the wheel. She handed him the rest of her money. He stuffed it in his trouser pocket and turned a key in the ignition and the big hearse rumbled, throwing a great cloud of smoke that engulfed the vehicle.

'Away we go,' he said, and stuck the hearse in gear. 'Hing on.'

The hearse shook and rumbled and tossed her around in her seat. There was no belt to hold her in place, but what did she care?

'Right old fuckn boneshaker, eh?' the man said. He laughed, a smoker's crusty laugh, and scratched his chest constantly as the hearse went roaring and vibrating along Edinburgh Road.

She shut her eyes.

She felt a deep rage gathering. Fuck you

Chuck. Fuck you. Sending me there. How could you do that to *me*? Ship me out to that place.

She knew what she'd do. She'd go to her flat, toss some things quickly in a bag, and leave. And Chuck wouldn't know where she was. Stew, Big Man.

She listened to the roar of the hearse. Street lamps flitted past, yellow in the night. The driver kept trying to tell her jokes but she wasn't listening.

Knock knock who's there?

Knock knock, who's there, who's behind the door?

Something dreadful —

She stared straight ahead with her hands clamped in her lap and her mind emptying like suds carrying unthinkable thoughts down a sink.

26

Early morning, Perlman drove to Govan. He'd expected word from Betty, but she hadn't phoned. She may have gone directly back to her flat after the morgue. He thought about her as he travelled west along Govan Road. Sunlit morning, but not for Betty, not for her.

He parked his Ka and locked it outside the fire-damaged tenement where Tartakower lived. He stood on the pavement with his hands on his hips and studied a group of kids who idled at the end of the block. They were the same young teenagers who'd scoffed at his attempt to kick a ball last time. They wore the regulation street corner threads, tracksuit pants and running shoes and jackets with upraised hoods. They watched him with tough-guy expressions.

These were in all likelihood the same kids who'd snaffled his wing mirrors. They sent vibes of malicious intent. He was reluctant to leave the car and go inside the building, God knows what they'd nick this time. Tyres? Hub-caps? They openly passed a joint around. In the old days he'd have given them a lecture on narcotics — but you didn't do that now, not in the new climate where these kids probably carried knives and had total contempt for the polis. Also, these wee bassas spouted the law. If you so much as laid a finger on one, or tried to intimidate them, they came back with smart-arse retorts about their rights and accusations of polis abuse.

A losing battle, Perlman thought. Glasgow belonged to wild kids.

He tested the door handles, checking the car was as secure as it could be. The kids were still eyeballing him, and shuffling around. Polis alert. They smoked the joint down to its brown bitter end where it fell apart in fading sparks. They whispered among themselves and kept glowering at Perlman, who was reluctant to enter the tenement and climb up through that burned-out gloom again.

One of the boys, the smallest, red-cheeked and cherubic beneath the hood, broke away from the group and walked straight past Perlman and kept going, gathering speed as he moved. He had the demeanour of a messenger, the kid who wasn't quite in the fold yet because he was too young, the menial who did what the others told him, stealing the ciggies, rummaging for money in his Ma's purse, whatever. He looked back at Perlman a second, as if to check whether the polisman was watching him.

Something's afoot, Perlman thought.

He turned to survey the other kids, who'd assumed a collective nonchalance. Polis is here, hee haw, we don't give a buggery. We just stand on the street corner and smoke dope, watcha gonny dae aboot it, Mister Polisman? Arrest us?

Perlman swivelled, saw the small kid vanish inside a corner shop at the end of the block. What was this wee angel up to? Perlman walked after him, reached the shop, which was barricaded with a roll-down steel window

213

peppered with manic graffiti. He peered through the doorway into the murk. The air smelled of boiled ham and spoiled apples.

A turbaned shopkeeper stood behind the counter, which was protected by strong wire mesh. He regarded Perlman with the air of a man who was thinking: *Glasgow or Calcutta, toss a coin.*

Lou was about to back out, wondering if maybe the kid's move was a clumsy ploy to draw him away from his vermilion car for criminal purposes. Then he glimpsed the kid whispering to somebody just out of sight behind shelves of canned beans and instant soup mixes and Bisto packets. He went quickly to the kid — and there, huddled like a fugitive, Tartakower lurked with a shopping bag in one hand and a ferret on a chain in the other. The small boy instantly did a runner, whipping past Perlman and out into the street.

'Hiding?' Lou asked.

Tartakower was flustered, and working not to show it. 'Just gathering a few grocery items, Perlman. Is this now against the law?' He wore a threadbare ex-army coat and a tattered scarf knotted at his neck. His dirty brown shoes were cracked and the soles flapped.

'Is that really a ferret, Tartakower?'

'Sshh. She thinks she's a dog, Perlman. This delusion I encourage.' Tartakower rattled the creature's chain.

'And the wee smout who ran away, what is he? Your lookout?'

Tartakower shrugged. 'A lonely man takes his

214

friends where he can find them.'

'My heart flows over like a cheap cistern. He came to warn you I was here.'

Tartakower ignored the remark, and dragged both ferret and the grocery bag out into the street. Perlman followed. The kids on the corner whooped and cheered and shouted *Issy! Issy!* And then they came pounding along the pavement, all loose laces and happy faces, toward Tartakower. They jostled Perlman aside.

'For Christ's sake,' Perlman complained, only just keeping his balance.

The kids huddled around Tartakower, patting the ferret, and firing Perlman glares of contempt.

'What is this, Tartakower? Your gang?'

'Fuck off polis bastart,' one of the hoodies said. A big kid this one, maybe fourteen or older; you could imagine his future mug shot, a composition in resentment and disobedience.

Perlman said, 'Shut your pointy face, scruff.'

'Make me. Come on.' The boy held his hands out, inviting Perlman forward to fight. 'Come on then, big baws. Feart, eh?'

'Feart? Aye, right.' Perlman stared at the boy and saw in those eyes the bare aggression imposed by the blight of the city. He'd seen the look thousands of times, more than. These were the city's children, brought up in doomed housing, failed by parents and teachers and priests, and all those useless theorists and planners of civic order, shrinks, sociologists and politicians. These kids didn't give a damn, there was no future, tomorrow, fuckit, they might be dead. They lived in a world they knew to be volatile and cruel-hearted. They saw their unemployed parents' promises of better times vanish in a litter of useless lottery tickets or discarded betting stubs or racks of empties. They grew up with racial and religious intolerance, casual thuggery, older brothers imprisoned or dead — and who could say that some blissed-out terrorist, dreaming of an afterlife of willing virgins, might not just fly over Glasgow one fine day and drop a fucking bomb?

Tartakower, surrounded by this army, said, 'Issy is popular. He's a hero to these boys.'

'And you're what, Fagin?'

One of the kids said, 'Issy's the fuckn greatest,' and picked up the ferret, smothering it in an embrace. The creature looked alert suddenly, pink tongue dangling. The kid kissed the ferret on the mouth.

Perlman addressed Tartakower over the bunch of hoods. 'Why the hell do you keep a ferret?'

'You'd prefer I kept a caged parrot? Curtail the movement of living creatures. Lock them in cages, throw them in jails. This is what you love.'

The big kid who'd tried to provoke Perlman said, 'You're yella.'

The others laughed and stamped their feet. 'Yella bassa polis,' they shouted.

Perlman looked at Tartakower, lord of this urchin legion. 'Can you discharge your warriors, Ben? All I want is to talk.'

Tartakower gestured at the pale faces surrounding him. 'I don't control them, Perlman.'

'Come *on*,' Perlman said impatiently. He

didn't enjoy the idea of a serious confrontation with these kids and the possibility of concealed weapons appearing. He tried to get closer to Tartakower but the phalanx of hoodyheids stood firm. A bloody preposterous stand-off, blocked by a circle of adolescent scoundrels. What has the world come to. He had an urge just to shove them aside, assert authority, get Tartakower all to himself. The kids stared at him grimly. All these faces that should have been innocent. What happened to childhood. What happened to street games. He remembered peever and girls skipping ropes and singing, and he had a memory of playing ring-bell-skoosh or mooshie — marbles!

The ferret was being passed around like a beloved gang icon, stroked, caressed, kissed.

Perlman took his mobile phone from his coat. 'I've had enough of this nonsense. Clear these kids away, Ben, or I call for some assistance. I can have backup here in minutes.' Pure bluff. Nobody from Force HQ would come to assist him even if he was in a gutter, dying with a blade in his ribs.

'Some solution,' Tartakower said. 'More cops.'

'Bring em on,' one of the kids said.

'Aye bring yer polis pals here,' another said.

The kid who'd called Perlman big baws laughed. 'We don't move. Right boys? We don't fuck off.'

A chorus of agreement. Right, we don't move.

Perlman sighed. They were ready for war, patrol cars and black marias, and a fresh entry in their juvenile records.

'Is this what you want, Ben?' he asked.

'Like a root canal.'

'Then tell your enforcers to scatter.'

'We don't fuckn move,' the enforcers chanted.

In another age they might have been choirboys, Perlman thought.

Tartakower plunged a hand into a coat pocket and pulled out a fistful of coins and notes and held them up in the air. 'Boys listen to me. I need a little time with this polis. OK?'

The kids formed a huddle, and conferred. 'We take Issy,' one of them said to Tartakower.

'For one hour only,' Tartakower said.

'The whole day. Look at her, Tarty, she needs a shampoo, and a fuckin good brushin. You neglect her, so you do.'

Tartakower considered this. 'Until tea time.'

'You let us have him the whole day a coupla times. Even overnight wan time.'

'Not this time, boys. Seven o'clock. Plus a few coins.'

Tartakower thrust money into the hands of the big aggressive kid. Somebody scooped up Issy and that was it — a collective whoop, an army jubilantly demobilized. They ran off along the street like they'd been blown by a sudden wind, shouting words that were incoherent to Perlman, a private slang, a personal language. And then they vanished round a corner, but not before a couple of them had pounded fists into the bonnet of Perlman's Ka.

Tartakower passed his grocery bag from one hand to the other. 'OK. Talk.'

'When did you form the army?'

'Issy's their talisman. He's a symbol. A wild

218

animal in a city. You don't think they connect with that?'

'So you give them some money and the occasional ownership of Issy and they become your Praetorian guards. And sometimes they ferret-sit a whole day. Or all night.'

'What can I do? They adore her. They wash her and clip her nails, things I don't have energy for.' Tartakower started to walk in the direction of his close. 'A loose arrangement I have with these boys. I tell them surgical tales. They enjoy uplifting yarns about some schmuck leaking to death on an operating table. Amputations also they're fond of. And vivid descriptions of gunshot wounds. I keep their attention half an hour or so, which is more than their teachers.'

Tartakower's Hoodie Army. Perlman said, 'That was my money you gave them.'

'I remind you, mister, that was money we negotiated for information.'

'Information that was pure shite.'

Tartakower took an apple from the bag, bit a chunk, offered the fruit to Perlman, who declined.

'Let's talk about Jackie Ace — you *fucking* knew what he was. You knew he was a *transvestite*. You misled me by failing to say this — '

Tartakower had apple bits in his beard. 'You come, you ask me for a boy not so right in the head. So I give you one. You saw him. He's not *strange* enough for you? In my estimation he's cracked all right . . . Plus he's no transvestite.'

'I saw him. *Her*.'

'You saw Jackie Ace, sure. You just got your terminology wrong. He's going *all the fucking way*, Lou. Imagine that.' Tartakower was simmering with glee. Saliva dripped from his lips. 'This is sex-change we're talking. This is the big transformation, Mister Smart Polis.'

'Is this another fable?'

'Take it leave it. One day years ago he says he's never felt he was a man. Always a woman inside, he says. I'm his priest? He's saving his money for a series of operations that don't bear thinking. My guts turn over. They'll cut off his *schlong*. Castrate him. A vagina they'll dig him out. Uh . . . This sounds to you sane behaviour?'

He watched Tartakower's face, all bearded guile. 'Are you lying again?'

'And tell me what I gain by lying?'

'More fucking amusement.'

'You deserve a kick up the arse now and again, Perlman. I sat four years in jail with all the scum of Glasgow, you think I'm jack-in-the-box eager to help you? So I throw you a body-swerve. Jackie Ace. You think a man. Then you find a transvestite. Now I tell you he's on some other evolutionary stage. I amuse easy at my age.'

Perlman said, 'The hand was cut from somebody living.'

'Somebody living? You sure?'

Perlman caught Tartakower's arm. 'No more silly fucking games, Ben. No more daft jokes to inconvenience me, OK? I want a name or else you can get in my car and I'll drive you down to HQ and you can explain why you're impeding a police investigation into possible *murder*?'

220

'I'm allergic to cars. Small spaces in general.'

'I'm waiting.'

A pleading sound entered Tartakower's voice. 'How many years now I knew your family in the old Gorbals. Your mother and father. One time I took your Aunt Hilda across the Govan Ferry to Partick. A journey that takes a minute, for her a transatlantic crossing.'

'Ben, this is a woman who crossed God knows what rivers to escape the Nazis? She's going to think the Clyde's a transatlantic crossing? It's a pish of a river.'

Tartakower ignored this point. 'Tartakowers and Perlmans, neighbours. Did we not exchange sugar in rationing times, buckets of coal, this and that, an easy flow between families. But you grow up, become a polisman and you dismiss history with a cruel stroke . . . '

Perlman said, 'Get over it. I want a name. You don't give me one, fine, my car's over there. We'll go now.'

'Wait . . . just wait.'

'For what? More bullshit?'

'Look, I got other possibles. I had this kid who loved cadavers, *loved* to get his fingers way deep inside the *kishkes* — '

'Save the gory stuff for your gang of commandoes.'

Tartakower clutched Perlman's sleeve. 'Also I had a girl about twenty I just remembered. Short-sighted, ugly as one of the Cinderella sisters, a wallflower, tells me amputation is her thing, she's done a couple of gangrened limbs in Africa or somewhere . . . this is one deranged *shiksa*, Perlman — '

'Your chop-shop was chock-a-block with headcases,' Perlman said. 'I'm tired listening. Just get inside my car.'

Tartakower looked tearful. 'OK wait. Maybe I go over the top. Suddenly I remember another boy, skinny kid, all fingers and thumbs, big glasses, he comes to the surgery, he hangs around, he's checking this, checking that. He's keen to cut, I never saw anyone so keen. Maybe some potential skills but he's no Jackie Ace with the blade.'

'So?'

Tartakower drew Perlman closer. 'He starts following Ace around like Ace is some kind of fucking god. This kid's smitten. Thinks Jackie Ace craps gold bricks. Ace takes the kid under his wing and teaches him some rudimentary skills. I see them together, they whisper in corners.'

'So what kind of relationship is this?'

'He's attached to Ace like Darwin to fossils, Marconi to radio waves — '

'Did this boy have a name?'

'Harry Houdini. He was with me six months, seven maybe. Then one day gone, *pouf*, like his namesake. He's worth finding, Lou.'

'And you're saying Ace would know?'

'He might.'

'You could have told me this before.'

Tartakower coughed and hawked up a chunk of phlegm and expelled it through the obstacle of his beard. It hit the pavement.

'I could,' he said. Was that a sneak of a smile behind the enormous beard.

'Fucker,' Perlman said.

27

Ron Mathieson drove the six-seater minibus along Paisley Road West. In the passenger seat Big Rooney smoked a cigarette and told a joke about a drunk man who confused nuns with penguins, but Mathieson wasn't paying attention. In the back of the bus Stip and Wee Vic laughed at the punch-line.

Take them to HiCon, Chuck had said.

Mathieson looked in the rear-view mirror. Wee Vic was slugging a can of Tizer and mouthing down a sausage roll. His acne was particularly red and raw-looking today. A pustulated face, like a pitted blood orange. Stip, a quietly spoken man with one eyebrow that met above his nose, studied a racing paper and talked about a horse that was a dead cert at the Kelso National Hunt meet tomorrow.

Rooney, formerly an amateur boxer, looked out the window and said, 'I fought a coloured boy somewhere around here. I hammered him half-deid in the second round. Hamid somebody.'

'Hamid and eggs,' Wee Vic said.

'Scrambled eggs when I was through with him,' Rooney said.

Stip closed his newspaper and said, 'For any youse diddies interested, this nag's called Yarrow Water. Two o'clock race. SP will be about four, but you can get him today at six or seven.'

'The last tip you gied me is still running,' Wee Vic said.

Mathieson turned on the radio. He preferred some brain-dead pop music to the clunkety chatter going on around him. He just wanted to get to HiCon and be rid of these morons who'd fucked up a simple job and landed him in the shite with Chuck.

Wee Vic said, 'Here, that burd was gemme, eh?'

Rooney said, 'I've had better.'

Wee Vic said, 'Lying big tosser. You never get crumpet. No like her anyway.'

'I've had more fucking crumpet than you've had sausage rolls, wee man.'

'Aye right sure ye have.' Wee Vic leaned forward and tapped Mathieson on the shoulder. 'So how long did The Boss say we'd be outta town?'

Mathieson said, 'A month, mibbe six weeks. Until things quiet down.'

Wee Vic said, 'Fuckzake. Six weeks in Newcastle.'

Rooney said, 'I know burdz in Newcastle.'

Stip rattled his newspaper. 'Six weeks, long time.'

'Orders is orders,' Mathieson said.

He drove down a narrow industrial road between warehouses and haulage companies until he saw the wire fence that surrounded HiCon. A galvanized-steel building, surrounded by long brown stalks of weed, sat in the centre of a gravel compound. The building itself hadn't been used for years. The sign HiCon was weather-battered and hung askew above the main door.

Mathieson got out, unlocked the door in the fence, then drove the minibus through the weeds. 'This is where we get off, boys,' he said. 'You'll be picked up here and taken down to Newcastle. You'll get expenses, plus a bonus.'

'Now you're talking,' Wee Vic said, rubbing his hands together.

'I have the money right here.' Mathieson patted the inside pocket of his jacket and then unlocked the door of the building. The three men followed him inside a large space filled with flattened old cardboard boxes which bore the company name.

'What's HiCon anyway?' Rooney asked.

'Used to make computer bits, I think.' Mathieson strolled round the big room.

The three men explored. Wee Vic kicked at some of the cardboard slats and a couple of mice scurried out from under them. 'How long are we meant to wait here?'

Mathieson said, 'Five minutes, mibbe ten.'

'So how come *you're* no taking us to Newcastle?' Rooney asked.

'I don't have the time, Rooney.'

'The Boss keeps his boy jumping,' Stip said. 'So where's this bonus?'

Mathieson took three envelopes from his pocket and handed one to each man. Rooney ripped his open immediately, and counted. 'Five thou. Nice.'

'Plus your hotel's paid for,' Mathieson said. He looked at the wire mesh that had been erected inside each window. 'Stay in the hotel, lie low, don't make a public nuisance.'

'And what if we do?' Wee Vic asked.

'I'm passing down orders, boys. That's all.'

Rooney said, 'Stupid cunt hung herself and we have to take a hike to England.'

Wee Vic was pissing in the corner. With his back to the room he said, 'This is gash. Newcastle. Fuck that. They talk funny doon there.'

Mathieson said, 'It's not like you're going to jail.'

'My girlfriend's pregnant,' Stip said.

'Away tay fuck,' Wee Vic said. 'What do you want kids for? Always under yer feet, always greeting and then they need clothes and shoes and you're handing out money all over the place. Nappies. Bibs. Clothes. What the fuck else.'

'We fancy having a wean,' Stip said quietly.

'Who's the daddy,' Wee Vic said, zipping up. 'You better hope it has your eyebrow.'

Stip said, 'Ha bloody ha.'

A vehicle drew up outside. Mathieson heard the wheels crunch gravel and then the sound of two doors opening and closing. He went outside.

'Here, where the fuck's he going?' Wee Vic asked.

Rooney looked through a window. 'He's talking to a couple of guys who just got out a minibus.'

'Two drivers?' Wee Vic approached the window. 'Who needs two drivers to take us to Newcastle?'

'Mibbe only one of them's a driver,' Rooney said.

'So who's the second punter?' Stip was at another window, peering out. 'Anybody know them?'

Nobody did.

Stip said, 'Mibbe one's a minder.'

Mathieson reappeared in the doorway. 'I'm off, boys. Have a good trip. Stay out of trouble, mind.'

'Aye, I promise,' Wee Vic said, putting his hands behind his ears and making them stick out like donkey flaps.

Mathieson walked back to his minibus. He climbed in behind the wheel. He watched the two newcomers go inside the building. They were a hard pair with Fife accents. The taller of the two wore a flat bunnet, the other was bald and one side of his face swollen the size of a golf ball from a gumboil.

Imported talent.

Mathieson heard one of them shout, 'Right, boys. Ready for the big journey, are we?'

Followed by three gunshots in rapid succession.

Mathieson closed his eyes until there was silence again. Then he got out of the bus and went back inside the building. The two Fifers were checking the bodies for movement. There wasn't any. Mathieson went around gathering the envelopes. The one he took out of Rooney's limp hand was streaked with blood. Wee Vic lay alongside Rooney, face turned away. The side of his head had caved. Stip had a look of displeasure.

'Swift,' Mathieson said. He stuffed the

227

envelopes back in his inside pocket.

One of the gunmen said, 'We come, we go.'

The one with the swollen face said, 'We aim to please.'

Mathieson said, 'If I ever need you again, I'll know where to find you.'

The bald gunman said, 'Any time you're in the East Neuk, pop in and say hello.'

The other one added, 'But don't sneak up behind us if you know what's good for you, eh?'

The two killers laughed, and high-fived each other.

'I'll make a point of knocking first,' Mathieson said.

28

Perlman went back to Egypt. He didn't expect Betty to be there, but he called her name anyway when he entered his house. No answer. She was probably with close friends and family, seeking solace. The drab silence disappointed him just the same. He picked up his post from the floor and sifted through it; a bank statement, a *Concern* appeal, an invitation to an opening of something called The Furniture Depot: *BUY THAT BEDROOM SUITE YOU ALWAYS WANTED. PRICES SLASHED DRASTICALLY!!!!*

I need a futon, he thought.

The last item of mail was a postcard from Miriam.

He tossed the other crap back on the floor and went inside the living room to read the card.

He had a pain behind his eyes. Maybe the effect of the contacts, maybe tension. He found his painkillers in a drawer of the sideboard. He took one, throwing it back without water. He noticed his supply was dwindling — out of thirty prescribed, he'd devoured twenty-seven. He ought to be cutting them out instead of gobbling them.

He sat in the armchair and lit a cigarette, and fingered the smooth surface of the card a moment before reading it. Why postpone it? What are you afraid of? Bad news, distressing revelations. *Lou, I met somebody ... he's changed my life utterly.*

Or, *I'm marrying Mario.*

Or, *I was in a car wreck and I'm in hospital.*

He had the selfish thought that her hospital-ization was preferable to the idea of her finding love. Shit, what was he doing — wishing pain on her, for God's sake?

He read the card, which had been posted five days ago from Barcelona, and the message was short: *Nice town. Who needs Glasgow? Fondly, M.*

Still the fondly.

So Barcelona now. Maybe Mario had been replaced by Juan or Pedro. What a mover she was. The world, oy, was her oyster.

Who needs Glasgow? He translated this as Who needs Perlman?

Definitely a brush-off.

It hurt, he'd be a liar to deny it, but a little less than it might have pained him once. It was more a pen nib to his heart than a dagger. Just the same. Absence blunted hopes and dreams, always the way. I should have dreams, at my age.

He got up and walked back down the hall to pick up the items of mail he'd dropped. Clean as you go. Don't leave a mess. He put the post in a drawer, then paced the room, smoking and still holding Miriam's postcard.

Which he read again.

She writes this five days ago. Or at least she posts it five days ago. Maybe she's long gone from Barcelona by now. He set the postcard down on the shelves where his CDs were stacked. His mind drifted to the photograph in the loft, the one parked beside the bed, Colin and Miriam, happy partners. Latta, it had to have been Latta who put it there, because if Perlman believed one thing Miriam had told him before she'd flown out of his world it was the fact she despised her late husband, there was no love left between them —

He remembered Tartakower's latest little story: he'd do something about that, he'd get on it now — but he couldn't drive the shimmering mirage that was Miriam from his mind. He called the telephone company and asked when her connection had been cut off. A woman told him the line had been severed seven weeks ago, non-payment. He rang the electricity company and was informed by a man with a high-pitched voice that the electricity was paid quarterly and the next payment was due in a week.

OK OK. The phone was disconnected because she hadn't paid. Forgetfulness? Or because she knew she wasn't coming back? But if she'd decided she was staying away, why hadn't she said so in one of the cards, and why had she left so many possessions behind — including her paintings? Had she just abandoned them? Unlikely. Maybe she was undecided. Maybe she hadn't made up her mind if she was staying away forever —

Do I care? Do I fucking care?

Drawn back to the postcard, he picked it up. He studied it. A boring picture of crowds on a beach, sun umbrellas stuck in sand, palm trees. She hadn't even troubled her arse to choose an interesting postcard, something artsy, say, a picture of something built by that guy — Perlman fished for the name.

Gaudi.

Because she didn't care, or because she thought Perlman was blind to art and architecture. I wasn't her equal.

Suddenly he was angry, angry that he'd nurtured such a fragile hope for such a long time, angry that she'd gone without a fucking word of goodbye, and infuriated by allowing himself to be *seduced* by the postcards, which were like a form of slow faux striptease where she never took off a single garment, even if he was daft enough to believe that one day she might.

He ripped the postcard down the middle, slicing the sun lovers and the sands and the sea, then he tore these pieces a second time, and a third, and the scraps fell from his shaking fingers to the coffee-table.

He didn't hear Betty McLatchie come into the room. He raised his face, looked at her, and stepped around the coffee-table as if to conceal from her the sight of the dismembered postcard.

She wore a black overcoat, a black headscarf, black glasses, black Levis. Only her grey shirt and maroon Docs alleviated the severity of her appearance. 'I should've phoned,' she said.

'No, no matter, it's OK.'

She sat in one of the armchairs and stared at the floor a while, then raised her face to look at him, and her sadness, so evident in her posture, crushed him.

'It wasn't Kirk,' she said.

For an uneasy moment he thought she was speaking factually, a terrible mistake had been made, the dead boy wasn't her son. But no, she was talking in metaphor, the way you always did when you spoke about the dead. Passed on, passed away, popped your clogs.

'Kirk would have sat up and said April Fool, Ma. He liked practical jokes. But it's the wrong month, the wrong bloody month.' She opened her small black leather purse and tugged out a cigarette. Perlman lit it for her. She inhaled deeply.

He sat on the arm of her chair and laid a palm on the back of her hand. 'I'm sorry,' and wondered what else he could say when it came down to the extremities of feeling. Grief needed a new lexicon.

She shook her head, blew a stream of smoke angled upward. 'There's this wee corner of me that's always been optimistic. It's like a candle burning away at the back of my head. I try to keep it going because I want to think the best of people and enjoy life. How the fuck do I keep that candle going now?'

Perlman wanted to say it would take time, but the sentence was a candygram. He got up and fetched an ashtray from the dresser and took her dying cigarette from her hand and stubbed it. She appeared not to notice.

'Do you believe in a God, Lou?'

God made Perlman uneasy. As a kid he'd thought Rabbi Friedlander, with monumental beard and authoritarian voice, had been God. 'I have good days when I imagine there might be some benign power out there. Most days no. Like today.'

She got out of the chair and wandered the room, ran a hand across the CDs as if checking for fresh dust. She paused at the coffee-table and looked down at the destroyed card. He wasn't sure if she was reading fragments of it, or if the card was just an indefinable object in her field of vision.

Betty said, 'I was brought up to believe. But I got tired of the blether of ministers, Lou. All they can do for me now is bury my kid.' She raised her face to him. 'Why are some people . . . '

'Just downright evil?'

'Yeh. Why are some people *like* that? For God's sake, Kirk was . . . harmless. Just a harmless boy. He had his faults. But he had no malice in him, Lou. None.'

Harmless boys get murdered, the innocent die. Perlman sensed a slight reaction from the painkiller, not the normal mild detachment he experienced, but a contraindication, a sharpened awareness. Maybe the need to concentrate on Betty's situation nullified the power of the anodyne.

'Let's get out of here,' he said. 'Get some air, go somewhere for a coffee.'

'Why not.'

He walked with her down the hallway. Outside, she moved along the driveway in slow contemplative steps, pausing now and again to adjust her glasses or her headscarf. He was about to open the passenger door of his Ka, but she said, 'I feel like walking, Lou.'

'Sure. Whatever you want.'

They went some yards in silence. She slipped her arm through his without looking at him. He felt comfortable with the connection. She needed support, he'd give it.

Perlman suggested a stroll in Tollcross Park, a fine expanse of greenery at the edge of Egypt, and Betty agreed. The thin sunlight lying across the park glowed pale against the big glass structure of the Winter Gardens. A group of runners in coloured singlets and shorts moved along one of the paths. Athletic crew, vibrant with energy.

They went toward the Winter Gardens. He saw himself and Betty reflected in glass. Anyone looking at them would assume: *long-married couple*. The deceit of appearances. He held the door open for her. Inside, the building was warm. Exotic plants flourished in a rage of rare colours and strange shapes. Perlman led her into the café, where they sat at a table and drank coffee under a window streaming with condensation.

'I must be keeping you from something, Lou.' She held her cup in both hands.

'Nothing that can't wait.'

'Who's working on Kirk's case?'

'A man called Adamski.'

'Will he go at it hard? Will he find who did it?'

'He's dedicated.'

'That's not answering my question — '

'He's got safe hands and some good people working alongside him.'

235

'How long did you say your sick leave is anyway?'

'It feels like from here to eternity.' He knew what she was thinking: she wanted somebody familiar in charge of hunting her son's killer. 'I'll stay in close contact with Adamski.'

'I'd appreciate that.'

She lit a cigarette despite the No Smoking sign.

What the hell. You could take a day out for your grief, you could say fuck off to the rules.

'I hate the taste of these things. I don't know why I bother.' She dropped her cigarette into her half-finished coffee. 'You know what's so bloody *heartbreaking*? The thought you'll never see somebody again as long as you live.'

He was edgy, anxious to move. Coffee, too many smokes, too little food. A transistor radio played somewhere, a penny whistler blowing 'Tunes of Glory'. Without a word, Betty got up and went outside and stood motionless in the sunlight.

Perlman followed. In a different mood she'd notice life bursting out all around her, she'd see the muscles of the world flexing. She'd see the runners break into a sprint far in the distance, or notice a small hawk rising graceful and free above the tree-line. She'd smile at a gaggle of young mothers going past with their toddlers in a ruction of unfettered laughter and hear a yellow plastic windmill in a kid's fist whir.

Betty, hands deep in pockets, was quiet. Perlman swept aside a strand of her hair where it had fallen upon the frame of her glasses. She took off her glasses and turned to look at him as if she wanted to thank him for his company and support, but she said nothing. She just rubbed her eyelids with her fingertips then stuck the glasses on again, but not before Perlman glimpsed that extraordinary blueness, which made him think of clear arctic skies. She'd been crying. There were veins of red in the whites of her eyes, but the blue was intact. She inclined her face against his shoulder and sighed.

'Walk me back to my car, Lou.'

'Of course.'

She slipped her arm through his and they moved across the park. Halfway toward Wellshot Road she said, 'Miriam's the one who went away.'

Out of nowhere.

'I noticed the torn postcard,' she said.

'She's the one, the endless tourist.'

'Your aunts mention her sometimes. They don't approve. I remember reading something about her court case. You spoke up for her.'

'I believed she was innocent.'

'That was the only reason?'

The question was close to the bone. 'I hate injustices,' he said. *I hated to see Miriam, vulnerable and lovely, harassed and harried by a fuck like Latta.*

'You must have pished some people off.'

'I shop there regularly.' He looked at her, but she'd gone into fade mode again, drifting in and out of the immediacy of things, a woman sleepwalking.

She paused, stared the length of the street as if

she'd seen something, or somebody she recognized, directly ahead. He noticed nothing out of the ordinary. A man opening a car and tossing a walking-stick into the back seat. A woman entering a tenement with two bulky Tesco bags. A white van approaching, a young man at the wheel. An orange cat ran across the street, streaking close to the wheels of the van. Rubber squealed as the van swerved to avoid it. The cat bolted between the railings that edged the park, and disappeared into shrubbery. The van drove on.

'Close call,' Perlman said.

'Nine lives,' Betty said. 'Pity people don't get so many chances.'

'Some people,' Perlman said.

They reached his house. Outside, Betty unlocked her car.

'Thanks for your company,' she said.

'Any time.'

'Call me if there's anything . . . '

She patted his arm. 'I will.'

He watched her go, realizing he wanted her to stay.

★ ★ ★

Indoors he felt solitude. He walked to the coffee-table and looked at the shredded post-card. In the drawer where he'd stuffed his unopened post he found the previous cards he'd received from the Wandering Miriam. He spread all three cards on the coffee-table, piecing together the jigsaw of the one he'd torn apart, and compared the handwriting on each. It was the same flamboyant script, great loops between the letters, a fandango in pale blue ink. He went inside the kitchen and removed the unreconstructed picture he'd pinched from Miriam's bedroom, took it into the living room and contrasted the handwriting on the back of the photo with the postcards. Same handwriting, different sentiments.

What had he expected to find?

More than terse messages at least.

He looked at the postcard pictures. The scene she'd sent from Florence was of tourists wandering in sunlight along a street where every vendor sold leather jackets. It wasn't enthralling. Sunburnt faces and racks of leather. Where was the Duomo? The Ghilberti Doors? Did she think he was a fucking hick? *Oh, he'll accept anything I send.*

The card from Copenhagen showed the railway station covered in snow. Stunning, right. Not even The Little Mermaid, for Christ's sake. Did she just dash inside a tourist shop and pick up the first card she saw and scribble some words and post the damn thing?

To keep me nibbling.

He sighed, then gathered the postcards and the scraps and the anniversary picture and stuck them back in the drawer. He listened to the silence of the house. The place felt empty, detached from the world. He left, locking the door behind him.

He drove away in his funny wee car: voices were calling him.

29

On the steps of the Number One Fitness Centre Reuben Chuck called Ronnie Mathieson on his mobie.

'How'd it go?'

Mathieson said, 'Done.'

'No problems, eh?'

'Clean as a whistle, Mr Chuck.'

'See this as a part of a learnin process, Ron. One that never stops. Remember.'

Chuck cut the connection and went inside, climbed the stairs to the upper gym, and walked into Glorianna's room at the back, thinking of the three dead men: it didn't matter if they'd hung the woman or she'd done it herself, the point was simple — he had three less problems. And if Montague could describe any of these thugs, so what? The corpses were locked in a building that had once belonged to Gordy Curdy, and had lain empty for more than two years. No estate agent had the place up for sale or rent.

Glorianna wasn't in her room. She's late, but she's never been late in her life.

Chuck went into the stockroom. He'd find her conducting an inventory of supplies, towels, chemicals, or the vitamin compounds on which the Centre made an indecent profit. She wasn't in the stockroom. He walked back, glanced at her empty lounger and a copy of last week's *Scotland on Sunday* on the floor.

She read this rag avidly: it's important to stay informed, she told him. Chuck hated this particular publication because it had run a series of articles on Glasgow's 'underbelly': *Dear Green Place In Hands of Mobsters*. Pure shite, Godfather stuff that would have the S-o-S readership deluded into thinking there was no form of commerce in the city, from casinos to football teams to day nurseries, that didn't have criminal personalities involved. His own name was mentioned as a former 'associate' of the late Curdy — notorious insurance scammer, embezzler, loan shark with 'attachments' to mobsters south of the border and beyond. Chuck had been outraged and wanted to sue the paper, but his lawyers advised against it on the grounds that he really didn't need the public exposure a legal action would generate.

They were right.

As he moved downstairs, he called Glorianna's flat. Her recorded voice said *I'm not here to take your call. Have a great day.* He tried her mobile but she must have switched it off. First time ever, he thought. She was a mobie devotee, called it her life-line. He sat for a while and wondered if she'd spent the night at Dysart's. He was uneasy with this idea.

He overheard Tommy Lombardo in the gym putting a dyed-blond gay guy through his paces with the weights.

'Oh *you*, Thomaso, you make this so hard for me, you *cruel* boy.'

Chuck gazed at the front desk where Zondra was signing some first-time customers in. He watched money change hands, then when he was satisfied she was running it through the cash register — and not into the pockets of her tight white shorts — he entered Lombardo's little office and closed the door. *I should be beyond this, watchin pennies. I own an empire.* Old habits, picked up in poorer times when he was an ambitious kid low on the totem and countin change, died slow.

Chuck used his mobile to call Rick Tosh's number.

Rick Tosh answered, 'Howdy.'

Chuck said, 'Here's the stuff you need, Rick. The Azteca Bank of Aruba. Account: 957 8671-045. Password: countdracula. You got that?'

'Countdracula one word?'

'One. You have the code I gave you for the transfer.'

'Sure do. I'll arrange the wire now. The money will be in your Luxembourg account tomorrow, less my commission. You're cleaning house, man. Bigtime.'

'Cleanin and accumulatin.'

'Things move forward, Rube. No life in stagnant water, right? How's the weather over there?'

'What do you expect? I suppose you're baskin in ninety degrees.'

'It's a sweet eighty in the shade. You gotta come over some time, Rube. I'll lay on a barbecue to end all goddam barbecues.'

'One day. Call me when you've made the deposit.'

Chuck said goodbye. *A barbecue, burning*

dead animals and brushing them with brown sauce. He sat with his elbows propped on Lombardo's desk, which was strewn with glossy body-building magazines. The models on the covers were all steroid cowboys. Restless, he tried Glorianna's two numbers again with the same results. Was this the morning she took off for her voice lessons? He checked the date on Lombardo's desk calendar.

No. She went Mondays. This isn't the day.

He felt a touch of depression. All this death was disturbing. He wondered how much of it he could absorb and what he'd have to do to offset it in karmic terms. He needed to see Baba and get himself centred. He needed a quiet presence, a reassuring spiritual encounter.

He made another phone call, this time to Dysart's number.

'Hallo.'

'Dorco, how did you and Glorianna get on?'

Dysart said, 'G-get on?'

'Did she *relax* you, Dorco?'

'Oh, ah, y-yes.'

'What time did she leave?'

'I d-don't remember. I fell asleep.'

'I presume she got a taxi.'

'I woo-would think so, Mr Chuck.'

'Hard to find taxis out there, is it?'

'I n-never use them.'

Reuben Chuck was silent, trying to imagine Glorianna looking for a cab in the wilderness. Maybe she phoned for one. She'd have more sense than to walk the streets in that part of the world.

243

Chuck changed the subject. 'Incidentally, Dorco, my man was delighted with the last shipment you delivered.'

'Oh that's g-great.' Dysart giggled.

'Just keep the stuff comin.'

'Definitely I w-will, I will.'

Chuck hung up. Dysart's giggle pestered him. The giggle, the stutter, the chopped sentences: Dysart was definitely odd. He needed to be odd in his line of work.

Chuck got up. He had a memory of himself and Glorianna making love in the toilet of a plane on the way to Corfu. She'd been pressed up against the wash-basin, her dress hoisted up and her panties down to her ankles and he saw his face in the mirror behind her. He could recall the jet roaring in his head and how the image in the mirror was no longer himself but that of a man experiencing ecstasy . . . Wonderful, out of this world — but brief, too brief. That was the problem with sexual rapture. It died about as quickly as it flowered.

Never mind, he missed the intimacy and the thrill of mutually explosive release, and the clinging together after and the pleasure he felt in satisfying her and seeing that dizzy outerspace look on her face. He pictured her massaging Dorco.

He couldn't see it somehow.

★   ★   ★

Ron Mathieson drove him through the red sandstone tenements of Hyndland. Outside the

Temple of Personal Enlightenment, Chuck told Mathieson to wait, then he went inside.

The place was empty. He noticed Baba's big pillows on the floor and saw that Christ's broken eye had been repaired and that the leak-catching bucket was no longer around. What did he do now, just wait for Baba to materialize? He walked to the pile of cushions and stared at the curtains drawn across the wall a few feet further back.

He circled slowly round the room. *I ordered the deaths of three men, Baba. I instructed a man to supply organs ripped from human beings.* How much simpler it all was when you could say twenty Hail Marys and go off to the pub with a clear conscience. You don't even have the escape route of booze anymore.

He heard a sound from behind the curtains. Baba was probably back there, maybe meditating. You don't interrupt a meditating man. Often the Baba retreated back there when he meditated with a group of acolytes — mainly peely-wally spotty young men and women who looked like vampires had been drawing their blood. Chuck didn't like that young crowd, tended to avoid it. They were even more intense than Baba.

Wait a minute.

What was that crunching sound?

He wandered close to the curtain and listened. He caught a smell he knew, but he discounted it because its presence here was incongruous. He touched the curtain.

He heard Baba's voice, pitched quietly. 'I am in no position to pass judgement.'

245

Another voice, almost as low, asked a question: 'Is he truly serious?'

Baba said, 'Many people come to me in times of despair, when their souls are endangered.'

'Seeking refuge, taking flight?'

'These are one and the same thing.'

'Not necessarily.'

I know that fuckin voice, Chuck thought. He parted the curtain and peeped into the spartan room beyond. Baba, squatting on the floor, turned his face to look at him with a small smile of surprise. Chuck's attention was drawn from Baba down to a bucket of Kentucky Fried Chicken that sat on the floor between the guru and his visitor, who stood with a greasy drumstick in his hand.

'Scullion,' Chuck said. 'Well well.'

'I'm here to question the diverse ways of God, Reuben.' Scullion nudged the bucket toward Chuck with the tip of his shoe. 'Leg? Wing?'

'I'll pass,' Chuck said, annoyed and troubled finding Scullion in the Temple.

Baba said, 'Mr Scullion has questions, Reuben.'

'Has he now.'

'I've been telling him how generous you are.'

'Practically a saint,' Scullion said.

'I said no such thing. I simply told Mr Scullion how much you give to our Temple and how hard you strive to find the way.'

'Because you're a lost soul, apparently,' Scullion said.

Reuben Chuck looked at Baba. 'He's a polisman, Baba. He's tryin to pin some crimes on me.'

'Is that what I'm doing?' Scullion looked innocent.

Baba said, 'He mentioned no crimes to me, Reuben. He was making a general inquiry about what we practise here, and your name came up, as names sometimes do.'

'So this cop's a student of religion and my name just sort of *popped* up, did it?' Chuck looked at the KFC bucket. 'You actually eat that crap, Scullion? You know it's poison, don't you?'

'Most polismen don't have time or money for top dollar bistros. Some of us make do with quick takeaway shite.'

'I am detecting tension, an unpleasant vibration,' Baba said.

'Not from me,' Scullion said.

Chuck said, 'You come in here pretendin to be interested in the Temple and all you're doin is sneakin into my private life gatherin information, Scullion.'

'Your paranoia's showing, Chuck. Baba was telling me you donated a special bus to the Temple. Very worthy of you. I take it you're the rightful owner of the vehicle?'

'Come again? Of course I am.'

'Do you have legal title to the bus, Chuck?'

Chuck felt flustered. 'What are you tryin to pull? I just telt you I was the owner.'

Scullion said, 'You'll have a document of ownership then.'

'It's with my lawyers, because they're preparin transfer of the vehicle to the Temple.'

'Roman, Glebe and Hack, right?' Scullion bent, nabbed a wing, bit into it like a wolf into a lamb's throat. 'Smart boys. Slick movers.'

'You want to see that document, talk to them,' Chuck said. How much pryin had Scullion done into my life? What does he know behind that smug polis face?

Had Baba slipped, and told him too much? What did Baba know anyhow? Not the secrets of Chuck's life, not the blood-lettings. Chuck had never revealed these.

Scullion held the relic of the chicken wing in his hand. A slick of grease dripped to the floor. 'Where's the rubbish around here?' He asked this question of Baba, but he was looking at Chuck.

'There's a receptacle at the side of the building,' Baba said.

'Fine. I'll take my bucket and my bones and I'll be off.'

Baba said, 'Thank you for calling in.'

'I enjoyed our talk,' Scullion said. He looked at Chuck as he parted the curtain to leave. 'See you around.'

'Not if I see you first,' Chuck said.

Scullion stepped out, the curtain fell back in place. Chuck was furious. Some days begin bad and just get worse. He thought of the fleet of buses he'd 'inherited' . . . what the hell, it was only a matter of paperwork. Gary Hack could eat Scullion for a bedtime snack.

Baba rose. 'Trouble with the law, Reuben?'

'Not me, Baba.'

'You're stressed, I see.' Baba touched his shoulder. 'Always remember: everything you think permanent is transitory.'

248

'Including a bus?'

Baba smiled as if answering a child. 'Yes, including a bus.'

'Right,' Chuck said, disturbed. He knew where Scullion was coming from. If he can't nail me for somethin big, he'll sneak in the backdoor sniffin for somethin small. Paperwork, legal documents, deeds, tax returns, bank statements.

'You look weary,' Baba said.

'Unclog my head, guru.'

'I am not the instrument, Reuben, only the guide. Sit. Close your eyes. Do the deep breathing exercise I taught you.'

Chuck sat cross-legged. He sucked in air slow and deep, filling his lungs, then expelled slowly. He blanked his mind, a condition he managed to maintain for a mere ten seconds before he began thinking about Glorianna. If she left Dysart's place in a taxi, he could locate the driver easy enough. Make a few calls. And then Montague came waltzing into his head, babbling to the cops. Then Scullion. Before long, Chuck's head was a cauldron bubbling with all kinds of rabble — chlorine, bowling-alleys, Kentucky Fried Chicken, Montague in polis custody, hired gunmen, old geezers on sportsbikes, the bistro, Zondra's tight white shorts, Glorianna and what it had been like to *fuck* her and how much he'd love to do her again, *possess* her, never let her go . . .

'Escape yourself,' Baba said.

O, I'm tryin, Chuck thought.

30

Perlman entered The Triangle Club in Cadzow Street, where he was greeted by Rhoda.

'Can't stay away?'

'Moth to a flame, love,' Perlman said. 'I just want a wee word with Jackie again.'

'Oops, wrong night.' Her skin was silvery under the mirrored disco balls. 'Jackie's off.'

'Where could I find her?'

'I'm not supposed to give out personal details.'

He winked at her. 'I'll never tell.'

'She's not in trouble, is she?'

'Do I look like trouble?'

She laughed. 'You look like my grandfather. Same hairstyle.'

'You call this a style? I'm honoured.' Perlman smiled, although the grandfather word niggled him. He didn't want to look like anyone's Grandpa.

Rhoda went behind her desk and tapped a computer keyboard. 'Here, check for yourself. Then nobody can ever say I told you.'

Perlman looked at the screen and memorized Jackie Ace's address. He thanked her

'Visit us again,' she said.

'Be sure of it.'

Perlman left. Outside, the sky was turning toward evening, leaving behind a few melodramatic streaks of the afternoon sun. He drove in this crepuscular light up through the city centre, crossing Sauchiehall Street at the Dental Hospital, where he cringed at a bad memory of the old Jab and Stab dental college that operated years ago out of a Victorian building round the corner in Renfrew Street. He fantasized about Latta putting in long hours at this place of torture, spending painful afternoons at the hands of cack-handed students who bludgeoned your gums using ancient rotating drills that rattled every bone in your body, and injections that froze your mouth for days afterwards. You always departed the old dental college worse than you arrived. You went for a filling and left with three extractions.

He turned up Hill Street. He found the tenement he was looking for, dark stone, sombre as a funeral director's face. He parked his car. He was close to the Art School where Miriam used to teach. He thought of her paintings hanging unnoticed in the empty loft —

Fucksake, banish the woman or be haunted all your days —

He checked the doorbells, saw *J Ace* on a typewritten slip of paper, and he pressed the buzzer. A voice came through the intercom.

'Yes?'

'Perlman. Got a minute?'

A pause. 'I'll buzz you in. Second floor.'

Perlman pushed the door open when the buzzer sounded and entered the narrow tiled passageway leading to the stairs. He climbed quickly. The door to Ace's flat was glossy rich red wood with bright Rennie Mackintosh stained-glass inserts.

251

He saw Ace's outline on the glass before the door opened. 'Come in, Sergeant.'

Perlman tracked Ace down the corridor. The living room was simple — a turn of the century writing-bureau, a couple of nineteenth-century upright chairs, two lilacs in a thin blue vase, quietly poetic. A slatted red blind hung at the window.

Perlman lowered himself into one of the chairs. It was uncomfortable. He leaned forward.

'Awful chair, right?' Jackie Ace smiled. 'How did the Victorians ever get comfy?'

'Think this is hard? Try my Aunt Hilda's biscuits.'

Jackie Ace smiled. She wore eye make-up and lipstick and her hair was long. It didn't look like a wig, Perlman thought. It was too loose, too natural. She'd grown out her own hair. She was dressed in a simple maroon cashmere dress; he, she, Perlman wasn't sure how to think of Jackie Ace: a halfway person. She looked a little more angular, a little less feminine, than she'd done at the Triangle Club — but not by much. The word castration popped into Perlman's head, and he crossed his legs, imagined the act of gelding. I wouldn't let them have my balls, he thought. He wanted to ask Jackie Ace about the strenuous surgical procedure that lay ahead, but some places you just didn't poke your nose.

'Can I get you a drink, Sergeant?'

'No, I'm fine.'

Jackie Ace plucked a cigarette from a red cardboard box. A du Maurier, a brand Perlman hadn't seen in years. She didn't light it. He remembered she'd told him in The Triangle that she didn't smoke. 'How did you find me?'

'Sorry, I'm not at liberty,' Perlman said.

'A mystery? How inscrutable you are. Now you're here, what can I do for you?'

'A couple of questions I need answered. Then I'm off. Tartakower mentioned a guy who used to hang around you in the old chop-shop days.'

Jackie Ace appeared surprised. 'One in particular?'

'All I got is he was desperate to learn, skinny, wore glasses and attached himself to you.'

Jackie Ace stared at the unlit cigarette. 'No bells ring.'

'Think a minute. Take your time.'

'What else did Tarty tell you?'

'Just you and this kid were close. I got the impression he worshipped you.'

'An unknown disciple? I think I'd remember somebody like that.' Jackie Ace moved to a rack of stainless-steel shelving where a sound system had been installed, and pressed a button. The music was solo jazz piano. Perlman recognized it immediately.

'Monk.'

'You're a fan?'

'Years.' He listened to Monk plink out a simple version of 'Dinah'.

Jackie Ace smiled, as if she detected some little surprise, hitherto unnoticed, in the tune. She looked more feminine when she relaxed into the smile. Perlman could see her as she would be in the future when, with all the procedure behind her, she'd pass without problem as a woman. In

clothing emporia, at hair-stylist's, or experiment-
ing with make-up and perfumes the way women
did in the House of Fraser and all the big
department stores.

She looked at Perlman and shrugged. 'Sorry, I
just can't think who this mystery person might
be.'

Drawing a blank, Perlman thought. Everything
Tartakower says, it's a wrong turning. Was he
capable of opening his mouth without lying?
Even when he yawns, I bet it's a lie. But he'd
been so scared of enclosure in Perlman's car, so
spooked by the idea of going down to Force HQ,
that Perlman was *convinced* he'd been telling the
truth. So if he wasn't lying, then Jackie Ace was.
To what end? People lied for protection. So was
Jackie protecting herself, or the alleged old
friend, or both?

Jackie Ace put the unlit du Maurier back in
the box.

Perlman got up from his chair, sighed,
straightened his back and looked at her for a
moment. *She wants me to leave*, he realized.

It's in her position, the arms folded tightly
across her chest, the fingers of the left hand
kneading the biceps of the right arm, as if to
suppress a tic. Also the smile's gone stiff, too
fixed, and a slight impatience was forming ice in
the eyes.

'I'm thinking of something that would be
really helpful to me, Jackie . . . A meeting
between you, me and Tartakower, clear the air.
Your story. His story. I'm uncomfortable with
discrepancies, always have been — '

'There's absolutely no way I'd want to meet Tartakower again.'

'It would make my investigation a whole lot easier. If he sits down with you, maybe he can fill in some details of this kid. Refresh your memory.'

She shook her head. 'There's nothing wrong with my memory.'

'You're not afraid of *meeting* the harmless old duffer, are you?'

'No, certainly not.'

'I didn't imagine you would be. Somebody like you facing serious life-altering surgery, you've got to be brave.'

'Who told you that? Tartakower?'

Perlman nodded. 'It sounds rough.'

'It's no picnic.'

'You're seriously going through with it.'

She had a bright pride in her eyes when she spoke, and a determination. 'You're damn right I am. I've been serious for years. Oestrogen. Electrolysis. Female facial construction. Castration. I'm going for it the whole way.'

'Like I said, you're a brave man — '

'Woman. Soon to be.'

'Woman, aye, sorry. So meeting old Tarty for a few minutes might help me take a step down the road to solving this case — and it shouldn't be hard on you.'

'I just don't want to remember those times. They belong to another person's life. Surely you can understand that?' Jackie Ace made urgent, dismissive movements with her hands, as if rasped by a wasp.

'I'm investigating a crime, Jackie. I don't have the luxury of sparing your feelings about the past. I'm sure Tartakower wouldn't be as sensitive as you.'

'I don't believe he'd want to look back either.'

Perlman patted his coat pockets. 'Can you lend me one of your cigarettes?'

'Help yourself. I haven't smoked in eight years. I like the idea of having them around. In case there's a sudden lapse. Or a need. Or something.'

Perlman took a du Maurier from the box on the bureau. He rolled the cigarette between his fingers before he lit it. He liked the crinkle of tobacco inside paper. 'I'll arrange a meeting.'

Jackie Ace said, 'I don't think so.'

'I need clarification.'

'Of what? You're dealing with an old man's memory, and how reliable is that?'

Perlman said, 'My problem is I smell shite, Jackie.'

'Then your nose is too near your arse.'

It wasn't a ladylike remark, Perlman thought, and it shocked him unexpectedly. How weary he was of obfuscation and the great dissembling roil of humanity in general. Deceptions, sleights of hand, smoke bombs. He strolled the room, looking for a place where he might dispose of the du Maurier, the taste of which he didn't like. He flicked it carelessly into the open fireplace — and noticed too late that it was no longer a working fireplace, but a small whitewashed cave with designer pretensions, an arrangement of bonsai trees, glittering seashells and chopsticks balanced carefully in the shape of a steeple and dried herbs hanging from strings hidden in the chimney-piece.

'What the hell are you *doing*?' Jackie went down on her knees and scrambled to retrieve the burning cigarette end. 'I worked hours on this.'

'Oh shit,' Perlman said. 'I just did that without looking. Everywhere I go, I leave a mess. Is it OK? Nothing lost?'

'It's fine.'

'I'm so haunless sometimes. Just last week I left my new contacts on the edge of the wash-basin and I reached behind me for a towel — you know, groping blind. And just as I grabbed the towel, my free hand knocked the contacts down the sink,' and Perlman, demonstrating the backwards stretch for the towel, clattered into the delicate vase that contained the lilacs. Water slicked across the surface of the bureau and the vase cracked and the lilacs slid in the stream of spilled water to the floor.

'Oh Jesus, I'm sorry — '

'That vase was a *gift*,' Jackie Ace said angrily. 'It had sentimental value for me, Perlman.'

'I'll clean it up, let me, show me where you keep — '

'I'll do it myself.' Jackie Ace picked up the flowers. She rushed into the kitchen and came back with them in a drinking-glass half-filled with water.

'At least you saved the flowers,' Perlman said. 'But not the vase.'

Perlman sussed the orderly room, thinking it was just the kind of organized living-space he disliked. So fastidiously arranged, so empty of charming clutter. It needed a touch of shambles.

Ace placed the lilacs on the mantelpiece and stood with her hands on her hips. The look she gave Perlman was one of deep contempt.

'You're a bit of a disaster.'

'I'm not much of a guest, Jackie, granted.'

'Technically you're not a guest at all, I never invited you.'

'I know, I came barging in . . . ' Perlman gazed at the red slatted blind. 'I meant to say, I love the blind, eyecatching.'

'Don't go near it. Please.'

But Perlman reached out, fingered a slat. Jackie Ace, panicked, edged between Perlman and the blind to protect it. 'I'd like you to go. I'm asking nicely.'

'I don't blame you,' Perlman said. 'It's funny how I can come into somebody's flat and turn their world upside down in a minute, Jackie. Born clumsy.'

'I think you do it on purpose, Perlman.'

'No no, I wouldn't do that.'

Perlman's face was close to Jackie Ace's. He smelled aniseed on her breath and saw turmoil in her expression. He felt a surge of pity for her — poised as she was in uneasy balance between sexes, and facing the trauma of intrusive surgery, the long months of healing.

'I'll leave, give you some time.'

'For what?'

'Remembering.'

'You might have a very long wait.'

Perlman let himself out of the flat and closed

258

the door. He was sweating. The light on the landing threw his shadow, grotesquely distended, against the stair wall. He rubbed his eyelids, took a few steps down. His shadow altered. He held the banister, his palms damp on the wood. Clumsiness was hard work. Sometimes it helped, because it created agitation, and dented politeness, and people often said what was really on their mind.

He half expected Ace to have a change of mind and call after him. It didn't happen. He reached the bottom of the stairs, then walked the tiled close to the street.

★　★　★

He sat in his car and thought for a time about Betty and how she was coping. The need to see her overcame him. He imagined her sitting in a room with dimmed lights and drawn curtains.

He phoned The Pickler. 'Are you sober?'

'I'm just back from seeing Gers play Motherwell. Shite game.'

'That doesn't answer my question.'

'I'm sober enough.'

'I want you to do something for me. Now.'

'I was just about to watch a boxing match — '

'Forget it. Meet me in Hill Street. I'm parked near St Aloysius'.'

'You joining the Jesuits?'

'I've got enough problems without having to sit round and analyze them all day long. Get a taxi. I'll pay.'

'What's the job?'

'I'll tell you when I see you.'

There was a sound of bottles falling. Obviously The Pickler was in the act of standing and had collided with a pyramid of empties.

'I'm on my way.'

31

Chuck made a point of visiting The Potted Calf once a week. Mainly he wandered from table to table, glad-handing, saying hello, playing the host. He didn't like the smells from the kitchen, otherwise he might have come more often. Pieces of animals sizzling in butter, the pungent stench of the Basque stew that was a favourite with the customers. Sometimes he had Pako Sg, the chef, make him up a small bowl of noodles with vegetables, or a simple salad, and he ate standing close to the back door, which he always opened a little way.

Tonight he had no appetite. He was restless, his session at the Temple hadn't cleared his head or diminished his concern about Glorianna. He'd sent Mathieson to her flat with a pass-key and he'd come back to report there was no sign of her. Now Ronnie was checking the taxi companies, searching for the driver who'd picked her up from Dysart's place.

Chuck shook hands with the maître d', a smooth silver-haired man called Rory O'Blunt who'd worked some of the best rooms in Europe — Paris, Florence, London. O'Blunt was about fifty but had one of those seamless shiny faces that suggested years of self-control and careful diet.

'Evening Mr Chuck.' O'Blunt pressed the

meat of Chuck's hand between his own. The Sandwich Shake.

'Busy the night.' Chuck surveyed the room, which had been decorated by an Edinburgh interior design firm called LaScala, fussy painstaking fudgepackers who squealed a lot over books and paint samples. *Oh we must go with this, we must we must.* Chuck had spent four hundred and thirty-nine thousand pounds on making The Potted Calf luxurious and comfortable. The textured light tan wall covering looked like calfskin. There were small pen and ink portraits here and there of famous Scots. He hadn't wanted these, but the interior design people jabbered on about the importance of a Scottish identity. Chuck grew bored reminding them that the menu was a mix of European and Asian cuisine.

Rory O'Blunt said, 'Booked to the rafters, Mr Chuck.'

'Excellent.' That was one hundred and forty covers at an average of just over one fifty per cover. Some of this money was cash and could be disappeared very easily.

Chuck listened to the buzz of diners and the clack of cutlery and the easy laughter of people half-cut on silly-money wine. He worked his way across the room, a little more quickly than he normally did, nodding and smiling, shaking hands, tapping a shoulder here, an arm there, dropping an occasional joke. It was what you did in this biz if you wanted to be a success, the human touch. He wasn't much up for it tonight.

Chuck spotted Chief Superintendent Tay in

the far corner, seated with other high-ranking polis, mainly overweight men in anonymous suits. Tay was slurping soup du jour, pulped lettuce and ginger in a wine and beef stock broth, on which slivered leeks floated.

'Everythin OK, Super?'

Tay slowly raised his big boulder of a head like a man interrupted at prayer. His tiny mouth eked out a smile. 'Interesting soup. Not too leeky. I'm not a leek man.'

'The chef's always on the leek-out for new tastes,' Chuck said.

'You're a card,' Tay said and went back to his soup.

The other cops regarded Chuck with interest. He knew they'd arrest him in an eyeblink if they had evidence. A strange situation, and unsettling, as if there were two Reuben Chucks, one a respectable restaurateur, the other a criminal.

As he looked at Tay, Chuck imagined Scullion saying to the Superintendent *I'm digging deep into Chuck's background, getting warmer . . .*

Fuck Scullion, he thought.

'What's your main dish tonight, Super?'

'I chose the game pie.'

'Enjoy.' Chuck drifted away, but not before he noticed three bottles of fine wine — marked up seventy-five per cent from the dealer's price — on the Super's table. And the money rolls in. He nodded to O'Blunt, then left the bistro, which was discreetly concealed by willows. Once upon a time it had been an exclusive little hotel favoured by rich old ladies who liked its seclusion from the traffic on the main road.

He walked toward the Jaguar. He had two minders track him. They wore black leather jackets and black slacks. They were attuned to sudden, inexplicable movements. Chuck felt protected — and yet not, bothered again by thoughts of fuckin Scullion. *Keep on him, don't let up*: did Tay say somethin like that? Did they confer on a daily basis and devise strategy and sift such evidence as they might have gathered?

What fuckin evidence, they don't have any. They don't have beans.

He saw Mathieson in the car, and climbed into the back seat.

Mathieson said, 'I checked the taxi companies.'

'And?'

'Nobody remembers picking her up.'

'Somebody has to. Mibbe one of them gypsy cabs. Start askin some hard fuckin questions. Get on it as soon as you drop me off at Hack's.'

Mathieson glanced in his rear-view mirror and said he would.

Chuck thought: holy fuck did I just hear myself *curse? No*. Like an alkie taking a drink after years of abstinence, he felt regret and shock. He'd been careful with his language. He'd watched over it like a puritan at a witch-trial. I let myself down. I looked away. *Shit*. Baba said find the still space at the heart of the storm. Get a grip.

Mathieson drove until he reached Woodside Place, near Charing Cross. He parked outside a refurbished Victorian house.

Chuck said, 'Wait for me. Work the phone. Get

out the word to these gypsy cabs.'

'I will,' Mathieson said.

Chuck went inside the building, which had a brass plaque on the door that read: *Roman, Glebe & Hack, Solicitors*.

Mathieson thought: Chuck isn't himself today, not by a country mile.

★ ★ ★

Gerry Hack was a dyspeptic man who wore gloom as if he kept remembering he'd been dragged into the world by a pair of surgical forceps. He essayed a smile whenever Reuben Chuck entered his office — which was hung with degree certificates — but he wasn't a smiler by nature. Chuck paid him a retainer enormous enough to lighten his heart, but sometimes Hack had to do some deft paddling to get around the fact that Chuck lived in rough waters well outside the legal limits.

Chuck sat facing Hack across a desk carved in Acapulco by Mexican craftsmen. This desk, with its Aztec faces and configurations, had been written up in style sections of Sunday newspapers. It was spectacular, twelve feet long by nine deep, a size that served to keep some distance between Hack and his clients, most of whom were villains.

Chuck said, 'I hate that desk.'

'Only because you covet it.'

'It's a piece of Mex crap.'

'I turned down your last two offers. Don't waste my time.'

'It would make great kindlin.'

Hack's smile widened. He might be the essence of flexibility when it came to that borderline where Crime met the Law in a tangle of contentious issues, but in the matter of the Acapulcan desk he was granite.

He laid his hand on a bundle of manila folders. 'You spawned every one of them. Whenever I think of you and these files I'm reaching for the Zantac.'

The whites of Hack's eyes were a jaundiced colour. He suffered from alopecia which had destroyed his eyebrows, and all the hair on his head.

Chuck always thought he was an odd sight. 'I pay you enough. You could throw in the desk for what I pay you.'

'This fucking desk stays where it is. As for your paying me. I cost you an arm and a leg because I'm the best and I keep your arse out of jail. If it wasn't for me, do you think you'd be able to stroll around town like a man with a halo? Buses for the handicapped. Donations to religious charities. Free sessions for senior citizens three nights a week at your health spas. Instead of sitting in a cell, you're at liberty to glow in the darkness of Glasgow, Rube, like one of those electric Christs I nearly bought at Knock.'

Knock, Chuck thought. He knew Knock all right. It was a form of low-grade Catholic Vegas, a place where the depressed and the maimed laid bets on the wheel of fortune they called Faith, cap F. 'Don't talk to me about Knock, Gerry.'

266

'Right. You had a falling out with God.'

Chuck eyed the stack of files. 'How's your security here?'

'Your files are safe, Rube.'

'What if the cops raided this place?'

'You don't think I *store* the files here, do you?' Hack lit a thin brown-papered cigarette. 'So Scullion's bothering you.'

'Gettin on my tits. Has he asked you about that paperwork?'

'Not yet. When he does, he'll get it.'

'How?'

'Don't meddle. I don't reveal trade secrets and I never name connections.'

Chuck imagined he'd figured out Hack's methods: a conspiracy of lawyers and clerks in Government offices was involved, what else could it be? Hack played footsie with Stoker's lawyers, and Curdy's as well. They traded documents and deeds, every doc doctored in the appropriate places, a legal stamp here, a signature there, whatever it took to construct an appearance of legality. When they heard the first whisper of the big changes coming in the map of lawless Glasgow, they smelled huge profit in paper-shuffling. Chuck could see them hold clandestine meetings in quiet country hotel rooms where they hatched treachery. Bram and Curdy were on the skids ... who'd want yesterday's men for clients? Who'd want to be associated with losers?

The smart money follows the winner every time.

This was the way Chuck liked to see it, an

association of bent lawyers looking out for themselves. And, incidentally, his neck too.

Hack pointed his cigarette at Chuck. 'Scullion's covered for now.'

'For now — what does that mean?'

'I mean he might come up one day with a request I can't fulfil. Highly unlikely, but in the realms.'

'Wait a minute — '

'What worries me is your mindset. Think in advance next time you decide on a flamboyant takeover.'

'It was planned like a military op, Gerry.'

'More Keystone cop.'

'The amount of schemin that went into — '

'I don't want to know,' Hack said, singing the words in a thin funny soprano, and covering his ears and closing his eyes. 'What I'm telling you is this, consequences are easier to deal with if you root out loose ends before they become loose ends.'

He's Baba in another form, Chuck thought. 'Somethin might throw you for a loop, is that it?'

'Who knows? Bottom line, I'm only telling you if you have future plans put them on hold. Let things cool.'

Chuck was quiet. Future plans. All he wanted was peace. He couldn't stop thinking about gypsy cabs. You couldn't trust them. What if some bandit picked up Glori and took a shine to her? Rape was always a possibility. A desirable young woman alone in an unlicensed cab with some horny fuckin Romanian or Greek at the wheel on a stretch of dark isolated road and who knows what.

Hack shook his head. 'Here's my best advice. Keep your hooter clean. Do some more low-level charity stuff. Be Mister Nice.' Hack pushed his chair back from the desk. 'Go home. Relax. Count crystals or whatever you do.'

Chuck snorted. '*Count* crystals? Shows what you know.' He got up from his chair. He needed to have faith in Gerry Hack. He needed to believe there was no angle Gerry Hack couldn't cover. 'Scullion's a fuckin pancake. You could snaffle him for breakfast, right?'

'With my ulcer?' He stood up and walked Chuck to the door.

They shook hands and Chuck left, feeling not the reassurance he'd come here for but a little dissatisfied and insecure. How good was Hack really? And if he was capable of entering into a conspiracy of lawyers, how could Chuck know that something similar might not happen in the future — only this time *he'd* be the one conspired against?

A weird thought, I'm replaceable.

He went outside. Ronnie Mathieson was in the passenger seat of the Jag, talking into his mobile phone.

Chuck slid into the back.

Mathieson said, 'I'm still chasing gypsies. Not a sausage yet.'

Chuck jammed his hands into the pockets of his camel's hair coat 'Where is she.'

'She'll turn up.'

Chuck, fighting anxiety, said nothing.

32

Betty McLatchie's sleep had been shallow. No calming black sea had come to claim her, despite the bottle of Chilean red she'd drunk, and a couple of Dalmane tossed back. She rose unsteadily, glanced at the bedside clock: nine forty-five. Morning, evening. Did it matter?

Her throat was dry and she felt she was listing at a peculiar angle. She pulled on a long unflattering woollen robe and put on her slippers and left her small darkened bedroom. From the living room window she saw streetlights glow. So it was night, not morning. She switched on a table lamp, blinked. Traffic rattled past along London Road. She drew the curtains.

The doorbell rang.

She hoped it wasn't another neighbour with flowers or words of solace or oh my God a home-baked cake. Why did they feel they had to bring food anyway. They knew she wasn't going to sit down and stuff herself with sponge cake or rhubarb pie. Kindness, simple human kindness motivated them, and she was touched, she really was. But even so she was reluctant to open the door and admit another face white with shock and sympathy.

She wouldn't have minded if it was Perlman. He'd been so kind to her earlier, walking with her in the park, taking her arm, saying little — his presence was comforting. He had a quality she liked. More than just sympathy, an unexpected gentleness. He looked as if he was forever on the edge of a gruff mood, but that wasn't the real man.

She knew that much.

She didn't recognize the young woman on her doorstep for a moment. Her mind needed time for memories to slot into place. Slowing down, sluggish, wine, medication, grief. It was a fuck of a concoction.

'Betty,' the woman said.

'*Annie?*' Betty was surprised. She lost her bearings, time collapsed around her. How long was it since she'd seen Annie Cormack? Years, how many years, she couldn't calculate.

'Have I changed *that* much, Betty?'

'No, no, love, it's me, I was out like a light, and I'm fuzzy-heided. Come on in, come in, oh it's so good to see you — '

'I can come back another — '

'I wouldn't dream of it,' and she hugged Annie for a time, then led her inside the sitting room, thinking the light from the lamp was just about right. Stronger illumination she couldn't take. She must look as haggard as she felt.

Annie, slender little thing, kept a tight hold of Betty's hand. 'I had to come. I saw it on TV. It's so . . . oh Christ, unbelievable. What can I do? There must be something I can do.'

What can I do? They all said that. All the sad-faced neighbours. And then they all said, *You think of anything, let us know.*

She wanted to tell them, *do this for me, resurrect my boy.*

271

She kept to herself the gruesome details of Kirk's death. Why impose them on others, on well-wishers who were shocked to know he'd been *murdered*, but not by the way he'd been mutilated — which hadn't been broadcast on TV or in the newspapers? Yet.

Annie and Betty sat on a colossal sofa Betty had bought at a going-out-of-business sale. It was unfashionable, beige with a big floral print, and it was a bugger to move, but it was satisfyingly comfortable. You could lose yourself in its depths.

'I always cared for him, Betty.'

'I know, I know. Sometimes things just don't work out.'

Annie was so pretty, Betty thought. She always had been. Now she was even more so, but with an authority to her looks. She'd grown up. One time, Betty had hoped that Annie and Kirk would go the distance — but Annie drifted in other directions. It happened.

Annie said, 'I heard he got married.'

'He chose the wrong one.'

'I'm sorry.'

Betty had seen daughter-in-law Debbie somewhere during the blur of the afternoon, when people were coming and going. Debbie was tearful and crumpled. She didn't stay long. Bereavement suited her equine face. She'd want to do the whole widow thing, black clothes and a veil with a tragic inconsolable air.

Annie, dressed in baggy black pants, black sneakers and a rainproof black jacket with big pockets and a hood that hung at her back, played nervously with a tiny lace-edged hankie she took from her black leather purse. All this blackness — Annie had always preferred bright colours in the old days. She was uneasy, but Betty didn't ask why. Probably the situation made her tense. The death of Kirk, flashes of the past, and coming back to this flat when she probably thought she never would.

Betty felt herself space out, seeing the room and not seeing it. She was lost in a ball of lamplight reflected in the panel of the glass display case where she kept her good china and some other possessions dear to her, including a framed photo of her and Kirk taken on the beach at Saltcoats when he was about two, a tousled plump-faced boy in baggy swimming-trunks saddled on a stubborn donkey.

Annie went to the cabinet. She paused once, as if she felt pain in her leg.

'You OK?' Betty asked.

'I pulled a stupid muscle at my exercise class. Sometimes it twinges. It's getting better.' She looked at the picture of Kirk. 'He was a wee charmer, wasn't he?'

'Aye he was. I remember he couldn't get that bloody animal to move. Kicked it, shouted, even whispered in its pointy ears, but the donkey was going nowhere. He couldn't say donkey. The word came out as denka. *Denka, giddy-up, giddy-up denka.*'

Annie came back to join her on the couch. Betty patted her hand. She felt the need to keep a conversation going in banal everyday words, safe words that didn't have depth-charges

273

buried in them. 'How long has it really been?'

'Four years and a bit.'

'That long? Where does time go? How are you doing? Bring me up to date.'

'Oh, getting along.'

'Working?'

'I do a bit of this, a bit of that.'

Betty wondered what this meant. She didn't pry. 'So are you still living in the Drum?'

'No. Kelvinbridge. Up near the top of Belmont Street. Dead posh, so it is.' Annie delivered this, not in a boastful way, but as if she were ridiculing the neighbourhood for its airs and graces, and herself along with it.

Betty said, 'It's very nice there.'

'Aye if you like cheese shops and fancy French pastries.'

Betty still couldn't get over how strange it was to see Annie again. She hadn't even known Annie still lived in Glasgow. Twice she imagined she'd seen her on the street, but it was somebody else both times.

'Your parents, how are they doing?'

'Dad retired. Mum's busy as ever.'

'I can't remember what your mother does.'

'She delivers flowers. And Dad mopes, feeling old and useless.'

Betty waited a second before she asked, 'So is there somebody special in your life?'

'There was somebody.' A strange look crossed Annie's face. Betty thought it was indescribable, in part resentment, in part trepidation. 'Men can be so bloody disappointing. They're like weans. They want you to do things you don't want to do.'

'Aye and throw a fit when you don't.'

Annie said, 'Can I get you something to drink?'

'You remember where it's kept?'

'Unless you've moved it.'

'I'll have a wee glass of the vino if there's any. Wait, I should go if your leg hurts — '

'It's nothing.' Annie disappeared into the kitchen. Betty heard the rattle of glasses, a cupboard door opening on a squeaky hinge.

'I found some red and some white.' Annie carried two glasses. 'What's your preference?'

'You choose.'

Annie gave her the red and said, 'I was just thinking Kirk always liked movies.'

'His great passion.'

'We'd see a film and we'd come back here and sit in your kitchen and drink your wine.'

'So that's where it all went,' Betty said.

Annie smiled. 'It didn't matter if I fancied doing something else, he dragged me off to the cinema every chance he got. Always those action things, aeroplane hijack flicks, every one the same as the last. He thought they were the berrs. We used to come out trying to imitate Yanks. He'd say Let's kick ass. And I'd come back Hey whaddya say we go chill out wid a coupla brewskies.' Annie's impersonation was good. She laughed very quietly at the memory, but a sombre note lay submerged beneath the laugh.

Reconstructing Kirk. Fleshing out the dead. Betty put her glass down. She started to cry.

Annie hugged her. 'There there.'

Betty said, 'I'll be OK.'

Annie didn't release her. She seemed to want the connection as much for her own sake as Betty's. Annie's shoulders shook. She sobbed quietly.

Betty stroked her back. 'Ssshhh, sssshhh.'

'It shouldn't have happened.'

'I know, love.'

Annie drew back from Betty, and blew her nose into her hankie, and when she looked at Betty again her eyes were blurred with tears and her mascara was like black wax melting. 'Oh Christ, I'm supposed to comfort you. And here I am . . . dammit. I'm useless at this, Betty. If I'd married him — '

'Oh don't even think that.'

'I had other ideas, such big ideas, I wanted to *make* something out of my life — '

'And Kirk was happy enough just getting along from day to day.'

'He was sweet, considerate — '

'But no ambition.'

'Who says ambition's such a fucking great thing anyway?'

Betty was surprised by the sudden vehemence in Annie's voice. She sipped her drink and looked inside the glass at the purple disc of wine shimmering. 'I don't know about great, but my old ambition was to be a backup singer. I wanted to stand behind the guys and go ooobie do-wap-do.'

Annie crumpled her hankie. 'You went to Woodstock. I just remembered that when I came in tonight. The pictures in the hall.'

'Ah but those pictures don't tell the *whole*

276

story.' Betty plucked a cigarette from her pack of B&H and lit it. Her fingers shook so badly she was embarrassed. She'd smoked a lot today. She'd drunk too much coffee. 'Some other time.' She looked at Annie fondly, remembering better times. 'He once told me, Ma, I'm arse over elbow in love with this girl. He'd been drinking and he'd slipped into one of those God's honest truth moments. Then he said you'd found somebody else.'

'I thought I had.'

'He always felt he couldn't compete — '

'He was so good to me, Annie.'

'But the new fella turned your head. Was it love?'

'I don't know what love is. It's not all flowers and gifts, I know that.' Annie sounded bitter. Betty had never considered her as bitter or sour in any way; the break-up with the boyfriend had affected her. She wanted to ask but thought: *I'll mind my own business.*

'Kirk was never romantic, Annie.'

'And how would you know that? I could tell you a few things.' Annie nudged Betty's knee, smiled thinly, and then dabbed her ruined eye make-up with the hankie. 'Do I look like a washed-out rag?'

'*I'm* the washed-out rag, pet.'

Memories then tears. Was this the cycle of moods ahead? Betty finished her drink. She tilted her head against the back of the sofa, sighed long. Somehow you had to find yourself again. If you could. If you could put a finger on a place and say, *This is me.*

277

'Listen, want me to spend the night?' Annie asked.

'That's awfy sweet of you, Annie.'

'I could sleep here on the sofa. I'd like that.'

'I'll be OK. Really.'

'Seriously, I'm happy to do it.' Annie looked like an eager child. 'We'll sit up and chatter about the old days.'

Betty thought Annie's persistence probably rose from her concern, her willingness to be useful, but there was something just a little desperate in the way she asked — as if *she* was the one bereaved and in need of company. Betty considered the prospect of more hours spent dredging the past, every square inch of Kirk and Annie's lost love excavated, and more wine drunk. She liked Annie, she always had, but if she lingered it could only mean further reminiscences — and when these were exhausted they'd be recycled.

The doorbell rang. Annie jumped a little. She wants it to be just her and me, Betty thought. No outsiders, no strangers. Then it struck her: Annie's lonely, she needs to be here.

'I better see who that is, love.' Betty hauled herself out of the sofa and went out into the hallway where she passed under the famous old pictures of herself at Woodstock — coloured, fogged by time. That bright smile, the long hair middle-parted, the loud floral blouse and the mini-skirt up to here and the knee-high boots, youthful, you sexy beast. Hello world. A young girl who was ready to seize experience by the scruff. And she had. Jesus she had.

She opened the front door.

Perlman stood outside. 'Can I come in?'

'Lou, I wasn't expecting . . . ' She reached up and adjusted the twisted lapel of his overcoat. She couldn't help herself. She felt silly — maternal, but not entirely that. Somebody has to care for this man.

He appeared not to notice her rearrangement of his clothing. 'I just wanted to see how you're doing,' and with a shy movement he produced a bunch of flowers he'd been hiding behind his back. 'For you.'

'Oh Lou.' She took the flowers, a mix of carnations, a half dozen roses, a wedge of ferns. She suspected he wasn't a flower giver generally, if ever.

'Are they OK? Do you like them?' He looked so hopeful.

'They're beautiful.' She sniffed them. They had barely any scent. She'd never tell him that. Anyway, how long since a man had brought her flowers?

'I can exchange them if — '

'What for? Don't be daft. I love them.' She helped him out of his coat and hung it on a wooden rack. 'I've got company.'

'You want me to come back another time?'

'You will not.' She led him inside the living room.

Annie looked up at him.

Betty said, 'This is Annie Cormack. Annie, Lou Perlman.'

Perlman smiled, shook the young woman's hand. 'Nice to meet you.'

Annie slid her hand from the clasp. 'Likewise.'

Perlman stared at her, trying to place her. She was a little disconcerted by his scrutiny. She scratched the side of her face, shifted her position.

'Funny, you remind me of somebody.' Perlman narrowed his eyes.

Annie opened her purse and fidgeted with whatever it contained. Car keys, lipsticks, tampons. Rummaging and engrossed, she said, 'People always say that.'

There was a chill in the room, something that hadn't been there before. Betty felt tension, and it came from Annie: a mood swing.

Perlman said, 'An actress. What's her name?'

'What film was she in, Lou?' Betty asked.

'That film with whatsisname. Tip of my tongue.'

'That's helpful,' Betty said.

Perlman snapped thumb and middle finger together. 'Paul Newman — '

'She reminds you of *Paul Newman*? You got your contacts in, Lou?'

Perlman was obviously determined to unearth the name of the actress. Annie kept ploughing through her purse.

'That film where he's a boxer. Rocky somebody. His wife . . . Italian. Got it, Pier Angeli. Lovely girl.'

'I remember her,' Betty said. *Lovely girl*. The phrase bothered her. Perlman comes to see me, and here he is concentrating on Annie. How bad do I bloody look? If she'd known he was coming she'd have made an effort to be presentable, she'd have tossed the long boring robe, junked the carpet slippers. This mode of dress wasn't fetching — oh, come on, you've only known the man a matter of days and yet you're troubled when he compares Annie to a 'lovely' actress? Hold your horses, McLatchie. This is a bad day and your head isn't screwed on right and Perlman didn't come here expecting to find you done up like a nightclub hostess.

'Annie looks like her, Pier Angeli,' Perlman said.

Annie snapped her purse shut and glanced at Perlman. 'I've never heard of Pier Angeli. Is this an *old* movie?'

'Long before you were born, dear,' Betty said — too quickly, clumsily.

Perlman searched for a place to sit. *He couldn't find his way out of a paper bag,* Betty thought. She liked that about him, the way he bumbled, the vagueness that overcame him at times.

'There's a chair by the cabinet, Lou.'

'Oh right. Either it's the light in here or I'm going blind.' He sat down and propped his elbows on his knees and continued to look at Annie, who rose from the sofa and slung the strap of her purse over her shoulder.

'I was about to leave.'

Perlman smiled. 'The Perlman Effect. Want a room emptied? Call Lou.'

Betty said, 'You don't have to, Annie.'

'It's OK. I just remembered some place I said I'd be.'

'You wanted to stay ... ' Betty wasn't unhappy. She'd prefer Perlman alone. She was

281

curious about the change in Annie's manner — but on a day like this, so finely balanced on the edge of deep feelings, so turbulent under the false surface of putting a bold face on death, people went through all manner of emotional currents.

'I'll come back another time,' Annie said.

'Stay by all means.'

Annie took a small compact mirror from her purse and looked at her own reflection. 'Christ, I'm a sight.'

Betty said, 'You are not. It's me . . . ' I must look a ghost, she thought. She hurried from the room, saying she needed to find a vase.

Annie popped the mirror back inside her bag and walked to the living room door. 'Tell her goodbye. I'll phone her.'

'Wait,' Perlman said.

'I really need to leave.' She opened the door to the hallway and walked away. He went after her.

'Since when were you Annie?'

'Since the day I was born, Mr Perlman.'

'Call me Lou.'

She kept moving, and was halfway to the front door when he said, 'George Square. Two Christmases ago. Mibbe three. You'd been shopping, you had Armani bags — '

'You're barking.'

'Woof,' Perlman said. 'You and Chuck.'

She swung round to face him. 'Who? I've never seen you before in my life.'

'I don't leave much of an impression, but I'm good with faces. And yours is memorable. You have some reason you don't want Betty to know you changed your name?'

'I never changed my name.'

'I bet Chuck did it for you. He'd prefer Glorianna to Annie. More glitz. More flash. Myself, I think Annie's a nice name.'

She stared at him fiercely. 'Let it go. Leave it alone.' She raised a hand to her face, a fluttery gesture, as if to conceal an expression.

'What are you so afraid of?'

'I'm not afraid.'

She opened the front door, intending to go, then turned back to him. 'It was somebody else with the fucking Armani bag. Not me. Somebody else. All right?' And she left, shutting the door without looking back.

He lingered a second, then returned to the living room just as Betty came in from the kitchen with the flowers in a vase. She'd done something to her hair. The pile of yellow and grey had been combed quickly, and pins strategically inserted for control.

'Has Annie gone?'

'She'll phone. Told me to tell you.'

'God, she practically *fled*.' Betty placed the vase on a coffee-table, turned it this way, that, until she was satisfied. 'She said she wanted to sleep here the night. Then you showed up. You must have scared her.'

'I showed her my Frankenstein impersonation and she was out that front door like she'd been fired from a cannon.'

Betty looked at him in silence for a while, face tipped to one side. 'You have anything you want to tell me, Lou?'

'About the case? I wish. But nobody's been apprehended.'

She was quietly relieved. She'd had enough of death. It suffocated her. It dimmed every light in her soul. She needed to get beyond it, even if only for ten minutes, ten seconds, any amount of time would be welcome.

Perlman lit a cigarette. 'How well do you know Annie?'

'Well enough. She was Kirk's girlfriend for a while. I haven't seen her in a long time.'

'You know where she lives.'

'Why are you asking this?'

'Cop's habit. Excuse me.'

'She's from Drumchapel originally. She has a flat in Belmont Street.'

'Came up in the world. You know anything else about her?'

'She just broke up with her boyfriend, and I think she's hurting.'

'Who's the boyfriend?'

'I don't know. What's your interest anyway?'

He didn't reply. She saw deep preoccupation in his eyes. He sat down on the sofa, stretched his legs.

'You want a drink, Lou?'

He came out of his reverie as if startled. 'A wee dram, if you have it.'

'There's a drop somewhere.' She didn't make any move to fetch it for him. Let him find it for himself. 'Are you often like this? In and out. Off and on.'

'My head goes places.'

'All the time or only when a pretty girl's involved?'

'Pretty girls have nothing to do with it.'

'You come down to earth for food and water though.'

'I visit the planet now and then.'

Betty sat beside him, 'In the kitchen, top cabinet, you'll find a bottle of Black and White.'

He got up. She heard him clatter about in the kitchen. She wondered what he'd break as he foraged. Inevitably something would fall. He needs assistance. She entered the kitchen and saw him standing one-legged beside the open door of a bottom cabinet.

'I said top, Lou. Upper cabinet.'

'You didn't warn me about perilous domestic objects.'

He pointed to the foot he was holding up off the floor. A mouse-trap had clamped tight shut on the tip of his right shoe.

'That damn trap finally caught something,' she said.

She laughed, and the sound surprised her. Days since she laughed. She realized with something of a shock that she wanted to spend the night with him. She hadn't wanted a man in a long time. Not like this. She felt a warmth rush through her body. Betty, Betty: some night, but not this night, this isn't the time.

33

It was somebody else with the Armani bag.

Perlman was still preoccupied with Glorianna when he reached the door of his house. He caught a strong whiff of camphor. He knew only one man who smelled like this. And here he was, The Pickler, emerging from the shadows of the shrubbery and shoving some paper slips into Perlman's hand.

'Unwritten rule, cops and their snitches should meet in neutral places.'

'Nobody saw me, Mr Perlman,' The Pickler whispered.

'Remember in future.'

The Pickler sounded like a schoolboy chastised. 'I'm sorry.'

Perlman unlocked the door. 'What's this paper?'

'Taxi chits. You owe me thirty-two ninety. Round it off to thirty-five, if you like.'

'Where did you go — Inverness?'

He guessed The Pickler urgently needed to be reimbursed otherwise he wouldn't be here. Probably he knew a place where he could score some drink after hours. Perlman stepped indoors, and gestured for The Pickler to follow him. They went directly to the living room.

'Oh very nice place, very homey,' The Pickler said. 'Christ how many CDs have you got?'

'Fifteen hundred going on two thousand. Give

or take. I don't keep count.'

The Pickler yanked a CD from the stack. 'What's this? The Greatest Hits of Ray Charles. Here, I've got this myself. Very nice. Ray was King. Some say Elvis others Jerry Lee but — '

'Stick it back in the right place,' Perlman said.

The Pickler replaced it upside down. With uncharacteristic fussiness, Perlman righted it.

'He sang great for a blind man,' The Pickler remarked. 'I read there's a connection between loss of sight and musical abil — '

'Not all blind men can sing,' Perlman said. He was impatient and tired and overextended, as if the day behind him had been longer than twenty-four hours. He didn't need to hear the facts and half-digested theories stored in The Pickler's head. They came out of popular science or car magazines or the *Reader's Digest*, The Pickler's favourite reading material.

The Pickler plopped himself in Lou's velvet armchair facing the silent TV. Perlman, mildly resentful he'd chosen this chair, took out his wallet and gave him thirty-two pounds. His bankroll was thinning quickly.

'You still owe me ninety p. Don't worry, I won't sue.' The Pickler laughed and took the cash, then picked up the remote zapper and turned on the TV. *Make yourself at home.* The Pickler was one of those people who'd ask to use your toilet and flush the cistern to conceal any noise while he rifled your bathroom cabinet and siphoned off any pills he fancied.

Perlman immediately killed the TV.

'Force of habit, Mr Perlman. Sorry.'

'If I was a pregnant moth, your wardrobe would be the last place I'd drop my eggs. Do you bathe in that stuff?'

'I've got wan suit, Mr Perlman, and this is it. I don't want moths eating the heart out of it. Would you eh have a beer handy?'

'I never drink the stuff.'

'Too baaaad.' The Pickler farted, a genuine ripper. 'Sorry, Mr Perlman. That was a cheeky wee sneaker. Canny catch they softees.'

A cheeky wee sneaker? Christ, it was practically a whole wind ensemble. Perlman worried about damage to the fabric of the chair.

The air was heavy, almost chewable. Perlman opened a window.

'Chilly in here all of a sudden, Mr Perlman.'

'I'm a fan of fresh air.'

The Pickler rubbed his hands together and said, 'Here's the story. I folly him down Renfrew Street brisk-like. High heels, nylons, a lovely overcoat with wan of they high collars.'

'Skip the fashion report,' Perlman said.

'Just painting a wee picture. He heads inna general direction of the Buchanan Galleries. He meets this guy outside. The pair o them walk to a van. I got the licence number, by the way.'

'Good.'

The Pickler drew a stub of brown paper from his trouser pocket. 'There it is. So they get in the van. I'm left like a tosser looking for a taxi. They're never there when you want them, you notice that? Like the polis. No offence. Finally I find one and jump into it and the van's wheeching off toward Killermont Street right where the bus station is.'

Perlman smoked a cigarette. He gestured with his hands: get to the point.

'The van goes out Alexandra Parade, past Alexandra Park, then along Cumbernauld Road to Edinburgh Road. Past aw the housing schemes. My ex still lives there in Cranhill.'

'I don't need a family history.'

The Pickler asked, 'Did I no tell you I was married once? She was too hoity toity for me. Airs and graces. Fur coat nay knickers. Called me a guttersnipe. I wasn't putting up with that so I walked out — '

'We're past the housing schemes, then what?'

'The van drives inside the grounds of an auld house, a crumbling big place. High chimneys. Tall gates. I wait around for a while. It's no a pleasant area, Mr Perlman. This house is right up against the housing scheme and honest to God it's rough.' The Pickler frowned. 'I'm surprised the housing authorities didn't get a compultory purchase order to dynamite the house.'

'You mean compulsory.'

'When I don't have a bevvy in ma hand I mix up words. You sure you don't have a snifter of something?'

Perlman shook his head. One snifter would lead to another and then The Pickler would have to be hauled out of the chair with a docker's hook.

'OK, so the pair go inside the house. I sneak a look through the gates and watch. I'm there a while. I gave some thought to seeing if I could climb the gates — then these *shoooge* dogs come rushing at me. Wild? They're like Satan's fuckn messengers. I'm no suicidal, I'm no going over.'

'Then you came straight back here.'

The Pickler looked offended. 'No. I went into the scheme — '

'Brave soul.'

'I was a sojer once in The Black Watch, but that's another story. This scheme is kids hanging around corners looking dangerous, and some women punching the shite outta each other in a front yard and somebody's got a shotgun they're firing. Talk about entertainment. It's a dump you want to get the fuck away from quick-like.'

'Which you did.'

'Naw. Whatza point going aw the way out there and coming back empty-handit? Anyway look at me — you think I canny pass as a local resident? I fall into conversation with this punter, who's had a jar too many, lucky bastart, and he says there's a fuckn fruitcake living in that big house. The locals hate him. Oh and one other thing, the house is haunted. Don't look at me funny. I don't believe in ghosts, I'm only passing on what he told me. Guy who owns the house is called Dysart. Nobody seems to know what he does in there.'

'So the locals make up their own legends.'

The Pickler shrugged. 'That's for you to find out. I done my bit.'

'You did fine.'

Perlman looked at the registration number of the van scribbled on the scrap of brown paper. *Question time.* Why did Ace rush out to meet

Dysart almost immediately after Perlman left? Was Dysart the one who'd 'worshipped' Ace in chop-shop times? Did Ace hurry away because he was panicked and needed to warn Dysart that Perlman was snooping, circling a past they were anxious to conceal?

Until he talked to Dysart, he'd only be guessing.

The Pickler, who'd been fidgeting, got up from his chair. 'I'll head out then, Mr Perlman.'

'Right. And thanks.'

'My heid. I was nearly forgetting the address of that house. 3 Cobble Drive. Only house on the drive. Anything else, gie me a shout. I better find a taxi. I'll need — '

'Taxi fare.'

'You're a scholar and a gentleman.'

Perlman handed him a tenner and thought I'll be bankrupt at this rate. He walked him to the door where he said goodnight.

The Pickler stopped dead. 'Oh a coupla things before I forget. I saw the van again.'

'When?'

'I was looking for a taxi in Edinburgh Road when it went flashing past me, heading back in the direction of town.'

'Same van?'

'Same white van. Same reg.'

White van, Perlman thought — one nearly squashed the cat on Wellshot Road. Glasgow was full of white vans.

'What's your other point?'

'The drunk geezer I'm yacking with, right? He tells me the other night a bird came running out

291

that big house. Apparently in some distress. No shoes, crying, so I heard. Young bird, easy on the eyes. She's frantic, he says. So some kids arrange for her to get a lift back into town. A guy with a hearse obliged.'

'A hearse,' Perlman said. 'Did you get the name of the hearse driver?'

'Pudge is all I got. Then my source fell down dead drunk. No shame, some people.'

Perlman locked the door and went back inside the living room.

★   ★   ★

Alone, he almost sat in the chair where The Pickler had farted. Too soon to occupy that space, still warm and doubtless suffused with The Pickler's gaseous discharge.

He shook off his coat and lay on the sofa.

He stared at the ceiling.

Puzzled. Aye, but life was a puzzle. He smoked a couple of cigarettes and remembered Glorianna's haste to leave Betty's and how she'd denied ever having met him. Even denied her name. She'd fallen out with her boyfriend, presumably Chuck — if indeed Chuck was the current one.

A disagreement, an infidelity, any one of the stresses that afflict relationships, who could say what had caused the falling-out?

And why was she afraid?

Connect it to Chuck. If they'd split up, Chuck would be worried that she knew too much about his life. She talks out of turn somewhere, let something slip, something damning. If Chuck thought that — she'd be in danger. She might have been threatened already and decided to go back to her old name, low-profile.

No more Armani bags.

Speculation. Sometimes it opened doors.

She'd been with Chuck long enough to know something about his operations. And, who knows, she might be in a mood to tell. A woman scorned. *If* she'd been scorned. Maybe she was the one who'd dumped Chuck.

Perlman lit a cigarette and thought: I owe Sandy. When he first offered assistance in the matter of the hand, Perlman had promised to pass on anything of interest he happened across. And even if the investigation of Chuck had no connection to the discovery of the Ziploc bag, he should talk to Glorianna anyway — who knows? If she was responsive, maybe he could extract something useful about Chuck's operations to give Sandy. On a platter. Here, add this tasty scallion to your busy plate, Inspector.

A scallion for Scullion.

He went up to his bedroom and, kicking his shoes off, lay down fully clothed. His mind refused to shut off. The foundry pounded, the pistons pumped. He thought of a sleeping pill, but remembered he'd given his last to Betty.

He had the urge to phone her. Almost 1 a.m., he'd be interrupting her. He recalled sitting with her on the big couch and holding her hand to comfort her, and trying as gently as he could to steer the conversation away from death and loss. Sharing grief was demanding — but he enjoyed being with her even in dire moments, and there had been a few of those. But she laughed in her raw unfettered way when the mouse-trap snared him, and the sound delighted him, because it was a sign of life. Then she cried some more.

Talk to me about your life, Betty. In a nutshell: she'd never married. She'd been a middle-range secretary at the Grey and Dunne Biscuit company and then they'd cut staff back. After that she'd temped in one office after another. Finally she decided she'd make more money cleaning. And keep her own hours.

She fell asleep on the couch before he left and he'd kissed her forehead lightly, then he'd gone.

Now he wondered if she'd felt it.

34

Dysart scrubbed his hands in very hot water transformed by Dettol into the colour of thin milk. Nurse Payne handed him a towel, a pair of gloves, and tied a surgical mask over his mouth.

Scalpel, Dorcus said.

He surveyed the young man's white skin. He had a perfect navel, a little masterpiece of symmetry. His hair was gold and clean and his face unblemished. Dysart had seen him walking down Springkell Avenue near Maxwell Park, alone, pensive, loping along unhurriedly just before daybreak. He was an easy take, barely a struggle.

Scalpel, Nurse Payne.

Nurse Payne was slow today, mind elsewhere. She's worried.

He knew that.

He made the incision. The flesh yielded without resistance to the blade. This was his portal. From here he could go inside the boy's hidden places, advancing through an astonishing world of blood and tissue and organ.

Kidneys. Liver. Scarlet, rich in blood, protein.

He worked quickly.

Nurse Payne collected each organ after removal and wrapped it in sterilized cloth, and placed it in a blue plastic cooler stacked with packets of ice.

The heart was the last. The precious heart.

The surgical power saw buzzed in his hand as it carved through bone. Once inside the chest cavity, that cunningly fortified chamber, he carefully removed the heart, freeing it from its anchorage, the pulmonary veins, the sinus venarium, names he'd loved as a student. Before he got drummed out after pre-med. Rejected, denigrated. Don't have the right temperament, Dorcus. The Examining Board is sorry, but ... He remembered their smug faces, fake sympathetic comments, their criticism of what they called his 'temperament'. Not everybody makes it, Dorcus ...

Forget all those old farts.

He liked to hold a hot human heart in his hands. The life source, the vitality. Beating day and night. Whether its owner was awake or asleep, this miraculous device went on and on. Even when you took it out of one body and planted it in another it continued to work.

He removed his smock, gloves, mask and dropped them on the floor. He washed his hands in steaming water.

Nurse Payne took the cooler out of the surgery into the hallway. She set it down and looked at Dorcus. 'We have to quit for a while. We're running too many risks.'

'We need the money — '

'I'll postpone my plans for a time.'

Dorcus felt a quick fizz of anger directed at Glorianna. 'I should've refused when Mr Chuck offered to send that girl.'

'You couldn't. Why derail the gravy train.'

'If she hadn't sh-shown up so bloody early — '

296

He was conscious of time pressing him, he had to move the cooler, deliver it.

'Get over it. What worries me is Glorianna telling Chuck what she *might* have seen. Maybe all she got was a very *quick* glimpse of me through the steam, and nothing else.'

'If you'd *locked* the door,' Dorcus said. He picked up the cooler. He imagined he heard the heart beat weakly inside the container.

'I didn't *expect* her to come prowling upstairs, did I?'

'All I'm saying is *if* you'd locked the door — '

'Arguing doesn't change the facts. She might tell Chuck something *else* about her experience here — like how you totally lost control and smashed her phone. And he might think fuck you, Dorcus, nobody treats my girl like that, no more work.'

Dorcus was flustered, felt a tightening in his chest. He imagined dire possibilities. No more money from Chuck. And then there was the cop. 'I h-hate that old f-fuck Tartakower putting the cop on to you. Now there's this business with the hand.'

'I've thought about Tartakower. He'd be easy enough to find and old enough to scare.'

Dorcus could still sense Glorianna in this house. 'She didn't have to show up when we were work — '

'One of you got the wrong time. Pointless to argue.'

'I better go.' Dorcus went inside the bedroom, changed his clothes hurriedly.

When he came back out again she looked at

him and said, 'You need a haircut. I'll do it when you come back, love. That coat's on my dump list too. You need new clothes. You need to feel good about yourself . . . '

'First my hair, then my clothes.' He moved toward the stairs, and Nurse Payne followed him. As they descended Dorcus said, 'We never shouted at each other before. I didn't like it — '

She said, 'Neither did I.'

'I rushed out after her, I wanted to c-calm her down.'

'You don't radiate calm, Dorcus. All you had to do was *pretend* you enjoyed her touching you. Instead you left her alone to — oh, drop it.'

In the hallway she placed her hands on his shoulders and squeezed, as if to give him reassurance in a world that wasn't always charitable to him. 'Sometimes love isn't enough to get us through. We need to be practical . . . '

She was planning something, a precautionary measure, whatever, he knew that scheming light in her eyes. He loved how it gave her an authority he couldn't match.

He kissed her forehead. 'My precious lady.'

Jackie Ace smiled at him in an absent way, but she was elsewhere, gone to that place where she did her thinking.

★　★　★

Dorcus hated leaving her. It was as if he abandoned not only her but his strength. With her at his side he hardly ever stuttered or stammered.

298

Alone, he was at the mercy of language.

Dorcus in duffle-coat and glasses, the deliveryman. She was right. It's time to look different. A more mature look. He hadn't had his hair cut in three years. He hated the duffle-coat. He looked silly in it, like a simpleton who'd lost his bus-pass, or his library card.

He drove with the cooler on the floor at the passenger side. Every so often he glanced at it. Heart liver kidneys in an icebox. He had a thought he didn't like. If Tartakower could set that cop loose on Jackie, maybe he could also direct him to *me* . . . A cop at the gates.

Don't think that.

He reached The Gallowgate, turned up Melbourne Street. He was near the old abattoir. Every time he passed here he imagined cattle being herded inside to receive the stun-gun direct to the brain. He saw the animals going down on their front knees and then the slick slice of knife that slashed their windpipes.

He took a left along a narrow street and parked at the end of a lane where a company called Kanga Textiles was located inside a pristine cream-painted one-storey stone building behind a metal fence. A small grey car was parked beside the fence. Dorcus pamped the horn three times, which he'd been instructed to do by Mr Chuck at every delivery. A man came out and walked toward the van and opened the passenger door.

Dorcus said nothing. The man was a grave Oriental of about thirty-five. He was brisk, all business. Dorcus was glad he never demanded conversation. The man didn't ever look inside the cooler, never conversed. He was always in a rush.

Dorcus wondered vaguely about Kanga Textiles. There was never any movement inside the building. It's none of my business. I deliver, I get paid, the money goes to a good cause, the rest isn't my problem.

I won't be coming back again for a time.

The man took a thick white envelope from the pocket of his coat. He handed it to Dorcus, who didn't open it.

The man took the cooler. He got inside his car, squeezed it past Dorcus's van and drove off at speed. Dorcus stuffed the envelope inside his glovebox before he headed homeward, thinking overlapping thoughts — the pathetic cat he almost hit the other day, and the possibility of the cop coming into his life, but mainly of Jackie and how they'd protect one another and keep this sorry world's putrescence away.

35

Chuck walked through Glorianna's third-storey flat in Belmont Street. Noon, and still no sign of her. He hadn't heard from her since she'd gone to visit Dysart and that was about forty hours ago. He checked the bedroom first, thinking — what? He'd catch her with a man?

Would you be jealous —

No way — *me* jealous?

His brain was rumbling.

Four-poster bed empty, unmade, panties and bras in a white wicker laundry basket, a pile of skirts and blouses on an ironing-board. So where is she, where is she? Where's my wee Glori?

He wandered back out to the big open living room. He stared at a row of browning bonsai trees. How long since they'd been watered? He tested the earth with his fingertips. Dead dry.

Books lay in disturbed stacks. She reads, she reads. Does she ever finish a book? Most of them had strips torn from newspapers as markers. He scanned titles. *The Ultimate Self-Help Book. A Guide to Acting. The I-Ching For a New Age.* He recognized some of the titles as books Baba had recommended to him, none of which he'd ever read.

He saw piles of CDs and magazines and discarded T-shirts and jeans tossed aside. A mess, how different from the person she was at the Fitness Centre, where she was fastidious:

301

everything in its right place. He didn't know this side of her and somehow it caused him an ache — the Glorianna he never saw. The few times he'd come here in the past the flat was always spic. She must have cleaned it before he arrived. Look how nice I keep things, Rube.

The bathroom had knickers and towels on the floor. He bent, touched the towels, they were just slightly damp. So she'd bathed or showered — but when? After returning from Dysart? The questions, questions.

On the kitchen table a half-eaten Chinese take-away lay in congealed cornstarch. The noodles looked like dead flatworms.

He thought: She leaves Dorcus when? Early a.m., late p.m. — and no cabbie remembers picking her up and Mathieson squeezes no juice out of the gypsy cab people either and she hasn't answered my phone messages.

Where the fuck is she?

Angrily he kicked books around and knocked over a couple of plants and ripped some oriental scrolls from the off-white walls.

There. Fuckin cunt.

Leave me hangin, eh? Leave me without so much as a word, eh?

He stopped, breathless, heart going like a machine gun. He was furious with himself. For losing control. For sending Glori to Dysart in the first place, using her like she was just another bit of office equipment, an adding machine, a laptop.

Baba once said, *Arise each day, cherish your body, but remember you are foolish, ignorant and without understanding.*

That's me, he thought. Ignorant and without understandin.

All this time on the planet what have you learned?

He sat down, shut his eyes, inclined his head.

This mood was useless. He stirred himself, took his mobie from his coat and dialled Mathieson. Nothin. Why couldn't he get anybody on the fuckin telephone? Mathieson had dropped him off and then asked to use the Jag to run a quick errand, back in fifteen mins to pick you up, Mr Chuck, oh aye, so how come you're no answerin your mobie?

Mibbe Dorcus had lied.

What would Dorco gain from lying?

Where did he live? It was somewhere way out in the east of the city. He had it written down in his address book. What should he do — go out there with Mathieson and apply a wee bit of shoulder to the stutterin doc and see if he was holdin somethin back? Like what. A suspicion threw a wicked shadow across Chuck's mind. No, Dorco would *never* dream of applying his skills on Glorianna, not in a hundred years, a thousand. He'd be signing his own death-warrant, for Christ's sake.

Nobody was that stupid.

He called Mathieson again.

This time Ronnie picked up.

'Where inna fuck you been?' Chuck asked.

'I stopped to collect some shoes I had mended.'

'And you use the Jag for that? A fuckin trip to

the cobbler?' This anger was no easy thing to shake off. Veins popped in his neck. *Forchristsake cool down*.

'Do something useful, Ronnie. Check the hotels. Remember she could be usin her real name.'

'Will do,' Mathieson said.

Chuck clicked the off button.

He rolled up the shades and looked down into the street and saw two uniformed cops stroll past. Beat polis, doin the neighbourhood thing. We're your friendly Glasgow polismen. Need any help? Cat stuck up a tree needin rescue?

Fuckin windowdressin.

He suddenly remembered Rick Tosh. Tosh hadn't phoned to verify that bank deposit. This worried Chuck — were there problems Tosh hadn't told him about? He found Tosh's number on the Contacts list of his mobie and punched it in, without thinking of time-zones — night or day in Texas? was Tosh asleep? Who gives a shit.

The phone was answered after two rings and Chuck said, 'I wake you, Rick?'

'I never sleep,' Tosh said. 'What's the skinny over there?'

The *skinny*, Chuck thought. He didn't even try to keep up with Yankee slang. Fuck, why should he? When Tosh was in Glasgow he didn't ask what a *rammy* meant and *stoater* went right over his head. No curiosity, some of these Yanks. The whole world was America to them.

'What news of that transfer,' Chuck said.

'Yeah, been a slight delay, sorry.'

'Delay. What are you tellin me?'

'Don't sweat it, Rube. Seems like there's a holiday of some kind in Luxembourg, so even though the money's been wired, the banks are empty.'

'I thought it was all done automatic these days.'

Tosh said, 'Well, there's automatic and there's automatic, if you know what I mean.'

'Millions of dollars waitin for some fuckin clerk to punch a button or two, what kind of set-up is this? Just keep a very close eye on it, Rick.'

'My eyes are never shut, Rube. Now you come to Texas, you hear?'

'When that cash arrives, you never know.'

'You ever eaten barbecued dillo?'

'Zat one of they prickly fuckers?'

'Tastes like sweet pig. Fingerlicking good.'

'Aye, well, you call me,' Chuck said, and hung up.

A delay in Luxembourg. Some days were bad from the start. What if Tosh was a con? OK, Tosh had supported the overthrow of Stoker and Curdy because *his* bosses told him they wanted a younger man to run some of their interests in Glasgow: guys like Stoker and Curdy were getting old and lazy. But that support didn't mean a bucket of pish in this world. Tosh's bosses, whoever they were, could change their mind at the drop of a wee jobby. He imagined them sometimes — overweight Americans, big fucking rings, western cowboy's suits, bola ties, mirrored aviator sunglasses, pompadour hair-cuts.

He didn't like wondering if Tosh was on the level. It was more clutter than he needed. I want a Valium, sort myself out, calm myself down. He searched the bathroom, rummaging through all Glorianna's mysteries. Skin moisturizers, talc, creams, false nails. Tiny glass tubes of essential oils — why were they *essential*? Dr Bonner's Peppermint soap. Fuck this, where are the meds?

Glorianna come back to me, doll.

He spotted a handful of prescription bottles tucked away at the back and pulled them out. He sat on the toilet and read the labels. What was Celebrex and Zithromac and Aciclovir and Buspar? Was Glori using this stuff? He recognized none of these names. This was useless. He only wanted common everyday Valiumsky.

OK. Another solution. He'd get a taxi, go to the Temple, seek out Baba. So it wasn't a quick fix, maybe no fix at all. Plus he'd sworn off fuckin drink, pills and sex — and look at the state of him, squattin, surrounded by drugs like a junkie, turnin Glasgow upside down for a wee lassie whose heid was filled with Hollywood dreams.

Big fuckin man.

The city is yours — but not the girl.

He was about to rise when he heard a familiar voice.

Perlman said, 'There's a sight I would've paid money to see. Reuben Chuck on the toilet.'

Chuck looked up, surprised. 'What the fuck are *you* doin here?'

'A more interesting question is what are *you* doing there?'

'Looking for a headache cure.' Chuck thought, eejit, I didn't owe him an answer. Why offer one? Perlman sometimes put a question in such a fashion that if you didn't answer you left him an opening, which he often used to his own advantage.

Perlman glanced at the bottles, shook his head. He picked up a couple from the floor, shook one in each hand, making a sound like maracas. 'Cha cha cha. Tried aspirin?'

'Aspirins? Never crossed my mind.'

'Any chemist shop will have them. Just ask.'

'Right enough.' The indignity of Perlman finding him on the crapper was bad enough, but what the fuck *was* he doing here? He got up quickly.

'You left the front door unlocked,' Perlman said.

'And you just popped in.'

'I'm like that. Unlocked doors tempt me. You never know what you're going to find.'

'Depends what you're lookin for.'

Perlman scanned the bathroom. 'Smells like a high-class bordello in here.' He walked out of the bathroom and into the living-area. 'Ah, you had the demolition crew in, I see.' He picked up an overturned plant and righted it. I'm becoming Betty-like.

'It was like this when I got here,' Chuck said, wondering why he felt the need to explain *anything* to Perlman, when it should have been the other way round. Perlman could talk you into a dance, all the while pretending he was following your steps when in fact he was the one leading you. Smart fucker, it was so easy to be bamboozled by his sleakit manner and his battered coat.

You always had to be on your toes with the Jew.

Perlman sat on the sofa and placed his hands on his knees. 'Nice flat. Once you ignore the wreckage.'

Chuck said, 'You're trespassin.'

'I'm looking for Glorianna.'

Chuck thought: No, I'm no goin to ask why, no way, if he thinks I am, he's gonny wait a long time. I show this fucker too much respect.

Perlman said, 'You know where she is?'

'I always know where she is.'

'But you're not telling me.'

Chuck said, 'What's this, a polis state all of a sudden?'

Perlman yawned, didn't bother to cover it. 'That line's grown a beard, Chuck. Polis state — the evasion of last resort. You can do better than that.'

'I'm savin my best answers for another time.'

'I suspect you don't have any best answers, Rube.'

'Sez you.'

'You don't have the equipment.' Perlman tapped his skull. 'Somebody asks you a question you don't like, you jump on a slogan straight away. A polis state, there's a good example.'

'You piss me off sometimes, Perlman.'

'Another zippy riposte.' Perlman stretched his legs, crossed them. 'You're going out of your heid wondering why I want to see Glorianna

— or is it Annie — but you think it's a weakness to ask.'

'We've split up, Perlman. She lives her own life. Comes and goes as she pleases. I look like I give a fuck?'

'So why are you here rummaging through her medications?'

'That's my business.'

'You're peeing your pants to know if I had an appointment with her. You're gagging to ask. Does she have something she wants to get off her chest, something she needs to tell me? What a mystery. If I was you, I'd be chewing my insides.' Perlman got up and slowly roamed the room.

Chuck said, 'You're fulla shite. Why would she have an appointment with you when you've been drummed out the Force? If she had anythin she wanted the polis for, which I seriously doubt, she'd want a *real* polisman, and that rules you out, pal.'

'That's better, Rube. You're getting the hang of it.' Perlman got up, stared out of the window. 'Two guys are sitting in a car down there. They yours?'

'Mine?'

'Black leather jackets, serious expressions. Minders?'

'They're nothin to do with me.'

Perlman said, 'It's got to be a very shaky proposition running a gang, Rube.'

'Gang? Whit gang? You polis all live in a comic-book world.'

'Do you ever wonder what all these wee men are thinking about The Big Man? They must talk about you. The Big Man says this, the Big Man does that. Mibbe they're critical. Mibbe they don't like some of the things you do, the decisions you make. Mibbe some of them feel a little leftover allegiance to Citizen Stoker or the late Curdy — '

'You're a flowin river of shite.'

'In your shoes, I'd be lying awake at night wondering if I hear anything moving in the bushes, worrying about this guy or that guy, are they plotting against me? I'd be on a tightrope, Rube. I'd need a second army to protect me from the army that's already protecting me.'

Chuck laughed. 'Some imagination, Perlman. A second army. You're a comedian.'

'And I'd be worrying about the polis as well. What are they up to? What do they know? They're fucking sly bastarts.'

'You should know — '

'And their powers, oy. Search and seizure. Imprisonment without specifying a charge under the new terrorist laws.'

'I look a terrorist? You see a towel round my heid?'

Perlman sailed on. 'You don't know half the powers they possess. Oh the pressures. They'd wear anybody down so fine you could pour them through a salt-cellar.' Perlman strolled the room again, singing quietly to himself, 'These Sleepless Nights Will Break My Heart in Two'.

'I've heard craws with better voices, Perlman.'

'I wasn't aware I was singing.'

'Sign of old age,' Chuck said. 'I was about to

leave when you came in. You've cured my headache though.'

'I thought you had a guru for that.'

'Oh aye. Your mate Scullion's a nosy bastart.'

'He keeps an eye on you, Rube. He's manic when it comes to you.'

Chuck felt little thrusts of pressure in his head. 'He's got me aw hot and bothered, I don't think.'

'You should be. You're number one on his list.'

'Number one, eh? Top of the pops. I'm a hit.'

Perlman smiled. 'He'll get you, Rube. Don't have any illusions about that.'

'He'd need to be awfy sharp off the mark. He's on to plums, Perlman.'

'Sharp *and* relentless.'

Chuck clapped Perlman on the back as he edged him toward the door. Scullion, he thought. Perlman delivers rave notices about his old china. *He'll get you, Rube.*

Predictable pish.

'I'll walk out with you.'

On the landing Chuck locked the door, turning the key twice. He went downstairs with Perlman and into the street.

'Here, try my bistro some might,' Chuck said.

'What's it called? The Pissed Ox?'

Chuck released a big fake laugh. 'You know the fuckin name.'

'Too rich for my blood,' Perlman said. 'When I'm flush, mibbe.'

'The chef's a fuckin magician.'

'So I hear.'

Perlman walked toward his car.

Chuck laughed at the Ka. 'You driving a

purple flyin saucer these days?'

'I boldly go,' Perlman said.

Chuck watched him drive away. He didn't believe Perlman had a meeting with Glori. She'd never set up such a thing. Perlman was a liar, a good liar, but a liar all the same. What roused the hissing snakes in Chuck's head was the simple question he couldn't find an answer for: why had Perlman come here if Glori hadn't asked him?

Simple question, my arse. There's no such thing any more.

Complex world.

The Jaguar approached and braked beside him. Ron Mathieson got out and opened the back door for him.

Chuck got in. 'The Temple, Ron.'

'Right-o Mr Chuck.'

36

Perlman made a phone call to The Triangle Club from his car. A girl answered, sing-song little voice. 'Fi-on-a. How can I help you?'

Perlman had hoped he'd get the irrepressible Rhoda. 'Is Jackie working tonight?'

'She's here training some new dealers. Hang on, I'll get her for you.'

Perlman cut the connection. He'd have Dysart to himself. Good.

He travelled east through a heavy drizzle that had just begun. He thought about bumping into Chuck, the human smear test. The slick-haired douchebag had looked ill at ease, which could be ascribed to Lou's unexpected appearance — but more. Chuck was obviously undone because he couldn't find Glorianna, and it was twanging on his nerves like a truly awful country song. His tics came into urgent play. The hollow laugh, the way the eyes protruded, two black moons expanding from internal pressures. Chuck was running on low, and vulnerable, and his lies were as transparent as a school of jellyfish.

Reuben Chuck always left a sour taste in Lou's mouth, like he'd sucked on the heart of a lime.

So where are you, Chuck's golden girl?

He found the house much as The Pickler had described it, an unexpected red sandstone Victorian, high-walled, gated, austere in its dilapidation. Tall chimneys crumbled, chimney-pots were missing. He parked a few yards away from the gates. He heard dogs bark with the sound of hand-grenades exploding.

He could see, beyond the walls, the rooftops of the housing scheme with their satellite dishes. In the hardening rain the view was dismal. Maybe once, in the dreamy summer days before The Great War, the house had been enchanting and toffs came out to visit in their primitive motor cars or graceful horse-drawn carriages, and tea was served on the lawn by a cast of low-bred maids happy to be on tuppence a week. He'd always thought it curious how you never saw horse-droppings in old sepia tints of the city.

He hesitated before getting out of the car, checked to see if he'd brought his umbrella. A pair of old leather gloves, but no fucking *brolly*. He was going to get wet no matter what. He hated damp overcoats, leaky shoes, water dripping down his face. *I belong to Glasgow* — and yet. Sometimes the bones yearned for warmer places, blue skies, blue sea. He pulled on the gloves, his hands were chilled.

He opened the car door, slammed it, caught his raincoat. Bloody rain was chucking down now. He opened the door again, freed his coat, hurried to the gate and pressed the enamel button set in the wall. Two big Dobermans appeared beyond the gates, white-fanged, barking with harsh savagery.

We guard this space. We are Dobes, the SS of dogs. My name is Heinrich, my chum is Rudi.

Nobody answered the bell. He rang again and made angry growling sounds at the dogs, inciting

314

them to jump. They obliged, rose on their hind legs, flattened themselves against the gates. They were six feet or more fully extended. Huge buggers.

A man appeared on the gravel driveway beyond the gates. He had a yellow plastic raincoat over his head and he ran hunched against the downpour. When he reached the gates he calmed the dogs while he scrutinized Perlman's face.

Perlman introduced himself. He uttered his name and rank in the stern tone of a debt-collector. He knows my name, Perlman thought. Jackie told him.

The man wore glasses and had the expression of a worried scholar interrupted on the last page of his monumental PhD thesis. 'What is it, s-something w-wrong?'

A stutter. Perlman always had a soft spot for anyone even slightly disadvantaged. 'You're Dysart?'

'Doctor Dysart.' He uttered his title proudly, without faltering.

'Doctor Dysart, eh? I'd like a word.'

'With me?'

'You see anyone else? Do I have to stand out here getting drooned?'

Dysart offered a small awkward smile and said, 'M-my manners. I don't get a lot of company. In a place like this,' and he gestured with his head toward the housing scheme. 'I k-keep to myself.'

'Understandable. A rough element.'

Dysart unlocked the gates. He grabbed the

315

Dobermans by their collars and yanked them aside with enormous effort. They eyed Perlman and snarled.

I am top of their foodie wish-list, Lou thought.

He stepped through the gate, which Dysart immediately locked. Still straining with the dogs, Dysart led the way up the drive toward the house. He released the dogs, shooing them off with wild hand gestures, and they scudded away into the rain.

Dysart went inside, dropping his mac on the floor. Perlman followed him along the hallway, noticing a pair of gloomy oil portraits that seemed to scrutinize him, as if they suspected an admission fee was being avoided.

'In here please.' Dysart showed Perlman into a room with drawn blinds. An old rolltop desk, a couple of worn leather chairs, a wood floor badly wormholed. Dysart switched on a desk lamp, which gave a frugal light.

'I leave the b-blinds down . . . for privacy. Sometimes Slabbite spawn climb the walls.'

'Slabbite?'

'From over there,' and Dysart nodded toward the scheme. 'They try to see in. They g-give me a hard time.' He sat down and grinned unexpectedly, as if a funny thought had popped into his mind. It gave his mouth a lopsidedness. Perlman had the impression of a man not entirely attuned to the exchanges of everyday life, but trying hard to figure them out for the sake of sociability. The smart navy blue blazer and grey flannels he wore seemed to make him uncomfortable. He sported them as a dummy in a tailor's window might.

316

Perlman was drawn to a diploma on the wall: University of Glasgow, the degree of Doctor of Medicine conferred on Dorcus Dysart, June 1997. 'Are you in practice? Here, maybe you can advise me about these painkillers I'm told to take, personally I think they're far too strong — '

Dysart interrupted. 'I used to w-work in hospitals. But n-not now. I don't like them.'

'Hate them myself. What's your reason.'

'They're t-too impersonal. I n-never felt at ease.'

Perlman didn't probe this line. He suspected he knew where it would lead. He'd learn that Dysart wasn't really a team player. Something about him suggested the nervous loner who wandered the night shift corridors, riding the lifts as much as he could, trying to avoid the nurses who jokingly flirted with him.

Dysart asked, 'What can I do for you, Sergeant?'

'I have a report of a woman seen running out of this house a couple of nights ago. In some distress, it seems. Tell me about it.'

'A woman? N-no woman was *here*.'

'So the report is false.'

'Yes certainly *yes*. A complete lie. A Slabbite lie.'

'They do this kind of thing often?'

'Oh they do much w-worse. Trash my yard. S-say all kinds of things. They call me a p-pederast. Or I'm a junkie doctor struck off. My hou-house is haunted.' Dysart shrugged and waved a hand as if to dismiss the effect the Slabbites had on him.

'Haunted, eh? Ghosts and things that go bumpetty in the night?'

'I suppose so . . . They don't know any b-better, Sergeant. Poor education, b-bad health system. Society fails so many people.'

He tolerates the unwashed plebs, Perlman thought. Nice guy. What could it be like to live in a house this alienated from its neighbours, a house from another era? You'd be the object of all kinds of suspicion and scandal. It was a tradition — yobs united against the big house, which symbolized a resented upperclass. Name-calling, spreading rumours, throwing shite over the walls: Perlman could see it. One day they'd probably torch the place. History was relentlessly cyclical.

'You seen anything of a supernatural nature yourself?'

Dysart shook his head. 'I'm a realist.'

'What do you mean by realist?'

'I mean . . . I b-believe in what I c-can see and touch.'

'And nothing beyond.'

'A . . . such as?'

'Faith, for instance. In God.'

'I don't have faith in any God.'

'A godless man, eh?'

'That m-makes me sound t-terrible. Call me agnostic.'

'So you're waiting for proof, or divine manifestation, or a deathbed conversion.'

'Any of the above.' Dysart smiled and seemed pleased with himself, visibly a little more relaxed, as if Perlman's questions were part of a test he'd been rehearsed to pass.

Perlman thought, Basic Conversation, Book One.

'Live alone?'

'Yes.'

'Monster house for one,' Perlman said.

'M-most of the rooms don't get used.' Dysart ran a hand across his short hair.

'I'd really enjoy a guided tour.'

'There's n-not much to see. Unless you have a taste for damp empty r-rooms — '

'Damp, give me damp over dry every time. If I enter a room that isn't damp my body cries out, Turn around, get out, we'll turn into a prune, Lou.'

'You need a certain amount of m-moisture in the air. For health.'

'Exactly.' Perlman smiled, removed a glove, took out his small notebook and wrote something down, then replaced the glove. Scribbling in a notebook sometimes caused people to become ill at ease. They felt they were being recorded for an inscrutable official purpose, and so they became nervous and garbled. He wrote: *bollocks*, underlined it, and shut the notebook.

'So you make a living how?'

'I was left some m-money. And the house of course.'

'Big upkeep.'

'It's a weight, granted.' Dysart's hand flew to the knot of his tie as if he'd suddenly discovered a growth beneath his larynx.

Doesn't like neckties. Only wears them

— when? Social gatherings? Restaurants? Why was he wearing one today? Expecting company? 'I assume the legacy you got isn't enough to cover everything that needs repairing.'

'There's wet rot in the basement — '

'Wet rot? *Christ*. Talk to me about wet rot. You don't get that seen to, it spreads like the plague. I had some in my own cellar. I live in an old house myself, not huge like yours, but a total pain in the arse maintaining it all the same.' Like I try. Perlman shook his head in sympathy.

'I have plans,' Dysart said, brightening. 'I've t-talked to architects and b-builders about restoration. This house d-deserves to be restored. It really d-does.'

Perlman wrote in his notebook again. *Call Betty*. He wrote it on the page where he'd placed Kirk McLatchie's snapshot, which he'd meant to return, but forgotten: holes in his memory nets wide enough for schools of dolphin to pass through. 'Forgive my curiosity, awful habit. Has it ever crossed your mind to sell, since you don't have the wherewithal to maintain?'

'Are y-you trying to give me financial advice?'

Perlman laughed and made it sound hearty, two pals enjoying a chuckle and a coupla pints. 'I'm the last person, Dorcus. All right if I call you Dorcus?'

'Feel free.' Dysart clearly wasn't sure it was all right.

Lack of trust. He's unhappy, a cop in his house. Most people are. Most people have some secret they'd prefer to keep. What's yours, Dorcus?

'My bank manager pulls a paper bag over his head and tries to hide every time I enter the bank,' Perlman said.

Dysart issued a thin laugh and ran his fingertips down the sharp creases in his trousers. Good hands, Perlman noticed. Sensitive fingers, such as you'd expect to find on a violinist. The nails had been buffed and trimmed. Recently, too. They hadn't had time to become imperfect. So, a necktie he isn't accustomed to wearing, a new manicure, throw in the good blazer and flannels with creases you could cut yourself on, *plus* the neatly laced sensible black shoes built to outlast ocean liners — is Dysart dressed up for going out, or waiting for somebody to come in? Such finicky questions. The polisman's mind, all fluff sticks. I'm DS Velcroheid, pleased to meetcha.

Dysart said, 'Are you done with me?'

'Just about. I wonder if you'd mind,' and Perlman suddenly tugged the chord that released one of the blinds and it ravelled at velocity, exposing window, overgrown gardens, tops of the towers. He needed a sense of the outside. The melancholy atmosphere of this house was a weight on him.

'I t-told you I never raise the b-blinds.' Dysart blinked several times, and got up from his chair and walked quickly into the hallway.

'Sorry.' Perlman went after him. 'A wee bit of light just helps me see better. We can talk here, I don't mind.'

'I thought w-we were finished — '

'Two minutes, I promise. So you don't want to

sell up. Old family home, emotional bonds. I understand. But this place is a money-pit, and if your inheritance isn't enough I assume you work at something else. Odd jobs here and there, this and that.'

'I h-have just about enough to live on. But n-not enough for all the planned r-repairs. I'm talking to some people from the National Trust, b-because they often finance this kind of work.'

'Civil servants. Paperwork. It's a mire sometimes.'

'They've b-been very optimistic about funds.'

'I hear it's a lottery. I hope you get lucky.' Perlman gazed into the room he'd just vacated. Rain thudded into the grass and bent the branches of trees and blew over the towers, causing the satellite dishes to quiver. 'Does Jackie kick in a few pounds now and again to help?'

'Jackie?' Dysart looked as if he was about to deny knowing anybody called Jackie. 'I n-never ask Jackie for anything.'

'I just thought since you and her have been friends a long time, mibbe she'd lend a hand. I imagine she makes good money at The Triangle.'

'Don't think I'm rude, Sergeant, but I answered what you c-came to ask me, and I d-don't feel easy talking to a stranger about m-my m-monetary situation or p-personal matters.'

Perlman coughed into his gloved hand, then took a packet of cigarettes from his pocket and eased one out. 'You mind?'

'I do m-mind as a matter of fact. But s-smoke

if you n-need to. All smokers are selfish.'

'I won't smoke if you don't want me to.'

'No, smoke.' Dysart moved toward the front door and bent down to pick up his wet plastic mac. 'You c-could quit if you had the willpower.'

'If I ruled the world.' Perlman lit the cigarette and quietly admired the layered patterns of rising smoke a moment. 'You got an ashtray?'

'I don't *s-smoke*. Why would I have an ashtray?'

'That's a very good point, Dorcus.'

Dorcus slung the mac over a peg in the wall. 'I th-think the rain's letting up.'

He wants me out, Perlman thought. Jackie Ace was the same, wanted him out. I'm a serpentine presence, he thought. A suit filled with rattlers.

'When you worked with Jackie at Tartakower's chop-shop, what did you do there? Some cutting, a little butchery, this and that?'

'T-Tartakower — is that wh-why you're really here?'

'In a roundabout way, aye. But do me a favour, drop the big astonishment act. One, you're no good at it. And two, I know Jackie's told you we talked and Tartakower's name came up.'

Dysart had the expression of a man who'd always hoped his past misdeeds had been forgotten, only now somebody had come along to expose them. He was the kind of *schlemiel* Perlman always *wished* he could give a break, not just because of the stutter, but because he transmitted rays of old hurts, the strange guy routinely singled out for mockery by careless

323

teachers and cruel school-mates and, later in life, by heartless nurses or callous professors. What did he feel when he heard laughter behind his back or when somebody impersonated his impediment?

'I'm not interested in anything you did in your Tartakower days, Dorcus.'

'You're not?'

'Far as I'm concerned, that's bygones.'

'Then w-why are you here?'

Perlman walked in deliberate little circles and talked in a patient manner about the severed hand. He explained he was following up this information, he wasn't here to make accusations or bring charges, this was — oh that dear wrinkled old chestnut plucked from the fire — routine. Did Dysart understand?

Dysart had been leaning against the wall with his arms tightly crossed and his eyes fixed to the floor all the time Perlman talked. Only when Perlman finished did he raise his face and look at him. 'So the w-woman you said y-you were looking for, that was a pretext — '

'No, that was a genuine report.'

'Now you're talking about s-something t-totally different. I c-can't follow you. I never c-cut off anyone's hand. I *never* did anything like that.'

'I'm not accusing you, Dorcus.'

'B-but you're thinking I did — '

'No, no, I told you, I'm only making inquiries.'

'T-tartakower's c-crazy. You can't b-believe anything he ever says. He tells ter-terrible stories and . . . ' Dysart faltered, brain-blocked.

324

This stutter was agony to Perlman: so what was it like for Dysart, who heard his own mangled words echo in his ears? Perlman wished he could grab him around the chest and perform a kind of Heimlich that would free the wordjam. 'I didn't say I *believed* Tartakower, Dorcus.'

'How can I t-trust you? It s-seems p-peculiar you come here about one th-thing and then suddenly move on to something else — '

'Sorry if I give you the impression of a deception.'

'You set t-traps. That's wha-what you do.'

'Is that what you think?' *Trapper Lou. Snowshoes and caribou pelt and an Eskimo wife called Nanda*. He was finished with his cigarette. He wondered where he could put the stub. He raised his eyebrows at Dorcus, who was conscious of Perlman's little predicament but offered no suggestion.

Perlman said, 'No ashtray, no sweat. Smokers are ingenious. I can hold it until it dies completely, then I can stick it in my pocket.'

'A smoker's d-dilemma,' Dorcus said.

'One among many.' Perlman smiled his biggest smile, the one reserved for the admission of his own weakness.

'Think of your lungs.'

'I never stop,' Perlman said.

'Think of emphysema. Then you need a portable oxygen supply if you g-go out. I'm only p-pointing these things out as a doctor.'

'Your concern's noted. You're just not the kind of guy who'd inflict a needless cruelty. Like cutting off somebody's hand.'

'N-never.'

Perlman felt a floorboard move underfoot. Joists creaked. All this talk of cigarette diseases screwed with his head, accentuated his own lugubrious fears. And the house was having a disquieting effect on him too, as if in other rooms people were sharing whispered secrets. It was like a weird dream — you hear whispers, you burst into the room, nobody's there, just a circle of empty chairs still warm from recent use. But no evidence of anyone. He was tuning in to the sounds and rhythms of an old house dying, that was all. Every ancient house had its own terminal illness, its idiosyncratic gasps and sighs as extinction loomed.

The portraits glowered at him. *What are you really here for, Perlman? Have you come to bully our son?* The woman seemed to be fading into a mauve nothingness, a lavender afterlife.

Perlman asked, 'Your parents?'

Dysart said yes.

Perlman regarded the portrait of Dysart's father, the sterile blue of the eyes. He edged a little further down the hall. A staircase rose into dusky uncertainty.

'So what kind of shape is it in up there?'

'Y-you won't be happy until you g-get the tour, will you?'

'Honest, I wouldn't mind a gander. OK with you?' Perlman shook the handrail and then, without Dysart's approval, climbed the first four or five steps. The staircase was infirm, but it wasn't exactly on the edge of collapse.

Dysart caught up with him. 'Wait.'

He doesn't want me to go up here. And yet — Perlman had the inexplicable feeling that for some reason Dysart *did* want him to explore. Why the mixed signals, the scrambled radar? The atmosphere of this house, the brooding light, Dysart's stiff awkwardness, his *strangeness* — a combination of them all, who could say?

Perlman paused on the stairs and let Dysart lead the way up.

At the top Dysart said, 'There's r-really n-nothing of interest.' He moved down a long hall that stretched into a series of closed doors.

'You could have a bowling-alley here,' Perlman said.

Dysart opened the first door he came to, and showed Perlman a room, bare and carpetless, walls with faded spots where mirrors or pictures had hung.

'This was my f-father's bedroom,' Dysart said.

'What did you do — hock the furniture?'

'I had no n-need for it . . . '

'You and your Dad got along?'

'We g-got on all right. He was a judge.' Dysart was fidgety. He fiddled with the tie knot a couple of times, then adjusted the buckle of his belt.

'You like this room, Dorcus?'

'It's j-just a room, a b-bare room.'

Problems with Dad, Perlman wondered. Fair to assume? The portrait downstairs was of an aloof man, a severe man who maybe didn't have time for a kid. A judge, for God's sake, what could you expect? Perlman had never met a judge he liked. They were all black-cloaked gods of their own demonic little worlds.

He followed Dysart back into the hall.

Dysart opened another door and showed him a room similar to the judge's — no furnishing, no carpet, bare walls. Acrid mildew permeated both rooms.

'This was m-my mother's room, b-before . . . '

'Before what?'

'She g-got sick and we h-had to s-send her to hospital.'

Bad memories of mother. Sickness and loss. Perlman didn't feel like lingering in this room. He was cold. The deeper you went into this house, the colder it seemed to get. He felt a draught from somewhere. He surreptitiously dropped his dead cigarette-end on the floor.

'How do you heat this place?'

'There's an oil central-heating s-system that n-needs a new boiler. You don't notice the cold after you've lived h-here a while.'

I'd notice if I lived here an eternity, Perlman thought, and moved back into the hall and turned the handle of the next door he reached. It didn't yield.

'Oh that r-room's locked, Sergeant.'

'What's in here?'

'It's only s-some old stuff.'

'Got a key?'

'I have a k-key, yeh.' Dysart reached into his pocket and produced a ring of keys. He inserted one into the lock, click, pushed the door open.

Perlman said, 'After you.'

Dysart stepped into the room, where half-open slatted white blinds allowed strips of insipid grey light to enter. Perlman was instantly struck by two layers of scents, one the cloying perfume of an air-freshener liberally applied, the other an underscent of disinfectant that reminded him of the time he'd spent in hospital with the gunshot wound. He was also conscious of smooth white walls, a bed with a white lacy quilt, a stainless steel sink with long-stemmed taps. Beside the bed was a wooden locker painted white. Halfway up the wall a shower head had been installed behind a frosted glass partition, the door of which lay open. Inside was a sponge in a ceramic dish, a bar of Nivea soap still in its box, and a full bottle of Pantene shampoo.

White-tiled floors and a mix of scents and soap in a box.

This room troubles me. It's not right. Or maybe it was just Dysart's presence that made him feel this way. Something about Dysart, a quality of combustibility, say, as if inside his head a lake of lava simmered.

He looked up at the ceiling and saw two light fixtures that contained no bulbs. Then he turned and noticed a wheelchair folded in the corner, beside a small white sitz-bath.

The thought popped: Somebody died here.

He looked at Dysart and asked, 'Your mother?'

Dysart said, 'When she c-came home from Hairmyres Hospital this was her r-room. My father had it specially prepared for her. He didn't want her dying in a hospital. We had a p-private nurse for her. The room's pretty much as it was when she passed away.'

Makes sense, who wants to die in a hospital.

He looked at the bedside locker. 'Mind if I take a peek?'

'I don't know why you'd want to. But g-go ahead. It's not l-locked.'

Perlman opened it. Inside lay some personal items, presumably the property of the late Mrs Dysart. He found a slender silver watch, a well-thumbed deck of cards, a spray-bottle labelled Essence of Rose, and a book called *A Life of Elizabeth the First*. A long-dead rose was stuck somewhere in the middle, a withered bookmark. Mrs Dysart hadn't finished the book. She probably knew the ending anyway.

Dysart looked at the stuff. 'She suffered. It w-was so t-terrible to watch.'

'I can imagine.' The unbearable nature of human endings. The way death ate through tissue day by day, the erosion of the will to endure.

'She c-couldn't breathe. My f-father brought in cylinders of oxygen. I watched the n-nurse put a mask on her face. She fought for life, you know. She didn't j-just give in. M-my father spent hours with h-her in this room. Sometimes he fell asleep sitting on the edge of the b-bed.'

'Devoted.'

'Completely. He n-never believed she really died. He always thought she c-could be contacted.' Dorcus looked alarmed, stung by the pain of an old memory. 'He h-held s-seances in the d-dining room all the time. I w-wasn't supposed to l-look b-but I sneaked in.'

Seances. Congregations of optimists. 'Ever see anything?'

'People lighting candles and h-holding hands and praying. My f-father never knew I was w-watching. I h-hid behind a curtain, s-scared — all these p-people praying to the spirit w-world and calling out m-my mother's name. And my f-father would sink h-his head into his hands and s-sob, it was . . . terrifying. I k-kept thinking oh these are all g-grown up people, they kn-know what they're d-doing, so I expected m-my m-mother to appear, I always did. I w-watched shadows in the l-lamp and imagined I could s-see her b-but it w-wasn't her . . . '

A small kid gatecrashes a seance. A child on the edge of a world of mysterious suggestions, candle flames flickering, the company of adults who believed in the penetrability of the other side. How did this experience affect a kid's mind?

Dysart said, 'This room is an unhappy place.'

'So why keep it this way?'

Dysart shrugged. 'To remind me. I s-suppose.'

'My own feelings about the dead. You bury them. You remember them. You move on. You don't linger the way you do.'

'I d-don't c-come in here and t-talk to her or anything c-crazy like that. I d-don't come in here at all in f-fact.'

'Unless you have a janitor, you must come in sometimes. I don't see any webs, and I don't see dust. And obviously you disinfect. I'd say you disinfected quite recently. Then you sprayed something else to cover the pong, Dorcus.'

'W-well, of course, I come in now and then to c-clean.'

'I'm wondering why you spray the place this heavily.'

'Because I remember this r-room *always* smelled of rose oil. It smothered m-me. After my father died, I s-started to use the d-disinfectant. Sometimes the d-disinfectant is too s-strong so I spray something s-sweet over it. But not r-rose, n-never rose.'

A panoply of scents. Perlman folded his arms across his chest, and rocked very slightly against the wall. 'You and Jackie — do you ever come in here?'

'No.'

The Pickler said he saw this room *lit* the night Jackie was here. Unless he was dreaming or deluded. He'd been sober that night.

The room was cold and had all the welcome of a deep-freeze. Perlman pictured Mrs Dysart in this bed, covered by the white quilt. Death was everywhere in the air here — the mother, the seances actively seeking to communicate with her, the house itself dying.

'You don't really use this room for anything.'

'Right.'

'But you lock it.'

'Yes.'

'Why? What's to steal? Anyway, what burglar's going to get past the mighty Dobermans?'

'S-somebody might.'

'Did you bring the girl to this room?'

'G-girl?'

'Girl, Dorcus. The one who ran away?'

'N-no, I never brought h-her in here.'

'You admit she *was* here, right?'

'N-no, I d-don't admit that, I don't.'

'She was seen. She was heard shouting.'
Perlman paused a moment on the cusp of a lie.
Go for it. 'She already told me you brought her
here.'

'I d-don't believe you. There's no g-girl.'

'Why was she so scared, Dorcus? What did you
do to terrify her?'

'If you t-talked to her, why don't you ask her
y-yourself?'

'I want to hear it from you, Dorcus. Tell me
what you did. Bring her in here and tell her some
ghostie stories and scare her? Maybe you had her
witless and trembling. She's susceptible, she
believes your stories — '

'P-Perlman, no, how m-many times — '

'Mibbe I'm wrong about ghost stories. Mibbe
you keep some of your old instruments from
Tartakower days and you dragged them out and
scared her shitless. You might even have tied her
down on this bed and pretended she was a client
at Tartakower's and you just couldn't help
yourself, trip back in time, memory lane, good
old days at Tarty's, eh? Just a game, you told her.
And you had the scalpels all ready and shining,
and maybe some chloroform handy, and let's say
she was too drunk to resist, too snookered to
know it was only a harmless game.'

'No, n-no — '

'Speak to me Dorcus. Speak.'

'I d-don't have anything to say — '

Perlman stared into Dysart's eyes. What did he
see there — fear? Sickness?

Old instruments from chop-shop days.

The idea kicked and turned inside his head. Ill-shaped mirages shifted disconcertingly at the back of his skull. He had a vibe of the kind he'd had a thousand times in his career, and it was something he'd learned not to ignore. *Old instruments.* Sometimes the phantoms took shape, sometimes they didn't, then the vibe, the instinct, call it what you like, vanished.

But he had something. He knew it. He wished it was clear.

'I n-need to f-eed the dogs, Perlman. It's that time — '

'The dogs can wait. Answer my questions.'

'*I n-need to feed them.*'

Perlman couldn't shake the smells of this room. They wrapped themselves around him, choked him. He remembered lying in a hospital ward, his shoulder burning, his mind swept out to sea on the good ship pethidine. The smell of the ward. The nurses floating like apparitions. He had a sudden flash as the fog dispersed and the mirages took recognizable form in his head and he saw Kirk McLatchie lying in the morgue, neatly stitched.

A bed. Scalpels. A place to drain away the blood.

He looked at the shower head, at the sink set in tiles. You'd need a rubber tube attached to the sink to carry blood from the body on the bed. This room could be transformed in minutes, halogens attached to the sockets in the ceiling, a saw that was easily portable, instruments that came in their own nifty cases, and somebody who knew not only how to use these tools, but had the *desire* to do so.

Could Kirk have been brought *here* and butchered? Was he drugged and dragged to *this* place and sliced open and his organs cut out and ferried to wealthy buyers awaiting transplants and his blood sluicing through a rubber tube into the sink and down and down? *No, it's unreal.* And then the body was driven away in the van and dumped where two young people on a date found him? *No this isn't the way to go.* He was agitated, his mind surfboarding, this wave, that wave, this current, that. He reached quickly inside his jacket. He took his notebook from his pocket and opened it at the page where Kirk's photo was placed, and slipped the snapshot out and shoved it under Dysart's face.

'You seen this man before?'

'No.'

'Look carefully.'

Dysart glanced, then said, 'Never.'

'You're sure?'

'I'm sure.'

What else could Dysart say? *Yes, I worked on this man, I cut his heart out.* Perlman thought: I'm jumping to conclusions like a fucking salmon leaping upstream without knowing why he's making the bloody effort in the first place. Kirk McLatchie might never have been here — it's wild, wayward, my head catapulting me into no-go areas, thickets of nonsense, the sensors are off target.

Let it go. Leave it.

He heard rain scour the house and remembered the van.

'I want to see your van.'

'I d-don't know why — '

'Humour me, Dorcus.'

They left the room and went down the stairs, Dysart a step below Perlman.

'The v-van's in the g-g-g — '

'Take me there.'

Dysart led him along a narrow passage that opened into a huge kitchen where fresh flowers had been artfully arranged in a crystal vase on the table, and potpourris of dried herbs lay in open glass dishes, scenting the air with thyme, rosemary, sage. On a window-ledge a couple of avocado pits were suspended by toothpicks in old jamjars half-filled with water.

A woman's touch, Perlman thought. The mark of Jackie Ace. She came here — how often?

Dysart led him through a scullery to a door, which he opened. He switched on a light, illuminating the garage where the van was parked, a large space filled with storage boxes, garden tools, a couple of old tyres, folded deckchairs, ropes, lanterns, camping gear, big bags of dog food.

Dysart unlocked the van.

Perlman peered at the two front seats. Immaculate. No rubbish anywhere, no scraps of paper, no pencil stubs, pens.

'Show me the back,' he said.

Dysart sighed, unlocked the back doors.

An interior light clicked on. Perlman scanned inside, which was as clean as the rest of the vehicle. Only one thing was out of the ordinary, a chain welded to the panel.

'What's that for?'

'S-sometimes when I have to take a dog to the vet, I l-lock the chain to the dog's collar. S-so the dog d-doesn't bounce around — '

'And if you have to take both dogs?'

'Oh, that's easy. It's a l-long enough chain.'

Perlman tried to imagine two Dobes on this chain. Chain looped round the neck of one, then fed round the neck of the other and what — padlocked? It could be done. The chain could be used for a number of purposes — if you had something or somebody whose movements you wanted to restrict.

He stood a moment, surveying the inside of the vehicle.

A chain in a van, it was nothing. And a room that was some kind of homage to a dead woman — OK, mildly eccentric, maybe a touch morbid, but a long way from criminal. He continued to gaze at the chain.

He still had Kirk McLatchie's photo in his hand. He held it toward Dysart. 'Try. One more time.'

'I've already t-told you I d-don't know this person. I don't n-need to *f-fucking* l-look. Y-you th-think you can do anything, you p-police . . . You ha-harass Jackie, y-you go to her place of work, y-you go to her home, she's going through d-difficult times and y-you — '

He stopped suddenly, victimized by word-lock. His mouth was open and he stared at Perlman with the angry look of a man desperate to speak but struck mute. A flow of red raced across his face, rising from his neck and up through his cheeks, flushing as high as his forehead.

Perlman spoke quietly. 'Dorcus, I understand what she's going through. I never harassed her. I asked some questions she didn't like, and I wasn't satisfied with the answers.'

'Y-you b-broke s-stuff in h-her f-flat you c-can't l-lie about that.'

'I'm clumsy. I'm sorry.'

'No you're not. Y-you're persecuting us.'

Persecuting *us*.

He heard it loud and clear in Dysart's anguished voice and was annoyed with himself for failing to pick it up before. Tartakower had almost been right. *Those two are close*. But he'd never walked the last few steps. He'd never said love.

Ace and Dorcus, hearts entwined. Love, of course: who could explain love? He thought: We're all love's victims in some way, giving our hearts freely, usually with complete disregard for consequences, often with no hope of reciprocity — look at me, love's nebbish. Prime instance.

'Your private life doesn't interest me, Dorcus.'

Dysart said, 'You say that, you d-don't mean it. At every t-turn there's p-persecution. If it's n-not you, it's somebody else. All the t-time. I d-don't need this, P-Perlman. I f-fucking d-don't need this.'

Perlman thought, *And neither do I*.

'Please, please l-leave us in p-peace.'

Perlman stared at Dorcus but he had no more questions for him. Some other time. 'You want peace, you got it. Walk me out as far as the gate and make sure those dogs don't think I'm an appetizer.'

'Scared?'

'Of a few things,' Perlman replied. Including my own mind where the spectres pass through whispering seemingly sound advice as they go, and the jury in my head deliver verdicts. *I thought I had it: they told me I had it*. But it slipped away, whatever it was, and what can I prove?

Raining outside still. Smells of wet grass and sodden leaves. The dogs came thundering out of a hiding place and Dysart, with the mac over his head and shoulders, shouted them away. He unlocked the gates and Perlman went outside.

Perlman turned as Dysart closed the gates. A metallic clang echoed, then faded. 'Thanks for your time, doc,' Perlman said.

'No problem.' No stutter, no exasperating struggle from Dysart.

Perlman walked to his car and sat behind the wheel and watched Dobes, vigorously shaking water off fur, come running at Dysart and leap affectionately around him.

The dogs love him too, Perlman thought.

37

Mathieson parked outside the Temple.

In the back seat Chuck had been thinking about the night he'd first met Glori in the Arta and how he knew from the start they'd make harmonious body-music together. She was light in the dark, joy unexpected —

You find joy, don't let it go.

'Here we are,' Mathieson said. He got out of the Jaguar and held an umbrella over Chuck and walked him up the steps to the door. Hard rain bounced off the pavement with the sound of pebbles.

Mathieson said, 'I'll get on the mobie and check hotels.'

'Do that.'

Chuck approached the door and didn't immediately see the notice stuck to the inside of the glass pane. He reached for the handle, and then his attention was seized by the sign:

CLOSED UNTIL FURTHER NOTICE.

What the *fuck* is this — *closed*?

Baba is sick, maybe: but no — gurus lead good lives, *spiritual* lives. They meditate and pray. They eat nuts and berries.

Chuck in panic pressed his nose to the glass, although the notice impaired his range of vision. But he saw enough: the fat pillows were gone and the curtains at the back had been taken down and the tapestries were gone and so were the statues.

A man with a broom was sweeping the floor.

Chuck rapped the glass. The man paid no attention.

Chuck found a pound coin in his pocket and hammered it against the pane. The man turned and looked at him, adjusted his hearing-aid, then opened the door.

Chuck swept into the hall. 'What's goin on here?'

'Place is for rent,' the man said.

'*What?*'

'For rent. Former tenant shot the craw.'

'Who the fuck are you?'

'Here, watch your language,' the man said.

Chuck grabbed the man by the collar of his blue overalls. 'Where the fuck's *Baba?*'

'Hey, I'm only the janitor.'

Chuck squeezed the man's scrawny throat. 'When did he leave?'

The janitor spluttered. 'Last night — packed up his bus — end of.'

Chuck released him.

'Christ, you nearly choked me, mac. Nay need for that.'

Packed up his bus and gone. Like that. Chuck paced up and down the hall, his footsteps echoing sharply. 'He leave an address?'

'No according to the owner. Took his curtains and his pillows and off he went in his bus. He owed rent.'

'How could he owe rent, for fuck's sake? He was well supported here.'

The janitor shrugged. 'I only know what I telt you.'

Chuck fizzled.

Fucker conned me. Conned me all the way. And took the bus.

He stood directly under the stained-glass Christ. Rainwater dripped into the bucket at the place where Farl the roofer had allegedly made repairs. Chuck had a chain of explosions in his head — *canny trust priests, canny trust gurus, canny trust roofers, canny trust Texans, canny trust yer granny, canny trust* —

The janitor said, 'Ask me, I think this guru was a flyman.'

'Who's askin you.'

'Hey, mac, just my opinion.'

'Shove yer opinion down yer fuckin throat.'

Chuck walked to the door, peered at the rain. Who on God's earth can I depend on?

★   ★   ★

Ron Mathieson found Glorianna on his seventeenth call. She was listed as A Cormack at St Jude's Hotel in Bath Street. He asked to be connected to her room.

'Nice room, Glori?' Mathieson asked.

'Ronnie . . . oh *shit*.'

'Chuck's looking everywhere — '

'Oh for God's sake *please* don't tell him I'm here. Don't.'

Mathieson saw Chuck come out of the Temple. 'You think I'd give him the satisfaction?'

'Swear to me on your life,' Glorianna said.

'On my life.'

'You're a doll, Ronnie.'

'You deserve better than Chuck,' Mathieson said, and cut the connection and rushed up the steps with the umbrella and held it over Chuck's head.

'Fuckin Baba took a hike,' Chuck said. 'A fuckin toe-rag. Untrustworthy sneaky bastart baggashite . . . ' Chuck slid into the back of the Jag, thinking about trust. How did you know when to trust somebody? Was it in the way they looked, the way they spoke? Was it an instinct born into you?

If so, his was seriously jiggered. He felt despondent. Lower than that. Low as a tic up a centipede's arse.

'Any word o her, Ron?'

Mathieson said, 'I'm up to twenty hotels so far, and nothing, Mr Chuck.'

'Right. Keep it rollin, Ronnie. Don't give up.'

Glori, my girl. Come back.

38

Perlman drove into the housing scheme and parked his car outside a wire fence surrounding a tall water-tower. He was glad to be out of Dysart's house. He scrutinized the rainy streets. There were no people about, no wet pets: the place might have been abandoned. A row of small shops was open directly in front of him — a grocery store, newsagent-tobacconist, a hair salon called The Cutting Zone where an empty row of conical hair-dryers was visible through the window. Bad hair day, all this rain.

He walked inside the newsagent's. A wire cage, erected the length of the counter, kept customers away from the cigarettes and the cash register. A couple of female assistants behind the counter watched him enter. He saw in their eyes a cool assessment. He wasn't a regular, a local. An object of curiosity.

Neither woman asked him if there was any-thing he needed. He surveyed the stacks of tinned goods, the big jars of sweets, the bottled lemonade. A man in a long raincoat and flat cap came in and started scanning stacks of newspapers.

'This is no a readin-room, Charlie,' one of the women said.

'I'm buyin, I'm buyin, haud yer horses, *Jesus*,' the man answered.

'You always buy the *Evening Times* early edition, Charlie.'

'Well mibbe I'll buy somethin else,' Charlie said assertively.

'Aye when the moon's cheese,' one of the women remarked.

The other laughed and took a drag on a cigarette that had been burning in an ashtray.

Charlie selected an *Evening Times* and took it to the counter and paid for it. Perlman noticed the headline: *Was Victim Butchered?* He wanted to grab the paper out of Charlie's hand.

'See this,' Charlie said. 'Somebody carved up, another body dumped. What's the polis doin?'

'Whit d'ye expect em to do, Charlie.'

'Fuck all as usual.' Charlie coughed. 'Gie's ten Senior Service.'

A packet of cigarettes was slid under the wire to him. He pushed some coins across the counter. Then he left, tucking his paper inside his coat.

Perlman picked up a copy of the same newspaper, checked the front page story as he approached the counter. He was shocked to see Kirk's face stare out at him. Behind the counter one of the women, her big round face stained with an oblong purple birthmark, looked at him. The other, small and rotund, flipped the pages of *Woman's Own*, and pretended Perlman didn't exist.

'I'm looking for somebody called Pudge,' he said.

The women stared at him with a surly lack of interest.

Tribal protection. 'He drives a hearse.'

The woman with the birthmark said, 'See the

sign outside? Does it *say* Funeral Home?'

Perlman said, 'Bin the patter. I'm in a hurry.'

The other woman slowly raised her face from her magazine. 'Aye everybody's in a hurry these days.'

Perlman wondered if he should show his ID, but he figured these women had sussed him anyway. 'Where do I find Pudge?'

'You know any Pudge, Margaret?'

Margaret scratched her birthmark and looked at Perlman defiantly. 'And what if I do?'

Perlman sighed. 'It's a shite day outside and I've been on the go for hours, ladies. So please don't fuck with me.'

Frannie said, 'Threatenin, int he? A wild man. Disny look it.'

Perlman grabbed and shook the wire cage and it rattled. 'An address — then I'm history.'

'That cage'll faw doon,' Margaret said.

'Why don't you just tell him, Margaret? Then we're shot of him.'

Margaret said, 'Out here, first left, first right. You'll see the hearse parked in the street.'

Perlman went outside. He read the story quickly. Rain fell on his newspaper. Kirk McLatchie, twenty-five, was the alleged victim of criminal surgery. *Police are refusing to confirm details, but this reporter understands that the victim's kidneys, liver and heart had been removed.*

This story shouldn't have seen the light of day in this form. Some source inside Pitt Street had provided this story — and was handsomely paid by a snooping journalist for the info. It was inevitable. Nothing stayed private for long inside Force HQ. The place was a church of talkative cops.

The picture was one he'd never seen before; Kirk on his wedding day, arm linked through his wife's, a small smile on his face.

He called Betty. She took a long time to answer.

He said, 'I saw it.'

'Oh Lou, why did they print *that?* Why did they put Kirk's picture on the front page? Don't they have any feelings?'

'Feelings don't come into it, Betty. You're news.'

'I've had reporters camped on my doorstep since first thing this morning. The doorbell hasn't stopped ringing. And the phone. I can't take it, Lou. I just cannot take it. What do they want from me? They've got their bloody news. My son's dead. Isn't that enough?'

'They'll hound you until you weep.'

'They can go to hell.'

'Lie low. Keep your curtains shut. Don't answer the door, don't answer the phone. If I call you, I'll do the old two ring hang-up and ring again routine. Same routine if I press your doorbell.'

'OK.'

'I'll come by later. I wish I could tell you exactly when, but I don't know. Meantime, do what I just told you.'

He cut the connection and walked to his car and tossed the paper on to the passenger seat. Poor Betty, exposed to the hawks, those tenacious fuckers. They were pitiless and unrelenting and they dug into fresh wounds without mercy.

The directions he'd been given were misleading. First left first right turned out to be second left second right, and he only saw the hearse after he'd circled a couple of blocks. It was parked outside one of the towers. Long, black and rust-eaten, bald tyres, a hairline crack on the windscreen — this hearse had shed its original purpose long ago.

He got out of his car, locked it, walked quickly through the rain and entered the building. The hallway floor was puddled. There were doors on either side, and a stone staircase ahead. He knocked on the first door he came to.

A good-looking young man answered. He wore a bandanna and in his right hand he dangled a plastic sword.

'Zup,' the young man said.

'Where can I find Pudge?'

A smell of hashish drifted out of the room. Inside some girls giggled. Perlman heard one of them say *I'm no carryin his wean it'd look like a turnip. Fancy the nurse's face she sees a turnip comin oot between ma legs.*

The young man said, 'Tell me honestly. You think I look like Johnny Depp?'

'Depp? Aye, well, there's a resemblance, definitely.' Perlman knew nobody with the name of Depp, but what was the point disagreeing?

The young man laughed and shouted back into the room. 'Telt youse I was a double for Johnny Depp!' He turned his face round to

Perlman, posing as if for a picture. 'Pudge, eh? One up, on the left.' Then he slammed the door.

Imagining a turnip-like baby, Perlman climbed the steps. The world is unreal. He stopped outside a wooden door that had its paint scratched by the long claw marks of an animal. The letterbox hung at an angle. He knocked on the door, nobody answered. He lowered his face and yelled through the letterbox. 'Anybody home?'

A voice inside the flat shouted back. 'I'm buyin nothin, no insurance no charities no hairbrushes no vacky cleaners nothing, so pish off.'

'I'm here to see Pudge.'

A long silence. At the foot of the stairs rap music started up, loud and repetitive.

The door opened and a heavy man in a stained white singlet appeared. He was unshaven and his braces hung outside his shiny black trousers. On his bare arms were a couple of faded shamrock tattoos.

Perlman asked, 'You Pudge?'

Pudge frowned defensively. 'Mibbe. Or I could be his brother Fudge.'

'Let's assume you're Pudge. Did you drive a young woman into Glasgow the other night? She was running from Dysart's old house — '

'Anybody in their right fuckn mind would run from that place. So what's your interest?'

'Where did you take her?'

Pudge rubbed his chin. There were tiny shamrocks on the backs of his hands. He eyeballed Perlman, assessing his cash potential. 'This'll cost.'

'Business as usual.' Perlman put his hand in his jacket pocket, fumbling for his wallet. He took out a twenty. I'm a cash cow — Tartakower, The Pickler, now Pudge.

Pudge said, 'Make it fifty. A round five-oh gets you the whole setta bagpipes and no just the chanter.'

Perlman wondered about his bank balance as he watched two twenties and two fives vanish into Pudge's shamrocked hand. He was on basic sick-leave pay, which left him very little after the hand-outs he was constantly splashing around.

Pudge said, 'I took her to the top end of Belmont Street.'

Belmont Street. Perlman felt a flutter in his heart. 'You dropped her off and left?'

'Naw naw, she asked me to wait. I didny mind, she's a looker. Nay sense of humour, didny laugh at any of my jokes, but a right wee stoater. She goes inside a tenement, five six minutes later she comes back down, hair wet, clothes changed. She's carrying a bag.'

'And?'

'Asked me to let her out at the corner of Bath Street and Campbell Street.'

'You see where she went after that?'

'I watched her a wee minute in the mirror. She went back down the block, and I started to drive away. I checked the mirror again, didny see her this time. I'm guessing she went inside one of the buildings along that stretch. There's a hotel there she might have gone into. She wouldny want to be seen getting out my hearse right in front of a hotel, aw no. No good enough for her.'

Perlman tried to remember hotels located in that part of Bath Street. 'Did she say why she was running from Dysart?'

Pudge shook his head. 'She barely said two words to me, mac. She just wanted the hell away from here. Scared blind in my opinion.'

He thanked Pudge.

Pudge said, 'Any time.'

He went downstairs and back to his car. He turned the key in the ignition and thought of Glorianna, *scared blind*, running, riding a hearse in the night.

39

Mathieson drove to The Potted Calf, listening all the way to Chuck mutter in the back seat. Sometimes he tuned Chuck out like a Scottish dance band radio station he didn't want to hear. Sometimes he only caught key words.

Got to be somewhere. Tried all the hotels. Checked the Y. Checked her friends.

'I turned the city over, Mr Chuck.' The fuck.

Chuck nibbled on his knuckles. 'She'll show up. Bound to. How many hidin places are there for fuck's sake?'

Thousands, Mathieson thought. But only one.

Chuck was miserable. Heartache and regret, heavy loads. What had he done in his past life to deserve all this?

What past life? Oh aye. That fuckin guru was talking shite.

The onslaught of rain darkened his mood. Glasgow was awash. Foaming rain rushed down gutters unable to cope with the deluge. The street lamps were lit and rainwater changed reflected light into quicksilver. Rain like this, you could scrap the Jag and get a fuckin Ark.

Chuck got out of the car in his parking space behind The Potted Calf and went inside his office at the back of the restaurant. Mathieson followed. Chuck's room was small, lime-green walls, a mahogany desk, two expensive black leather chairs. An electronic map of Glasgow

352

hung on the wall facing the desk.

Chuck sat. 'That fuckin garlic again. Smell it?'

Ronnie Mathieson said aye, it was strong. I'm not smelling anything, Ronnie thought. The Big Man's fucked.

'The system's flawed, Ronnie. Those cowboy installers never got the plan right. The smell should bypass my office *entirely*, but there's a loosely fitted pipe some fuckin place or a leak so small you'd never see it with the naked eye. Get these cowboys back, Ronnie, even if you have to hold a fuckin shotgun to their heids to make sure they do the job properly.'

Moans, the Big Man is all moans. Chuck crumbles. When you smelled things that weren't there, wasn't that a sign of some brainbox junction on the blink?

Chef Pako Sg came in, carrying a bowl of noodles in a vegetable broth, and set it down on Chuck's desk. Chuck looked at the dish, then at Pako Sg. The wee man's uniform was spotless white, his hat black with a chequered black and white band.

'*Beef*,' Chuck said. 'Take this gruel away.'

'You want *beef* Mister Chuck? *Beef*?'

'My body's tellin me, gimme *beef*. The bloodier the better.'

Pako Sg smiled. He twinkled. He twinkled a lot. Too much for Chuck's liking. *Man who twinkles isn't always a star.* Where did that come from? Confucius or Baba, the Holy Wanker?

'I sear you some very fine fillet of Aberdeen Angus, free-range, no antibiotics, no ho-mones. Just so perfect.'

353

'Bring it on, cookie,' Chuck said. He fell silent a second, thinking — a drink to fire his spirit, keep him buoyant. 'Ah, throw in a bottle of gin, Pako. And make Ronnie a sandwich or somethin.'

'Gin?' Pako Sg hid his surprise. He bowed, picked up the soup.

'You all set for the special tomorrow night, wee man?'

'Under control. nine p.m. seating. Fifty covers.'

Pako Sg went out, still bowing. Still *twinklin*.

Chuck thought about the Special, a private affair held every month or so — depending on circumstances. It always brought in big spenders. People with money to pish away. People with diddybrains and cash up the khyber. Some travelled miles to attend.

He pressed a button on a remote control device that lit the map of Glasgow. Red sensors blinked, each denoting a property that had, so to speak, come Chuck's way. There were also yellow sensors, which indicated a property he was thinking of acquiring — by legal means, thus obeying the mandate of his lawyer: keep your head down, don't make any loud noises, and do nice things for charity.

Chuck rose, walked to the map. 'Ronnie, did you know Glasgow has eightysomethin parks? All that space wasted on fat wee women pushin prams and boys wankin in the bushes and doddery old tossers walkin their fuckin dogs.'

'Eighty parks, news to me.'

'Aye, but not for long, because . . . ' Chuck

winked. 'I intend to buy a few of them. Startin with Elder Park here, very handy for the Clyde Tunnel. I let some time go past, then I get plannin permission from those crookit flyboys on the City Council, and I build a small development of seven or eight de luxe executive houses in one corner of the park. I'm thinkin steel and chrome and bagza glass, a new look. Then . . . ' Chuck paused, engrossed in his vision. 'Park Executive Properties, that'll be the company name. Like it?'

'Terrific.'

'I buy another park and I do the same thing. See here,' and he jabbed the map. 'Linndale Park, nice acreage adjoining Carmunnock Road and close to King's Park, which has a golf course attached. I'll develop these parks very carefully and with style. Maybe six classy semis in Linndale, then a *second* wee development in Elder, and probably a coupla mansions in King's Park eventually.'

Mansions. Mathieson listened to this scheme, then said, 'Can you actually *buy* public parks, Mr Chuck?'

'I can buy fuckin well *anythin.*'

'I thought the parks belonged to the people — '

'The *people*? Ho ho. Them scruff don't deserve parks. They shag in them, they vandalize the gardens. Christ, even if I end up purchasin half a dozen, they've still got enough parks left for their dogs to shite in. Everythin is locomotion, Ronnie. They'll have a statue of me one day in George Square.'

355

Mathieson said, 'I can see that.' The Big Man. Pigeons crapping on his stone heid. Chuck would never be able to buy a public park, for fuck's sake. He was going to the dugs. He never had balls enough to be The Big Man anyway, in Mathieson's opinion. He had insecurities as pronounced as open sores. He felt menace in empty stairwells. He heard gossip behind his back when nobody was there. He fought these enemies with bluster and bravado and a touch of Baba — but who was he kidding?

And now Baba was away.

Chuck stepped back from the map. All these streets, these railway lines, these parks and ponds and colleges and monuments, they seemed unfamiliar to him for a second — *where in all this strange jumbled city is she?*

Pako Sg returned carrying a tray and a bottle of gin he set on the desk. A fine grilled steak for Chuck, and a ham sandwich for Mathieson. Chuck cut into the steak and blood flowed rich and oleaginous over the plate. When you lose your beliefs, you turn back to all the things you've been foolish enough to deny yourself.

Includin sex. Booze.

That bastart Baba swizzled me. Nobody does that to me.

Pako Sg waited for approval.

The beef dissolved in Chuck's mouth. Delicious flavour, texture of silk. Chuck was blissed. 'It's like a fuckin slice of Christ,' he said.

Mathieson chewed resentfully on his ham sandwich.

'Very glad Mr Chuck is pleased,' Pako Sg said.

'I'm in heaven, Pako.'

'In heaven, ah, very good, very good.' Pako went out with a slight bow.

Chuck finished his steak, wiped his lips with a napkin, and drank a good mouthful from the bottle of Gordon's. How long since he'd had booze? It went like a dragon's flame to his head. Woo, not such a bad feelin. He'd missed that blast and roar somethin terrible.

'I keep comin back to that weird git. He knows somethin.'

'What weird git?' Ronnie Mathieson mumbled, mouth filled with dry white bread, shredded lettuce and some fatty bits of ham. A ham sandwich, well fuck, thanks a lot. All the things I do for you. And not an offer of a drink.

Chuck glugged another fair measure of gin and belched softly. 'Comes back like perfume . . . sweet as a lathered twat. Fuckin Dysart. I'm gonny do somethin about him.' He stared at Mathieson with that chill, slicing look he sometimes used. It was X-ray and cut through steel. Then he held the gin up to the light and admired its clarity. 'Mother's ruin, down the hatch,' and he jammed back another mouthful.

Ronnie said, 'Mibbe Dysart knows nothing. Mibbe she'll show up tonight.'

'Aye. With some story. Some long complex explanation. I'd just be glad to see her, honestly. Just to see her and know she's safe. No questions asked. This gin, you know it comes from berries, Ronnie?'

'Junipers, aye.'

'Right, jupiters,' Chuck said. 'It's a hell of a kick.'

Mathieson said, 'I'm sure Glorianna's OK.'

Chuck clapped a hand on Mathieson's shoulder. 'She's got me goin like banjo string, Ronnie. I swear to God. Somethin I wasn't expectin. I'm feelin sixteen again.'

Mathieson, unaccustomed to hearing Chuck express any depth of emotion, observed his boss's face, which was flushing from the booze. He saw a kind of forlorn hurt in Chuck's eyes, which he'd never witnessed before. He almost felt sorry for him. He almost said, I know where she is. I'll get her for you, Big Man.

Almost.

But he wouldn't give Chuck the sweat from his oxters. He looked at his watch. 'What do you want to do, Boss?'

Chuck wrapped his lips round the bottle, drank, then laughed as if everything was a big joke. 'I have some restaurant dockets I need to discuss with O'Blunt. Between you me and Paisley Road Toll, I have a funny feelin he's skimmin. Tenner here, fifty there, soon adds up. Then I want to make sure the kitchen's runnin right for tomorrow. After that . . . check on Dorco.'

Long drive to the edge of the city, Mathieson thought.

Chuck downed more gin. He drank like a man with yesterdays to forget. 'One thing, Ronnie. Any time in the future I tell you I'm off to see a fuckin guru, you have permission to castrate me. OK?'

Mathieson dutifully laughed. I'd cut your balls off cheerfully.

'Now, where was I?'

'Dysart, Boss.'

'Right. Take a wee drive out there and see what's the score, eh?'

'Why not.' Mathieson took the Jag keys from his pocket. 'Ready when you are, RC.'

'Wait,' and Chuck tilted over a little. Whoops —

Ronnie thought, he's never had the head for booze. Never. It went through him like pish through a tennis racket.

'First O'Blunt. Then . . . there was somethin else. Slipped my heid. Ah, shite, Blunt can wait. He's goin nowhere. It's Dysart I want to see. Gimme the keys.'

'Keys?'

'Whose fuckin Jag is it?'

Ronnie tossed them. Chuck bent for the keys, laughing at his failure to grasp them first time.

'Your licence is out — '

'A piece of fuckin paper ten months out of date doesn't make a man a bad driver. Don't wait up for me, Ronnie.'

'Boss, should I come along just in case?'

'Ah fuck off. I'm capable.' Jangling the keys, Chuck stepped boldly to the door. 'Is this Jag automatic Ronnie?'

'It is. You know your way?'

'Matter of fact yes I do. Cobble Drive.'

Mathieson shrugged. It's no my funeral, he thought.

40

Perlman parked in Bath Street as close as he could to the place where Pudge said he'd dropped Glorianna. The rain was like rivets shot from the sky. He ran half a block with his coat over his head, then rushed dripping inside St Jude's, a 'bijou' establishment with about a dozen bedrooms and a restaurant. It was the only hotel in the block. Two youthful waiters stood just inside the door of the dining room — spiky-haired and earringed. They stared at Perlman in his shapeless raincoat, as if they expected him to be followed by a retinue of ragamuffin street people asking for alms.

A slender black girl worked the reception desk. She wore a red mini-skirt and a white blouse. She smiled at Perlman nicely, which blunted the edge of his mood. He was flustered on account of circuit overload — a measure of dread about the outcome of the DNA test, persistent uncertainties concerning Dysart, and worry, of course, over Betty. He needed focus, but the film running through his head-sprockets was all over the place.

'What can I do for you, sir?'

Perlman said, 'You might have a guest here I want to see.'

'Name?'

'Try Cormack.'

The girl checked her computer screen. 'I'll call her room.'

'I'll just go up.'

'Oh.' The girl was apologetic but firm. 'We don't allow that, sir, unless the guest agrees. So I have to call ahead.' She reached for the phone.

'Wait,' Perlman said. He showed his ID.

The girl examined it closely. 'Is there going to be trouble? I mean, anything that would generate bad PR for us?'

'I'm not here to drag her off in handcuffs, if that's what you're worried about.' Perlman offered this lightly, but the girl's response was a frown.

'OK . . . room 12.'

Perlman moved to the staircase, climbed. He wanted to look back and just for the hell of it say *Special Services team right behind me, love, grenades and bazookas, duck.*

Up he went. It had been an afternoon of stairways and climbing.

He knocked softly on the door of room 12 and called out his name.

A silence. 'What do you want?'

'Five minutes of your time.'

She opened the door an inch, saw that he was alone, then slipped the security chain off.

Perlman stepped in, Glorianna shut the door, replaced the chain.

'Busy reading?' Perlman said, looking at the mass of glossy mags on the bed.

'Very observant. No wonder you're a polisman. I'm just killing time.'

'Until what?'

She lit a cigarette and walked barefoot to the window. She dropped her lighter in the pocket of her white terry robe and turned to him. She was better looking without the make-up, more attractive than the day he'd met her in George Square. Untouched, pale, her skin had a natural luminosity.

'Do I call you Glorianna or Annie?'

She shrugged: who cares?

Perlman said, 'Annie has a certain purity about it.'

'Purity?' She blew a smoke ring. 'You're not here to talk shite are you?'

'Why are you hiding from Chuck?'

'What makes you think I'm hiding?'

'He wouldn't be looking for you otherwise.'

She opened the mini-bar and took out a small bottle of ginger ale, which fizzed as she uncapped it. 'OK, I don't want Chuck near me.'

'And what did he do to deserve the heave-ho?'

'As if that's any of your business.' She was bold on the surface, but Perlman sensed underlying anxiety, tension — the same guarded nervousness she'd projected at Betty's.

Her clothes lay scattered around. 'Messy,' he said. 'Just like your flat.'

'When were you ever in my flat?'

'Earlier today. Ran into your boyfriend there.'

Annie lit a cigarette from the butt of the old one. Her hand shook. She had difficulty docking the cigarettes. 'What was my former boyfriend doing there anyway?'

'Like I said, looking for you. He's unravelling faster than a cheap cardigan.'

'And what were *you* doing?'

'Same as Chuck. Looking for you.'

She sat on the bed. 'Why?'

'Just mooching around, Annie. You probably picked up a fair amount of knowledge about Chuck's business over the past couple of years — '

'How much more *transparent* can you get? Me and Chuck might be on the skids, but you think I'm going to tell *you* anything? Newsflash — wrong girl here. I don't know the way he operates and even if I did I wouldn't tell a soul, and definitely not a polisman.'

She's a tough wee number in some ways, Perlman thought. He opened the mini-bar and plucked out a bottle of mineral water.

'Help yourself, why don't you,' she said.

'I will. Thanks.' He drank some, then sat in a chair facing her.

She asked, 'How's Betty?'

'Griefstricken. Stressed.'

'I've always liked her. She doesn't know anything about my life as Glorianna. I never told her.'

'I gathered that.'

'God only knows why, but she's fond of you.'

Perlman said, 'I like to think we've become friends.'

'Friends — that all?'

'Friends, right.' Perlman shuffled his feet. He wasn't here to talk about Betty. It had been a couple of hours since he'd spoken to her — he needed to see her, and to know how she was handling the gannets of the local press. Soon, *soon*.

Annie looked at her wristwatch, which lay on

the bedside table. 'Your five minutes are ticking away.'

He took another glug of water. 'What's it like to travel in a hearse.'

'Who told you that?'

'Tell me what Dysart did to scare you.'

'I don't want to talk about Dysart.'

'Why?'

'Because.'

'Because isn't an answer, Annie. You went to his house why . . . start there. I'm a wee bit puzzled about what you and Dorcus could possibly have in common.'

'Absolutely nothing. Believe me.'

'But you went all the way out there anyway? So you're a student of old houses. Or you love the quirky charm of housing schemes.'

'Yeh, right. They're so picturesque, so *very* sophisticated. Bookshops, espresso scenting the air.'

'You ran screaming from that house, Annie.'

'That's a lie.'

'I'm only reporting what I heard. I'm assuming Dysart threatened you in some way.'

'Assume what you like.'

Perlman was quiet, then changed the angle of his approach a little. 'It's a bloody scary house, Annie. You expect the Munsters to greet you. The locals say it's haunted.'

'Ballocks. I never noticed a thing.'

Stonewalling. Perlman had talked to bags of cement more forthcoming. 'Did you get a tour of the place?'

'No, and I didn't ask for one either.' Annie

opened the drawer and removed a nail-file and began to work her nails.

He leaned against the wall. His coat was heavy with rain, and he felt dampness seep through to the bone. *I'll come down with something.* 'I'm beginning to wonder if you're protecting Dysart for some reason. Or is it Chuck you're trying to shield?'

'I'm looking out for myself, Perlman.'

He took off his coat.

'Don't get any ideas about staying,' Annie said.

'I'm only trying to dry out my coat a wee bit before I leave.' Perlman slipped his mobile phone from a wet pocket, then placed the coat over a radiator. 'I hate to waste time, Annie. I bet Chuck feels the same way.'

Annie held one hand out and checked her nails, then peered at Perlman between her fingers. 'I don't have any idea what Chuck feels.'

'He's thinking he's wasting a fuck of a lot of time looking for you, dear. He's sitting at his desk, I bet, waiting for a call.'

She saw the mobile in his hand and read his intention immediately. She raised her face aggressively, and muscles tensed in her neck. 'You *wouldn't*.'

'I wouldn't want to, Annie.'

'Don't call him, Perlman.'

'Then suppose you *talk* to me.'

He watched her go to the mini-bar and remove a half-empty bottle of white wine. She poured some into a glass and sat cross-legged on the bed. She lit a cigarette, a Camel, and was silent for a time, weighing choices.

The mobile rang, vibrating in Perlman's palm.

Annie jumped. 'Is that Chuck?'

Perlman saw the caller's identity on the screen: it was the number for Force HQ. He signalled Annie to be quiet and answered the phone. 'Perlman.'

Annie was still agitated. She bit her thumb nervously. She mouthed the question, *Is that Chuck?*

Perlman shook his head at her.

'Jack Wren here, Lou.'

'Jack, you old schmoozer. You still serving Glasgow's finest?'

'Still the reliable Constable on the desk, Lou.'

Perlman had a fondness for Jack Wren. They went back years together. 'What's the story, Jack?'

'You're expected here at six sharp. That's coming from upstairs.'

'From the pinnacle, eh? You any idea what for?'

'The day they tell the downstairs staff anything is the day I'll croak. See you at six, Lou. Mind how you go.'

Perlman closed the connection. Six sharp, Tay's office. Why were they calling him in unless they had news they wanted him to hear about the DNA result? And they wouldn't ask for his presence to tell him anything cheerful, damn right. They'd never summon him for a glass of sherry and sing 'For He's a Jolly Good Fellow'. So? What lay ahead? It could be something other than the DNA, he realized — the official pink-slip, a reprimand for punching Latta, or —

Don't borrow from the future.

Annie was sipping her wine. 'I'll make you a deal, Perlman. I'll tell you what went on in that house, or as much as I remember — but I won't answer any questions about Chuck's business interests. Which isn't an admission I know every move he makes. Remember that.'

'Fair enough.'

'I also want *you* to promise me you won't tell Chuck where I am. Swear that.'

'Such delicate negotiations,' Perlman said. 'What do you want, Annie? An oath? I swear it, OK?'

She stared at him, as if she might find an element of trustworthiness in his face. 'Maybe Betty goes for that just-been-dragged-in-by-the-cat look you do. You *seem* sincere. I hope she's got your number right, Perlman.'

Dragged in by the cat. This was probably similar to *just-out-of-bed* — maybe some women saw him in this light: a stray to be sheltered, a waif to be fed. He wished he projected suave, man about town.

'I could cross my heart, if that would help,' he offered.

Annie didn't take him up on this offer. She drank some wine and fidgeted with the stem of her glass. 'I do massage, Perlman, I'm fucking good at it. I make home calls once in a blue moon. I know what you're thinking.'

'No you don't.'

'Oh come on, everybody leaps to the same snide conclusion when I tell them — massage plus home calls equals sex. They always say *oh, I suppose you offer extras at a price*. Well I don't, Perlman. I went out to that house to give Dysart a massage. No strings. No extras. I want you to understand that.'

Annie Purity. 'I believe you. How did Dysart contact you?'

'I did it as a favour.'

'For who?'

'Doesn't matter — '

'I'd still like to know.'

'Jeez, you're *pushy*. I hate pushy. I did it because Chuck asked me to give Dysart a good massage. And it's important to be nice to Dysart because Chuck . . . '

'Chuck what?'

'There's some kind of arrangement between them — don't ask me what. I'm not hiding anything, I just don't know.'

Perlman heard the ping of a tuning-fork vibrate in his head. Were Dysart and Chuck connected in some form of commerce? He couldn't begin to imagine it: an 'arrangement'. What were their conversations like? Chuck speaking clipped hardman Glasgow, with that characteristic nasal edge, Dysart stammering in his agitated manner. Odd socks, so how did they match?

Annie said, 'Dysart's a bagga nerves right from the start. He doesn't want me there. But since Chuck sent me, maybe Dysart doesn't like to offend the Big Man. Not many people do. Chuck's displeasure isn't always welcome . . . I've massaged some uptight people in my time, Perlman, but this guy — this was like trying to revive a corpse in an advanced state of rigor. Think OK, I'm wasting time, I'll split, so when I decide to call a taxi he goes weird on me and smacks my mobie out my hand and it breaks on the floor . . . I'm not happy about this, obviously. I'm thinking, uh oh, this is not a cool place to be.'

'This was upstairs or down?'

'Downstairs. The room was just a couch, a small table. He had all these big thick medical books. He's a doctor. He *says*. Oh — and he delivers office supplies on the side.'

Office supplies? Ding dong. Dysart hadn't mentioned that. His only income was seemingly from the legacy. *I have just about enough to live on* . . . The house was a demanding and ultimately insatiable mistress; she needed great wads of money. And delivering office supplies wasn't going to provide enough to appease this harridan, nor the depleted relics of an inheritance, nor help from Jackie — if in fact she provided *any*. Then he thought about her surgical expenses and wondered where that kind of cash was coming from. Insurance? Or did she also have a legacy?

'Does he deliver these supplies to Chuck?'

'I said I wouldn't talk about Chuck's business.'

'Right, you did.'

'But I don't believe that's what Dysart does. I know where Chuck gets his office supplies, and it's not from the Doctor.'

'What happened after the phone demolition?'

'Strange. Suddenly he turns pale and he *flies*

369

upstairs. I hear a door slam and then the sound of him being violently sick. I mean *violently*.'

'So you took this opportunity and left?'

'How could I leave when Dysart had the key to the gates? So I went looking for him.'

Brave girl. Perlman waited. She's confused, the ordeal's a puzzle for her, give her time.

'If this comes out jumbled it's because it's how I remember it . . . I walk along the hallway, tapping on doors, I can't find him. I think OK I'll go back downstairs, it wasn't rational thinking, because I didn't have the key, maybe I imagined I'd be able to climb the gates. Fucking daft, eh? So downstairs I take a wrong turning and find myself in a room where mice are running over the keys of a piano. *Mice*. I swear. And there was this old wingback chair and somebody was sitting in it and he started to get up . . . very slowly.'

'A man?'

'A man, I think, I didn't see a face. I don't know if I imagined it. I was beginning to panic, Perlman. I ran out of the room and found the hallway and then I was outside, and Dysart was coming after me and shouting . . . maybe I *did* scream, I don't remember, but anyway. He's still shouting and he's coming behind me. I also hear dogs and I lose my shoes. Look at my feet,' and she kicked off her slippers and showed him her soles, which were covered with strips of Band-Aid. 'Blisters.'

'Nasty. What was he shouting?'

'He's sorry, he wants to apologize, I don't remember.'

'OK, you still have the gates to get over.'

'The fucking gates. Some kids tossed me a rope and I climbed.'

'Kids?'

'Little kids. They had a whacky plan to climb the gates and poison the dogs.'

'But instead they rescued you.'

'Thank Christ they did. I climbed and climbed and my hands hurt like hell. Then these kids took me to the guy who owns the hearse.'

Perlman had the feeling she was skipping something. 'Roll it back a bit, Annie. Dysart went inside a room to throw up. Did he unlock that room?'

'I never knew which room he went into because I couldn't find him.'

'You knocked on a couple of doors in the upstairs hallway. And he didn't respond.'

'Right . . . I remember a smell.' She wrinkled her nose.

'A strong disinfectant by any chance?'

'Very strong . . . ' She held a hand to the side of her face and closed her eyes. He wondered where she'd drifted.

'You smelled this upstairs mainly?'

'Upstairs, yeh. But also on Dysart's clothes. He reeked of it.' She looked at Perlman: something clearly distressed her, because she grabbed the hem of her robe and twisted it, curling it round her fingers.

'What else do you remember.'

'There's this other room . . . The smell was stronger . . . '

'Was this room locked?'

'No . . . I thought he might be in there because of the smell, and I wanted that key to the gates, Perlman. I had to have that fucking key. What was I thinking? He'd hand it over to me? Here, let yourself out . . . was I thinking that?'

'Slow down, take it easy, Annie.'

'This room was different from the rest of the house.'

'What way.'

' . . . the floor. No carpet. It was tiled.'

'White tiles.'

'Right.'

'Was there a bed?'

She hunched forward over her glass. Her body seemed to have locked, as if she'd become paralyzed in this awkward curved position.

'A sink . . . I remember a sink. I think I found a light switch and turned it on and I saw this steel sink.'

'What else?'

'A naked woman was standing at the sink . . . she was running hot water very slowly out of the tap into a cloth, and she was washing her hands and body and her hair was hanging over her shoulders . . . the room was clouded with steam.' She caught her breath. 'I feel giddy.'

'It's the wine, the tobacco.'

'There's a breeze following me around, and footsteps in the distance but nobody's coming. And the person getting out of that chair . . . He isn't real, he's kind of shadowy, like he's almost transparent . . . Maybe the place is haunted after all.'

Perlman tried to redirect her. 'Go back to the room with the tiles, Annie.' He sat on the bed. She was trembling.

'I don't need to go there, Perlman.'

'Try.'

'Easy for you to say . . . ' She blinked rapidly. 'The woman turns and I think she sees me and she's surprised because she drops her towel. And that's when I see.'

'See what?'

'This woman has a *cock*.'

'You saw this for sure?'

'Not for sure . . . I look away because I'm what? Embarrassed, shocked? I don't know, Perlman.'

'All this took a few seconds,' Perlman said.

'You think I was looking at my watch?'

'You see the woman's actually a *man* and you look away quickly.'

'I think I did . . . yes . . . '

'You step back out of the room? Come on, I want this through your eyes, Annie.'

'I turn my head because I'm looking away and . . . Remember there's steam, a lot of steam . . . but I see a bed, a kind of a bed.'

Perlman waited. *A woman who's a man. A kind of bed.*

'There's a bundle on the bed. I don't know, it's laundry wrapped up in a sheet, ready to be taken away . . . That's when I turned and ran down the hallway.'

'A bundle of laundry. Why would it scare you?'

'The room's spinning, Lou. Hold me or I'll float away.'

373

He put his arms around her. 'Take your time. Just take your time.' He was talking in the hushed reassuring voice he'd use to a frightened child. 'Tell me about the laundry.'

'I thought laundry. It passed through my mind in a flash. It's a white sheet soaked with blood, it's bulky, because it's laid across something. But I realize it's not laundry, Perlman. It's not.'

'You can tell what this *something* is?' Perlman felt tension rise inside.

She looked at him, dazed. 'The shape I see under the bloodstained sheet is human.'

'Human? Covered all over? No view of the face?'

'Covered totally. Head to toe. In this bloody sheet.'

Perlman got up from the bed and walked to the window and looked out into the rain. It fell miserably: the city was draining away. He thought of Kirk McLatchie's photograph. He thought of Dysart showing him this sickroom where he said his mother had died.

How many others had died in this room?

A bloodstained shroud. Only now the bed isn't a souvenir of his mother, her deathbed — something else. He moved back to Annie and for a moment saw the vulnerable child in her, the kid from The Drum drawn into a world she didn't comprehend.

She stared at him. 'How could that bastard Chuck send me to a place like that? How could he do that to me?' Now she was angry, outraged — but also perplexed. She'd been let down, she'd been sent out and abandoned inside a bad dream, and she couldn't figure why.

Flecks of spit gathered at the corners of her mouth. She drew back from Perlman. 'You don't ship somebody like me to a guy you know fuck all about. And that room, Christ that *room* . . . I dreamed it, I want to believe I did.'

'I know you do.' Perlman listened to the screaming rain assault the window.

41

He was already running late when he left St Jude's. He wasn't looking forward to HQ, passing through the front door and watching faces turn to clock him, or catching sneakit smiles and hearing sly whispers. Nobody inside Pitt Street had forgotten Miriam's trial, and most resented Perlman for his actions. He had few friends in this place.

PC Jack Wren was one of the few. He stood at the reception desk when Perlman came in and peered at him over the rims of his specs. He'd shaved off his walrus moustache.

'Evening, Lou,' Wren said.

'I turn my back, you get a face lift,' Perlman said.

Wren winked. 'Flattery will get you anything.'

'I live in hope,' Perlman said.

'You really think it works?'

'What — hope or flattery?'

'The shave, Lou. The *shave*.'

Perlman said, 'I swear, ten years younger, Jack,' and headed for the stairs.

Wren said, 'Good to see you. I mean that.'

The warmth Perlman felt at Wren's greeting faded as he climbed, hurrying past figures coming down, some who looked openly hostile, or merely nodded, others who pretended they were involved in conversation and didn't see him. Fuck them.

He reached the landing, paused to collect himself. He listened to the beat of his heart and he thought of Annie's story. Was it enough to take to the Proc-Fisc's office for a search warrant? Dysart's house was in Adamski's territory. Maybe Adamski would think he had sufficient to go on. If there was a body in that house, he'd want to move in with a crime-scene team before all evidence had been destroyed. You couldn't wipe everything away. Hairs, blood in the septic system, something damning always remained.

And now he had Tay, and no time to think of anything else —

He looked along the landing at the flight of stairs leading up to Tay's eyrie and he had the stab of a sudden headache. He was queasy and tired, and couldn't remember when he'd last eaten.

Tay's door was shut. He straightened his back, knocked and went inside without waiting for a response — politeness wasn't expected of him, so he'd live up to expectations.

The room was lit only by a small desk lamp.

Very Gestapo, Perlman thought.

Tay sat behind his desk, big hands clamped. Because of shadow, Perlman could see only half Tay's face — it was like a rock fallen from a sea cliff and eroded by tides into an impressionistic human countenance. One eye one nostril one ear. *Tay by Picasso.* Perlman ransacked the gloom.

There was Latta, in his Sunday best, a dark brown serge three-piece number and a necktie of horrible red and yellow stripes. Latta's chair was drawn close to Tay's desk as if he might feed off any fallen crumbs of authority. And in the corner, bearded and taciturn, sat the long-armed Tigge, gazing at Perlman with a frown. Tigge's nasal passages made a quiet squeaking sound as he breathed.

The gang's here, Perlman thought. And they know something I don't. He was at a disadvantage, which was the way they'd want him to feel.

Tay made a mighty show of looking at his watch. Wait for the sarcasm. Tay never disappointed. *Harumph.* 'Glad you could see your way clear, Perlman.'

'I've been busy.' Perlman noticed an empty chair but didn't take it, although he longed to sit. Upright, he hoped he gave the impression of self-confidence.

'We'll take your word for that.' Tay had a folder in front of him, the only object on the desk except the lamp. He opened it slowly, tapped the papers inside with his stub of an index finger. 'These are the conclusions of forensic examinations carried out by Sidney Linklater,' Tay said with measured formality, needlessly adding, 'Doctor of Medicine.'

He leaned over the sheets. Latta tilted himself slightly forward, ever closer to Il Duce, and turned his face briefly to Perlman and there it was, that bitter glint in the eye, a provocation: *let's see you walk away from this, Perly.* The desk lamp buzzed curiously, a weird glitch in the stream of electricity.

This hand was violently amputated from the body of . . .

Perlman heard him intone Miriam's name and he lurched. He experienced a ghost pain sear his own arm. Sweet Christ no, Miriam, no, he was hearing this wrong, picking up distorted signals. Tay's voice became a dirge that rendered language as blocks of grievous sound, like a pibroch.

This hand . . . amputated pre-mortem . . .

Perlman swayed a little. He had to remain upright. Don't reveal anything, don't let an emotion show. They'll come in for the kill if you do. You're wounded, and in pain, and they smell blood —

Wait, back up, how did they *know* the DNA sample from the hand was *Miriam's*? How the fuck did they know *that*? He'd come here anticipating what? At most — to be informed that the hand had belonged to a woman or a man, that was all. But he saw now that had been a vain expectation, they wouldn't bring him in for *that* scrap of news, never, not in a hundred years, they'd leave him outside the loop. Perlman, pah, he's nobody. Tell him shit.

No, he was here to be led in another cruel direction.

He stared at Latta, who had a look on his face of assumed innocence. 'What the fuck did you pull?'

'Pull? In what way?'

'The fucking DNA way, Latta. If this is Miriam's hand, you ran a comparison.'

'A hair from Miriam's hairbrush,' Latta said.

'Nicked from the loft.'

Latta didn't respond.

Tay looked at Perlman with his dishwater-grey eyes. 'When did you last see Miriam?'

He couldn't remember. Some time after the gull crashed into the skylight — where and when, he didn't know. That history was lost to him all at once. His head was like a gaunt tenement abandoned and he was wandering empty rooms dreamlike. Tay's office had gone silent, and the world with it — no phones rang anywhere in the building, no traffic moved along Pitt Street.

He broke this insufferable quiet. 'How does that matter?'

Latta said, 'It matters.'

Now Perlman was beginning to hear odd little echoes when other people spoke. He was coming down with something: a flu, no, more a case of serious alienation. The pain in his head raged. He yearned for one of his painkillers, which he'd left at home. 'I'm not evading anything, Latta. I just don't think it's any of your fucking business when I last saw her.'

Latta looked at Tay as if to say, *see what we're dealing with?*

Tay made a chubby steeple of his fingertips. 'Don't take that attitude, Perlman. Not here. Keep that for your pals in the streets.'

'Oh please forgive me,' Perlman said and feigned a cringing humility. 'By pals in the street — d'you mean pavement scruff, losers, dossers, wasters? Is that what you think populates my sad wee corner of the world, Chief?'

'Don't push my bloody patience,' Tay said and gave Perlman a homicidal stare. Sometimes he looked like a mug shot of a serial killer. 'Frankly I'd prefer to be at home at this time on a Saturday evening instead of sitting here.'

'Or tucking into grub at The Potted Calf,' Perlman said.

'Is that a dig at my personal life? I warn you, Perlman — '

'Warn me? Oh God what will you do, Chief? Get some uniforms to throw me into the street? I'm already on the fucking street, which is where you sent me months ago.'

'And where you deserve to be,' Tay said, collapsing his steepled fingers.

Perlman stepped toward the desk, glaring at Latta. 'You fucker, you think you can railroad me?'

Latta smiled. 'I do? Where?'

'Into that rusty depot where you store all your fucking stupid fantasies and your petty spites. More than your teeth that's corrupt, Latta — your soul.'

Tay wagged a finger at Perlman. 'Enough. You're here to answer some simple questions. Why is everything always so bloody *personal* with you, Perlman?'

'She was my fucking sister-in-law, of course it's *personal*. We're not talking about some *scruff* sleeping under a railway bridge — '

Ignore Tay. He was irrelevant and insensitive, a stupid man. This was about Perlman and Latta. This was about Latta's dementia.

'Let me guess your Christmas wish list, Latta.

381

One, absolute proof of Miriam's crime, *two*, evidence that I was her partner in this wrongdoing and *three* — since the hand was found in my bloody house, I was obviously the one that cut it off.'

Latta pinched his nose like he was locking a laugh down. 'It'll take an awfy big stocking.'

'Why else would you ask for a DNA comparison test? On the basis of your sick suspicions, you steal a hairbrush from her loft because you so desperately *want* that hand to be hers, it clears the way for you to poke one of your hirsute fingers at me. Perlman did it, Perlman's got a saw or a machete, ya ya ya, the *meshuga* butcher — '

Tay said, 'Nobody's accused you of severing this woman's hand, Perlman.'

'I'm sure Latta has another point of view. Right, George? Do me a favour and unlock the shrivelled wee walnut that passes as your heart and squeeze out the truth.'

Latta said, 'I don't want to contradict the Chief — '

'Oh heaven forbid — '

'But I'd be derelict in my duty if I didn't take you into account as a possible perpetrator. I emphasize possible. You had motive.'

'Oh aye, the loot I drooled over,' Perlman said.

'And you obviously had opportunity.'

'Opportunity galore, Latta. But explain this, because I'm getting slow in my old age — why would I cut off her fucking *hand*? What's the point in that? Mibbe you think I administered one of those barbaric medieval punishments

— because she tried to screw me out of the bounty, right? So tell me, where did I get the saw and the expertise?'

Latta said, 'Maybe your old friend Benjamin Tartakower supplied you with an instrument. You've been spending time in Govan, after all.'

Perlman thought: *so they watch me.* Why should he be surprised by anything now? Men in doorways, passers-by, characters you wouldn't look twice at, a city of spies. 'Seeing as you know so much about my fucking movements, Latta, did you ever *observe* me leave Tartakower's carrying a suspicious implement? Or did that happen on your day off? Or maybe you don't have days off?'

'And maybe Tartakower gave you *instruction*, Perlman. Showed you the best way to handle a surgical saw. It's not beyond possibility.'

'Aye, and it's not beyond possibility we'll wake one morning and the Clyde will be flowing in reverse.'

'So why did you visit Tartakower anyway? What have you got in common with a felon?' Latta smiled tight-lipped, showing no teeth.

Paint me in black, Latta. 'I'm his fucking spiritual advisor.'

'He must be in an awful bad way then.' Latta glanced at Tay, then looked again at Perlman. 'I understand he's got some kind of gang connection.'

'Sorry, I'm overlooking that. He's well in with a mob of vicious thirteen-year-old boys in hoods.'

Flustered, Latta skipped Perlman's response.

'What about this cleaning woman?'

'What's she got to do with anything?'

'After she'd been working for you a few days her son turned up dead, didn't he? One of those so-called surgical victims we've been getting.'

'You think I had something to do with that?'

'Only following the threads, Perlman.'

'And making silly patterns.'

'I don't know if they're patterns. Just pointing some things out, that's all.'

'You forgot to mention I haunt casinos and hang out with some questionable people.'

'I was getting to that — '

Perlman interrupted. 'So if I'm a right bad bastard that sawed off her hand, what did I do with the rest of her?'

Nobody responded. Silence consumed the room again. It had menace in it, the charged stillness in a landscape before a storm. He sensed waves of suppressed emotion roll toward him all at once. Then out of the quiet emerged a gathering of tiny sounds: Tigge's whistling nose and Tay, in a move he might have rehearsed, sliding his folder toward Latta and Latta taking something from it.

I'm excluded from this conspiracy of small noises.

Latta said, 'Here, look at this.'

Perlman reached for the object, a photograph, a coloured shot of fresh earth and tangled roots awry and broken blades of grass. The arrangement puzzled him a moment.

Look at the centre. Look at what the busted earth reveals.

384

Look at what they've *really* brought you to HQ to confront.

He was drawn down into the picture, into its pixels. Making sense of the chaos. Trying to. Not wanting to. The appetites of bugs, the blind explorations of worms, all the seething turbulence that fed and thrived a couple of inches under the surface.

Tigge said, 'She was discovered last night by some kids digging for worms. The precise location was ah now . . . ' He picked through his notes. 'Close to St Peter's Cemetery, some grassy waste ground . . . primary examination of the remains indicate she'd been dead for about two months, perhaps longer. Cause of death not yet established.'

'St Peter's Cemetery,' Latta said, as if he'd only just realized a damning fact. 'Across London Road from Tollcross Park. Isn't that your part of the world?'

The photograph in Perlman's hand shook. He willed his fingers to be firm. He had that flu-like sensation again: an inner shivering. Give these buggers nothing, nothing, never give them a sign, a sniff of what you are going through, whatever it is. 'Is there positive ID?'

'Yes,' Tay said.

'How can you be so damn sure this is who you say it is?'

'The body's missing a hand,' Tay replied. 'Not conclusive in itself, of course. But it led us to check dental records, which establish beyond any doubt that this is the body of Miriam Perlman.'

Perlman looked back down at the picture. Not

for long. Long enough to see the matted frizz of lifeless hair, the ruined face, the bones, a few of them still fleshy, in disarray. Who needs to scrutinize such a horror? Out of the earth. What was once human. He tossed the picture back at Latta, who caught it.

They'd brought him here to bushwhack him. They'd brought him here to batter him into submission: the hand is Miriam's, but hold on a minute, that's only a tasty appetizer, we've got more, open the box, here's a corpse for you as well. They were dealers in the craft of malice. They knew how to twist the knife.

'And so conveniently close to where I live,' he said quietly.

Latta said, 'Remarkable.'

'And that makes me a suspect.' He affected nonchalance, amazed by his own ability to hold at bay the babbling chorus he knew waited for him in the ante-chamber of his consciousness. An effort of will: dig deep, Lou.

'It puts you neatly in the frame,' Latta said.

'And am I alone in this frame, Latta?'

'For the moment. Others may turn up in due course.'

'You'd like me to confess now, and save you all some time. Where I got the saw. Did I use an anesthetic and how did I know how to use it. Did I buy equipment from a surgical supply store. Where did I do the cutting and what really caused her death. How did I transport her. What sort of spade did I use to dig her grave. Bladdy bladdy. So many little details you have to gather. It's work.'

Tay said, 'In your own interests, you may want to seek the advice of a lawyer, Perlman.'

Perlman wasn't about to pause and acknowledge this eejit's suggestion. No, he'd fly through the storm as long as he could. 'All these intriguing little details aside, we haven't explored motive, have we? Was it because she was this greedy cow that Latta likes to imagine, and she was stealing money. Was it because she scorned my advances and broke my patient heart. Or what about — she found herself a lover and I was deranged with murderous jealousy. There must be others.'

Tay leaned across his desk. 'A lawyer, Perlman. A good one.'

Perlman couldn't stop himself. Silence was his enemy. 'You might as well book me. Look at me, so mild and compliant, I'm helping you build a fucking case. I want to be a model suspect. I don't want to get unruly and smash up the room. Am I doing well, Latta? Tell me.'

'Champion,' Latta said, without enthusiasm.

Perlman felt his energy dip but he wasn't letting that stop him. He extended his arms, offered his wrists to Latta. 'So cuff me. Come on, Georgie, the cuffs. What kind of cop-shop is this where you don't whip out the cuffs? Stick em on me. What's your problem, Latta? Forget your cuffs? Leave em at chez Latta?'

Latta looked uncomfortable. 'It's not — '

Tay interrupted. 'This isn't the way it works, Perlman, and you bloody well know it.'

'All I know is I want cuffs. I have a right to be cuffed. How about you, Tay? Cuffs in your desk there? Get them out, here's my wrists, lock me up and throw away the key. Yodel-ay-ee-dee. Model suspect, model prisoner, all in one package. Any cuffers on offer here?'

Tay rose. 'I advise you yet again to talk to your solicitor.'

Perlman took long exaggerated steps toward Tigge. 'Where are your handcuffs, King Kong? Here's my wrists. Stand up and be counted, Tigge. Be bold. Cuff me. Fucking cuff me.'

He was into it now, the crazy dance of the cuffs, turning this way and that, his arms held out and flashed under Tigge's beard and then, spinning, he offered his wrists to Latta, who pushed them aside, and then he confronted Tay, rolling up the sleeves of his coat and opening his hands. 'Come on, Tay, cuff me.'

Tay said, 'Stop all this silly-bugger stuff and go home. You'll be advised of our further investigations in due course, and when we move you'll be the first to know. Now get out of my bloody sight.'

Perlman walked to the door. 'You're sending me home. You sure?'

Tay said, 'Yes yes go. Get legal help.'

'Mental help more like,' Latta said, grinning.

Perlman was about to turn on Latta, but he let it go. He gripped the door handle. He was reluctant to turn it. It's easier to stay in this room, he thought. Out there alone, dear Christ. Who knew what. He kept moving. Blood roared in his brain. He shut the door behind him — and then his whole life appeared to be in silent rewind, he was moving in reverse down a flight of steps and along a corridor and out past the reception desk where Wren was talking backwards and then he was back in the street with the rain blowing into his face, and he was walking to his car, the entire world arse-backward . . . if he kept going in this direction he'd make it down through all the years to the womb, a foetal mote and finally nothing. This was grief, this reaching back to a hiding place where you were safe from scarring.

He reached his car, lost his balance, slumped against the chassis. He remembered saying to Miriam that night long ago in the loft that his heart was a harp silent half a lifetime until she'd come along. And she'd pressed a finger to his lips and simply said *Lou* — maybe with affection, maybe not, he'd never know now.

All he knew was he'd loved her once, dreamed of her for long years, and daydreamed of her, until she turned to mist, a figure he saw only on the far-off edges of his vision. And then he failed to see even that, she diminished gradually, faded daily, reduced to the isolated essence of a person — an impression he received through a sensory organ he never knew he possessed. Love rots in neglect and unfulfilled longings. And Miriam. Miriam was twice-lost to him — the first in love, the second in death.

He sat in his car, and realized he was weeping quietly.

He wiped his eyes with his knuckles and the thought bludgeoned him: who sent the fucking postcards?

42

Rick Tosh sat in the lounge of the Cameron House Hotel and drank Guinness slowly. He'd been in Scotland for two weeks, what they called a fortnight here, and was damn homesick, although he was acquiring a taste for the black bevy. Scotland was scenic all right, the Hotel was conveniently close to Glasgow, but the grey skies over Loch Lomond depressed the crap out of him, and the rain, oh Christ the rain. He was leaving first thing in the a.m. Back to Texas, back to heat and dry air and the things he knew.

He raised a hand when he saw the man he'd been waiting for come into the lounge. 'Over here, Willie.'

Willie Boyd, a thin man in blue jeans and a rain-stained khaki windcheater, walked to Tosh's table.

'Drink, Willie?'

Willie Boyd sat. 'A wee Auchentoshan would warm the bones.'

'Is that a whisky?'

'Lowland single malt,' Boyd said.

'You Scots and your malts.' Rick Tosh scanned the room for a waiter, didn't see one. 'Fucking service here.' He stuck a hand inside his pocket and removed an envelope, which he gave to Willie Boyd.

Boyd opened it with his nimble bony fingers and looked inside.

'It's all there,' Tosh said. 'Airline ticket. Bank draft in the sum we agreed. Plus, lo and behold, one genuine green card.'

Boyd checked the contents. 'Good.'

Tosh continued his search for a waiter. 'Whadda you plan to do?'

'I'll check out Noo Yock City, then see.' Boyd smiled. 'America's a big country and Baba's future is infinite.'

'Yeah, I guess it is,' and Tosh laughed in his silent head-nodding way.

Boyd rolled his eyes so the whites were all Tosh could see.

'That's some fucking trick,' Tosh said.

'Piece a cake, part of the gig. The real downside is all the shite you have to spout, and the warpaint's a bastart to get off.'

Tosh spotted a waiter, hailed him. 'Gimme an — what was it, Willie?'

'Auchentoshan,' Boyd said.

'Right away.' The waiter, whose face was squirrel-like, scampered off.

Tosh said, 'My people are grateful to you.'

'You're paying for it. My honest opinion, Chuck's feet don't touch the ground any more. He was OK operating mid-level, and he had ambition, but as soon as he got the nod to take over, the changes started. Big anxieties about trust, worries about his underlings. And big big dreams, the kind despots get before their downfall — including a statue in his honour in George Square. A fucking statue! Reuben Mussolini, for Christ's sake. He's got major fault-lines ready to blow. You don't want that.'

Tosh shrugged, 'Wouldn't be the first bad pony we bet on. Cut losses, move along. What about this girl?'

'She lost most of her interest in the whole guru babble, but Chuck bought it lock stock and knicker-elastic. That tells me she's smarter than Chuck. Or less gullible.'

'She a problem for us?'

Willie Boyd stacked beer mats on the table. 'My opinion, no. She's always had dreams of her own that'll take her far away from Glasgow.'

Rick Tosh's cellphone rang. He looked at the caller ID. 'Talk of the devil.'

'Zat Chuck?'

Tosh killed his cellphone. 'Bye bye Chuck.'

The waiter came back and Boyd smelled his drink before he tasted it. 'Good doing business with you, Rick.'

'Hey, real pleasure for me.'

Willie Boyd scarfed his Aucky and stood up. He shook Rick Tosh's hand. 'I spose you'll deal with Chuck.'

'Board level decision,' Tosh said. 'We'll see what they say in Dallas.'

'May your karma be good,' Willie Boyd said.

'Same to you.'

Willie Boyd walked a few paces and turned, 'Ronnie Mathieson has his heid screwed on the right way. Matter of interest.'

'Noted.'

Tosh watched Willie Boyd — one-time child actor and later ringmaster for a self-motivation bandwagon that conducted sessions on How to

Develop Your Total Human Potential — walk out of the lounge and into darkness. Good actor, Tosh thought.

Shame about Chuck.

43

The rain had let up when Perlman stepped from his car and saw two TV vans with satellite dishes parked at the kerb outside the tenement where Betty lived. A dozen or more murky figures, some with cameras at the ready, crowded him as he headed for the door.

'Is that not Perlman?' one of the figures asked.

'Or a dead ringer,' said a runty little guy in a herringbone coat.

'Scatter, you lot,' Perlman said, thrusting through. 'I'm in no fucking mood for inky malingerers. And get these vans to fuck outta here.'

'Come on, Lou, a little cooperation, some of us have been waiting hours for an interview,' the runty man whined. 'Free press, Lou, basis of a democratic society.'

'Democracy, feh. Shite-hawks, every one of you. *Tell me how you feel about your son, Mrs McLatchie*. How do you *think* she feels? You scadges have pestered enough victims you could write this off the top of your heads without *kvetching* about an interview.'

One of the journos remarked, 'Every story has a different heartbeat.'

'You'd know something about the heart, would you?' Perlman recognized this wavy-haired guy from the *Sunday Mail*. He'd been present at Miriam's trial.

'Just get your arses outta here. Go on. Give the woman a break.'

The *Sunday Mail* scribbler said, 'Is Mrs McLatchie a *personal* friend or is this police business?'

If this was innuendo, Perlman chose to ignore it. He turned to search for Betty's bell among the others on the door.

'Suppose *you* tell us about the dead boy, Lou. I've got to file something. I'll do a tear-jerker. Not a damp eye in Glasgow.'

Lou looked round. 'You think I don't *know* your style? Ghouls and flesh-eaters, every one of you.'

'Hold on there, Lou.' The man in the herringbone coat protested. 'Speaking as a citizen and not a scribbler, as you put it, lemme ask you to tell the people of Glasgow what's going on, this isn't the first body — '

'No fucking comment. Print that. And spell my name right.' Perlman found Betty's bell, pressed twice. He waited in agitation, pressed it again, holding his finger down. The journos crowded him with the hungry persistence of gulls swarming a trawler.

A man switched on the blinding lights of a TV camera perched on his shoulder, and hunched forward, and a young woman draped in a fur-trimmed pashmina wrap was testing her microphone. Lou recognized her from a local news show. She thought she was Queen of Glasgow TV. She was always in gossip columns, linked to this actor or that wealthy footballer. She began to glide forward with the self-important air of one who lives in the public eye.

Questions pepper-sprayed Lou. *Tell us what you know. Tell us is if you're still suspended from duty. Tell us tell us is there any truth in is the rumour this the work of a lone madman or do we have a crime syndicate killing for human body parts . . .*

Betty opened the door a crack, enough for Lou to get through — just as a camera flashed and turned Betty's face fluorescent.

'Bugger it,' she said and grabbed Perlman by the arm, drew him inside the close, and slammed the door.

She led him into her flat, shut her door, locked and bolted it.

Perlman said, 'I'm later than I expected — '

'I can't go out, can't even open my curtains. I sit in the kitchen and hide. The doorbell keeps ringing. The phone.' She covered her ears with her hands. *'Jesus.'*

'They're savages,' Perlman said. 'They eat their young.'

Inside the kitchen an overburdened ashtray sat on the table next to a teapot and a half-eaten packet of McVitie's chocolate digestives. Perlman helped himself to one, ate it hungrily.

The phone rang. He picked it up and said, 'Fuk Yoo Chinese Takeaway,' and left the handset off the hook.

* * *

'You look weary, Lou. Sit, I'll pour some tea.'

Perlman sagged into a chair. Betty filled a cup with dark tea, pushed a bowl of sugar and a jug of milk toward him. Perlman snagged another biscuit and devoured it.

'You hungry? You can have anything you want providing it's eggs. Boiled, fried, scrambled. I haven't been able to go to the shops.'

'Scrambled sounds good. You don't mind?'

'Coming up.' Betty cracked eggs quickly into a bowl, salt and pepper, whisked the mix. Into the frying pan with everything.

The doorbell rang and rang.

She said, 'Tell me they'll get tired and bugger off.'

'Not yet. The energy of werewolves is boundless,' Perlman said.

Betty set the eggs down in front of him. 'I hope they're OK.'

He ate like a man rescued from a remote island after many years on a diet of raw turtle. He finished fast, laid down his fork, wiped his lips with a paper napkin. 'Thanks. Delicious.'

She sat, lighting a cigarette. She was watching him — a little warily, he thought. Wondering about something. Did she detect hesitation in him? Or a depth of sadness? The blue eyes were bright, and in receiving mode. There was no way he was going to unload the story of Miriam on her. Later, not tonight. She'd never met Miriam, but she'd heard the Aunts talking. Those two old dears rambled on about family matters from the minute they rose until they went to bed again, recycling stories with the patience of women crocheting.

The Aunts would be devastated when they heard about Miriam, even if they harboured no great affection for her. Another murder in the family, first Colin, now his widow. Shame and gossip in the community, scandal. People stopping to ask them questions in local shops, on the street, in the park, Rabbi Grossman coming round to offer spiritual comfort but also to pick up the latest tittle-tattle.

Perlman got up, wandered the kitchen.

'Heebie-jeebies?' Betty asked.

'Wired.' The world jostled him. The postcards. The places. Amsterdam. Copenhagen. Florence. Who wrote the words? He leaned against the stove. The fridge hummed. The doorbell rang again. Something fizzed in the ashtray, a discarded match maybe. He wanted to stay in this flat, shut away from the bawsacs on the pavement, the world in general. He wanted to believe the ID of Miriam was an enormous forensic misinterpretation, an error so gross the slacker should be crucified.

'Your coat looks damp.' Betty was promptly on her feet. She felt the fabric. 'Lou, it's practically *sodden*. I'll put it in the airing cupboard.' She helped him out of the coat, but not before he'd removed his mobie from a pocket. She stashed the coat in a closet on the other side of the room.

'How are your shoes? They damp as well?'

'A wee bit, but nothing — '

'Let's dry them,' she said. 'The socks too. Don't want you getting cold.'

Perlman bent obediently, removed his shoes. He rolled off the socks, relieved to see they matched. Betty stuck shoes and socks in the cupboard where she'd put the coat. Perlman glimpsed the interior — a big brass hot-water cylinder, towels and bedsheets folded neatly on shelves.

Annie's vision, laundry. The sickroom. It reared back at him. He should phone Adamski, let Joe and some crime-scene specialists make something of it. How long was it since Annie had seen the bloodied sheet? A full forty-eight hours anyway — which was more than enough time for Dysart and Ace to do a thorough cleaning job.

'Fancy a drink? Scotch?'

'Sounds fine.' Perlman was conscious of his white blue-veined feet and the unusually long middle toes. Betty brought him a tumbler of Scotch and laid it on the table. She sat, a glass of wine tilted in her hand. He liked her maroon shirt and blue jeans — she'd set black aside, as if she might create a space, however transient and illusory, between herself and the garb of grief.

'The last barefoot man in this flat was a Spanish accordion player called Yglesias . . . New Year's Eve 1990.'

A barefoot Spaniard playing an accordion. *Barcefuckinglona* — can't get away from Miriam's destinations, her fabled odyssey. And all the time she'd been lying motionless under the clay of Glasgow, less than a mile from his house. And he'd imagined she'd found a lover, or she'd been in an accident or who knows what his wild head created —

He drank his Scotch a little too quickly.

She pushed her chair back from the table and stretched her legs, and made a connection — her slippers against his bare feet.

He drew back, and so did she, and she said, 'Ooops.'

But he felt the pleasing frisson he'd had before with her — the closeness of lips a few nights ago, the almost-kiss. Wrong time then, wrong time now. Life was askew. He was a collection of unanswered questions. But those sympathetic eyes and that lush mouth drew him.

Except the dead were present in this room. The dead remained to be salvaged.

Betty was speaking quickly, as if to diminish any significance there might have been in the contact. 'I get a kick working for your Aunts, Lou. They're funny sometimes.'

'They're a pair of old eccentrics all right.'

He listened to Betty talk about Marlene's noontime habit of spiking fresh lemon juice with crushed cloves and a thimble of port. He enjoyed the imitation she did of Marlene, catching exactly the rise and fall of the old woman's voice and gestures.

Easy street, Lou thought. Let's talk about family all night. But his mind was peeling off elsewhere.

Split-level brain in action.

Somebody sent those cards. Somebody killed M. One and the same person — or two? One who'd committed the act, and an accomplice who travelled Europe? But why only three postcards in all that time? Why not once a week, twice a week?

Because you received just enough to make you think she was alive, OK, but that same irregularity served another purpose — *she doesn't entirely think the world of you, Lou.* And the messages, aloof, devoid of sentiment, were designed to underline the fact she didn't care to divulge anything of her feelings and plans. Even the fucking pedestrian images were an insult, postcards somebody would pick out if they were in a hurry, and sent to a recipient of no importance.

You were meant to be hurt. Somebody schemed your anguish. Somebody as black-hearted as Latta.

Maybe Latta's the one. Killed Miriam, forged the cards, popped out of the country a couple of times and mailed them. But Latta, despite his malicious cunning, his desire to hammer Lou down, would be reluctant to leave Glasgow — why would he turn his back on the city and neglect his obsession? God forbid, he might miss something. A clue, a hint of Miriam and Perlman's complicity. Also there was the loft to keep under surveillance, and although he had a paid informant to do it he needed to be in a place where he could easily be reached.

OK, imagine Latta had an accomplice post the cards —

Lou's head ached.

Betty was still going on about his aunts. She obviously found the subject neutral territory, a place she could wander safely. 'I once asked Hilda why she never married. She said she never met the right man. She 'walked out' with a young guy called Barry Bernstein for a time. The Nosepicker. Always hiding behind a hankie, finger as far up his nostrils as he could shove it.'

'Guaranteed to win a lady's heart.'

Betty smiled. 'After the Nosepicker there was the Slob.'

Perlman heard this even as he drifted to Dysart and Ace, wondering if *they'd* dragged Miriam randomly off a street, drugged her and tossed her in the back of the van, chained her, and then . . . How else did they find their victims other than by snatching people walking alone down dark empty streets? It was a job too risky to do in daylight. And they had the cutting implements, the means — if Annie's story was right. But Miriam didn't fit into what he assumed was their purpose: cash, working for profit — Jackie's operations had to be paid for, the upkeep of that house, even in disrepair, devoured money. So how did it benefit them financially to cut off a hand?

Click! Was it possible *Latta* had hired Ace and Dysart?

This leap plunged him deeper into thickets of associations — how did they meet, what was the arrangement? But what did Latta have to gain by Miriam's death — when all he really wanted was to *rub her face in a crime*, and Perlman's along with it? In public, where he could scream *I was right all along*.

You couldn't find that gleeful fulfilment if your quarry was dead.

Betty said, 'Hilda doesn't speak much about him.'

He'd lost her thread. 'The Slob you mean? I never heard of him.'

'He ate with his mouth open as wide as the

Clyde Tunnel. Always stuffing it full and food would drop into his lap.'

'Hilda's choices were impeccable,' Perlman said.

The doorbell rang again. Some dickhead on the pavement kept his finger to the button. Perlman asked for directions to the toilet.

'Through the living room and down the hall. First door on the right.'

The toilet was a small cubicle Betty had prettified with some dried flowers in a vase, and small prints of old Glasgow on the walls. He peed, flushed, washed his hands, dried them on a dark green towel colour-coordinated with the pale green walls. He saw himself in the oval mirror, *oy*, whose face is that? Eyelids puffy, bristle on his jaw darkening by the day, expression *farklempte*.

Perlman, feeling your years.

He turned from his reflection and took his mobile out of a trouser pocket. He punched in the number for Adamski. Saturday night, what chance? An automated voice said *Your call is being redirected*. He waited.

Adamski's voice came through. 'Hello.'

Perlman said, 'I'm not disturbing you?'

'I'm sitting in front of the telly watching reality shite.'

Perlman told him about Annie's experience, then asked, 'Can you get a search-warrant, Joe?'

'Do *you* believe she saw this body, Lou?'

'She saw something. I'm *inclined* to believe it was a corpse.'

'Inclined's iffy. I'd like to talk to this lady.'

403

'She's scared, Joe. She doesn't want a certain person to know her whereabouts.'

'And who is this scary person?'

'Reuben Chuck.'

'No wonder she's feart. Am I to take your word for what she said?'

'My word's gold.'

Adamski was quiet a second. 'Forty-eight hours have passed since she claimed to see this corpse. You know that body's long gone, Lou.'

'I know. But I only learned about it this afternoon. Then I was detained by another matter.' Another matter, but he was locking a door on that wretched encounter in Latta's Theatre of the Cruelty. Sometimes all you can do is keep swimming through the slime.

'I'll need to dig somebody up at the Proc-Fisc's office, *and* a Sheriff who doesn't mind getting off his arse on a Saturday to swear out a warrant. Then I'll have to scratch around to ferret out a couple of forensics people.'

Ferret. A verb, an animal. Perlman remembered Issy. A drab sorry creature, dead eyes and lacklustre coat. Who keeps a fucking ferret? He lowered his voice in case Betty had some reason to come along the hall. 'It's possible, but no certainty, that Kirk McLatchie was inside that house at some point. Mibbe he was butchered there. I stress mibbe.'

'This a hunch?'

'A feeling, Joe.'

'I'm working on the testimony of a girl who won't talk, plus Lou Perlman's feeling. My lucky day, everything so stacked in my favour.'

404

'Nothing's easy,' Perlman said. 'One final thing. Two serious Dobermans roam the grounds.'

'Dogs? I love dogs,' Adamski said.

'Not this pair. Thanks, Joe.'

'Thank me after I get the warrant,' Adamski said. 'But don't expect it to happen too soon.'

Perlman cut the connection.

Inside the kitchen Betty was checking the condition of his coat in the airing cupboard.

'Another wee Scotch?'

Perlman thought about it, but said no, just as his phone rang. He checked the screen: Scullion's name.

'Excuse me.' Half-turning away from Betty, he spoke into the mobie. 'Whatsup, Sandy?'

Scullion said, 'I just heard about Miriam. It's fucking awful. I can't believe Tay and Latta keelhauled you like that — '

'After they made me walk the plank.'

Scullion said, 'I don't think it's funny.'

'You hear laughter from me?'

'The whole thing's fucking deplorable, Lou.'

Perlman glanced at Betty, who'd risen to water a plant on the window-sill. 'They're masters of finesse.'

'That fucker Latta doesn't have a case. You know that. It's all sound and fury fuelled by his spite.'

'I don't intend to lose sleep over Latta. Believe me.'

'They'll drop it eventually, of course. But at a cost to you.'

'I resign the Force.'

'That would be Tay's asking price.'

'And Latta wins.'

'He'll think it some kind of victory, sure . . . it's a clumsy question, I know, but how're you feeling?'

'I'm tired, Sandy. How are things with you?'

'We lost our banker. Totally mental. It was a dead giveaway when he looked at three hundred mug shots and identified *every single face* as one of the fuckers who invaded his house. On the up side, we're raiding the offices of Chuck's lawyers this very night.'

'Legally?'

'How else? These are hot-shot lawyers. You don't go near them without the right paperwork. Chuck gave a freebie bus to Ragada, and the guru tried to sell it to a sharp-eyed dealer . . . who knew the docs of ownership were fake. Good fakes, just not good enough. The guru has disappeared.'

Perlman said, 'These are the days of false prophets, Sandy.'

'Call me in the morning, Lou. Better still, drop round about midday, we'll have a beer.'

Lou closed the connection, massaged his eyes.

Betty said, 'What was that about resigning?'

'Pah, politics.'

'In other words, don't ask.'

He got up from his chair. His feet were so cold they might have been welded to the floor. 'It's the usual polis shite, Betty. I'm not keeping anything from you.' That comment, he knew, might come back to haunt him.

'You're in trouble, Lou,' and she touched his hand softly.

406

'This is new?'

'I wish I could help.'

'It's time I was leaving.'

'You don't have to go. Unless you have other places . . .'

'And miles to travel,' he said.

He fetched his coat and shoes and socks. The coat was warm but still damp, the socks were tolerable. 'I'll kick some arses out there before I go. I'll also disable the doorbell. You can put your phone back but don't answer unless I give you the signal.'

She was downcast. She didn't want to be alone. He hugged her briefly, kissed her cheek, then went down the hallway, where he paused to reach up and yank the bell-wire from the wall before he continued into the street.

The scribblers were still milling around. Dogged crowd, hunting in packs. They clamoured for answers. They had readers to titillate, viewers to please.

Perlman drew them together. 'Pay attention, youse lot. Mrs McLatchie is now sedated and sleeping. The phone's not being answered and the doorbell's disconnected, so unless you break a window to get to her — which let me remind you is seriously against the law — there will be no statement tonight, and no interview. Awright? Got that? Now let me see you scatter, boys and girls.'

'Aw fuck,' somebody said.

The Queen of Glasgow TV was snippy. Her diction slipped. 'Been freezing my bloody arse off for hours here.'

'Here's a wee suggestion, dear. Go home to bed and crack open a good book.'

'Don't *dear* me, Perlman,' she said. 'I'd like to do a story on the stalling tactics of the local police, starring you.'

'He's no even on the Force,' the guy with the wavy hair said.

Perlman stared at the guy belligerently. 'That's a fucking rumour, you turnips will swallow anything. Now move, move along. Give the woman a break.'

The hounds began slowly to disperse, muttering.

Perlman waited, rattling car keys and change in his pocket, until the last of them had gone and the TV van had pulled away, before he walked to his car and sat behind the wheel, watching vigilantly for anyone who might chance his arm and sneak back.

Nobody did.

Driving home, he mourned Miriam silently.

44

From the kitchen window Dorcus looked at the lit towers. Grievous Saturday, damp dark Slabland. Sometimes a hundred or more empty beer cans and bottles were tossed over the wall on Saturday nights. Saturday was a pagan Glasgow festival, football in the afternoon, drunken fans rolling home hours after the game, rowdy and violent whether their team won or lost, car windows and street lamps smashed with stones, and always at least one murder, usually from stab wounds or head blows with a heavy instrument or just a damn good kicking.

The Dobermans howled. They always knew when it was Saturday. They went berserk Saturdays.

Jackie Ace, dressed in a yellow chenille robe, was fashioning a head full of long ringlets with her curling iron. 'I want you to know — I'm very proud of the way you dealt with Perlman.'

'I just stood my ground, I told him he was wrong about that photo.' Dorcus wished he still had long hair. He missed it, the feel of it against the side of his face. He watched how deft Jackie was with the curling iron.

'That's all it takes. Stand your ground, don't give way.'

She set the iron down and took Dorcus's hand, stroked it. At times she wanted to hold him, never let go. 'When you showed him the

409

OR, he accepted your story.'

'I had your help — '

'Oh, all I did was take some of your Ma's old things out of the attic.'

'But it was good — '

'I'm just so brilliant.' She laughed and wrapped her arms around him. She was filled with a longing to protect him. She kissed his forehead and was impatient for the day when she'd no longer be this incomplete creature.

She raised a palm to the side of his face. 'You can do anything.'

'Only when you're with me.'

'I'll always be with you. Have I ever let you down?'

Dorcus couldn't remember a time. All the way back as far as the Tartakower days, he'd known Jackie would be his life-partner. How eager he'd been to befriend Jackie, following him around, fetching his surgical instruments, watching the way he operated. He'd learned so much observing Jackie with a scalpel. He'd marvelled at Jackie's nimble hands. And card tricks — Jackie could create illusions that left you laughing and baffled. Cards vanished without trace inside hankies, spades turned to diamonds, clubs to hearts, cards cascaded randomly out of his hands and yet always ended in the appropriate suits, cards set on fire in one place were restored from ashes in another . . .

He loved Jackie instantly. Or if not instantly, then the day after.

One night Jackie said, *I need the operation. I need it for myself and for you.*

Dorcus remembered that with joy.

He looked into her eyes and said, 'I'll sell this house.'

'Let's not go there.'

'Somebody will buy it. Even if they only want the land and demolish the p-property — '

'No.' Jackie was touched whenever he suggested this. She saw how eager he was, how love and generosity brightened his face.

'It makes sense — '

'No, love, no, this is something I want to do through my own efforts.'

Dorcus opened his mouth to make an objection, but Jackie said, 'I mean it. My decision . . . But there's something you *can* do for me, sweetie, drive me to work later.'

'I always do,' he said.

Jackie slipped into a light-hearted mood, snapped her fingers and gyrated her hips this way, that way, and laughed from the back of her throat. '*Arriba arriba!*'

Dorcus was delighted whenever she danced. The house shed its dull trappings, and for a few lively minutes became a place free of the past, rescued from ruin.

★   ★   ★

Reuben Chuck didn't know how long he'd been driving. What he did *know* was that he was lost in a part of Glasgow he rarely visited, deepest Cathcart. This isn't east, this is aw wrong. He wished he'd brought Mathieson, oh but he was damned if he'd phone Ronnie and ask for

411

directions — total loss of *face*.

Besides he was fucking *stocious*.

Backing up drunkenly in a quiet side-street, he ran over somebody's lawn, demolishing a wooden fence and squadron of garden gnomes. Tut-tut-Tutenkamen. On the sort of impulse experienced by inebriates and loonies, he got out of the Jag and seized one of the decapitated gnome heads and set it on the passenger seat, buckling the seat belt round it.

He needed a pal. Wee cheeky pink face, whiskers, red lips, pointy ears.

He drove away at speed. The gnome's head, fixed by the belt, stared forward.

'Been in a Jag before, wee man? Naw? Sit back and enjoy.'

Chuck played ventriloquist, squeaky voice. '*Thanks for the lift, I was very fed up in that garden.*'

'Life canny be interestin just standin there all day.'

'*Aye it's a fuckin bore, Mr Chuck.*'

'Want some gin?'

'*I swore off the booze, Mr Chuck.*'

'Aye me too, me too, wee man. But I was fuckin miserable without it. Zatza fact.'

By the time Chuck reached Daldowie Cemetery he'd finished the last of the gin and was lost again. The city was all unfamiliar intersections. For a minute he thought he'd somehow travelled into another city altogether, one he'd never seen before. He drove into a petrol station, narrowly avoided a pump, then went inside and asked for directions.

A surly young guy with a pearl in his oil-stained right ear lobe was totting up the take, watching a paper-roll spit through an adding-machine.

'Tryin to find Cobble Street,' Chuck said, stumbling into a Coca-Cola machine. 'Ooops. Or mibbe Cobble Drive.'

The guy didn't look up. He snarled, 'Make yer mind up. And stay a few feet away, wid ye? I could smell the booze on you coming in.'

'Fancy that. I musta been drinking. So what. None o your business.'

'I've a mind to call the polis and tell them. Drunk driver on the loose.'

Chuck thumped the counter. 'Cobble *Drive*. Put a lid on the attitude, jim.'

'Oh pardon me.' The guy raised his face and stared at Chuck with intense animosity. 'What are you gonny day about it? Eh? *Eh*?'

'This.' Chuck reached across and grabbed the guy by his earring and drew his face down, pressing it into the laminated counter. Dazzlin motion, speed and agility. Wasted he might be, but he could still move fast. He imagined this was Baba he was cramming into the counter. Take yer karma and shove it ya fraudulent fucker.

'Ah-*wouch*,' the guy moaned.

'You're what's wrong with this fuckin city, too many rude bastarts, too many toe-rags like you.' He gave the earring a twist and the lobe bled freely. 'Geeza directions then I let you up.'

The guy, lips kissing laminate, said, 'Leave here, take a right, you're headed for the M73.

Keep going until you reach the M8. Follow the signs for Easterhouse . . . Once you're there, stop and ask somebody.'

'M73, M8.' Chuck memorized this much. His brain was an imploded soufflé. 'So you don't know exactly where Cobble Drive is.'

'No, but listen, you'll be in the general area. Ask anybody.'

Chuck stepped back, releasing the earring. 'That's all you had to do in the first place, sonny. Instead o this surly act. A wee bit cooperation goes a long way in this life. Know what I'm sayin.'

The guy said, 'You hurt my ear.'

'I coulda yanked it right off yer *fuckin face*, ya wanker. Think about that.' He kicked the Coke machine and left the building, crossing the concourse and passing under tall blindingly bright lamps.

He reached the Jag. Inside, he fumbled with his belt-buckle and looked at the gnome. 'Some people,' he said.

'*There are bad-mannered gnomes as well, Mr Chuck.*'

'In all walks of life bad is what you find more than anythin else,' and Chuck gave the big car some instant pedal and zoomed out of the station and zipped quickly through oncoming traffic, screeching past flashing lights and angry horns — so much fuckin *rage*, just because he nipped in front of a few cars. Rudeness everywhere. He cruised the M8, dipping in and out of lanes as he fancied. He burst into loud song, *This Jaguar's so fast and sleek, it could run for a fuckin week . . .*

When he reached the housing scheme he drove between tower blocks, passing people on unlit corners doing sneaky wee deals in the dark, and boys and girls smoking hash. He braked, tyres squealing, and rolled his window down and asked some kids the way to Cobble Drive. They gave him directions that sounded simple enough.

'Izzat a gnome's heid in there?'

Chuck looked at the young girl who'd asked. She was pretty, but blurred in his gin-whacked vision, as if she was underwater. A nimbus hung around the crown of her head. He was reminded of catholic icons. He remembered tossing cash at the RC Church, and that pederast Father Skelton. *You'll get your reward when you're in heaven, Reuben.*

'Lassie, come here, closer. You tell me. What the fuck is it about holy men, eh?' he asked.

'Uh?' The girl poked her face inside the open window. She popped a bubble out of her chewing-gum. Chuck imagined it was a small balloon-like extension of her tongue.

He said, 'Priests and gurus, total shite. Total shite! The lotta them.'

'So they are.' The girl giggled. Her friends were gathering around, a bunch of teenage girls with bloodshot eyes.

'Priests and popes and fuckin bishops,' Chuck said. He understood he meant to warn these girls of some impending evil in the world, but the intention fell apart like faulty scaffolding. 'You lassies keep an eye open. Know what I mean?'

'Whiddye doin wi a gnome's heid anyway?'

Chuck moved his lips, did the squeaky voice. *'Hello girls, I'm Gregory and I'm gnomeward bound.'*

High on dope, the girls found everything hysterical, doubling over and throwing their heads back and hooting at the sky.

'Night girls,' the gnome said.

Chuck drove off and found his way to Cobble Drive, where he saw the house set back from the road. *Sticks out like a plook on a fashion model's nose Mr Chuck.* A couple of windows were lit. He braked, gazed at the high walls, the big iron gates. He stepped from the car, walked to the gates. Lockedy-locked. Two big dogs rushed through shrubbery, frantic canine energy, slavering. Fuck the fuckin dogs, Chuck thought. He rattled the gates.

Dr Dysart, I am here to see you.

The gates shook but wouldn't yield. He kicked them. *Come on.*

Easy solution. He got behind the wheel of the Jag and reversed. He told the gnome to hang on, changed gear to drive, and flattened his foot on the pedal and smacked the big car straight into the gates, which swayed, then buckled and finally snapped under the force of so much horsepower. He broke a headlamp and ruined his grille, but kept going, clattering through a clump of shrubbery and over a series of grassy bumps and then a stretch of gravel that crackled under the wheels and there he was — right up at the front door, Jag scratched and dented, fender bent, two dogs howling at him, and the gnome's head, which had fallen from the passenger seat, broken in many pieces on the floor.

I lose friends, Chuck thought. I lose my girl.

He rolled down his window and looked at the big dogs. 'Fuck off ya beasts.'

Staggering, Chuck took a gun from the glove compartment and got out of the Jag and fired the weapon in the air and the dogs scampered off terrified. He walked up the steps to the front door and kicked it open, roaring *Dorco, hey Dorco, where are you?*

★ ★ ★

Jackie saw him from the window of the sickroom and said, 'Company, Dorcus. In a Jaguar. With a gun.'

Dorcus peered out. 'Oh G-god, it's Chuck. What'll we do?'

Jackie Ace was already planning a course of action. She squeezed Dorcus's hand. 'Can you go down and keep him occupied?'

'Occupied? You *kidding*?'

'A minute's all I need, Dorcus.'

Dorcus trembled. A gun. He'd never even *seen* a gun. 'I don't think I c-can d-do it, Jackie.'

'Stop stuttering. You can do it. I won't let you come to any harm. I promise you. Go, before he comes upstairs.'

Dorcus felt cold fear. He trusted Jackie with his life, but even so. What if Chuck shot him right away, no questions asked.

From below Chuck yelled *Where's my girl, Dorco?* His big blustery voice rattled through the hallway.

417

'Stall him. Tell him you don't know where she is,' Jackie said. 'Look at him with confidence, right in the fucking eye.'

'C-confidence?'

Jackie Ace said, 'The way you were with Perlman.'

'Perlman didn't have a gun.'

'Do it for me, Dorcus. Show me.'

Dorcus stepped out into the hallway and moved as if through marmalade to the top of the stairs. Brave and bold, right, he wanted to show Jackie he was worthy, he wanted to be manly. *Nobody comes into this house and threatens me with a gun.* He descended. He sweated. His eyeballs felt numb. He had the feeling he'd piss his trousers any moment. He'd done that years and years ago, hiding behind the curtain and spying on the seance, the creepiness of it all.

He reached the landing and looked down and shook and tried to conceal his fear. *Jackie promised.*

Red-faced, swaying, Chuck was looking up at him.

'Where's my girrel, Dorco? What have you done to my lovely Glor-ian-na-na?'

'She's n-not here Mr Chuck.' His bladder swelled. His throat was so dry his words felt like wads of cotton. *I'm coming apart, Jackie.*

Chuck blasted the gun at the ceiling, hitting the chandelier, which burst in a fine shower of glass rain and Dorcus flinched, covering his ears with his hands. C-c-confidence.

'Where the fuck you keepin her?'

'D-don't shoot me, Mr Chuck. I'm coming d-down.'

'Tell me about my girl, ya bastart!'

'I t-told you — ' Dorcus was halfway. Going all the way, can't stop now. He reached the bottom step. He slipped into a kind of trance. He heard his mother ask for a kiss, he smelled roses, he imagined the assembly of ghosts might rise to support him.

'Tell me again!'

Chuck advanced in a staggering mode along the hallway and fired at two oil-paintings that pissed him off. A pair of ugly fuckin faces starin at him. They slid from the wall, and their wood frames cracked as they tumbled over and down slowly, step by step. Then he turned and followed Dorcus, who'd hurriedly retreated inside a room where a lamp lit a piano and a wingback chair, both covered in white dust sheets.

'*Where's my fuckin girl?*' He fired twice into the piano, shooting through the dust sheet and the keys, and the soundboard vibrated like a choir of crones tuning up their dehydrated pipes. He booted the wingback chair, and it fell over, and a mouse streaked out from a hole in the upholstery.

'Rodent problem,' Chuck said, and fired at the moving mouse and missed.

★ ★ ★

Briskly, Jackie Ace tossed a few things in a big blue canvas bag. Timing was important. Had to act quick. She heard the sound of gunfire and

419

Chuck's upraised voice. She walked to the top of the stairs, descended softly to the first landing, looked over the handrail.

Chuck grabbed Dorcus and forced him to the floor, pressing him down, knee crushed into his chest.

He shoved the gun at Dorcus's throat. 'Did you do a nummer on her, Dorco? Did you gie her the scalpel treatment?'

'N-no way, Mr Chuck.'

'Cut out her heart and sliced that lovely young body, didya? Stuck her innards into an ice-box and delivered her, did you did you did you. Tell me where she is, you fuckin faggot. I'll rip this fuckin dump apart if I have to.'

Dorcus felt the barrel against his throat. He saw in Chuck's eyes a world gone berserk. Why hadn't the spirits of the house come to help him? 'I n-never t-t-t-touched her, M-m-mr I s-swear . . . n-never a ha-hand on her.'

'Lyin faggot peeza shite. Tell me the fuckin truth Dorco or my next bullet goes — guess where, fudgepacker? Right between your fuckin eyes.' Chuck stared at him, but his line of vision was skewed so that he seemed to be looking directly at Dorcus's left ear.

'D-don't . . . t-to t-tell . . . M-m-m . . . Chuck . . .'

'You're for the b-b-bad fire, Dorco. You're for the heavenly choir, soprano section.' Chuck held the gun at Dorcus's forehead. 'Never touched Glorianna, eh?'

'No nev nev n-never!'

'Last chance, Dorco.' Chuck pushed the gun hard into the bone between Dorcus' eyebrows.

Dorcus quivered and closed his eyes and felt he'd be transported any moment into that sphere where the Judge and his mother lived, that dank mysterious void where draughts cavorted in strange partnerships and somebody invisible shuffled endlessly up and down the hallways —

His back to the door, Chuck had no idea someone else was gliding quietly into the room. If he'd turned he'd have seen her, but he was preoccupied with Dorco's fate and his senses were kaput anyway.

When he felt a jab at the back of his neck his first thought was a bee, a wasp, a gnat —

He imploded, sagged and slithered away from Dorcus, and the gun slipped out of his hand. He rolled face down and lay very still.

Dorcus said, 'I th-thought you were never coming.'

'I said I would.' Jackie Ace looked at Chuck for a time. 'You were brave, Dorcus.'

Brave. Dorcus was trembling and white as a freshly laundered sheet. 'I know what you're thinking.'

Jackie said, 'Let's get the van.'

45

Perlman shucked off his coat and tossed his shoes and socks aside and flopped down on the sofa, closing his eyes and seeking sleep. But the persistent sparrowhawks of the day soared through his mind, buzzing him relentlessly. He kept hearing whispers of Miriam. He sat up, smoked, fingers trembling. He flipped the TV on, saw highlights of one of the afternoon's football matches, mince, players who couldn't pass a ball, goalies who flapped at space.

As I flap at space, he thought.

He switched off the box, went upstairs. Inside the bathroom he took one of his painkillers. It eased pain, also promoted sleep. And oh he wanted sleep, he wanted forgetfulness. The two pills left in the bottle looked like the remaining survivors of a crew of thirty that had foundered on the reef of Perlman's broken hopes. He worried about a Habit. At this time of life, oy, a dope fiend. He took off his trousers and shirt, and lay down in his boxers, drawing bedsheets and quilt over himself. He listened to wind shake plants in the backyard.

I used to have a Habit called Miriam.

He floated down a gradient into sleep and dreamed of a forest where a bear was stalking him. He called his father's name for help and woke suddenly, panicky, as if he sensed the beast's presence in his room, wet fur, rancid meaty breath. He raised his head and stared at the black window and thought he saw the outline of a huge animal pass in front of the glass. Bear dreams.

His mobile phone was ringing. What hour of day or night was this? He rose and went in a glazed manner downstairs to the living room. Christ it was *sharp cauld*. He picked up the phone and heard a relentless hammering, like the voice at the other end of the line was talking to him from a factory where machines pounded.

'Who is this? I can't hear. Speak up.' He switched the TV on with the remote and checked the time on SkyNews. 3.20 a.m. The groggy hour. He'd taken his contacts out and the image on the screen showed a newsreader and his blurry twin.

'Come rescue me, Perlman. You owe me.'

'Owe you . . . ' Perlman thought: this is part of the dream, the bear wanders inside a factory and finds a phone and speaks human.

'I'm in fucking serious trouble, and you I thank for this.'

'Tartakower? You know the time?'

'Time I don't have. You put me in jeopardy.'

'How did I manage that?'

Tartakower snorted. 'You gave my name away, *schlemiel*. What I told you in trust, you broadcast, and landed me in a pile of jobbies.'

'How did I land you — '

'Ace and Dysart, fool! You want them to kill me? I give you their names to help you, is this repayment? Thank you, thank you. I'm afraid, Perlman.'

'You never said you wanted your name kept out of it — '

'Some things I took for granted; confidentiality one of them. Now they're coming for me, Perlman.'

'How do you know this? They phoned you? Or they're coming up the stairs, how?'

'They came to my door, they were pounding on it only a minute ago, they shouted threats at me.'

'Are they outside your door now?'

'Perlman, be a *mensch* one time, save me, just save me.'

There was more banging again, like hammers booming as they rose and fell against Tartakower's door. 'I'm in terror, Perlman.'

'Call the Govan cops, they're closer.'

'Polis would come running for an old con like me?'

'Try them. And where's that gang of yours?'

He heard Tartakower shout, *'Go, fuck off, leave me alone, I don't need trouble from you oh Christ, Perlman come please — '*

The line died. Perlman checked his incoming call register and immediately dialled the number Tartakower had phoned from. There was a monotonous whistle, which stopped after a few seconds, and then silence.

How had Dysart and Ace located Tartakower? It didn't matter. They'd found him anyway. He couldn't believe they'd want to hurt him — he was old, poor, pretty much harmless. But Perlman wasn't entirely convinced by Tartakower, whose word wasn't always sound. He

424

dialled the number again; again dead. Then he thought about the search warrant Adamski was applying for — if Joe Adamski had been granted one and served it, then maybe he had Ace and Dysart in custody for questioning.

Which would make Tartakower's story yet another load of toalies.

He called Adamski, who answered curtly. 'What?'

'Did you get that warrant, Joe?'

'Eventually.'

'Did you serve it?'

'I wish. No sign of Dysart or Ace. And the front gates have been battered down. Somebody rammed a Jaguar through them.'

'A Jaguar?'

'Strange, eh? The car's registered to a certain Reuben Chuck. Only there's no sign of Chuck either. And the car's been stripped. Wheels, hubcaps, sound-system. The local yobs saw the broken gates as an invitation to come in and help themselves. Right now my team's going through this place. I'll call back when I can.'

'Wait, is there any sign of a white van?'

'None.' Adamski hung up.

Perlman imagined Chuck had gone there to look for Glorianna, or at least information about her — why else? What happened after that? Chuck in a rage bulldozed the gates down, and then what — did he find the house empty, Dysart and Ace gone? And where did he go after that? Or was there a confrontation between Chuck and the lovers? He imagined a number of possibilities, at least one of which might be ghoulish. He tried Tartakower's number again — but the same silence persisted.

He massaged his eyelids, felt a weight settle on his shoulders. What obligation do you have to the old guy? He thinks you betrayed him. He's living in fear. You don't like him particularly, but you never set out to bring his world down around him, never dreamed your questions would *imperil* him. You should have foreseen that possibility, and soft-pedalled a little, and kept his name private, but no, ah no, you were burning to get back into an old vibe.

So now you're responsible. We're all slaves of our own deeds.

He hurried upstairs, dressed quickly, slid his contacts in. Back downstairs, he put on shoes and socks, grabbed his coat, headed out to his car, which was sluggish to start. Going down Wellshot Road it picked up some speed and by the time he reached the Gallowgate it was moving smoothly along.

Glasgow, Sunday, 4 a.m. The dregs of Saturday night revellers were chasing taxis. High Street was crowded with scores of kids in their best shagging gear stumbling out of a nightclub, raucous, wasted.

He crossed the river, pricked by a smouldering needle of guilt. He owed Tartakower, OK OK — enough already. I admit the debt. I admit it, I was careless, unintentionally so, careless all the same. Govan Town Hall went past, then he was travelling Govan Road parallel to the Clyde. He parked his car and locked it in the narrow slumbering side-street where the charred tenement

426

was situated. Nothing moved. No sign of Tarta-kower's hoodies.

Where were they when Tartakower needed them?

He reached the entrance to the close. Darkness extended unbroken ahead of him. A blind man could see better than this. The smell of recent fire was sickening, throat-catching.

If black had a smell, this would be it.

Hurry. Hurry. How do you hurry when you can't fucking see? He remembered he had matches and he rummaged in his coat pocket for the box. He shook the box — it sounded like he had only a few matches at most. He opened it, groped around inside. Three fucking matches, *threc*. He struck one, and it went out instantly. He edged toward the stairs, fired a second match, which burned long enough to allow him a glimpse of stone steps. He climbed a few, the match singed his fingers and he let it go. Darkness again and an after-image of flame behind his eyes. One match left.

How many flights up? Recollection eluded him. He was losing the specificity of things. The day had depleted him — and here he was, still moving, working off an obligation he'd brought on himself. Guilt was always easy to find, if you knew where to look.

He felt a tickle of fear at the back of his neck. Feh. *I should turn around, flee.* All this blackness without apparent end chilled him. Climbing the stone stairs, seeking the handrail, hearing the crunch of broken bottles under his feet, pieces of newspaper, and a couple of tin cans which rolled out from under him with the sound of cymbals. I move through the garbage of the city. I gave a lifetime to this. How did I ever convince myself that Miriam would have fitted my world, with all its journeys into the sordid, coping with the incorrigibly bad, the injured, the dead?

Does the haunting go on long after the love is ash? Or is it brief, like a flash bulb on a retina?

He heard something from above. A groan, a moan, animal, human — he couldn't tell. He hesitated on the landing. He lit his last match. Another flight of stairs lay ahead. He saw them rise in angular shadows. He tossed the match before it seared his fingers. Darkness coagulated: you couldn't imagine another sunrise when you were in dark this dense.

He continued to climb, a hand extended for the purpose of finding invisible obstacles. He wasn't breathing well. The air in here was bad, and he had a taste in his mouth of burned timber. He coughed, heard an echo of his own noise. Then he saw light — the enfeebled flicker of a flame just a few steps above, which faded a second before it rekindled, a thin oily glow. He smelled paraffin. He moved toward the light source, a gap in a door, and the paraffin was stronger, abrasive.

He pushed the door and stepped into a room lit by an old-fashioned glass oil-lamp. He recognized the dented tin tea pot on the table from his only other visit to Tartakower's. In this light everything was hallucinogenic. The tea pot seemed to be melting. A couple of chairs had

428

been upturned, one missing a leg. The TV lay on its side, the rabbit-ears mangled out of shape.

He heard moaning again, and found its source beneath the plywood window. Tartakower was on the floor face down, arms slack at his sides.

Perlman picked up the lamp and held it over Tartakower, who whispered, 'Don't . . . not again please . . .'

'It's me. Perlman.'

'Perlman? You came.' A croak, a crocked voice.

Perlman bent, aware of the ferret nearby in the cardboard box. 'How bad is it? Is anything broken?'

Tartakower whispered. 'I don't know . . .'

Perlman leaned nearer. Tartakower moved his head a little, then swiftly sucked air, as if swallowing his pain. Perlman brought the lamp even closer. There was blood on the floor beside Tartakower's head. He needs a hospital, treatment, God knows what's been busted. Porous old bones snap as easy as dry kindling.

Perlman touched the old man's shoulder. Tartakower lifted his head an inch or two from the floor, and swivelled his neck to get a sight of Perlman.

'Where does it hurt?' Perlman asked.

'Name any part of me.'

'You need help. I'll phone an ambulance.'

Tartakower's beard was red-stained. Blood trickled from the corner of his mouth. 'You think I can move?'

'They'll carry you in a stretcher.'

'*Schleppers* will bang my head on the steps taking me down. Oh Christ how I ache.'

Tartakower raised an arm very slowly and grabbed Perlman's sleeve, then let his hand flop back to his side. 'Ace and Dysart . . . they break in, kick me in the balls. Beat my head with I don't know what. You did this, Perlman.'

'You want me to beg forgiveness?'

'You're beyond.'

Perlman set the lamp on the floor. He listened to Tartakower's stricken breathing. It was the sound of an iron lung. 'OK, right, absolution's not for me, but I better call a hospital. For your own good.' He searched his coat pockets for his mobile.

'Waste of time,' Tartakower gasped, and dragged a hand to his beard, then squinted at the blood that discoloured his fingertips.

Perlman took out his phone. The battery indicator was low. He watched the ferret rearrange itself and its glossy coat reflected flame. The hoodies must have shampooed it lately. Tartakower moved, grunting, turning very slowly over so that he lay on his back. He raised his hand up to touch Perlman's phone and streaked it with red from his fingertips.

'Don't phone, Perlman.'

Perlman ignored him. He started to punch the keys for emergency service. The blood was sticky on the plastic case, the keys gummy. Tartakower wrapped his hand round Perlman's wrist.

'You deaf as well as blind?'

Something troubled Perlman. He couldn't think what. Something about his phone. Those fucking pills make me old. Those fucking painkillers inhibit my reactions. He stared at his phone, then looked at Tartakower. 'I never gave you my phone number, did I?'

'You're in the book.'

'No, this *phone*. I never told you what it was. But you called me on it earlier.'

'Phoo, a mobie number is easy to get, if you look in the right places. Keep in mind what you see isn't always what you get.'

'What are you talking about?'

'Illusions, Perlman.'

'You brought me here to — '

'Ah no. You brought yourself here, Perlman.'

Perlman thought he heard movement from far down the stairs. But then there was only the sound of Tartakower's breathing and the ferret licking its paws and a whine in his own ears. What was this now, tinnitus, a disease that afflicted drummers and people who listened too long to music screaming through earphones? I've been listening to the discordant symphony of this city for too many years: Glasgow-itis.

Tartakower sucked the blood off his fingertips and seemed to smile, although it was hard to tell through the massive beard and the poor light. 'Blood tastes sweet,' he said. 'Our families.'

'Our *families*?'

'Call me sorcerer, Perlman. Call me necromancer.'

'You're losing it.'

'Did Lazarus recover so quick?' Tartakower got to his feet. A bone cracked in his leg, but he moved with no apparent difficulty.

I'm back in bed, this is a weird dream and Tartakower is the bear, Perlman thought. 'You apparently don't need help as bad as you claimed. Nobody beat you up, did they? Nobody came here and kicked you around.'

Tartakower, whose shadow on the wall was vast and menacing, ignored the question. 'Your aunt, St Hilda of the Blessed Virgins, she rebuked me.'

'You fucking duped me into coming here for an ancient history lesson?'

'Ancient and *less* ancient. You never knew she rebuffed me?'

'No, never,' Perlman said. Hilda and Tartakower, what a strange pair, a strange idea.

'She deemed me unfit. She wants a man who is tidy. *Tidy!*' Tartakower gestured round his room, his pathetic possessions. 'Even flying high, I was not such a man. So I marry somebody else — a fucking *khazer* — but did this waken jealousy in Hilda's heart?'

There was a wildness about Tartakower suddenly, his eyes bright, his beard glittering, his hands slashing the air.

'Hilda obviously didn't like your table manners,' Perlman said. 'You're wasting my fucking time. I'm going back home to sleep.' He started to move toward the door.

'I spook you into leaving, Perlman?'

'No, it's been a fuck of a day and I'm not at my best.'

Tartakower tugged on his beard. 'Maybe I mistakenly thought you'd be sympathetic. We have in common being spurned. Broken hearts.'

'I don't know about your heart, Tartakower — '

'Colin's burial.'

'What about it?'

'I was present that day.'

'I don't believe it. I never saw you there.'

'The reason is you have google-eyes only for the lovely widow, holding her elbow just so at the edge of the grave, I was reaching for my hankie. This is a memory I cherish. Lou Perlman, crazy in love with the widow.'

Perlman stepped away from another effusion of black smoke. He didn't want to imagine Tartakower at Colin's funeral, spying, an uninvited guest. There was a police presence that awful day, keeping away a rabble of vulpine onlookers curious to see the burial of a dead gangster whose misdeeds had been trumpeted in all the local rags. Maybe Tartakower had been kept at a distance by this cordon. Perlman remembered little of the burial, except Miriam's wan expression and the black of her coat and the hole in the ground where they laid his brother down.

'Broken hearts,' Tartakower said again, and uttered a sigh.

Lou said, 'Fine. We share a sadness. So what.' He took another couple of steps toward the door.

Tartakower smiled. 'Didn't I follow her trial in the newspapers and see Lou Perlman put the boot into his own team? An own goal you scored, Perlman. Such a spectacle of yourself. But what does it matter you're a turncoat to your colleagues so long as the untouchable Miriam flies free with the gelt intact.'

'The money was hers,' Perlman said, slowly rising to an anger for which he had no energy. Hauled from bed, rushing here with a kind of mercy in mind. To look at life through an old man's kaleidoscope of grudges?

'A lover's eyes see the world different. It's a golden condition.' Tartakower sniffed the air with the expression of a man smelling a very fine wine. 'Has this sweet love flourished, is she to become Mrs Perlman a second time?'

Heavy sarcasm in Tartakower's question. But more, a mean tone, spite and smugness. 'You want to taunt me about Miriam? I don't need this. I'm gone.'

'Miriam tells me her favourite places. She says she likes Florence best in all the world. So artsy, how she speaks. So la dee da, a lady. My soul is easy in Florence, Miriam says.'

'She told you this? When?'

'On a day we talked.'

'You talked, you and Miriam? And I came up the Clyde on a water lily.' The paraffin flame stuttered almost to the point of extinction, then flared again in a shroud of black smoke that belched through the top of the lamp.

'Miriam, so lovely, but alas a heart of ice.' Tartakower bent, stroked the ferret's head. 'Issy, Issy.' He stretched his hands forward, extending the fingers. 'See. I don't shake so much. Some days I tremble a little, other days not.'

'I'm impressed.' Perlman heard a sound once again, a shuffling from afar, movement inside the tenement. He found this room, this building, oppressive. And yet he stayed because Tartakower was guiding him somewhere, there was a story here, and it was unfolding at the old man's pace.

Tartakower was watching him with a look of loathing so strong it existed apart from the man, a malice of such force it became an entity that occupied a space all its own. 'One day I looked inside myself and saw a truth. The fucking Perlmans have cursed me. One Perlman wrecks my heart, another puts me in jail. Your family is a toxic cloud over my history. The Perlmans are agents of darkness.'

'This is such fucking nonsense. As for meeting Miriam, I'm not buying — '

'I put on my good suit. You surprised I have one? We go to the Willow Tea Rooms. Very nice. She has green tea and a tiny sandwich. She nibbles, doesn't eat the crusts, this woman of delicacy, this great love of yours, this *passion*.'

'How did you get her to meet you? Tell her your life was in danger?'

'What works for you isn't going to work for her. I phone her, I say I need to see her on a matter of some importance. She demurs. Ladies like Miriam always demur, Perlman. But I know the lure. I say I have information about Colin's money she should know about. Only then is she anxious to meet. And sweet all of a sudden on the phone.'

Miriam and Tartakower at The Willows. A picture Perlman couldn't see. 'And then what.'

'You want to hear? Ah, Perlman. I conjure visions until her eyes gleam. This is a venal lady. I say Colin asked me to hide for him considerable sums of money. More than I want to count. I'm uneasy, Miriam, I don't need the responsibility. She doesn't ask why her husband chose me, she doesn't ask a single practical question, not one, avarice has consumed what common sense she might have had. Money — what it does to a greedy person. She glows, Perlman. You may have seen this look. She burns.'

'I don't remember seeing her look like that,' Perlman said. But maybe he had, and denied it. Love sees what it wants. Tartakower's story was rolling into a stormy place, and he felt the dread of a landlubber on a ship during rough seas.

'We left the Willows and I took her to a place,' Tartakower said. 'A place where I kept this cash that was such a burden to me. She's delighted to come along. She floats like light on water.'

'Where did you take her?'

'Is not important.' Tartakower opened a cupboard, a door with no knob, and reached inside. He produced a black case, about the size of an attaché case, though deeper, and put it on the table, making space by pushing aside unwashed cups, a bowl that contained relics of a cereal, dirty cutlery. He clicked the case open.

'Before your eyes the sorcerer's tools.'

Perlman saw a series of velvet slots, each measured for a specific purpose. Tartakower reached in and removed a metal tool that was yellow by lamplight, but silver in ordinary light. 'My beautiful souvenirs. See.' He turned the blade in his hand. 'This you will recognize. The common or garden scalpel.'

Perlman forced himself to look closer into the

436

box — scalpels of different sizes, different shapes. Also something else.

Tartakower removed an implement and said, 'A prince among tools.'

Perlman found himself looking at a handsaw, some twelve inches long, steel blade smooth and wicked. He had an unhealthy urge to touch it, but Tartakower was a little quicker, and held the tool at his side.

'Justice in steel. Realignment of imbalances. In an unjust world, this saw is the equalizer.'

'You talk so much shit.' Disturbed by the saw, Perlman heard movement again outside, the shuffle of feet, whispers.

'Such a sceptic, Perlman. And the postcards, you don't believe either.'

The postcards.

Perlman felt an alteration take place in the atomic structure of his world, a cosmos turning on its axis. He was in an upside-down reality. *A handsaw, justice in steel, postcards Miriam never wrote.*

'In my one good suit I took some short trips. Planes if you book them at the right time are cheap and quick. I had a little money saved. I had a key to her loft, I had her handwriting down to a t. Also her hand off, you should pardon a crude witticism. Don't believe? From this encounter you hope to wake up safe and warm in your bedroom, Perlman? So many old newspapers. What a fire hazard.' Tartakower laughed and chopped the air with the handsaw. 'Compared to my suffering, she suffered nothing. Is this consolation for you?'

437

Perlman felt sick, oily smoke in his throat and his stomach, as if he'd drunk the stuff. He listened to the sounds rise through the building, then a boy's low laugh.

'A sceptic always needs proof.' Tartakower reached down toward the ferret and stroked its neck gently and whispered its name and then, with an unpredictable agility and an expression of utter indifference, drew the blade across the creature's throat.

'For *Christ's* sake,' Perlman shouted.

The animal howled and tried to move but a second draw of the handsaw cut its windpipe and it bled copiously from the throat and looked at Tartakower with what Perlman thought was a kind of misplaced pity. Perlman was about to grapple the saw away from Tartakower just as they entered the room, fifteen of them, probably more, how could he tell by this nightmare light? They wore their hoods upraised and they emanated the menace of an unholy monastic order that has strayed from the true church to align itself with an older ally, and as they shuffled through the doorway they saw Tartakower pluck the dying ferret from the cardboard box and hold it up by the scruff of its slit neck. Blood flowed out of the wound and down his hand and arms.

'*Issy. Jesus fuckin Christ*,' one of the kids said, anguished.

'What inna name o fuck have you done?' another asked.

Perlman watched Tartakower, whose face changed, exultation yielding to the anxiety of a

438

man who sees a scheme go awry, make an indeterminate gesture to the hoodies. 'This is the polisman who forced me to kill Issy, boys.'

'Forced ye? How did he force ye? Held a gun at yer heid, did he? You fuckin old cunt. I saw you. You cut her throat.'

This group seemed to have one voice, one vision. They moved across the room in a rabble, propelled by a rage they were only beginning to feel. The big kid who'd challenged Perlman days before, plucked the animal, his talismanic symbol of freedom, from Tartakower's hands, and shoved the old man back against the plywood window with a force that popped out a couple of nails.

'Boys, *boys*, calm.' Tartakower pointed a finger at Perlman. 'This man is *polis*, this is Perlman who forced me to use the saw on poor Issy. This is your *enemy*. The saw is the *weapon*. And this polis, I told you what he did to me — '

The creature bled dying in the boy's arms. Its body spasmed. The boy who huddled over it was moaning *Issy Issy*, while Tartakower rambled on like an orator facing an incredulous crew — the polis Perlman brought about the cruel death of the beloved pet, get *him*, do what you're supposed to do, go, *do it*.

Perlman attempted to get himself between Tartakower and the hoodies. But they were a swarm, and their energy thrust him aside. He lost his balance and slid back, tripping over the TV on the floor. He struck his head against the wall — a tiny explosion of pain — then he returned to the fray, attempting to rescue

Tartakower even as the hoodies crowded the old man, pummelling, kicking him, grabbing his beard and twisting it, poking fingers into his eyes — no, not fingers, Perlman realized with shock, but steel knitting-needles with sharpened points. Tartakower screamed and screamed. Perlman tried to claw his way through the hoodies, dreaming he might save Tartakower, who was covering his face from blows, and bleeding from his punctured eyes, and diminishing under the pressure of so much violence. Somebody had kicked the plywood loose and cold blew into the room, and the smell of the river. Tartakower, screaming to Perlman for help, was shoved toward the black space where the plywood had been.

And he was sucked out into darkness even as Perlman made a rush to grab him, a vain effort, because there were bodies in his way, and, besides, gravity was faster, gravity was always faster. He heard Tartakower's cry extinguished in the second it took for him to hit the ground, and then the sound of his body crashed on damaged windows stacked out back. Glass crackled like wood in a fire.

Perlman stepped away from the open window, horrified.

'Now *you* fuck off, polis,' one of the hoodies said.

The boy holding Issy said, 'Aye, fuck off.'

'We know how to bury the deid,' another one said.

'And we know how to unbury them.'

'Shurrup,' the boy with the ferret said.

Bury the deid, unbury them. Perlman said, 'You *killed* him.'

'He fuckin fell, it was a fuckin accident. Anyway how do you know he's deid?'

'Aye, how can you tell,' another kid said.

The big kid said, 'Unless you fancy havin a wee accident yerself, get to fuck. And if anybody asks what happened we just say you pushed him. We're witnesses. Right?'

Witnesses of something, yes. Participants in death and burial, yes, and disinterment.

Perlman was hollow and numbed.

He watched the boy's hand stroke the red wet fur of the dead creature. It was hypnotic and sad.

I am polis, I am law and order, I should speak, say something, act.

They looked at him. An incendiary situation; it would take only a couple of hostile remarks and these kids would explode inside their hoods. Still, he had an urge born from long habit to tell them a day would come when they'd have to make statements, that there would be an investigation. But he said nothing.

Then he thought the least he could do was explain the process of law — but he realized he knew as little about that as these kids did. And right at this moment he probably cared as much as they cared, which was not at all.

Leave, before they turn on me.

Some of the boys daubed their faces with Issy's blood. One of them tossed a steel knitting-needle at Perlman. It struck the side of his face and fell to the floor. A second needle followed, clipping his chin.

441

He didn't linger, he went out, reached the stairs and descended a little more quickly through the same dark he'd climbed slowly before — the same but different now: there had been a kind of resolution, and a kind of bleak justice, and the heart of a mystery had been punctured.

46

Dysart removed two ice-chests from the back of the van.

He gave them to the Oriental, who said, 'I see blood spilled inside your van. You work on wheels? What you call this? A travel surgery.'

Dorcus slammed the back doors.

'And the lady in the front seat, who is she?'

'My nurse,' Dysart said.

The Oriental carried the coolers to his car.

Dorcus thought: blood in the back of the van. Everything had been rushed, sloppy. They'd have to run the van through a car wash again. Hose it out, scrub it clean. He wondered what had happened to the dogs. Maybe they'd run away. He thought of the broken gates. He saw Slabbites wandering through the house, trashing stuff, stealing. They'd take the Jag, or strip it, leaving only the bones of a vehicle.

The Oriental came back with an envelope. He handed it to Dorcus. Dorcus stuck it in his back pocket.

The Oriental said, 'This delivery much needed.'

'People need parts,' Dorcus said.

The Oriental looked at him for a moment. 'Parts? Ah so yes they do, *parts*, very funny. Very funny. Parts.' And he got inside his car and shut the door, laughing.

It was the first time Dorcus had heard him

laugh, and he wondered what was so funny about parts.

He didn't want to hang around. The sky was lightening, a pale sun over Glasgow and a ghostly half moon fading in the sky at the same time. Church bells rang far off; an early Mass maybe. He got into the van and sat behind the wheel and Jackie reached for his hand.

She said, 'You know we can't go back.'

'Yes.'

'Absolutely no way, Dorcus.'

'Right,' Dorcus agreed.

'We need to dump these wheels first chance we get. How many people did Chuck tell he was coming to visit you? We don't know, do we? But I know this — somebody *will* come looking for him. And for us.'

Dorcus turned the van out of the yard. 'And what will they find?'

Jackie Ace said, 'They'd need to look a long long time before they find anything.'

Dorcus drove past the old abattoir.

'I think London, Dorcus.'

Dorcus thought about his dogs again. Somebody would find them, take them to an animal shelter, they'd get a good home eventually.

'Anywhere you like, Nurse.'

47

It was just after noon when Perlman arrived at Scullion's house in Drumbeck, at the edge of Bellahouston Park. Sandy, in off-duty blue jeans and loose-fitting v-neck sweater, led him into a glass conservatory. The room was airy and comfortable, armchairs covered with a bright floral motif. It looked out over a tidy lawn, a kiddy's swing, a rubber paddling pool.

Sandy picked up a copy of the *Sunday Herald* from a chair, and gestured for Lou to sit down.

'Where's Maddie and the kids?' Perlman asked.

'Church.'

'You don't go with them?'

'My faith doesn't quite fit churches. I'll tell you about it some time.'

That faith again: one day Perlman would ask for an explanation. 'All right to smoke?'

'I don't care, but Maddie hates the smell.'

'House rules, have to obey,' Perlman said. Smoking *verboten*: he knew he wouldn't stay long. He didn't sit in the chair Sandy had offered. Instead he walked to the glass walls and looked out and wondered if he would have been happy with this kind of life, the wife, the kids, the accoutrements and the obligations. He didn't miss it because he'd never had it. So there was no pang, no yearning, no sense of a lost opportunity to produce little Perlmans.

'Nice,' he said, watching the lawn in sunlight. And it was, if you liked the suburban way. 'How did your raid go?'

'We hauled away a fair pile of documents relating to Reuben Chuck's business enterprises. I don't believe we got everything. I have a feeling there's a stash hidden somewhere else. These lawyers are cunning. Meantime, the big man himself is nowhere to be found.'

Maybe you'll never find him, Perlman thought.

'Tell me how you are, Lou.'

Perlman shrugged, and talked quietly about going to visit Tartakower, and his experience with the man, which in recollection felt as if it had happened to somebody else — a Perlman in another dimension. He remembered the scorched darkness, and Tartakower dropping from the window, and it was like watching an illusion. He thought of the hoodies, and their martyred ferret. Issy's blood was sacred. Would they stuff her — or skin her and make a jacket for their leader?

Scullion said, 'Did Tartakower confess?'

'Confess? Not exactly. He *hinted*. He loved enigmatic statements. What he said wouldn't hold up in a court of law, but I'm convinced he *amputated* the hand.' He spoke the words, denied himself access to the image. 'He could've invented the story, of course, complete with realistic details. Maybe he wanted to feel important, maybe he needed a big performance in front of his teen gang . . . I don't doubt he was telling the truth about his feelings for my family, and I don't doubt he wanted me dead. But what am I left with — loose ends.'

'I know, you think you've got closure, then another door opens, and fuck knows where it's going to take you.'

Closure. Perlman thought the only true closure was death — and maybe not even then. Tartakower was dead. Chuck was merely missing at this stage. But Dysart and Ace, who knew? He wasn't worried — they'd show sooner or later, in another city, England or overseas. According to a weary Adamski, who'd called earlier, his team had rigged up lights and, working through the night, found human tissue clogged in the sewage system, and bundles of bloodstained decaying towels stuffed inside a basement furnace that didn't work, and so was useless when it came to destroying evidence. Dysart must have intended to have it mended at some stage, and procrastinated, or didn't have the cash, or never imagined anyone would go down there and look — and then it was too late.

It's going to be a long job, Adamski had said, and a fucking nasty one.

'We really *need* something to *wipe* in Latta's face,' Scullion said.

'If these kids would talk about Miriam's burial, the before and the after, we'd have something. But they won't talk unless somebody brings back the rack or thumbscrews. Hind-sight's a curse — I wish I'd had the presence of mind to grab the saw and take it with me, it might have helped Sid Linklater's forensic effort — assuming Tartakower's saw was the one used

447

on Miriam. But I just wanted out, Sandy. That's all I could think of, getting out. Getting away.'

Scullion strolled his conservatory with the confident step of ownership. 'Maybe we can retrieve the saw.'

'How?'

Scullion grinned. 'Some hard men in that part of the world owe me favours.'

'Sandy, you surprise me, travelling in rough circles.'

'I learned it all from you.'

'I take that as praise. Would these hard men bully a bunch of kids in hoods?'

'Kidding? They'd love it.'

Perlman saw sunlight flash on the surface of the paddling pool. 'Also it would be helpful if we knew where Tartakower performed the amputation. Linklater might like that, scratching round for evidence.'

'Leave it with me. You want a beer?'

Perlman patted his stomach, indicating gastric uncertainty. 'I don't think so.'

'One way or another we'll get enough to scupper that fucker Latta. It'll come together.'

'I believe that,' Perlman remarked, cheered by the possibility of Latta's disgrace and downfall. 'I'm not resigning. I'm definitely not resigning. Fuck Tay. Fuck Latta.'

'You sure about that beer?'

'Positive.'

Scullion patted his back. 'Next time. Maddie says you're coming to dinner this week.'

'So I am.' He'd forgotten.

Perlman drove to Betty's flat in London Road. There was no sign of the reporters who'd been there before. The value of news receded quickly, hot topics turned cold, the world rolled on in a series of fresh atrocities. He took out his phone and called Hilda.

'It's the prodigal,' Hilda said.

'The wandering Jew,' Perlman said.

'You should wander down this side of the city one day.'

Here comes the guilt express. He asked after her health, and Marlene's. This was risky, since it sometimes involved a catalogue of complaints. He was relieved to be told only that Marlene had passed a gallstone in the night without severe pain, just some small discomfort. End of bulletin.

He wasn't going to tell Hilda over the phone about Miriam. Such news meant a personal visit.

'So this phone call is what — just saying hello?'

'I was thinking I'd come over later tonight.'

'Say again what you said.'

'You heard me, Hilda.'

'So tonight I'll be baking?'

'Don't make a fuss, I'll bring something.' He looked at the curtains drawn across Betty's window. Was she asleep, awake? 'I have a question for you. Do you remember a guy you used to see . . . The Slob you called him.'

'Who told you about the Slob?'

'Was this Ben Tartakower?'

'Some questions you have no right to ask.'

Hilda's tone was clipped.

'He proposed to you. Yes no.'

'Here I close a door. Slam.'

'I was just *curious*.'

'And curious you'll stay.'

'Eight o'clock OK?'

'Eight is good. And don't forget the cheesecake, Louis.' She hung up.

She reveals herself in her refusals. Perlman put his phone away.

He got out of the car. Betty was on the pavement, smiling warmly at him. He followed her along the close to her flat. Music played quietly on her stereo. He recognized it, old Credence Clearwater.

'I've just made some coffee.'

She went inside the kitchen and came out with a coffee jug, cups and saucers, and a plate of assorted biscuits on a tray. She poured for him, and he sipped. She was waiting for his reaction to the coffee. He told her it was good, strong, the way he enjoyed it. Small appreciations pleased her. He liked this about her. He liked a lot of things about her.

'You look good,' he said.

'That's probably the first compliment you've ever paid me. Except when you told me how well I cleaned your house.'

'I've been remiss.'

'More like preoccupied.'

'Here's another compliment. I like the way you're dressed.' He was unaccustomed to making compliments.

'I've never worn this before,' she said.

'It suits you.' And it did — a well-cut dress of dark blue, knee-length. She'd done something to her hair, rearranged it, cut some of it, he wasn't sure how she'd made it different. Also she wore light make-up, subdued lipstick, a mere touch of eyeliner. So little, and yet it redefined her face, brought new light to her eyes.

She sat beside him on the sofa, holding her cup in her lap. 'I had a phone call this morning, by the way. From Annie. Remember? You were quite taken by her.'

'What did she have to say?'

'It was a goodbye call. She's going to America.'

'Good move for her.'

'She has ambitions,' Betty said. 'Music OK for you?'

'Takes me back.'

'That's what I like about it. Better days.' She drank some coffee, offered him a biscuit. He chose a chocolate bourbon.

He said, 'When I was a kid I used to eat the outside bits and leave the chocolate centre for the last.'

'Is there any other way?'

Barefoot girl dancin in the moonlight. He listened to the music and imagined Betty in her hippy days, and thought of her dancing shoeless like the girl in the song. He touched the back of her hand and then, beset by nervousness, drew it away.

'You're shy,' she said. 'Aren't you, Lou?'

'Uncertain more than shy. Maybe both in equal measures.'

She laughed. 'Do people tell you you're funny?'

'Complete stand-up,' he said.

'Sometimes I hear you think before you speak . . . I hear you weigh things in your head, trying to balance your words.'

'It's all show. Usually it's off the top of my head with no thought beforehand.'

'I don't believe that.'

'You don't think I'm madly impulsive?'

'You have impulses, I don't know how madly.'

He reached across and placed the palm of his hand against the back of her neck. She sighed, tipped her head back, enjoying the connection.

'Is this one of the mad ones?' he asked.

'Oh it could be, Lou, it could well be . . . '

He gently pushed aside a strand of hair and kissed her ear.

She leaned forward, set her cup down on the coffee-table. Then she turned to gaze at him. He saw it in her eyes — anticipation and hesitancy. And he thought: we're postponing an event that's waiting inevitably to take place. How does it happen, what whispered promptings of the heart tell you that one day, when enough time has passed to let cowls of grief and sorrow blow away, you're going to be lovers — even before you know it?

She wrapped her hands firmly round his. He understood. The dead still had claims on their behaviour. He kissed her again anyway and she yielded a moment and he realized how easy it would be to expel the dead, and how difficult.

His phone rang in his pocket and he was

tempted to leave it, but Betty had drawn slightly back from him, apparently lost in misgivings of her own, and so he answered.

The Pickler said, 'If you're still interested, Mr Perlman, I think I might have a wee lead on that heidless clown.'

We do hope that you have enjoyed reading this large print book.

Did you know that all of our titles are available for purchase?

We publish a wide range of high quality large print books including:
Romances, Mysteries, Classics
General Fiction
Non Fiction and Westerns

Special interest titles available in large print are:
The Little Oxford Dictionary
Music Book
Song Book
Hymn Book
Service Book

Also available from us courtesy of Oxford University Press:
Young Readers' Dictionary
(large print edition)
Young Readers' Thesaurus
(large print edition)

For further information or a free brochure, please contact us at:
Ulverscroft Large Print Books Ltd.,
The Green, Bradgate Road, Anstey,
Leicester, LE7 7FU, England.
Tel: (00 44) **0116 236 4325**
Fax: (00 44) **0116 234 0205**

WHITE RAGE

Campbell Armstrong

When an Asian entrepreneur dies in a suspicious fall from a balcony and an Indian teacher is gunned down in front of her class, it's clear to Detective Lou Perlman that he is dealing with racially motivated murder. The emergence of a group called White Rage and a growing sense of fear spreading across Glasgow mean that Perlman needs some answers quickly. And when he looks beneath the glittering new surface of the city in which he was born, he finds all sorts of ancient connections, some of them painful, some of them shocking, many of them disturbing.

THE LAST DARKNESS

Campbell Armstrong

Glasgow, December: In this city of biting sleet, icy pavements and Christmas street decorations battered by arctic winds, the body of a well-dressed man is found hanging from a railway bridge. Investigating the case is Lou Perlman, a detective whose idea of a good suit is anything that fits him. Perlman feels that this is no suicide, and that something about the corpse reminds him of his boyhood in the Gorbals. For Perlman is a man with secrets of his own and, as one death follows another, the hunt for the killer takes him into a territory of deceit and greed - a world of old allegiances that are lethal to reawaken.